GUARDIAN OF SHADOWS

NYX FORTUNA—BOOK TWO

MICHELLE MANUS

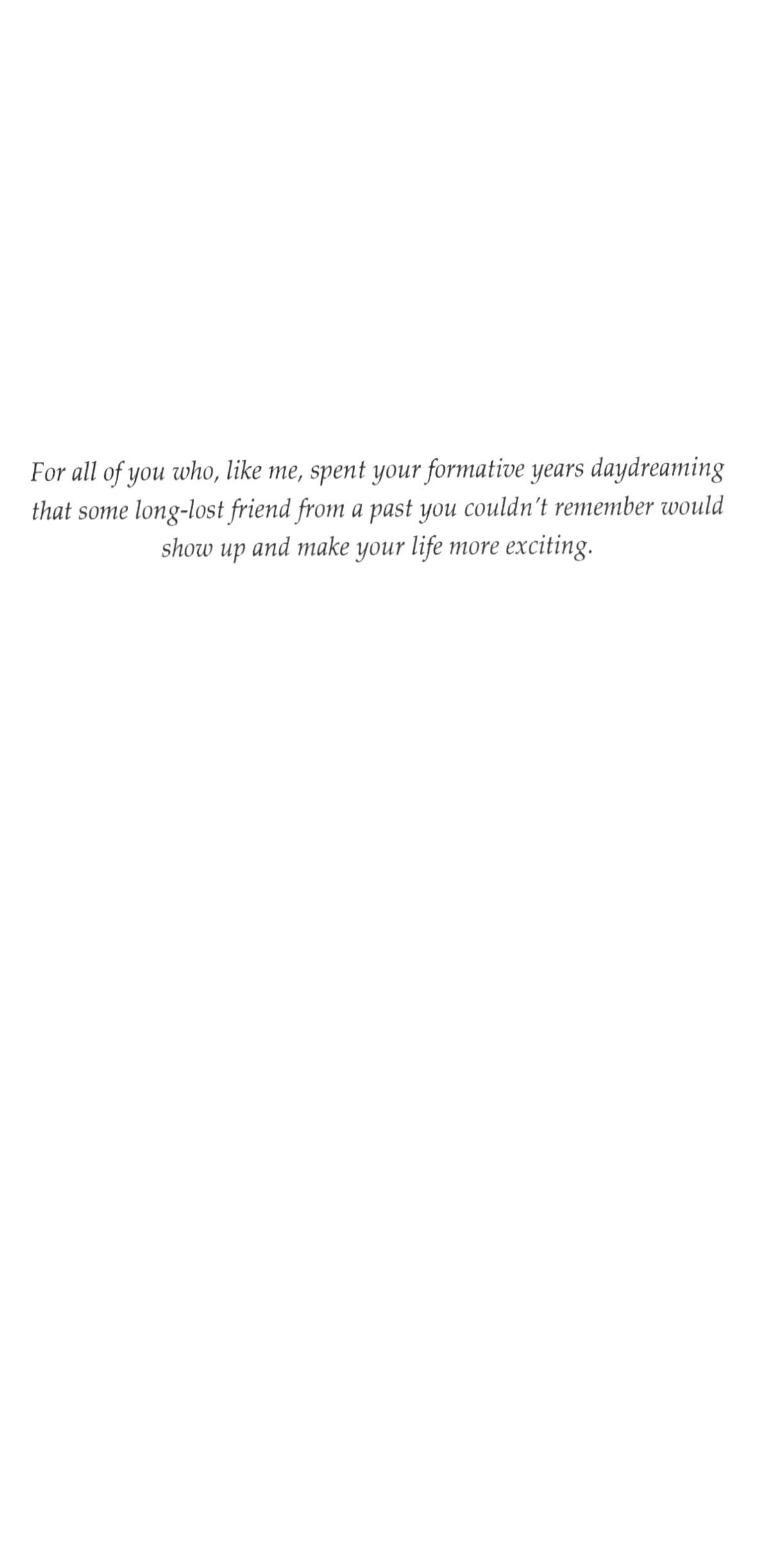

*For all of you who, like me, spent your formative years daydreaming
that some long-lost friend from a past you couldn't remember would
show up and make your life more exciting.*

1

————

The six silver spheres atop their posts, one for each point on the hexagon that filled the center of the Arrival Room, spun with dizzying speed, and a bone-deep thrumming echoed throughout Earth's Waystation. Nyx Fortuna, the Guardian of that Station, took her place atop the barstool behind a podium just as a figure emerged from the cosmic floor between those posts.

The new arrival shook off the ley dust of travel, revealing itself to be an Urthura, a lion-sized, winged feline race from planet Calkella. The Urthura cocked one ear and listened to the recording Nyx had made her very first day accepting Arrivals. The recording instructed arriving travelers to wait behind the *Line Starts Here* sign until motioned forward, and to help themselves to refreshments.

Nyx had experimented with a wide array of said refreshments, but her initial choice of cookies had proved to be the most popular across species, and she'd decided not to mess with a good thing. The Urthura snagged a chocolate chip cookie from the waiting platter—Nyx still hadn't quite gotten used to seeing opposable thumbs on a feline-based species—and trotted up to the podium when Nyx signaled them forward. The black dorsal stripe running down the Urthura's back marked it as a female, and she smiled shyly as she pulled her travel papers out of the little pack strapped to her back.

Nyx took down the Urthura's information, noting name, species, and home planet.

"How long will you be staying on Earth?"

The Urthura let out a series of yowls and hisses that Earth Between's translator spells allowed Nyx to understand as, "Two weeks."

"Is this your first visit to Earth?"

Growl, yelp, "Yes."

"You know the rules about hunting? Not allowed unless it's on one of the three registered game preserves or if you venture into Dead Earth proper." There were far too many sapient avian and small mammalian species across the galaxy that were appealing to predator species like the Urthura to allow the latter free-range hunting rights. After a close call in her second week, Nyx had started putting extra emphasis on the no-hunting clause.

While she had learned that Earth Between did have its own version of a police force, who would be responsible for determining guilt and possible punishment in such a case, she didn't want to be responsible for anyone's death. Besides which, after the aforementioned close call, one of Earth Between's investigators had paid Nyx a visit to sternly remind her that she had a responsibility to stress to travelers the importance of following local laws.

If it had occurred to Nyx that it was somewhat odd that Earth Between had an investigative task force, and yet *she* was the one the Council had assigned to find Morgen when he'd illegally come through her Station, she hadn't quite had the nerve to ask the stern-faced investigator *why* that had been the case. Said investigator had been thoroughly unimpressed by Nyx, to all appearances, and had continually made references to how such things as the near-death of sapient avians Simply Had Not Happened under the previous Guardian's reign. Nyx had taken her scolding to heart and tried to improve.

The Urthura before Nyx furiously nodded her understanding of the rules, even while her tail twitched in excitement at the mere mention of a hunt. Nyx handed her one of the visitor's guides she'd put together with the help of Earth Between's business owners and residents. "This lists all of the lodging and restaurants in the area, along with the locations of the gaming preserves and other recreational activities. Planet-specific laws are listed in the back. Please feel free to inquire here if you have any issues or further questions."

With an adorable purr-rumble of assent, the Urthura took the pamphlet and followed the yellow brick road out of the Arrival Room. The road had originally been a joke, but Nyx had ended up keeping it because absolutely no one understood the joke but her, and for some reason she liked that. She'd tried explaining it to her resident band of fugitive aliens but, while they'd grasped the plot of *The Wizard of Oz* just fine, they'd failed to understand why having a yellow brick road in her Station and telling people to follow it was amusing.

Thinking of said fugitives, her gaze went to the east wall, where three of their likenesses hung on four-foot wide floor-to-ceiling posters emblazoned with the word WANTED in all capital letters, and the All Council seal in the bottom left-hand corner. It was eerie to have Morgen's, Kaden's, and Maruca's faces staring at her while she checked in arriving travelers, but since they were hanging in every Waystation on every planet in the connected universe, it would undoubtedly raise questions if she took them down without being ordered to. Especially since the All Council already suspected she had something to do with the three's escape from the Arkadian prison planet.

They were right, of course, but she wasn't interested in proving it for them.

Her next traveler, a tall, dark-skinned male with the wispy

feathers growing alongside his hair that marked him as Kerian, the same species as the Between's very own Warlock, noticed her staring at the posters.

"They still haven't caught them yet?"

"Not that I've heard," she answered, beckoning him forward and taking his papers.

"You must get nervous, running a Station all alone with fugitives on the loose."

Nyx continued writing down his information and really, really hoped he wasn't hitting on her. She'd discovered, in her last few weeks on the job, that many people across many species apparently thought it would be cool to sleep with a Station Guardian if their species were sexually compatible.

"Not really," she replied flippantly. Since those wanted fugitives all resided in her Station, and she knew exactly where each of them was at every moment of the day, whether she wanted to or not, there was no need to be nervous.

"So you do run it alone, then?"

Nyx groaned internally, finished taking down his information, and handed his papers back to him alongside a visitor's guide. She forewent her customary smile.

"Enjoy your stay on Earth."

"Say, I was wondering if—"

"No." The word had been on the tip of Nyx's tongue, but it was Evra who uttered it.

Tall and exceptionally well-muscled, with bronze skin and blonde hair plaited down her back, Nyx's Amazonian assistant and newly-minted best friend always made a statement when she walked into a room. That statement usually translated to some version of *fuck off*. In case anyone missed that message, the excessive number of blades strapped to various parts of her person tended to get it across.

The Kerian looked from Evra to Nyx, muttered, "Figures," and walked on.

Evra clutched a bouquet of white flowers, fingers curled so tightly around the stems it was a wonder she hadn't sheared them in half. She stalked to the podium and thrust the flowers at Nyx. Several members of the growing crowd of travelers let out dreamy sighs and general *aww* noises as they, unable to see Evra's glowering expression, clearly thought this was a romantic gesture.

Nyx took the flowers. "Evra, really, you shouldn't have."

Evra leaned over the podium. "Morgen left them outside my door," she hissed. "Where *anyone* could see them."

"You did tell me to make sure he couldn't get into your room anymore."

"Because I thought he would stop leaving things then."

Nyx stuck her nose in the flowers and sniffed. They smelled divine, like honey, jasmine, and sweet almond had decided to have a collective lovechild. They definitely weren't Dead Earth native, and she made a mental note to find out where Morgen had gotten them.

"They smell amazing. I will, of course, treasure them forever." Softer, she added. "I'm about to have a riot on my hands if I don't start checking people through. If you really want him to stop, tell him to."

"I tell him to stop all the time."

"No, you grumble at him. It's not quite the same thing. Now, off you go, I have work to do." Nyx made shooing motions at Evra, who stalked out of the room like a Valkyrie set on vengeance. Nyx did hope Morgen would be mostly intact the next time she saw him. She'd grown rather fond of him.

Romantic gestures only got one so far in the customer service industry, and travelers were indeed starting to get grumpy. She waved the next in line forward and resumed her task of inspecting documents, logging information, and smiling. So. Much. Smiling.

All things considered, she liked her job. Even so, she was

always glad when she got to stop smiling for the day. When she'd taken down the last traveler's information she tore the log page from its clipboard and dropped it. It floated to the ground and vanished, on its way to the archives section of the Waystation's Den. Nyx stood and stretched and, activating the locking wards Griff had helped her install on the Arrival Room, made her way towards that Den.

She stopped off in the Station's little cafe to make herself a latte. At least, that had been her intention, but Kalvar, decked out in a black barista's apron, refused to let her do it herself. At seventeen, Kalvar was the oldest of the youths Kaden had protected on Arkadia, and he'd carved out a niche for himself at the Station, running the bookstore and the coffee bar. Technically, it probably should have been Evra's job, as she was the Station's official assistant, but the Amazon was ill-suited to domestic tasks of any kind, and Nyx didn't let her touch the espresso machine for fear she would destroy it.

Plus, it seemed to keep Kalvar busy. Nyx didn't know much about his past—just that he'd ended up in the hands of slavers and sold as a trading commodity to a prisoner inbound to Arkadia who could afford the black market luxury—and she hadn't wanted to bring up bad memories simply to satisfy her own curiosity. Already, he barely slept. He hid it well, his peppy facade made possible by a constant supply of free caffeine, and he threw himself into his self-chosen work at the Station in an effort to pretend everything was fine.

If she hadn't had to bond herself to the Station they all lived in, and therefore become privy to everything that happened within its walls, she might have bought his doe-eyed everything-is-fine act. Since she *was* bound to that Station, and hadn't yet picked up Griff's ability to tune out the goings-on inside it, every time one of her residents woke up in the middle of the night screaming from nightmares, she woke up too. Since four out of her six guests had spent significant time on a prison planet, they woke up screaming a lot.

It was making Nyx sleep-deprived and snappish. She'd tried to convince Kalvar, at least, to talk to someone about it. Nyx knew Tobi and Lauralyn, two of the other children who'd escaped from Arkadia, were getting professional help. She checked in regularly with their adoptive mothers, Ankira and Diana, who'd told her both of the kids were seeing a healer who specialized in emotional trauma, and they were slowly starting to respond to the sessions.

Kalvar had flat out refused to go. He insisted nothing was wrong. He was considered an adult by his people's standards, and Nyx wasn't going to take away his agency by trying to force him to go. She just wished he would talk to someone. She suspected the only time he was a fraction of his real self was when he was around Maruca. When he wasn't working, he followed the redhead around like a lovestruck puppy. Maruca pretended not to notice, probably because of the eleven or so years she had on him.

Kalvar set a cobalt blue mug down in front of Nyx. A perfect latte-art leaf graced the surface of her beverage. He'd gotten pretty good at it—at everything he did, really— in an astonishingly short amount of time, and her heart ached to think of what he could have done, could have accomplished, if his life hadn't taken the turn it had.

No, that wasn't fair. And it wasn't what she meant. He could still accomplish whatever he wanted, could still become whoever he wanted. Arkadia hadn't taken that from him. It had just altered the way he would get there, and probably the end result. She just wished, for his sake, that he'd never had to endure any of it in the first place.

Kalvar looked at the white flowers she'd placed on the counter.

"You know flowers only smell sweet because they're dying, right? Like, you are literally smelling their slow decay."

Ah, teenagers. So many different species, so many similar existential crises of youth.

"I did, and that slow decay smells wonderful." She stood and scooped up her mug. "I'll be in the Den if you need me. And Kalvar? Try to have some fun."

He gave her a mocking bow. Clearly, he'd been spending too much time around Morgen.

2

___

The Waystation's Den was a multi-room vault that housed all of the Station's records, along with every magical artifact ever confiscated by any of the Station's Guardians. Since the Station had been around for a few centuries and been through a number of Guardians, all of whom carried the secondary responsibility of relieving those who traveled through the Station from other planets of any illicit magical items, the Den didn't suffer from a lack of volume or variety of said items.

As such, one might expect time spent in it to be interesting. A week ago, when Nyx first came up with the brilliant idea of creating a thorough inventory of its contents, the array of magical swords, disappearing cloaks, cursed teapots and various other items *had* been interesting. Now that she had an inch-thick ledger full of them and was only a quarter of the way through the collection, the sheen of excitement had worn off.

She had been all for temporarily abandoning the project, but Griff, the Station's Avatar and very own griffin, had grumbled that they had started the project and might as well finish it. As a result, he had done the bulk of the previous two days' work on his own while Nyx detoured into trying to solve a series of questions the rest of the galaxy hadn't been able to answer in the last thirty years—where did the seemingly endless supply of identical Kumir assassins come from, how did they even exist, and how did they travel undetected throughout the galaxy? The answer to the last one might be able to explain how the Kumir had gotten into this very Den—supposedly the most secure room in the entire Station—when said Station had been shut down to ley line travel.

The Harvester of Worlds, as if it remembered that day with fondness, pulsed with a sick flare of warmth against her chest as she entered the Den. Nyx suppressed a shudder. She didn't precisely regret unleashing the Harvester. If she hadn't, everyone in this Station would likely be dead. When they'd fled from Arkadia, they'd been in no condition to tangle with the number of Kumir that had been waiting for them—not when the Station itself had been falling down around them.

Still, knowing all that didn't quell the queasiness that hit her stomach when she remembered the Kumir's skin dissolving, the organs and tissues beneath laid bare for a moment before they disintegrated and left only skeletons that turned to ash. In the second before they had disappeared entirely, the Harvester had taken—had harvested—something from each of them. Something that even now spun and whirred within the confines of the four interlocking spheres that formed the pendant that hung around her neck.

In the Den's spacious entry room, Griff sat on a long wooden table surrounded by objects, his tail thump-thumping on the lacquered wood. It had taken three weeks to convince him to return to his normal housecat size instead of remaining in the larger buffalo-size he'd grown to during the Station's troubles. Nyx had gently pointed out that he was the one who'd originally told her how difficult it would be to navigate the Station as an extremely large griffin, and he'd grumblingly shrunk back down. Whenever they roamed outdoors, however, he still tended to grow in size.

"What do those do?" she asked, approaching the table.

He sat in front of a pair of tall black boots, dictating to the inventory book that transcribed everything he said.

Griff pushed his spectacles back up his beak and closed the inventory book, pausing the transcription.

"They are boots," he answered casually. Too casually. Griff did not do casual as a tone.

"So what do they do?"

"Nothing."

"Nothing," Nyx repeated. There wasn't a single item in the Den that did "nothing." Even the table Griff sat on did something, it just fortunately didn't do it unless three or more people were seated at it for a formal dinner. "So you're telling me they're some previous Guardian's attempt at fashion?"

"Perhaps. I simply don't recall."

Nyx herself could not be said to be any judge of fashion, but the boots did hold a certain appeal. Actually, they held a lot of appeal. They were sensibly black, sensibly flat-soled, and she even liked the buckles up the sides.

"You know, they look kind of nice. Maybe I'll borrow them for a bit."

"No." Griff flung his wings protectively around the boots. Odd. He hadn't even objected *that* much when she'd asked to take the lightning sword out in the middle of a thunderstorm. The perks of sharing a bond with her sentient Station were that she could now remove a magical item from her Den without it immediately locking the Station down. The Station didn't particularly like her doing it, as it seemed to have a dragon-and-its-hoard kind of relationship with the objects in the Den, but it would let her.

"Why not?" Nyx asked, all pretend innocence. "If they do *nothing*, it can't be dangerous."

"You are the most difficult Guardian I have ever worked with."

"I'll take that as a compliment. Your other Guardians must have been *so* boring."

Griff mumbled something she couldn't understand.

Nyx cupped a hand around her ear. "What's that? I can take the perfectly harmless boots out for a night on the town?"

"They are mercury boots," he finally grumbled.

"Mercury? Like the metal?" Nyx repeated.

"No, not like the metal. They increase speed."

"Seriously? The big secret you're hiding is that the boots make you go fast?"

"You are *not* borrowing them."

"Fine. I don't like running anyway." It was even true. She went four times a week with Evra in the morning out of a principled interest in it perhaps saving her life if said life kept being as interesting as it had been when she first got here, but she didn't particularly enjoy it. None of that changed the fact that a pair of boots that could make her go really, really fast was still really, really tempting.

Maybe she would sneak down here later when Griff was distracted and—

"Don't even think about it." Griff snapped his beak. "If I even suspect you're coming after them later I'll drop them back in the endless trunk."

"You do realize you just told me where to find them?"

"Indeed. But it's the endless trunk. It will take you at least an hour to find them and by then, I will be here."

"You're no fun."

"Have you made any progress on the Kumir?" Griff asked, pointedly ignoring her statement.

"No." Nyx flung herself into a chair. "I've read absolutely everything there is to read on them. The factual stuff only details their confirmed sightings and hits, and the conspiracy theory stuff is too outlandish." She'd read theories that ran the gamut from people claiming the Kumir were an All Council experiment in magical cloning gone wrong, to the belief they were a hallucinogenic experience brought on by a rare micro-spore floating throughout the universe, and didn't actually exist. "I'd like to talk to Beauregard."

Morgen's uncle was semi-famous as a paranoid eccentric who thought the Kumir were out to get him. Nyx had met him once and he'd been a very pleasant, very reasonable individual with a nice castle and what might or might not be considered a small standing army.

Since Nyx had led a contingent of Kumir that had been hunting her and Evra right onto his grounds in order to utilize that standing army in their defense, she didn't feel like it was her place to judge whether anyone was paranoid or not. What she trusted Beauregard to be was an expert on Kumir. Unfortunately, he'd booked a ley line departure weeks ago and hadn't yet come back.

"Morgen keeps telling me he doesn't know when he's coming back."

"Morgen," Morgen said, dropping off the Den's entrance ladder four rungs up from the ground and landing with barely a whisper of sound, "is telling you the truth. I'm his nephew, not his keeper, and Uncle Beau's always been a bit of a free spirit."

Morgen strolled into the room with his usual swagger, which died when he saw the flowers Nyx had set on the table.

"Hey, those were for Evra! I had to order them direct from Caligula and you would not believe what shipping costs from that planet, give them back."

Nyx picked up the flowers and took a deep inhale from the petals before saying dreamily, "But she gave them to me. It was a very public, very romantic, gesture. How would she feel knowing I gave them to you?"

Morgen wilted, so much so that Nyx felt bad for teasing him.

"So she got them and she just…got rid of them. What does that woman like? I've tried everything. Weapons, jewelry, flowers. She just throws it all away."

For a fugitive hiding out on what amounted to a backwater

planet in the eyes of the universe, Morgen Drahl certainly seemed to have a large amount of disposable income and an easy means of accessing it. Nyx knew each and every item Morgen had gotten Evra, because the Amazon had flung each and every one of them at her with an air that demanded Nyx *do something*.

Nyx might have, if she hadn't known damn well Evra was capable of putting an end to all of it herself if she really wanted to. Besides, she knew that Evra had, despite very publicly tossing out the first thing Morgen had bought her—an extremely practical black-bladed tactical knife with a curved hilt and silver embellishments that screamed Evra al'Daemon—snuck out after everyone else was asleep to retrieve it and hang it on her wall.

Morgen was, apparently, still talking. "—and I'd say she wasn't interested but sometimes she gives me the most speculative looks and I would bet the entirety of my romantic career she's thinking about—"

"Something I definitely don't need to hear," Nyx interrupted.

"I guess you're right," Morgen said glumly. "So have you seen her around?"

"Not since she interrupted my morning Arrival to angrily shove these at me." Nyx waved the flowers. If Nyx could *feel* Evra's soles landing rhythmically on her/the Station's ground as Evra completed her daily afternoon run through the Station's woods, well, that wasn't information she had to divulge, was it?

Her altered bond with the Station was taking some getting used to. Learning to manipulate its physical layout was proving easier for her than controlling her awareness of it. She could blunt the things she noticed and felt, but she couldn't yet block them out entirely, no matter how much she might *want* to block some things out.

Like, say, the exceptionally attractive blond ex-Enforcer who was currently in the cafe with Kalvar and Maruca.

Morgen did not immediately leave to go find Evra. Instead, he looked around the Den like he was seeing it for the first time. "What are you doing down here anyway?"

"Inventory."

"You want some help?"

Nyx stared at him. "You want to do inventory?"

He ran a hand over his braids. "Sure, why not?"

"Weren't you going to go find Evra?"

"What's the point?" Morgen sighed. "I'm beginning to think I've made myself too available. Time to try the withdrawn and moody approach. Stars know it works for *some* people in this Station."

"Excuse me?"

"Oh, please. Don't act all innocent. If I have to watch you and Kaden sneak longing glances at each other while you think the other one isn't looking one more time, I may gag. Can't you two just fuck already and get it over with?"

"Precisely what I have been saying," Griff agreed.

Nyx choked on the sip of latte she'd just taken. "I have never once heard you say the word *fuck*."

"That is because it is a vulgar word. It is the sentiment of the statement I agree with. Tensions are running far too high and something must be done."

Nyx settled her coffee cup back on its saucer with a soft clink and tented her fingers against her forehead. "Just so I can see if I'm understanding this correctly, the two of you want me to have sex with Kaden for the sake of Station morale?"

"Yes," they chorused in unison.

"This is ridiculous. You" —she pointed an accusatory finger at Morgen— "I expect this sort of thing from. Griff, I expected better from someone of your years and supposed wisdom."

Griff, at least, had the decency to look somewhat embarrassed. Morgen did not.

"And you're both out of your minds. For one, my sex life—"

"Lack of," Morgen cut in.

"—is none of your business," Nyx finished with a glare. "And for another, even if I did sleep with him, it's not going to fix anything."

She had an Amazon and five fugitives holed up in her Station. Three of the latter were elite fighters, two were teenagers, and all were bored out of their collective minds. The building of tensions was inevitable. None of it was the result of her sex life. Or lack thereof.

"That's not exactly true," Morgen argued. "You're the Guardian here, so your mood infects everything whether you want it to or not, and Kaden has a domino effect on everyone. When he's morose, it makes Tamrin and Maruca cranky. When Tamrin is cranky, her and Evra butt heads. When Maruca is cranky, Kalvar is constantly on edge. Therefore everyone ends up in a vicious cycle of snapping at everyone else and poor, easy-going Morgen is caught in the proverbial crossfire. Not to mention Kaden is *no fun* these days and I miss my best friend. Conclusion, you should sleep with him."

"No."

"Why not? It's not like you haven't done it before." He paused, considering her speculatively. "You *have* done it before, right?"

"Not that it is any of your business but, yes, of course we have *done it* before."

Morgen threw his hands up. "Then what's the problem?"

"The problem," Nyx said, voice deadly calm because she was *done* with this conversation, "is that he *hurt* me. He abandoned me without saying goodbye and then I find out he lied to me about my entire life, used me to hide potentially the most dangerous object in the known universe, and after all of that I had to survive a bloody prison planet to get any answers out of him.

"Now he and his *charming* sister are more or less permanent guests in my home and I am understandably pissed off about all of it. Frankly, I think I've handled the situation pretty well, all things considered, only now everyone seems to think I should just *get over it* for the sake of everyone else's happiness."

Nyx was practically shouting by the end of it and they all

heard the soft scrape of a boot sole on the top rung of the Den's entrance ladder too late. Nyx had been so worked up she hadn't paid attention to the approaching figure, had noticed it only in a distracted way, like a fly buzzing somewhere in the back of her mind. Now that she paid attention to the Station's senses, it was only too obvious who had approached, who was even now softly retreating back out of the Den's entrance, disappearing through the Station's library like he'd never been there.

Kaden.

Mixed guilt and anger washed over her. She didn't *want* to hurt him. She hadn't said anything just now that wasn't true. She hadn't even said anything she hadn't told him before. But she could imagine how it must feel to walk up and hear her practically screaming about it. At the same time, she was angry at him for just walking away. For taking the easy path and avoiding her. Because whatever Morgen and Griff might say about her avoiding Kaden, it wouldn't have worked half so well if he hadn't been avoiding her too.

"You know what? You two do inventory. I have business in town. You can enjoy the Station's amenities without the unfortunate complication of my moody presence."

3

Nyx did not truthfully have business in the broader city of Earth Between, but she had popped over to Dead Earth last week to get more of the Cliff bars the Warlock liked to sell to tourists at outrageously marked up prices, so she decided she might as well drop them off. She felt the now-familiar twinge of separation and loss as she crossed the invisible boundary dividing the Station's grounds from Earth Between, half her senses disappearing as she stepped onto earth she was no longer connected to.

She followed Wayfarer's Way until it came to a fork, where a right turn took her to the ridiculously picturesque hill overlooking the city. A feeling of absolute belonging, of *home*, thrummed through her veins. Nyx had never been a wanderer. She loved reading books about grand fantasy adventures, but the thing she liked most about them, the thing they all had in common, was that at the end, the characters always came home. Because they had a home, a place they indisputably belonged.

Nyx had never had that, until now. Even as she closed her eyes and breathed in the cold, crisp air, alive with the scent of trees and growing things, so different from the air of metropolitan Phoenix that lay just sideways of Earth Between, she still couldn't quite believe she was here. That she belonged here.

She passed the blacksmith's forge just outside the city proper and Laila, her hair sheared close to her skull, looked up from inspecting a sword to grin and wave at her.

It hit Nyx hard every time someone did that. Every time someone looked at her and their eyes didn't just slide past her, unable to focus, unable to remember she was there. Nyx's mother—Nyx herself—came from a long line of people with the ability to Hide things, and her mother had Hidden Nyx so well that she couldn't remember her life before eighteen. Before she'd come to Earth Between, people could literally look right at her and not see her.

She was trying desperately to believe that her mother had done so for good reasons, but since she couldn't remember her and had no idea where she was, Nyx mostly just felt bitter. She'd been on the verge of poverty and desperation, unable to hold a job since no one could remember she worked for them, when she'd stumbled into Earth Between and become the Waystation's Guardian. That Guardian bond had done something to her mother's spell, anchored her in a way that allowed people to remember her. One unsanctioned ley line trip later, complete with a brush with a chaos pocket, and the chaos thorns now adorning Nyx's cheek had altered her enough that her mother's Hiding had started unraveling. She still couldn't access her memories at will, but every now and then something would trigger her and she would get a flash of memory, a little colored piece of her life before.

"Hey, Nyx," Laila called brightly, "Did Morgen get anywhere with the dagger?"

Hey, Nyx. So easy, so simple. But she had gone years where the only time she heard her own name was when she whispered it to herself in the dark, afraid that if she stopped saying it, she would forget it too.

"You made that? The black one with the silver trim?"

Laila's grin grew wider. "Sure did. Charged him an arm and a leg for it too. He didn't seem to mind."

"I'm sure it was worth every universal. Officially, I'd have to say he did not get anywhere. Unofficially, it might be displayed in Evra's room. And if you tell him that I'm probably dead."

"I'll keep it to myself."

"Any leads on cool metal bo staffs?" Nyx was still hopelessly in love with the lightweight, collapsible bo staff she'd taken to Arkadia. She was not, however, so in love that she wanted it permanently melded to her hand for the rest of her life. Which meant she wanted a duplicate version of it without that one's semi-sentient tendencies.

She'd taken it out of the Den long enough to show it to Laila, in the hopes she could forge her one like it, but the blacksmith had been completely perplexed by it.

Laila shook her head. "I've been looking through all the weapons dealers I know, and put questions out to the other makers I keep in touch with, but no one's heard of anything like it. Metal simply doesn't *work* that way. If I hadn't seen it with my own eyes I'd think I was crazy." She snorted. "Which is what all my colleagues now think of me. If I could see it again..." Laila trailed off, already knowing the answer to the request she'd made more than once.

"Sorry, but I could only borrow it for the one day," Nyx answered. She'd told Laila it belonged to a passing traveler, specifically so she'd never have to bring it out again. "Let me know if you come across anything."

"Don't hold you breath, Guardian."

Laila went back to work and Nyx went back to walking. The harpy who frequented the outskirts of the market square and hustled her wares didn't bother with Nyx as she walked by, as Nyx had become a familiar enough face for her to know it was a waste of time.

The noise of the square folded around Nyx like a comforting blanket, from the outdoor vendors selling everything from jewelry to paintings to decadent desserts, to the Gliblin handlers with their corrals full of the four-foot-tall birdlike creatures available for hourly and daily leases to take visitors around the city. They wore the most adorable cloth saddles, and Nyx had been relieved to find they were humanely handled and trained, though she still hadn't quite worked up the nerve to get on one yet.

Goren, the market goblin who hawked copies of *The Galaxy News*, saw Nyx and made a beeline for her. His species was not actually listed as goblin, but since Nyx couldn't pronounce the actual name, and he looked more or less like the mythical goblins of Earth folklore, it was how she thought of him in her head.

She pulled a few universals out of her pocket and handed them over as he pulled a rolled-up copy of the newspaper out of his satchel.

"And that's why you're my favorite customer," Goren said as he took the money. "You never quibble about price."

"It's only because I like you so much," Nyx answered. In truth, after going so long without much meaningful person-to-person interaction, the idea of haggling with someone over the cost of an item terrified her. She stuck the paper in the back pocket of her jeans and ducked into the bakery next door to the Warlock's shop.

Cain's Confections was presided over by a burly man who made the best desserts Nyx had ever tasted. Her current favorite was something she couldn't pronounce, as she lacked the appropriately shaped vocal chords, and for which the translator spells had no equivalent. They were the size of a brownie and the base layer was indeed similar, though the middle contained a layer of tart golden filling, and it was topped with whipped cream made from the milk of an animal that was definitely not a cow. The entire thing was dusted in a layer of fine, thin silver sugar.

In short, they were heavenly. Nyx got a box of twelve and tucked them under her arm, then headed into the Warlock's shop. She had once been exceptionally disappointed by its lack of dust, cobwebs, and other appropriately nightmarish paraphernalia, but she'd come here so often in the last few weeks that now it just felt comfortable.

Ankira, the Warlock in question, stood in the incense section, restocking items from the large crate settled on the ground next to her. Her adopted son, Tobi, still as quiet and reserved as he'd been on Arkadia and still clutching the same misshapen piece of stuffed cloth that was a prison planet's attempt at a stuffed animal, waved shyly at her when she walked in.

"Nyx!" Ankira, Earth Between's very own Warlock, turned, beaming, the feathers dusking her auburn hair fluttering. Her hazel eyes shone, and the happiness that radiated from her made her even more beautiful than the first time Nyx had seen her. Motherhood suited Ankira.

"Why don't you come upstairs for some tea? We were just about to close for the day anyway."

"I brought dessert." Nyx held up the bakery box.

"Then we are definitely closed." Ankira flicked her fingers at the shop's entrance door. The locking wards hummed into wakefulness and a beautiful, looping font scrawled across the glass to write, *Closed.*

Upstairs, in the Warlock's cheerful yellow kitchen, plants of all colors and species dangling from every available surface, Nyx immediately relaxed. She'd come to think of Ankira as a friend, and dared to hope the Warlock might feel the same.

"Where's Diana?" she asked. Nyx did not think she had much chance of making friends with Diana, the Warlock's fiercely protective wife, but she did think they were approaching something that bordered on mutual respect. Probably because Evra and Diana were becoming friends, and Evra liked Nyx.

"She's practicing with Lauralyn." Ankira nodded at the window while she bustled around the kitchen, making tea and arranging small sandwiches on a tray. It was the kind of everyday domestic bliss that made Nyx's heart hurt on reflex, so she wandered over to the window. It oversaw the small back-yard that lay on the side of the building opposite the market square, where Diana and Lauralyn sparred with wooden practice swords.

"She's good." Nyx didn't mean to sound so surprised, but of the four kids they'd rescued from Arkadia, Lauralyn was the one she would have least expected to attach herself to Diana. She had been meek and seemingly terrified of everything, more so even than Tobi, who was barely eight years old.

"She is, isn't she?"

Nyx didn't have to turn to hear the smile in Ankira's voice.

"They practice a lot," Tobi grumbled, "and then I have to fix her."

"Fix her?" Nyx asked, trying not to sound too concerned. She had seen Tobi heal a broken ankle in the blink of an eye, a young shaman tapping into an ancient collective power that called itself the Congregation and frankly scared the hell out of her.

"You know. Poultices—" he stumbled over the word but got it out "—and stuff. For bruises. Anki's teaching me to make them."

"Oh, good." Nyx hoped her relieved exhale was not too audible.

"Why didn't you come with Kaden? He came this morning."

"I had travelers arriving this morning," she said, glad to have a real reason so she didn't have to lie to an eight-year-old.

"He seems sad."

"I'm sure he's just adjusting to normal life again. Like you are."

"I still have bad dreams sometimes. He told me that's okay. That he still has them sometimes."

Yes, I know he does. They wake me up every time he stabs a knife into his mattress in the middle of the night, and then I can't go back to sleep. When it was anyone else's nightmares, she could. But every time Kaden's woke her up she ended up just lying there, feeling his heartbeat thump against the Station's mattress, and she couldn't go back to sleep unless he did, too.

He didn't, very often, and Nyx was getting the dark circles beneath her eyes to prove it.

She managed to find a smile. "Of course it's okay. They'll pass in time." She hoped the words were true.

She passed a pleasant half hour chatting with Ankira and Tobi, and then Lauralyn and Diana, who came upstairs sweaty and in good spirits. By the time she left, her mood was significantly improved, but the closer she came to the Station, the more dread and—curse Morgen—*moodiness* settled onto her.

This was ridiculous. It was *her* Station. She was just letting everyone live in it because they had nowhere else to go. It didn't mean she had to feel isolated in her own bloody home. If Kaden had been avoiding her and she had been avoiding him, well, maybe it was time to say enough was enough. If he wanted to avoid her, he could do it in the middle of a group of other people, and she knew just the two people to help her bring it about.

"You're both bored, right?" Nyx asked.

"Yes," Morgen and Evra chorused.

Nyx had tracked them both down and dragged them to the Station's library. Morgen hadn't given Evra a single flattering comment, bent on taking the withdrawn-and-uninterested course of courtship, and Evra kept frowning and sneaking sidelong glances at him.

"Great. Tomorrow, we're taking a field trip."

"You want to take a trip to a field?" Evra said slowly, brow furrowing further. "Is it a particularly interesting field?"

Morgen kept to the new aloof version of himself and did not cackle. Nyx was impressed. Taking joy in peoples' misunderstandings of other languages' colloquialisms was one of his greatest delights in life. Nyx was almost convinced he'd learned every language known to alienkind except, given the number of languages that existed on Earth alone, she couldn't imagine how many there were in the greater universe.

"We aren't going to see a field, we're—"

"You specifically said a field trip."

"Yes, it's an expression. When kids are in school, if their teachers decide to take them on a trip somewhere else that is interesting, it's called a field trip."

"But they aren't going to fields?"

"No, they're not going to fields."

"That doesn't make any sense."

"I would explain the origin of the phrase but I don't know it."

Morgen was enthusiastically bouncing his leg up and down, which told Nyx he definitely knew the origin of the phrase and very much wanted to explain it.

"The point is," she continued, "we are all going out to Dead Earth tomorrow."

Morgen's leg stilled. Evra quit frowning. Two sets of shoulders straightened and two faces leaned ever-so-slightly forward.

"You wouldn't be getting our hopes up for nothing, would you, little Guardian?" Morgen asked. "Because every time Dead Earth has been brought up, a certain individual in this room has always said *no*, and that individual is neither me nor Evra."

"I said no because it was always the kids asking and they can't go alone. I'm betting you know enough about Dead Earth to blend in, am I wrong?"

"Of course not, I'm a master of disguise." Morgen brushed invisible dirt off his shoulders.

"Uh-huh. So there's you, and then with me and Kaden along, we should be able to make sure no one gives away the secrets of the universe." *Or ends up in a mental ward,* as was the more probable outcome.

Silence greeted her.

"You and Kaden," Evra said carefully.

"We are the two that know Dead Earth the best."

"Yes, but the two of you have been avoiding each other like Bremman's Plague will break out if one of you is within a fifty foot proximity of the other."

"I would tactfully agree with that statement," Morgen said, "except someone bit my head off earlier for saying the same thing."

"You telling me I should sleep with him and her telling me we're avoiding each other are two very different things."

"Semantics."

"Do you *want* the field trip canceled?"

"No, he does not," Evra said smoothly, "so he isn't going to speak anymore. I will do all the talking. What do you need us to do?"

"Just let everyone know that we will be leaving tomorrow evening at four and make sure they read these." Nyx handed them a pamphlet labeled, *The Betweener's Guide to Dead Earth: Everything You Need to Know to Get By in a Non-Magical World.*

The pamphlet had been sorely outdated when Griff presented it to her and, since it hadn't had a listed author, Nyx had taken the liberty of updating it.

"No one is allowed to take visible weaponry. Small knives or daggers are permissible so long as they are hidden from view" —she wasn't so optimistic as to expect them to forgo weaponry entirely— "and Griff will have the Station leave Dead-Earth-appropriate clothing in everyone's rooms."

"What are we going to do?"

Nyx had considered this carefully. While going to a paintball course was probably more appropriate to all of their skill sets, Nyx had no intention of unleashing that on the populace of Dead Earth. Better to give them all an experience less like their daily careers anyway.

"We are going to a bar for drinks and dinner, and then we are going to see a movie."

Since Evra had asked about movies before, Nyx didn't have to explain them. Or pique her interest. She just begged the stars that something in the action genre was playing.

"Wonderful." Evra stood. "We will make sure everyone is prepared."

"Yes, prepared." Morgen continued to lounge in his chair. "And how much awkward avoidance followed by bickering should I warn the rest of everyone to be *prepared for* when you and Kaden are at last in the same room?"

"Field. Trip. Will. Be. Canceled," Nyx threatened.

At those words Evra grabbed Morgen by the front of his jacket and dragged him bodily from the room. He looked exceptionally pleased by this end result.

Nyx paced the floor in her bedroom, debating over and over whether she should go talk to Kaden before they all went out tomorrow. In the end she decided to leave it alone, both because she had no idea what she would say, and because she was beginning to suspect she was, at heart, a coward. If she didn't talk to him, they could both pretend everything was normal when they were finally forced to interact, and that would be for the best.

Despite reassuring herself of this fact, it took two and a half hours of tossing and turning before she came anywhere close to sleep. She was just on the verge of that blissful unconsciousness when she felt it: a subtle presence at the divide between the Station's grounds and the rest of Earth Between. As if someone knew exactly where the two separated and they lurked at the boundary, just close enough to brush against it and be felt, but not enough for Nyx—for the Station—to have any idea of who waited.

Nyx didn't move. She'd felt that presence every night for the last two weeks. At first, it had bothered her enough that she'd gone rushing out to try and catch whoever or whatever prowled at the edges of her territory. But every time she'd gone, the presence had vanished before she was halfway across the grounds, and by the time she reached the boundary there hadn't been a single trace of the Watcher, as she had started thinking of them.

Griff, too, had felt the presence, so she knew she wasn't losing her mind, but he hadn't been any more capable than she of identifying it.

Tonight, she didn't bother racing across the Station to try and catch them. She knew she would only fail. Instead, she closed her eyes and settled fully into the Station's senses, the *Station's* awareness, and let go of her own. Cold February wind whistled through her tree branches, rustled her grass. An owl landed in the branches of her oak tree, hooting softly into the night, talons gripping the soft edges of her bark.

Nyx slid her awareness away from the tree, from the owl, and down to the very air that marked the boundary between what was *her* and what was other. It was there that the presence lingered. Quiet, still, watchful. Always watchful.

It irritated Nyx that she couldn't *see* with the Station's senses. It had no physical eyes. Instead, everything was felt. Experienced. She felt only the soft exhale of the Watcher's breath against the boundary, felt longing and confusion wound together into the night. It was the longest the Watcher had ever stayed, once her attention fell upon them. As if they knew, felt, the instant her attention merged with the Station's and noticed them.

Only, tonight, they didn't leave. They stood on the other side, waiting, something in their presence and manner familiar. It frustrated her that she couldn't *see* them, certain that if she just had an image to go with the presence, the familiarity would make sense.

She longed to reach out, and the Station responded to her need, air condensing and packing together until it formed a palm and fingers. She reached out with her phantom hand and brushed the Watcher's fingers that just barely crossed the line into the Station from Earth Between. A sharp intake of breath stirred the air and those fingers pushed against hers, until the Watcher's palm pressed flat against her own.

It occurred to her that if she could grab their wrist, pull their body onto the Station's grounds, she could hold them. She shifted her fingers the slightest fraction, and as if that tiny movement had telegraphed the entirety of her intent, the Watcher jerked their hand back, retreating to the safety that came with the land outside the Station. Their presence lingered at the edge of her senses for a moment longer, then vanished entirely.

The Watcher was gone.

Nyx released the air that had formed her phantom hand, her physical fingers tingling even though *they* had not come into contact with the Watcher. She kept her senses focused at the Station's edge, feeling the wind shift through the grass and trees, and willed the Watcher to reappear.

Only when she was convinced they wouldn't did she let go of her direct awareness of that area of the Station's grounds and return her full attention to her *own* senses, and the mild headache she now had from manipulating the Station at such a distance. She had gotten better at doing so, but controlling the Station was still very much like flexing a muscle she hadn't known she had—most of the time, it hurt afterward.

She tossed and turned for over an hour before sleep finally claimed her. She dreamed memories that night, of a cabin nestled into a wide green valley, of a large vegetable garden, and a barn full of horses. But mostly she dreamed of laughter, silver and devilish and achingly familiar.

4

———————

Nyx spent the next day pointedly not thinking about the previous night's strange encounter. If it even qualified as an encounter. Her dreams had left her feeling restless and unsettled, and she'd thrown herself into inventorying the Den with a gusto that Griff had fully approved of. She'd worked straight through lunch and hadn't let herself consider the evening's outing until ten to four rolled around, afraid if she thought too much about it she might realize that taking a band of warrior-trained aliens into Dead Earth was a terrible idea.

Now that she was standing in the Station's kitchen, surrounded by said aliens, it was too late to back out. She appraised them all and decided it was seriously weird seeing them in Dead Earth clothes. It wasn't even that their normal clothes were *that* much different from what they wore now—at the end of the day, pants and shirts were pants and shirts—but she'd never once seen any of them besides Kaden in a pair of jeans before.

Griff, who had had the Station create their current clothes, apparently had an eye for fashion, because everyone looked great. Maybe she should let him make *her* wardrobe.

Putting Evra in black jeans and a sky blue v-neck sweater

with matching leather jacket somehow made her look more dangerous than she normally did in full combat gear. It was the wolf in sheep's clothing effect. The softness of the sweater made *her* look soft, but nothing hid the air of carefully controlled danger that emanated from her at all times. Or maybe it was just that Nyx knew Evra had a long knife tucked into a hip sheath inside her jeans, an ankle dagger in her right boot, a stiletto in her hair, and she was pretty sure those silver things on her bracelet were actually throwing darts. Knowing Evra, they were probably dipped in poison, too.

Morgen's jaw had literally dropped when she walked in, and he was obviously having a hard time recovering and trying to maintain his new aloof persona. The change in his attitude hadn't been lost on Evra, who kept frowning at him as if he were a blue box that had suddenly turned red, only she couldn't pin her finger on the change. She was also staring at him with an attention to detail that likely had something to do with the fact he looked like sin incarnate. His braids were freshly rewoven and oiled, pulled back tidily at the nape of his neck, and he wore a pair of jeans that were faded to such a light color they contrasted nicely with the darkness of his skin. Add a long-sleeved green Henley to the mix and Nyx wondered if it was cruel of her to unleash him upon the unsuspecting people of Earth.

Especially when she suspected Evra was more interested in his attentions than the Amazon was willing to let on.

Kalvar and Tamrin looked, for once, like teenagers. It was a good look on them, and she hoped they had fun. She thought they might be more inclined to have fun if they befriended each other, but since each of them only had eyes for a different Moor sibling, that wasn't likely to happen. Kalvar kept looking at Maruca, who looked surprisingly feminine. She wore a pair of olive green straight leg pants, sensible but cute flats, and an apricot blouse that nicely set off her red hair. Hair that she had taken the time to curl so that it fell in soft waves around her face.

Nyx would never have suspected in a million years that Maruca Moor had a feminine side, but then people were always surprising her.

As for the *other* Moor sibling, Kaden had yet to make an appearance, and Nyx hoped she was doing a better job of hiding her disappointment than Tamrin was. The younger Amazon looked absolutely crestfallen and kept glancing toward the stairs. Nyx didn't think she sported the crush for Kaden that Kalvar had on Maruca. It was more like Kaden was a lifeline she thought she would drown without. Nyx still didn't know the full details of what had happened to Tamrin when she first arrived on Arkadia, before Kaden had taken her under his protection, and she probably never would. She barely knew Tamrin and it wasn't her place to ask. What worried her was that she didn't think the girl had even talked to Evra about any of it.

It was probably why Evra hadn't yet forced the issue of finding a way to get Tamrin back to her home planet. She couldn't travel the ley lines since the All Council knew Tamrin had been on Arkadia, and sending her off from Earth's Station would be like lighting up a giant arrow pointing at Earth and proclaiming *Your suspicions are correct, fugitives here.*

Nyx was also trying not to glance too frequently at the stairs. Sure, she'd been relieved that avoiding Kaden since he arrived here hadn't been too difficult. But now that she'd offered the proverbial olive branch in creating this outing, it stung that he wasn't coming.

It doesn't matter. She certainly wasn't going to ask Evra what he'd said when she'd informed everyone of the agenda.

When the clock ticked over to four and he still hadn't appeared, Nyx decided it was time to get on with it.

"Okay, everyone remembers the rules, right?"

Morgen, eager as always, jumped in. "No talking about other planets, magic, or sword-fighting. No brawling. If we do forget and talk about magic and sword-fighting, we are to loudly say the word LARPing. The children are not allowed to have alcohol, and if the adults want alcohol we have to show people these cards." Morgen helpfully held up the driver's license Griff had made for him. It turned out the Station could make just about anything with the right materials, and it had managed to study Nyx's own Arizona ID and make thoroughly convincing fakes for everyone in their party.

"You show the waiter the card, if they ask for your ID," Nyx corrected. She'd never felt more like a kindergarten teacher in her life. "Okay, if everyone's good, I think we can go."

It was Tamrin who bit her lip and asked what Nyx wanted to. "Is Kaden not coming?"

"Evra, did Kaden say if he was coming?" Nyx asked neutrally.

Evra shrugged. "Not in so many words."

"He probably doesn't feel welcome," Maruca muttered, at a volume intended to carry and yet make it sound like she was only talking to herself.

Nyx gritted her teeth and bit back a retort. Maruca was taking her confinement to the Station with less grace than the others, if such a thing were possible, and she believed unquestionably that any problem Kaden experienced must somehow be Nyx's fault. It was the desire to thwart any satisfaction Maruca might take at Nyx's discomfort that made Nyx smile sweetly and say, "I'll go see if I can find him."

She took two token steps towards the stairs leading to the second level. Token, because she felt the Station's floors, and through them she felt Kaden's footsteps coming downstairs. He'd been up in his room, lounging on the small cot he preferred to a bed, and giving every indication he was going to stay there all day. Then half a minute ago he'd sat up as if possessed, shoved on his boots, and headed downstairs as if the All Council itself was on his heels.

"Am I late?" The bright sincerity in Kaden's voice was well-played, the perfect balance between genuine curiosity and slight worry, meant to convey a simple lapse in time-management.

His eyes held the ghosts of dark shadows, and the lines his face had gained on Arkadia, ones Nyx had expected would fade in time, seemed instead to have etched themselves more deeply into his skin.

"Right on time." Tamrin smiled, wide and bright. She looked so much like Evra it was easy to forget how young she actually was. The younger Amazon hid her worries well from her sister, but Nyx had awakened in the night to Tamrin's heart pounding wild against her mattress, to her sweat soaking her sheets through and her entire body trembling.

Kaden had protected Tamrin on Arkadia, and the younger Amazon associated him with safety and familiarity. Nyx suspected the only time Tamrin really relaxed was when Kaden was near. In fact, Nyx knew it was, because the Station felt Tamrin's tenseness right now, and felt that tension ebb when Kaden walked into the room.

"Great." Nyx said brightly. "Let's go before *right on time* becomes *late.*"

"Doesn't *he* have to recite the rules?" Morgen asked innocently.

Nyx did roll her eyes this time, because Morgen just brought out the childish in her. "He lived here for two years. I think he's got the rules down."

Shushing Morgen's reply, Nyx led her ragtag group of aliens out of the Station and onto their first field trip.

Nyx halted at the branching paths at the end of Wayfarer's Way. When she'd first followed it from Dead Earth on the day she'd become the Station's new Guardian, Wayfarer's Way had led only to the Station. Since then it had forked, the right path leading to Earth Between and the left fork to Dead Earth. Though Dead Earth was, as its name suggested, a mostly non-magical place, enough residual magic existed throughout the planet for Wayfarer's Way to deposit an individual anywhere in Dead Earth that was geographically equivalent to the parallel spaces Earth Between occupied.

Nyx did not actually know how much of Dead Earth that encompassed, and hadn't been able to find out. The few histories of Earth she had managed to dig up in the Station's archives only indicated that Earth Between had once held more purchase on the planet, but shrank over time as Earthlings' belief in magic continued to dwindle. As it dwindled, chunks of Earth Between became separated from the city as it was now, leaving pockets of magical space in various places throughout the planet. Inconveniently, said history did not include any maps or data on the current size of Earth Between proper or its isolated pockets.

"What are we waiting for?" Maruca demanded. The woman was physically incapable of asking a question politely.

"For me to concentrate so I don't dump us onto a street full of moving cars." Which was exactly what had happened the first time Nyx had returned to Dead Earth after coming to the Station. Well, the street part anyway. It had been one in the morning, so fortunately the street had been empty at the time.

Nyx closed her eyes and thought of Tempe Marketplace. More specifically, she thought of the west side of the parking lot near the Harkins theater, where the parking didn't usually fill up and it was unlikely anyone would notice them stepping out of thin air. If someone did see them, it should be a small enough number of people that the magic of the Between would convince whoever saw them that they'd simply been walking up from the street.

The forest surrounding the end of Wayfarer's Way blurred, disappeared, and was replaced by the black asphalt of the parking lot. The very packed parking lot. So packed, in fact, that when they stumbled through it was behind a line of parked cars.

The transition knocked the wind from her more effectively than any sucker punch. She'd been back twice since coming to the Station, and the transition wasn't any easier this time than it had been before. How had she lived here for years and never noticed how thick the air was? How claustrophobic the noise and pollution? It hurt to breathe, to think.

"It passes after a few minutes," Kaden said softly. He wasn't quite touching her, just standing close enough that he might as well have been, and Nyx's stupid heart sped up for no reason.

So, I guess he's speaking to me again.

"I know. It's not the first time I've come back." And then, because that sounded rude and she wasn't trying to piss him off, she asked, "What is it?"

"The absence of magic. I always wondered how you stood it here, being what you are."

Being what you are. Hidden. She'd just never known she *had* that magic before.

Nyx shook her head. "I never felt it before." But as she straightened her shoulders and sucked down a deep breath, she realized the words weren't quite true. It wasn't that she hadn't felt it when she lived here, it was just that she hadn't realized anything could feel different.

"What is that?" Evra stood ramrod-straight, her gaze riveted on a construction crane on the opposite side of the chain link fence edging the north side of the parking lot, its long arm poised high above a section of half-built apartments.

"It's a type of machine." Nyx had previously done her best to explain about machines. "People use them to move heavy objects when they're building things."

"It is safe to pass by?"

Only the dead seriousness of Evra's question kept Nyx from laughing. The crane was two-hundred feet away and quite obviously not in operation. Still, she could understand how, if you'd never seen a machine before, it might look somewhat like a great slumbering beast. Truth told, it even looked a little foreign to Nyx's eyes, now. The Between felt more like home with each passing day, and things like cranes and cars and construction zones were fading from her sense of everyday normality.

"It's safe," Nyx promised. "It doesn't move unless a person is operating it. Now," Nyx turned to address the entire group, "once we start walking we may pass some moving cars. They shouldn't be moving too fast through the parking lot but not everyone is a great driver, so stick to the sidewalks, follow me and you'll be fine."

"Spoken like a true leader. My little Guardian is growing up." Morgen brushed a nonexistent tear from the corner of his eye and was the first to follow Nyx as she led them along the perimeter of the parking lot.

How had she forgotten how loud cars were? The constant noise of them buzzing past her pounded abrasively against her ears. And stars, the *smell* of them. She thought of the crisp, clean air of the Station's forest and contemplated how she had lived for so long breathing in asphalt and pollution.

Nyx lead them up to the sidewalk that ran alongside Bar Louie at the Marketplace's eastern entrance. She had wondered how everyone would read and understand English without the translation spells soaked into Earth Between, but then Evra had reminded her that individual translator spells were a thing. Everyone except Kalvar had already had one, given their previous jobs took them all over the universe. Kalvar hadn't even blinked at the expense of purchasing one, probably because, since he had zero living expenses residing in the Station, he'd amassed a fair amount of money as Nyx's employee.

Nyx had gone with him to the tattooist who inked the spells in, and she now had her very own translator spell on her right wrist, opposite her Guardian tattoo. Not that she would need it in Tempe, but she'd figured she might as well go ahead and get it since she might, in theory, visit another planet some day. All planets had Earth Between-style translator spells in the main city hubs, Evra had told her, but if one wanted to travel at all off the beaten path, it paid to have a personal translator.

Her group read the brightly-lit store signs of Tempe Marketplace and promptly bombarded her with questions, which she happily let Kaden field, listening to him explain about things like Target, PetSmart, and the dozens of other shops in the complex. He did a good job of it and the telling of things livened him up, softened the lines on his face.

Lines she assured herself she was not worried about. *I am also not concerned about the fact he only averages three hours of sleep a night, or that those three hours are riddled with nightmares.*

She'd been an idiot to think that having him at the Station wouldn't affect her, wouldn't wear away at the numerous, very good reasons she had not to soften toward him. Reasons like deception and betrayal and the Harvester of Worlds hanging around her neck. There was a reason that when couples broke up, they tended not to remain friends—being intimate with someone for a long period of time made it difficult to maintain an emotional distance. It was practically impossible when she felt his every movement, though thank the stars he didn't know of her altered bond with the Station, didn't *know* he tortured her every waking moment.

Nyx led them past Bar Louie to the other end of the Marketplace. She had decided that only a bar would do for dinner, given the rough and tumble company she kept of late, even though she would have killed for a round of sushi. Though she liked Bar Louie, she'd settled on the Thirsty Lion, telling herself it sounded more rustic and would therefore appeal more to her companions. Plus, it would give them the opportunity to gawk at shops on the walk there.

That was what she told herself, and if it was technically true, it wasn't the whole of her reasoning. Bar Louie had been her and Kaden's pre-movie ritual, and she didn't feel like sharing it with anyone else. Or reliving the memories that going there would dredge up.

They reached the Thirsty Lion and Nyx, sending up a silent prayer to those benevolent gods she was pretty sure didn't exist, opened the door and requested a table for seven.

Despite the hostess looking at Nyx as if she were insane for her table request, she led them inside ten minutes later. "You guys got crazy lucky. A party of eight just canceled."

Nyx made a noncommittal sound. The restaurant was busier than she'd expected, packed so full that even all the stools at the bar were taken, with quite a few people standing, besides. Most faces were glued to the televisions hanging from the ceilings, the crowd sporting such an abundance of football paraphernalia it finally dawned on Nyx that they were in that time of year when football Sundays were all the craze.

Their waitress appeared five minutes after they were seated, a smiling brunette with large hoop earrings and an artistically crooked nose. "Hi, I'm Carrie, I'll be your server today, can I get you started with something to drink?"

Evra replied, "Ale."

The waitress took this in stride, rattling off a variety of beers whose title ended with *ale.* By the fourth variety Evra was sneaking covert glances at Nyx that clearly said, *What the hell?*

Nyx flashed an apologetic smile at the waitress. "They haven't been in the US long and their English isn't great yet. Kaden, do you think you could order for them?"

It wasn't that Nyx couldn't pick out a handful of beers. It was that she didn't want to be responsible for whatever Maruca ended up drinking. Kaden raised an eyebrow at her but he acquiesced, taking the simple expedient of ordering them all the same New Belgium Trippel Ale.

"Got it, I just need to see your IDs."

Morgen winked at Nyx and proffered his ID to the waitress with an embellished flourish. She giggled, looked it over and handed it back. She let her fingers brush his on the return, bending forward just enough to display the impressive cleavage popping out of her shirt. The exchange wasn't lost on Evra, who handed her ID to the waitress with an icy chill that would have sent the brunette scrambling for the first bus out of town if she'd had any idea what Evra was capable of.

Nyx ordered a Smithwick's, kept a watchful eye on Evra—whose hand was fidgeting with her poisoned-dart bracelet a little too much for Nyx's comfort—and ordered root beer for Tamrin and Kalvar. She hoped the name would mollify them somewhat, since the drinking age off-world went something like, "If they can swing a sword, they can drink a beer."

"Why is every—"

Nyx missed the end of Maruca's question as a collective roar went up from pretty much every patron in the bar. Fists banged on tables, glasses clinked together, and crowd energy rocked the room.

As a collective unit everyone at Nyx's table, save her and Kaden, jumped to stand on their seats. Nyx reacted just in time to halt Evra's hand before the Amazon could pull her long-knife out of its sheath. She yanked Evra back into her seat, a move which only worked because Evra allowed herself to be pulled down. Evra worked out her annoyance by dragging Morgen down with her.

Morgen, being Morgen, contrived to land in her lap. "My lady Amazon, if I'd known you were after a close encounter, I would have—"

Evra punched him in the kidney. He slid off her good-naturedly just as Tamrin and Kalvar figured out the roar of the crowd had not indicated impending doom and regained their own respective seats. Maruca stood a defiant two seconds longer than everyone else before settling down with the air of a monarch regaining her throne.

"What are they all yelling for?" Tamrin asked.

"To punctuate the realization of my idiocy," Nyx muttered. In all fairness to herself she didn't have access to the Internet in Earth Between, so even if she'd remembered the wretched event that occurred every February, she couldn't have known it was today. Turning to Kaden, she said, "It's Super Bowl Sunday."

Kaden was quiet for a long moment. Then he threw back his head and laughed.

ootball, it turned out, was fascinating to everyone at the table except Kalvar, who didn't understand, as he put it, "The point of running back and forth the same patch of green just to get your head knocked about."

Privately, Nyx agreed with Kalvar, but she wasn't going to bring it up since learning the rules of this "primitive war game" from Kaden kept her band of aliens too entertained to do anything spectacularly stupid. Like, say, throw a poisoned dart at the waitress, which Evra appeared to really, really want to do, as Nyx had to slap Evra's hand away from a certain bracelet every time the waitress came to their table. After the fourth time, Nyx announced, "I have to find the restroom. Evra, you have to come with me."

"I have to attend you to the privy?"

"It's a time-honored Dead Earth tradition. If a woman is in a bar and has to go to the restroom, another female from her party has to go with her."

Evra looked to Kaden, skeptical. "This is true?"

Kaden nodded, face serious, voice grave. "Think of it like traveling with allies through unknown territory."

Evra obviously wasn't convinced of the necessity but she shrugged and stood, stretching, the blue sweater riding up to expose a slice of taught golden skin. Despite the distraction of the Superbowl, men were *not* so drunk they didn't notice. Nyx couldn't blame them. Evra was a goddess in a sea of regularity.

Just keep it to staring, boys, Nyx thought, pointing out the bathroom and following in Evra's wake. Where Nyx would have had to dart around people and shove her way through because no one ever noticed her, the crowd naturally parted for Evra, and since no one was yet drunk enough to hit on her, they made it to the bathroom in record time. After a quick survey to conclude it was empty—a miracle in and of itself—Nyx propped her hip against the counter and leveled her gaze on Evra.

"Okay, talk. Who was it?"

"Who was what?"

"The asshole who broke your heart."

"If I had a broken heart I would be dead. It would have to be physically ripped from my body to be broken."

Nyx narrowed her eyes. "Don't play the, 'Oh, I don't understand Earth sayings,' card on me. I'm pretty sure a broken heart is a universal one."

"Fine. No one has broken my heart."

"Uh-huh."

"Did I really have to accompany you here to have *this* talk?"

"Yes, because we're friends. And friends don't let friends pine over hot half-sirens who are obviously mad for them without finding out why they won't do something about it."

"I am not pining."

"You kept the knife he gave you and you've thought about killing the waitress at least eight times."

"The knife was practical and well-made, and I've thought about killing the waitress twelve times. She is tawdry and annoying."

"And it has nothing to do with the fact she shoves her boobs in Morgen's face every chance she gets?"

A vein popped out along Evra's neck. "Of course not."

Nyx smirked. "You are definitely lying. And the only reason I can think of for a strong, self-possessed woman such as yourself not to jump into the lap of the hot guy she likes who quite literally jumped into *her* lap fifteen minutes ago, is that some asshole broke her heart. So who was it?"

"No one broke my heart. Can we go now?"

"Nope. Not until you talk."

Evra broke out into some *very* uncomplimentary words "There was no heart breaking. We had a difference of fundamental values and went our separate ways. I am past it."

"Good. Then you'll kiss him?"

"Excuse me?"

"Morgen. Kiss him. It will drive the waitress away effectively so you don't have to kill her and cause me a mountain of paperwork."

Nyx knew she was in trouble when Evra nodded. "Kiss him. Of course. And will you be kissing Kaden?"

"Excuse me?"

"Kaden. Kiss him. It will offer a hormone release and save the rest of us from the overpowering misery filling the air every time the two of you are in a room together."

Put that way, maybe Evra's love life was none of her business.

"Oh my, look at the time." Nyx tapped her watch. "Everyone will be wondering where we are." She turned and darted out the door.

She was halfway back to their table when Nyx felt someone's gaze on her and stopped abruptly, causing Evra to bump into her.

She followed the weight of watching eyes to the bar. A man leaned against the wall at the far end, his hair ink black, his chocolate eyes almost as dark, and they were staring directly at her. Except he couldn't be looking at her, because though the holes in her mother's Hiding had made it *possible* for people in Dead Earth to notice her, without the aid the Guardian bond gave her in Earth Between, it still took a lot of effort to get people in Dead Earth to see her. They certainly didn't do so from across a room.

Evra. He had to be looking at Evra.

Only, it didn't feel like he was looking at Evra, and something about him bothered Nyx, tugged at her.

"I'll meet you back at the table."

"Why?"

"I'm going to get a drink."

Evra frowned. "We have drinks at the table."

"I want a different one. And I don't want to wait for the waitress."

Evra looked suspicious, but she left when Nyx shooed her off. Nyx made a beeline for the bar. She slipped onto the miraculously empty stool next to the guy and pretended to try and catch the bartender's attention, which she knew from experience was a completely impossible thing for her to do. People didn't notice her in Dead Earth. Not bartenders, and certainly not dark-haired, dark-eyed strangers standing less than a foot from her.

The stranger leaned onto the bar. A black feather, like a miniature raven's feather, dangled from one ear, and a thin pendant swung from a golden chain on his neck. He looked directly at her.

"Buy you a drink?" He didn't wait for her to answer, motioning the bartender over in that effortless way Nyx had never been able to manage. He held up two fingers. "Tequila."

Plenty of people drank tequila, Nyx reasoned. So what if it was her liquor of choice? So what if he'd noticed her? Her mother's Hiding had simply frayed more since the last time she came to Dead Earth. It had frayed more, and it had allowed someone in Dead Earth to finally notice her. That was all.

The bartender brought their drinks and the stranger slid one across to her, some unexplained amusement in his eyes.

"So what brings you out today?"

"Isn't everyone here for the game?" Nyx ignored the shot glass he'd slid to her.

He shrugged, and there was something hard in his eyes. The pendant on his necklace glinted in the light, a long, narrow metal rectangle with raised symbols she didn't recognize even though she felt like she should.

"Why are *you* here?" she challenged.

He tossed his shot of tequila back. "Me? I came here to see an old… friend."

"Yeah? You should probably get back to them, then."

He made a noncommittal noise, then his gaze landed on her cheek, where the chaos thorns made their spiraling pattern. "Get into a fight with a thorn bush and lose?" he asked.

The teasing words irritated her, and even as she was thinking that something about this conversation wasn't right—or maybe was *too* right, she wasn't sure—and that she should keep him talking to figure out what it was, she found herself instead snapping out, "Was there something you wanted?"

He laughed, low and rich. "Oh, I want a lot of things, darling."

"None of them things she wants to help you with, I'm sure," came a voice behind Nyx. Kaden's voice. He stood behind her, close enough to indicate familiarity. Possessiveness.

Oh, for stars' sake, of all the useless, inopportune times for him to decide to acknowledge her existence again, he picked *now*?

The stranger looked Kaden over from head to toe. "Oh, I'm sure you're right about that." He picked up Nyx's untouched tequila shot and downed it, setting the empty glass on the bar with a thunk. "Nice talking to you, Nyx."

He stood and walked away. Nyx resisted the urge to immediately follow him, because one didn't just run after normal men in bars who had done nothing more irregular than possibly hit on her before her hulking ex showed up, except—

"My name," she breathed. "I never told him my name."

She ran, pushing her way through the crowd, Kaden a silent shadow in her wake. She darted out onto the patio, past the outdoor diners who gawked as she barreled past. She cleared the patio fencing in a single bound and kept going, because the stranger was running now, far ahead, swift like a shadow across the parking lot, sensing pursuit.

A name popped into her head, unbidden, and she yelled it before she could think better of it. "Seth!" She left off the *h* sound, saying it 'Set' like the Greek pronunciation of the Egyptian god.

He stumbled, stopped and looked back, something unreadable in his eyes. Then he was just…gone. She stopped abruptly,

Kaden next to her. Her breath came in harsh, jagged pulls as she stared at the space where the man had disappeared.

Disappeared, into Earth Between.

"Seth," she whispered again, knowing that it was right, that it belonged to him, and not knowing why. She heard a flash of silver laughter in her mind, saw herself leaning low over the neck of a buckskin mare, a bay gelding racing beside her, a younger version of Seth astride the horse, his dark eyes dancing with merriment.

"You know him?" There was something tight in Kaden's voice.

"Yeah." She didn't remember how or why or know what it meant, but she knew it was true. "I do."

5

Nyx stormed through the Station's front doors, her mood every bit as black as the night falling on Earth Between. They had searched everywhere, her little band of fugitives energized now they had a purpose that was familiar to them, yet they had failed. She had turned Earth Between upside down to the best of her ability—it might be small in terms of the universe, but it was large in terms of a few people searching it—but no one she'd spoken to had recognized Seth's description.

The others were still out looking, despite her telling them there was no point. Not in the dark. She was beginning to think there'd been no point in the light. Because something told her that Seth wasn't going to be found unless he wanted to be found.

"We'll find him, Nyx." Kaden followed her into the Station's kitchen. He'd been the only one to actually give up the hunt when Nyx said they should, following her back to the Station. She was surprised he'd given up, since she'd learned tracking was more or less his magical specialty. Maruca and Morgen had looked at him expectantly once they'd entered Earth Between, but after crouching for several minutes with his eyes closed, fingers splayed wide across the ground and the tang of magic filling the air around him, he'd stood and shaken his head. He'd then said a lot of words Nyx wasn't familiar with, but which she gathered boiled down to Seth had masked his trail and Kaden couldn't find it.

"You don't remember anything else about him?" he asked. Again.

"Just the name, that's all." *And laughter, and horseback riding.* She hadn't even known she knew how to ride a horse.

Kaden settled onto one of the kitchen barstools, leaned his elbows on the counter and laced his fingers together. Nyx considered the merits of continuing to stand, but decided she wasn't going to be deterred from sitting down in her own home simply because he was there. She could sit next to him. Which she did. She just left a seat between them.

"If you want to find him I need to know everything you know." Kaden seemed to be taking his tracking failure personally and was coping with it by interrogating her for information.

"I don't know anything that will help," she snapped. How many times could he ask her the same question? She wasn't going to miraculously find a different answer. "I'm sorry I can't tell you whatever it is you want to hear, but the only thing I can remember is his name."

He ran his hands through his hair. "I'm sorry," he said quietly. "I'm just trying to help. This must be…difficult for you."

Her fingers tensed on the counter, her veins running black as anger from the chaos thorns in her face flooded her body. She closed her eyes and shoved the anger down. Kaden *was* just trying to help.

"I just want to know who I am." She'd expected to sound angry but she just sounded tired. She'd been so hopeful, after she'd first learned her mother's name, and Viktor Hawthorne's, the man she thought might be her father. But she and Evra had searched and searched and come up with nothing. The only thing Nyx was certain of was that neither Elena nor Viktor had left Earth via this Station. Had they even left Earth at all?

"I thought I could let it go but now that I've seen him, now that I *know* someone knows who I am…" She trailed off.

She'd wondered so many times about her life before. What kind of person had she been? Had she had friends? Family other than her mother? She used to entertain herself by making up fantasies about what that life had been like. Of course, that had been before she knew about magic and other inhabited planets, so they'd all been normal fantasies, and she'd never bothered to explain her amnesia in any of them.

The joy had just been in pretending that she'd had a normal life. Like maybe she'd lived with her parents on a ranch in Montana and she had two brothers and a dog. Or, given her ingrained knowledge of the martial arts, maybe her parents ran a martial arts gym where she hung out after school and learned from all the instructors.

Stupid, silly fantasies, and she hadn't even gone the traditional route of imagining her family was wealthy in any of them, because money wasn't what had mattered to her. What had mattered was the idea that maybe, once, she'd had people she'd meant something to. People who remembered her and loved her. People *she* had loved.

Seth's name had settled into her like a missing piece, like it belonged there, like he *meant* something.

He'd been close to her. A brother? She discarded the idea almost as soon as she thought it. They weren't related, she'd bet on it, and yet she was almost certain she'd known him her entire life. That he knew exactly who she was, and if she could only track him down, he could tell her everything she wanted to know.

"If you think of anything else—"

"It's no use. I appreciate you helping me look, but there's no point in going over it again and again. Seth's like rain, anyway," she said, the certainty popping into her head. "Pray for it and it'll never show up, ask for clear skies and you'll get a downpour."

Kaden lifted an eyebrow. "That's oddly specific."

She shrugged. "If I could choose how my memory works, I would."

They sat in silence for a few minutes after that. It wasn't precisely awkward but she didn't know what to say to him, and he didn't seem to know what to say to her, either. She thought about apologizing for what she knew he'd overheard her say in the Den, but she wasn't really sorry. Sorry he'd heard it, yes. Otherwise, no. And if he wanted to pretend he hadn't heard, she was just fine with that.

"How long do you think the others will be gone?" she finally asked.

"Depends on how hard Morgen is trying to impress Evra."

"Maybe they'll be back soon, then. He's switched tactics from adamant pursuit to broody withdrawal."

Kaden smiled. "I'd give him a day before he cracks."

"So little faith." Nyx made a *tsking* sound.

Kaden snorted. "I've known him since we could walk. Broody has never been his strong suit."

No, she thought, *that would be yours.*

"I don't know. I think underneath that happy exterior he's genuinely torn up about Evra. I'd say he makes it at least three days."

"Want to bet?"

Nyx narrowed her eyes. "What do I get if I win?"

"What do you want?" His voice was a little lower, a little rougher, and it made Nyx's heart do things she wasn't ready for it to do around him again.

What did she want?

For you to never have left, she thought. *For you to never have lied to me.*

Her response came out flat and tired. "Nothing. I don't want anything."

She stood to walk away and he grabbed her hand. Sensation

jolted through her, the rough calluses of his palms rasping against her skin.

"Go on a date with me."

Nyx's mouth went dry. "What?"

"A date," he repeated. "Go on one with me."

"Why?"

"Because I miss you?" he offered. "Because we can't avoid each other forever? Because I'd like the chance to prove to you that I *meant* the time we spent together?"

That—that right there—was the core of her problem, wasn't it? The real reason she'd been avoiding him. After the initial shock of having him thrown back into her life, she'd come to the conclusion that she didn't *want* to know if they'd had anything real between them. She didn't want to find out how much of their relationship had just been him saying and doing whatever he needed to in order to keep her close, to make her trust him so that one day she would keep the Harvester Hidden.

What if she spent time with him only to discover they weren't anything, that there was nothing there? Before she'd come to the Station, the two years she'd spent with Kaden had been the only real happiness she could remember, the only connection she'd had to another person in a world incapable of noticing her, and finding out that it had been absolutely nothing at all? Well, she didn't know if she could handle that.

But finding out that it *had* been something—that might be even worse. Because then she might be tempted to look past the things he'd done, and she wasn't sure she wanted to. She'd been so naive, so desperate, thinking that the one person who could recognize her had actually fallen in love with her. Because whether he had or hadn't, it certainly hadn't been what he'd intended to do when he found her.

The voice of caution in her head warned her that Kaden always did what he felt was best, what he felt was his *duty*, and everything else came second. So what if he had loved her? So what if he still did? Did she really think he would stay here with her? Here, in this Station, where she was bound for the rest of her abnormally long life?

And then there was always the darker voice, the one that whispered that this could still simply be Kaden playing his cards carefully, ensuring that she was emotionally invested in protecting him and his sister and Morgen in the event he couldn't find a way to get them off Earth.

But then, who was to say she couldn't find out the answer for herself? She could let him think she believed him. Let him think she was still the same lonely, trusting woman who'd fallen right into his arms the first time, and then discover for herself whether he'd *meant* any of it or not.

She forced herself to relax. "All right. Fine. Let's go on a date."

Surprise flickered across his face, but he covered it over with a smile. "Good. And Nyx?" His thumb drew a circle on the back of her palm. "About what you said, about wanting to know who you are. You don't need anyone else to tell you that. But if you did, I could."

Nyx didn't move. She should have. She should have walked away right fucking then.

"You're smart and loyal and resilient."

No. No, no, no. This was exactly the reason she'd been avoiding him. Because as soon as he touched her, as soon as he talked to her like that, she lost all impartiality and wanted to jump him.

Focus, she ordered herself. *You're playing him, not the other way around.*

"You make me sound like a Labrador."

It was the first thing she could think of to try and make the moment less intense. The tips of his fingers had reached her palm, tracing little patterns. It had been a very long time since she'd been touched like that. She didn't count the brief time she and Kaden had kissed when he'd been half out of his mind and convinced she was a hallucination. That had been rough and desperate. Passionate, but also empty.

This—this was slow and intentional, his fingers tracing fire along her skin.

"That would make you the sexiest Labrador I've ever seen."

"Kaden…" She trailed off, not sure what she'd meant to say. What she *should* say.

Slowly, deliberately, without breaking the touch of his hand on hers, he slid off the bar stool and took two steps to her, until there was less than a centimeter of space between them.

"I miss you," he whispered. His other hand lifted to brush across the arc of her cheekbone. "If you don't feel the same way that's okay. I just need to know."

How was she supposed to know *what* she felt when he was standing so close? She wanted to bury her face in his neck and breathe him in, to have his arms wrap around her and feel even a fraction of the comfort she'd felt when they were together.

Because even though she wasn't alone anymore, the Station filled with people she considered her friends, there was a different loneliness that could only be driven away by being touched and held like she was the only person in the world that mattered. He'd always been good at making her feel like that.

"Nyx?"

Right. He was waiting for an answer. Nyx was so distracted trying to think of one to give him that she didn't feel the others on the deck outside. The front door swung open and Nyx jumped. Unfortunately, she jumped right *in* to Kaden, which would have sent him sprawling if he hadn't had the kind of balance that turned him into an immovable force. She bounced off the exceptionally well-muscled planes of his chest before sliding around him, slipping her hand from his and trying not to look guilty.

The way Maruca's gaze flicked between Nyx and Kaden before she glared at her with enough venom to fell an elephant told Nyx she hadn't been at all suave about her extrication.

Everyone else either didn't notice or at least had the decency to pretend they didn't.

"We found nothing," Evra growled.

"I told you it wasn't any use," Nyx said.

"You do not understand. I am very good at what I do. They," Evra indicated Maruca, Morgen, and Kaden, "are very good at what they do. And yet we found nothing. Not a single trace. Who *is* this Seth?"

"I wish I knew," Nyx murmured, even as a smile tugged at her lips because she was positively certain that somewhere out there, Seth was enjoying making them all run in circles, and there was a time when she would have been invited in on the joke.

<hr>

It took Nyx most of the night to fall asleep, and she woke not long after to something tugging at the edges of her awareness. Not her immediate awareness, but the Station's boundary again. It was a minuscule distraction, like a moth fluttering in and out of her peripheral vision, just barely crossing into it enough for her to see. She sat up, listening intently even though what she waited for wasn't a physical sound.

The Watcher. Except she knew, now, who the Watcher was.

As if he sensed he'd caught her attention, Seth stepped exactly two feet inside the Station grounds and stood, waiting. Nyx stumbled out of bed, groped for her clothes, and fumbled them on. Then she opened the sliding glass door to her balcony and jumped off it. She lived three stories up but had decided, in coming to terms with her new relationship with the Station, that given the price she had paid to be able to alter the things in a sentient building and grounds at her whim, she might as well be able to do it well. So she jumped off the balcony and grabbed hold of the fireman's pole that sprang out of the ground, hooked her leg around it and slid down, bare feet hitting the ground.

She'd mostly stopped going barefoot. The dual sensation of her feet feeling the ground and her ground feeling someone's feet was still a little much to take most days. Tonight, however, it served her purposes well. She felt through her feet, through the three miles of Station grounds to the spot where Seth stood. Terrified that whatever whim had brought him here would take him away just as swiftly, she reached for the space inside herself where her connection with the Station lay and took hold of it. Then she took the space where she stood and connected it to Seth's, drawing the two places together like the edges of a map, and folded space.

There was no rushing wind, no sense of traveling. One moment she was standing on the ground outside her bedroom and the next that same patch of ground was next to where Seth stood at the Station's borders. She stepped onto the ground near the border and let go of the piece she had folded to this spot, felt it snap back to where it should be like a released rubber band. The effort exhausted her—she was quite literally pushing the limits of a muscle she'd only just learned how to use, and maybe it was foolish, because she wouldn't be able to do anything of that magnitude again for a few hours at least, but she couldn't risk the possibility that if she didn't get to Seth right that moment, he would leave.

He leaned against a pine tree, arms folded across his chest like he was indescribably bored, and arched an eyebrow. "You always were full of surprises. How'd you land a Guardian post?"

Nyx leaned against a pine tree of her own and mimicked his pose, arms crossed and one foot hooked casually over the opposite ankle. Without knowing why, she was certain it would irritate him, and equally certain she made a habit of irritating him.

"Oh, let me see. I just wandered around for years with no idea of who I was and then, when I was living in what amounts to a hovel on the verge of eviction because I had no money, I stumbled into Earth Between, because apparently it's a place that takes desperation to find. But please, stop me if I'm telling you things you already know."

She could recall in minute detail the handwriting on the single note in her apartment when she'd woken up at eighteen with absolutely no idea of who or where she was. It had told her her name, her bank account and college acceptance information, and nothing else. It had been a precise, almost sharp, hand that had drawn the letters and, letting her gaze fall on Seth's elegant, tapered fingers, she was certain she knew who had written it.

Nyx caught the barest flicker of guilt across his face before he quashed it, before anger took its place.

What exactly did *he* have to be angry about?

"Did you consider working for a living? It's what normal people have to do. Or did Elena actually manage to drive any normality out of you?"

Nyx's heart sped up. *Elena.* Her mother's name.

"Oh, I worked. I worked every shitty job I could find but the funny thing is, it's almost impossible to get a job when people can barely remember you even when you're standing right in front of them. What jobs I did get I usually lost in a matter of weeks. Sometimes days, because no one could remember I existed.

"Do you have any idea what it's like to be a ghost in your own fucking life? You want to know how I got this?" She stepped forward, shoved the arm with her Guardian tattoo out. "Earth Between's Station chooses a person who has absolutely nothing left to lose. Someone no one will miss, because no one gives a damn about them. I got this post because I didn't matter to anyone, and I had nothing that mattered to me."

She felt footsteps on the path that led from the Station to here and recognized Kaden's loping run. How had he even known she was awake? Then again, his control freak tendencies probably meant he'd been on high alert ever since Seth's appearance at the bar. Kaden might not be able to track *Seth*, but he could easily track her.

Unfortunately, much like at the bar, Kaden's presence was the last thing she needed. Seth would run the moment he saw him. She reached out to the land, her mind screaming in protest at being asked to manipulate the Station to such an extent yet again, but she managed to slow Kaden's progress. Anything more, and she'd pass out.

She blinked through a haze of pain and turned her attention back to Seth, determined to get something from him.

"So now that I think about it, I guess I don't care who you are. Just tell me where my mother and father went and you can get the hell out of my life again."

"Your father?" He laughed and it was a harsh, jackal sound. "*Your* father? Oh, Nyxi, how screwed up are things in that pretty little head of yours?"

"I don't know," Nyx ground out, "why don't you tell me?"

Tell me something—anything—quickly.

Kaden, faced with ground that took twice as long to traverse, had simply doubled his speed.

"Nah, I don't think so. Trust me, you're better off without them."

"The thing is," she said, stepping in closer, "I don't trust you." Just an inch or so more and she'd be close enough to take his legs out from under him before he saw the move coming.

He leaned forward—

Just a little further.

—and twisted, pinning her against the pine tree with his body, his hands clamping her wrists. They were gentle, despite their iron grip. The musk and spice scent of him washed over her, familiar, like she'd smelled it every day for years.

"Oh, Nyxi," he murmured. "You must have forgotten I know all your tricks."

His attention shifted over her shoulder. Kaden was visible now, a mere quarter mile out. Seth sighed. "Does he always just show up like that?"

Nyx sighed too. "Usually, yeah."

"That's a shame."

"What are you even doing here? Why come back *now*?"

"I think—" He rested his forehead against the tree next to her, and his feather earring tickled the side of her cheek. "I think I missed you, Nyxi. I just didn't know it."

"Yeah? Well I think you're an asshole." Just another person who knew more about herself than she did. She'd gotten all the answers she could out of one of those people. She'd get them from this one too.

Seth laughed. "I think you're right. But I won't bother you again. Do yourself a favor. Elena and Viktor? Don't go looking for them."

Kaden was ten paces away. If she could just keep Seth busy, Kaden could make up for interrupting by tackling Seth.

"You've got a life here. Don't throw it away for them. They don't give a damn about us and they'll only bring you trouble."

Five paces away.

Seth leaped back, just outside the Station's borders. He pulled something out of his pocket, winked at Kaden, and crushed it between his fingers. An oval-shaped rip in the fabric of reality opened behind him, a portal showing the busy streets of another world, stone buildings built mostly into the red rock of a mountainside. Nyx dove for him as he leisurely stepped back into it.

She thought she might have had him, too, if Kaden's arms hadn't wrapped around her waist and pulled her back. The edges of the portal closed around Seth, and the only link to Nyx's past vanished.

Nyx clawed herself out of Kaden's grip. "What are you doing? I *had* him."

"You had a one-way ticket through a portal. Are you forgetting what happened to your Station the last time you left it?"

She opened her mouth to tell him the Station would be *fine*, remembered she didn't want to share the new details of her Station bond with him, and changed trajectory.

"He wouldn't have run if you hadn't shown up. Why are you here?"

"Because you ran out in the middle of the night, alone, to go after a stranger who appears to be stalking you."

"Seth would never hurt me."

Kaden closed his eyes, and if she didn't know for a fact he didn't believe in gods, she would have thought he was asking them for patience. "If you can't remember anything about him, how can you possibly know that?"

"Because he's Seth," she said, as if it explained everything. Because somewhere deep in her bones, it *did* explain everything. "And stopping me from going after him wasn't your call to make."

"Forgive me if I thought stopping you from jumping through a portal to the *Shadow Market* was the right thing to do. Next time, I'll be sure to let you go to the most dangerous planet in the known universe on your own, in the middle of the night, when you aren't even wearing shoes."

She looked down at her bare feet. The knowledge that he was probably right didn't temper her anger, or the certainty she felt that if she *had* followed Seth through that portal, he wouldn't have let anything happen to her. Now he was gone, and having the hope of finally getting answers disappear in a blink ripped open the old, festering wound that was her unknown past.

Seth had told her not to go looking for her parents. But that was easy for him to say. He knew everything. She knew nothing. And she wasn't going to let this opportunity slip away.

She fixed Kaden with a glare. "Wake everyone up. I want to know everything you know about this Shadow Market."

6

———————

"Why do you all look like you swallowed a porcupine?"

Nyx plunked the last latte she'd made down in front of herself. Aside from her, only Kalvar and Morgen had mastered the espresso machine; the first was bleary-eyed and still half asleep, and the latter she didn't trust with other people's beverages because he thought any drink under five espresso shots wasn't worth making. Because she wasn't completely heartless, and she'd roused everyone half an hour before dawn, she'd made them coffee before demanding answers about what, exactly, the Shadow Market was.

"What's a porcupine?" Kalvar asked sleepily. The tiger stripes on his skin, marking him as Tiagren, were prominent first thing in the morning, when he was sleepy enough to be himself and forgot to fade them back into his skin. She wished she could convince him he didn't need to hide them here. For being all of seventeen years old he'd had a rough life, and the only time he ever seemed happy at all was when he was around Maruca. Though how Kaden's flame-haired, condescending sister could brighten anyone's day was a mystery to Nyx. The woman didn't even like coffee.

"It's a small animal with quills all over its body. What's the Shadow Market?"

"It's where my parents sold me to Arkadia."

Nyx went cold at the matter-of-fact way Kalvar said it. She'd known, by the way he'd never expressed any desire to go home, to go anywhere, that he didn't have parents to return to. But she had hoped his parents were dead and he'd been picked off the streets. Because as terrible as that would be, it was better than being sold by your own parents.

"What?"

He shrugged at the fury in her voice, as if it wasn't a big deal. "We hadn't eaten in five days. Slaver recruiter came through and covered the portal cost for a seventy percent commission on my sale. I was only there a couple days, didn't see much."

No one else looked surprised.

"And this is legal?"

"Nothing's legal on Tenebris Umbra," Maruca said. "That's why it's the home of the Shadow Market. Drugs, weapons, forbidden magics, slaves, deviant sexual behavior—if it's illegal or distasteful in the known universe, you can find it on Tenebris Umbra for a fee."

Nyx ground her teeth together. "Isn't that exactly the sort of thing you Enforcers are supposed to put a stop to?"

Maruca fixed her with a superior sneer. "You try shutting down a planet with over one million inhabitants all crowded into a hundred square miles, most of it underground, where mass infiltration is impossible because the planet has no ley line or Station, and where windstorms up to a hundred miles-per-hour lift the regolith from the surface and blow it about like dandelion fluff, only it's harsh enough to flay the skin from every known species in the verse and so kills whatever unfortunate souls haven't found shelter when the winds pick up. You try it, and let me know what your success rate is."

Coffee, Nyx thought, *if she would just drink some damn coffee, she'd turn into a more reasonable human being.*

"Regolith?" Morgen repeated. "Really Ruca, you didn't subscribe to that word of the week newsletter again did you?"

Maruca, interestingly enough, flushed nearly as red as her hair. "It's the dust and rock and other loose materials on the surface of a planet. The *regolith*," she paused to glare at Morgen, "on Tenebris Umbra is very harsh. Hence the flaying of skin."

"Fine," Nyx said, "so it's a disaster of a planet and no one does anything to fix it."

"There is a branch of Enforcers dedicated to shutting down Shadow Market dealers and confiscating portal stones when they find them, but the universe is a big place," Kaden said. "We do what we can."

Nyx took a deep breath and reminded herself that other people had been dealing with the problems of the universe for centuries while she'd only known about other inhabited planets for a handful of months. "Okay. All right. So you can only get there by using these portal stones? How do we get one?"

This time they all looked at her like she'd offered them an entire platter of porcupines and suggested they try them dipped in hoisin sauce.

"Nyx," Morgen said gently, "trying to find someone on Tenebris Umbra is like looking for a specific blade of grass in a field of identical blades of grass. Since Kaden can't track Seth we could spend a year there and never find him, and that's if he's even still there. Most people only use it as a jumping point to get to somewhere else. Living there is prohibitively expensive and if you're even a third of a decent person you can't stomach it for very long."

"I have to try." Nyx's fingers clenched around her coffee mug. The chaos thorns in her cheek sparked, hot with her sense of helplessness, and the veins on the backs of her hands turned black. She practiced the box breathing she'd taken up when she found out she couldn't get rid of the thorns without killing herself: four breaths in, hold for four counts, four breaths out. Repeat.

The chaos thorns heightened all of her emotions but they fed her anger the most, and she'd made a few monumentally stupid decisions—like challenging an entire gang of convicts on a prison planet to a fight—before she'd understood what they were doing to her.

The breathing helped and the blackness in her veins faded. "So, where do I get one of these portal stones?"

"It's not like they grow on trees." Maruca flicked her hair over her shoulder and sipped her water. Imagine, drinking *water* first thing in the morning. "They're stones from Tenebris Umbra that have been spelled by a portal witch on that planet. Shadow Market dealers bring them to other planets, and I can guarantee you there are none of those on Earth Between. And, in case you haven't noticed, none of us can go ley line hopping all over the universe just to find one for you."

"Thank you, Maruca." Nyx's voice was pure caustic. "Now that someone has pointed out everything that can't happen, would anyone else like to offer a constructive suggestion?"

"Even if we could get one," Morgen said slowly, "how are you going to go? After what happened last time with Griff, I wouldn't think you'd want to risk it again."

Oh, right. There was that whole bonded-to-her-Station thing she hadn't told any of them about, and wasn't going to start now.

"That issue has been resolved," she said carefully. "Griff will be fine. But I do have to be back within one Earth week."

"Or?" Kaden asked softly. Too softly. The kind of soft that was just a little bit dangerous.

"I just do."

"What happens if you aren't back in a week?"

I burn through my remaining weeks of freedom, and after that, *I'm relatively certain I'll die and my Station will implode.* "Nothing you need to concern yourself with. So, who wants to look for portal stones?"

"There's no need. I can get you there."

Every head in the room swiveled to look at Evra.

"Just like that?" Maruca asked, her default bored expression sharpening with interest.

"I figured I'd have to go there eventually, to get Tamrin home." Evra sounded resigned and a little defeated. It was not a tone Nyx had ever heard on her before. "I've been looking for another way but there doesn't seem to be one. If you're set on going, Nyx, I'll take you."

"*You* have a portal stone to Tenebris Umbra?" Morgen's jaw was practically hanging open with slack.

"Yes."

"Moriana al'Daemon's daughter has a portal stone to Tenebris Umbra? *Moriana*. Practically the Creator of Rules, Moriana?"

"My mother trained you *once*, Morgen," Evra said coldly. "I have lived my entire life under that tutelage and I can assure you, you do not understand her *or* me. And whatever else I may be, I have not been Moriana al'Daemon's daughter for over sixteen months."

Tamrin shot out of her seat, her face white. "I *knew* you weren't telling me something. She severed your bloodline?"

Evra sent Morgen a withering look that said this slip of her tongue was entirely his fault, and he would pay for it later. "It doesn't matter, Tam."

"Of course it matters. What happened to me wasn't your fault. I'll talk to her, I'll—"

"You will do no such thing." Evra's voice was black steel. "I did not go to Arkadia to win back mother's favor. I went for *you*, Tam. You only have two years until you reach majority and mother still respects you. Do not ruin it by trying to change her mind about me."

"But it's—"

"Done," Evra said. "It is done, and it doesn't matter." She turned to Nyx. "When do you want to leave?"

Nyx hesitated, wanting to say something and sensing it wasn't the time. "The sooner the better. I get the feeling Seth doesn't stay put very long. I need to talk to Griff and settle things with the Station. Meet me out back in two hours?"

Evra nodded.

"Perhaps," Maruca said nonchalantly, picking at her nails with the tip of a dagger, "I'll come too."

Nyx must have heard incorrectly. "Come again?"

"I'm bored," Maruca answered, with an easiness that told Nyx she was lying. Well, not telling all the truth, anyway. Nyx was convinced Maruca lived the majority of her life in a state of bored indifference.

"What happened to danger, drugs, forbidden magic, and flaying winds?"

"I was listing the reasons *you* shouldn't go. Some of us are quite capable of dealing with trivial inconveniences."

Oh, of course.

"In fact, I think it would do us *all* good to get out and about the universe for a bit. Don't you, Kaden?" She looked at him pointedly.

"A brief excursion might be good," he said tightly, "if you're so interested in helping Nyx find Seth."

Maruca beamed. "I am all for helping the less fortunate. So we're decided then? Morgen?"

Morgen looked, of all things, sad. "You'd both be dead in two minutes without me. So yeah, I'm in."

Nyx looked to Evra since it was, after all, her portal stone. "Are you okay with everyone going?"

"I—" She looked at Morgen for a long second, as if there was something about *his* attendance in particular she found problematic. "Oh, why not? Perhaps it will be better this way."

Before Nyx could ask what the vague *it* was, Maruca gained her feet, bouncing on her toes.

"Wonderful. Then we'll all meet out back in two hours. No time to waste when we're tracking a fugitive." She bounded out of the kitchen, long, lithe dancer's body carrying her away.

Morgen shot Evra a pining glance—which wasn't at all

unusual, except it held that tinge of sadness that had been in his voice when he agreed to come along—and then he shuffled out as well.

Nyx waited until all of them except Kalvar were gone. He stared into his coffee mug without appearing to see it. The hands wrapped around that mug were no longer entirely human. Sharp-tipped black claws extended from his fingertips, black tiger stripes displayed prominently against his brown skin.

"All right," she said, "let's hear it, then."

His hands flexed, claws scraping against the sides of the mug with a nails-on-chalkboard sound that made Nyx cringe.

"I'm coming too."

"Okay."

"Okay?" He looked up at her, incredulous. "That's it?"

"What else would there be?"

"Oh, I don't know," he said sarcastically, and then mimicked Maruca's grave expression and tone of voice perfectly. *"It's a dangerous place, Kalvar. You're too young, Kalvar.'"*

"You've been through more at seventeen than most people go through in their entire lives, Kalvar. I'm not hypocritical enough to tell you stay here because of an arbitrary number some people claim defines when you're an adult. If you want to come with us, that's fine by me."

His eyes shadowed over. "Ru won't like it."

It still baffled Nyx how anyone called Maruca *Ru* and lived to do it again. "Well, it's not Maruca's portal stone and I don't think Evra will care. So if fire-hair has a problem with it, she can take it up with me. Okay?"

"It's your funeral," he said. But he said it less glumly, claws retracting and shoulders lifting as he went off to his room to pack.

Nyx went to find her Avatar.

G riff sat on a table in the Den, a book open in front of him, lion's tail thump-thumping as he flicked it repeatedly on the polished mahogany surface.

"I'm beginning to understand why these histories were banned," he said mildly when she walked in. "They're positively filthy."

He was stalling, and Nyx knew it. She had convinced him, now that she was bonded to the Station itself as well as he, to alternate nights of being "on guard" so to speak, so he could actually sleep. It was the first time he'd *slept* slept in who knew how many centuries, and watching his lion's paws and eagle's claws twitch as he dreamed had totally been worth it.

Last night had been her shift, so he hadn't been awakened by Seth's arrival. Still, her Guardian bond with him meant he would have come up to speed on events soon after waking up, and she was a little surprised he hadn't sought her out yet.

"If you aren't comfortable with me going, Griff, I won't."

Despite the reassurances she'd given Morgen, the idea of leaving scared her. Knowing that, theoretically, the chaos thorn she'd embedded in Griff, the one that held a piece of her life essence, would keep him from going insane when she went through a portal was one thing. Trusting an untested piece of magic she didn't understand to keep him alive was…another.

"I have no problem with you going, Nyx. I understand why you need to do this."

"Then what's bothering you? You haven't been yourself lately."

Not since the All Council had come to their Station. Not since *Jevryn* had come.

Griff closed the book, running his talons over the cover. "You do not remember your past because it was Hidden from you. For the last few centuries, I have not remembered mine because it was easier that way. What happened with the All Council, with you, it has made me ponder the wiseness of my decision to forget. And remembering…remembering has been painful. I apologize if my mood has been affecting you."

Nyx thought of the black ring etched with sapphire, the one that hung on the chain around her neck next to the Harvester of Worlds, and the member of the All Council who had given it to her. To her, because he was certain Griff would not take it or the promise of aid that had come with it.

Nyx went over to him and gently stroked his wings. "You're allowed to be sad, Griff. And if you ever need to talk about it, I'm here. Or if you just need to watch a sad movie or something."

"I'm still not sure what is so enjoyable about these movies you speak of."

"That's because you haven't seen one. When I get back, I'm going to Dead Earth and bringing back a DVD player." And a television, she supposed. She couldn't get the Internet in Earth Between, but electricity wasn't an issue.

It was still strange to her to know that she had the money to just go out and buy something like that. She was so unused to it that it had taken her an embarrassingly long amount of time to finally ask Griff if she got paid.

She could still remember his astonished tone of voice when he'd asked her, "Didn't you read the Guardian's contract?" He had looked so adorably disappointed in her.

In her defense, the previous Guardian had transferred the Guardian bond to her without explaining anything at all, and she'd then been promptly thrown into a manhunt. She hadn't much seen the point in reading the contract Griff had later handed her.

As it turned out, she had a safe in her room that opened with the Guardian ring, and her pay was deposited weekly. The extra cool thing about the safe was that it was also like a mobile bank and would automatically convert the money inside into whatever currency she happened to need. Everywhere in Earth

Between took universals, but it could handle Dead Earth currency too for her trips across the border.

There were undeniably cool perks to living in a sentient building in the heart of a magical universe. As long as she didn't think about that pesky little business of being tied to that Station for the rest of her life which, considering the Station was a Nexus, was now theoretically forever.

"Hey, do you know what currency's used on Tenebris Umbra?"

"You're going to the Shadow Market, arguably in the top five most dangerous planets in the known galaxy, and you want to go shopping?"

"What? They might have nice things." She'd more been thinking along the lines of how she would survive if she got separated from her group, but best not to worry Griff.

"Universals should work as well there as everywhere else. Try not to get robbed blind."

"I'll certainly do my best." She was almost to the ladder that led out of the Den when she saw the mercury boots still lying at the end of the table. She was surprised Griff hadn't stored them away somewhere yet—he was usually pretty prompt about that sort of thing—but since he hadn't…

"Say, Griff," she began casually, walking back into the room, "would you mind if I borrowed a few items from the Den?"

Before she'd bonded with the Station itself, taking an item out of the Den would have locked the Station down to ley line travel and the All Council would have been alerted of the status. Now, she was capable of working around that issue, and if the magical Den meant to hold dangerous magical items did not *like* having said items borrowed, it would let her do it, nonetheless.

Griff pushed his spectacles further up his eagle's beak. "You do recall that the last time you borrowed items you almost got a bo staff permanently melded to your hand?"

"Yes."

"And had to jump in a monster's lair to retrieve a dagger?"

"Yes."

"And nearly lost Morgen to magical plants?"

"Hey, I am older and more experienced now."

Griff sighed. "What were you thinking of borrowing?"

"The food and water pack I took to Arkadia? You know, just in case. Probably Veritas for the same reason and maybe the mercury boots." She rushed the last words in at a low volume. It didn't fool Griff.

"No to the mercury boots."

"Why not?"

"They are dangerous, Nyx."

"They make you go fast. That's it, right?"

"Yes, technically, that is it." He sighed.

"Please?" She drew the word out. "I am going to a bad, dangerous place with bad, dangerous people. What if I need to run away really fast? What if I am tragically killed and you're left here, slowly going mad and thinking to yourself, 'Oh, if only I'd let Nyx borrow the mercury boots like she'd asked, she'd still be—'"

Griff flung out his wings in exasperation. "All right, fine, you can borrow them."

Nyx let out a whoop of excitement.

"I should have guessed this would be inevitable from the moment you laid eyes on them." He muttered something else that Nyx couldn't make out.

She shrugged and bounded over to retrieve the boots. They were a soft black fabric with black buckles up the sides, all the way up to just below knee-height. She shucked out of her own boots and slid them on, waited while they adjusted, conforming to her feet for the perfect fit.

Stars, she *loved* magic. The soles were flexible, allowing for a closer-to-barefoot feel when she walked, but Griff assured her the material was impervious to most things she might step on. He watched her shift her weight from side to side and jump around a few times, getting used to the feel of them, and there was something in his eyes that made Nyx stop.

"Is everything okay?"

Griff had been acting so strange ever since the All Council visit. Not that it hadn't been traumatic and, yeah, he'd said he was thinking about a past he'd largely ignored the last few centuries, but it felt like there was something else going on. Sometimes she would look up and find him staring at her, his brow as furrowed as it could be in griffin form, like he was seeing her for the first time. Or like he was seeing someone else.

"Everything is fine." He fluttered a wing dismissively. "The boots are voice activated by Hermetic command. *Los.*" The boot buckles changed from black to bronze. "*Losa.*" Bronze to silver. "*Losara.*" Silver to gold.

Nyx memorized them, easy since they were all conjugations of the same verb. Near as the translator spells could manage, the commands translated roughly as *fast, faster, extremely fast.*

Whoever made them clearly had an appreciation for simplicity, an appreciation Nyx shared.

"How do I turned them back off?"

"*Exa.*" The buckles returned to black. "See that you remember it and *don't* take them above the lowest setting unless you want to break an ankle."

"What makes you think I'd break an ankle?"

"Not above the lowest setting, are we clear?"

"Yes, yes, we're clear."

She headed for the ladder out of the Den.

"Did you actually *want* the other items you asked for, or were they just a ploy to get the boots?"

She paused, guiltily. "I guess I will take Veritas." A truth-telling dagger had its uses, especially when she was going to the Shadow Market for answers. She retrieved it and stopped next to Griff on her way out. "You'll come see us off, won't you?"

He waved a talon in acknowledgment. "I'll be there. And Nyx? The boots suit you."

Nyx couldn't say why, but it felt like a more meaningful compliment than it appeared on the surface. "Thanks. You know I'm going to miss you, right?"

An eagle's beak could not curve up into a smile but it didn't have to. She felt it in his eyes.

7

―――――

I t took Nyx all of fifteen minutes to pack. She changed into pants, and a long-sleeved shirt made of Talorean cloth. The fabric held magic well and had been spelled so it wouldn't absorb dirt, liquids, or odors. She didn't bother to pack a change of clothes. She hoped to find Seth within a couple days and if she couldn't, well, she would have to return within a week anyway. The spells would keep her current clothing clean that long and save her the hassle of hauling a bag around on a planet where it might pay to be nimble.

She shrugged on the back sheath for the short sword she'd been favoring in practice lately, buckled it across her chest and adjusted the straps. The mercury boots laced snugly around her calves, leaving no room for a hidden knife sheath, so she strapped one to each thigh instead. When Evra had insisted Nyx pay the two-hundred percent mark-up for sheaths keyed to her magical signature, Nyx hadn't really understood why. Now that she was going to a planet no doubt crawling with pickpockets, she was grateful for Evra's insistence. The only thing worse than getting stabbed in the back would be having it done with her own weapon.

The only other thing she took was Gleipnir. She'd taken to

wearing the enchanted chain like a multi-layer bracelet. She didn't want to give it to the Den, because it was *hers*, and she didn't like the idea of stuffing it in a drawer somewhere. Besides, an unbreakable chain that was as slender as a fine necklace and could extend or retract to any desired length was bound to have a multitude of uses.

She met up with Kalvar in the Station's kitchen. He had packed substantially heavier than her, a brown pack slung across his back filled full enough Nyx was mildly surprised the ties holding it closed hadn't snapped. She didn't see any blades on him but she supposed when one's fingers shifted into claws at will extra blades weren't really necessary. She had expected him to look grim or nervous but he just looked resigned. He stood when she came in and they walked into the clearing out back of the Station together, a full fifteen minutes ahead of the arranged meeting time.

Of course, Maruca had managed to get there ahead of them, twin scimitars sheathed at her sides. Her expression was downright sunny until she saw Kalvar, and then the thunderclouds returned.

"Absolutely not."

Kalvar stepped back a pace. Nyx did not. She set her legs in a wide stance and crossed her arms.

"I beg your pardon?"

"He is not coming with us."

"I don't think that's your decision to make."

"And you think it's yours? He was *sold* in the Shadow Market. And you'd force him to go back there? For what? Some boy you don't even remember? Are you stupid or are you just as heartless as you treat my brother?"

Nyx snapped. She'd been putting up with Maruca's verbal jabs for weeks, not reacting because she hadn't wanted to cause a scene, to create any more tension when they all had to live together.

She hadn't wanted to be a problem. Well, she didn't think she was the problem now and they were about to go to a place where this kind of shit would only get them in trouble. Nyx could feel the ground beneath Maruca's feet without even thinking about it. Now, she became it. Hard earth turned fluid like quicksand in the space of a second and Maruca dropped through the ground up to her thighs. The soil re-solidified and held her tight.

Nyx hid the nausea brought on by calling on the Station's bond so soon after her previous night's use—why, for love of all the stars, hadn't she been smart enough to think of doing *this* to Seth last night?—and strolled up to Maruca, crouching down to bring her face level with the other woman's.

"The next time you decide to insult my intelligence," Nyx said softly, "take a moment to remember whose Station this is and by whose grace it is that you aren't in the All Council's dungeons. And as for Kaden, what goes on between us is absolutely none of your business."

Maruca didn't struggle to free herself. For a woman half-buried in the ground, she acted like she was still fully in charge of the situation.

"He doesn't think clearly where you're concerned. I saw the two of you last night. You've ignored him for months but now that you need something from him, suddenly you're throwing yourself at him."

Chaos pulsed in Nyx's veins. She wanted to punch that superior sneer right off Maruca's face, had a feeling she'd want that even if she didn't have a patch of chaos thorns in her face. She clenched her fingers into her palms and found the better angels of her nature.

"You don't know what you're talking about."

"I've seen your type before," Maruca spat. "And now you're dragging Kalvar into—"

"No one's forcing me, Ru," Kalvar interrupted. "I asked to go."

Nyx turned, surprised. She'd gotten the impression Kalvar

didn't want to have this argument and would be happy to leave her to it, but he appeared to have changed his mind. Maybe it had something to do with Maruca being buried in the ground. Whatever the case, if he wanted to go for it Nyx wasn't going to get in his way.

Maruca turned the full force of her gaze to rest on Kalvar. "Why would you do that?"

"I can't sleep, Ru. And it's not Arkadia that keeps me up at night. I *need* to go back to the Market. I need to face it, and I need to leave it again on my own terms."

"And if you don't leave it?" Maruca asked.

She could, Nyx noticed, talk through a clenched jaw just as well as her brother.

Kalvar shrugged.

"Because it is a very real possibility that you won't. This isn't a lark, Kalvar. It's not an adventure. The Shadow Market is as dangerous for free peoples as it is for slaves. Maybe even more so, because slavers have a vested interest in keeping their property alive."

"I don't care."

Maruca's entire body stiffened. "Go back upstairs and don't follow us."

For a moment, it looked like he was going to obey. Then he pulled his shoulders back and lifted his chin. "No."

"That's an order, Kalvar."

He shook his head. "We're not on Arkadia anymore, Ru. You're not my commander. I'm grateful for everything you taught me, but I'm done being told what to do."

Maruca looked like she'd been slapped.

Kalvar turned to Nyx. "Can you let her go?"

Nyx hid the strain doing so caused, noting with great satisfaction that dirt had rubbed into the fabric of Maruca's pants, which did *not* appear to be made of spelled Talorean cloth.

Kalvar took a step toward the redhead, another, until he was just inside the bubble of her personal space. Nyx felt awkward, like she was about to witness something better said in private, but her head swam and she had a feeling if she stepped away right then she might topple over.

"I'm not a kid, Ru. I wish—" Kalvar looked into her eyes and there was little of youth in him, and a strong hint of the man he was on the verge of becoming. "I really wish you would stop thinking of me like one."

Nyx felt for him. She'd been that young and lonely once. She just hoped, for his sake, that he got over this crush on Maruca sooner rather than later. Maruca obviously cared about him, it just definitely wasn't in the romantic way he wanted her to.

The back door banged open and Morgen, Evra, Tamrin, and Kaden spilled out, bickering companionably. Morgen, oblivious —or, more likely, pretending to be oblivious—to the tension in the air, walked up and slapped Kalvar on the back.

"Coming with us then?"

Kalvar held Maruca's gaze. "Yeah, I am."

Morgen's gaze swept over Maruca from head to toe. "Did you decide to roll in the dirt, Ruca?"

Maruca shot Nyx a look of pure venom and opened her mouth. At the same time, Nyx pulled on the Station just enough to tremble the ground beneath Maruca's feet, and the woman shut her mouth.

"So, how does this work?" Nyx asked, voice excessively bright. She was going to have the mother of all headaches in an hour.

The tension between Kalvar and Maruca finally eased, but only because Maruca turned away from Kalvar and acted like he no longer existed.

And the bitch called *Nyx* heartless?

"The portal stone is very similar to traveling through the ley lines, albeit in a more condensed fashion," Griff said, landing on her shoulder.

"What do you mean condensed?"

"I mean, think of compressing ten miles into the space of an eighth of a mile, and that's what traveling through a portal is like." His wingtip brushed her chaos thorns. "You also won't have to worry about picking up any more of these. There aren't any on the portal paths."

"That sounds nice. If portals are so nice, why don't we travel everywhere by them?"

"Because it's illegal," Morgen chimed in, "and has been for so long no one remembers when it wasn't. Which means they all operate from Tenebris Umbra, and there's wicked few portal witches willing to do that, as it takes a special kind of fucked up to live in that place."

"So how do we get back?"

Evra bent down and swiped a handful of rocks off the ground. "We pay a portal witch to spell these. My contact should be able to put us in touch with someone."

"Are you ever going to tell me who we're meeting?" Tamrin asked.

"No."

"You realize I'm going to find out anyway, right? Like, we will meet them and then I'll know."

Evra shot her a withering glare that younger sisters were apparently immune to. "Then you will know when you meet them." She turned to the rest of them. "Tamrin and I have to come through last or the portal will close before the rest of you make it through."

Evra stepped away from the group, pulled out a rock with the soft, powdery appearance of sulfur but with the red ochre coloring Nyx had seen in the portal Seth had gone through.

"Hold up," Morgen said, grabbing her hand before she could crush the rock between her fingers. "Portal magic won't work inside the Station grounds."

Evra frowned. "How do you know that?" Morgen still hadn't let go of her hand, and she didn't seem to mind.

He winked at her. "I know lots of things, lady Amazon. Think of it like competing dominance. You have two things that can portal—the Station and the stone—and only the stronger one will work. If you crush that in here, it'll just fizzle out."

Nyx followed Morgen as he led them all off the Station's grounds, thinking about what he'd said. Yes, Morgen *did* know lots of things, and, yes, magical theory did seem to be a hobby of his, but it was a little convenient how certain he was about the interaction of portal stones and her Station. It was convenient how certain Maruca had been that a portal stone couldn't be found in Earth Between.

Then there was Kaden getting all grim when Maruca had suggested they join the excursion, and Morgen looking so sad. The only reason for all of those things to come together was if they'd all been searching for a way to leave before now. Which shouldn't come as a surprise to her, only… well, she'd thought they would have told her. She'd thought Morgen, at least, would have told her.

They crossed the boundary that separated the Station from the rest of Earth Between, and Evra crushed the portal stone between her fingers. The air split open behind her and that void called to Nyx, pulsing out a beat that echoed in her veins the same way the ley lines did. She had learned to resist that call, to expect it when the lines opened for Arrivals and Departures, but she hadn't been expecting this portal to affect her the same way. She had thought her call to the Station's portal was because she was its Guardian and that this one, being a different mode of travel, would feel different.

It didn't. It felt the same.

Maruca strode to the portal and walked through. Kalvar, his face set in a combination of fury and determination, went through practically on her heels, and Morgen followed behind them. When Kaden didn't immediately follow she nodded for him to go through. He shook his head.

"I'll follow you."

She could argue with him all day or she could just go. She stepped up to the portal. Despite its hypnotic call, it was an unknown. She hadn't even asked how it worked, or if there were possible dangers in traveling through it.

Kaden stepped up beside her. "I can go with you, if you want."

"No, I'm fine."

So what if she missed her hexagonal Arrival Room with its cosmic floor and her absolute control over it? She could do this. She could just…step through and hope everything turned out all right.

What if it didn't? What if there was some unknown side effect of Guardians traveling through portals, different from the ones she'd experienced traveling through the ley lines? What if everything went wrong and something happened to Griff and—

She felt a hot whuff of air against her back and realized her Avatar was once again the size of a buffalo right before he said, "Everything will be fine," and pushed her through the portal with a gentle bump of his head. Kaden grabbed her hand and jumped through with her.

Damn it, hadn't she said she was *fine* on her own?

8

———————

Kaden landed on Tenebris Umbra with the perfect, level grace he seemed to do everything with. He reached out with the hand that wasn't clasping hers to put a steadying grip on her elbow. Nyx felt Maruca's glare before she saw it, and though she wanted to tell the redhead to mind her own business, she instead settled for disentangling herself from the many places she and Kaden were now touching.

They stood in the shadow of a red stone mountain, its sides worn smooth and glossy with the passage of time. The towering peak was one of many in the mountain range ringing the deep valley below them, the vastness of that depression filled with the noise and energy of the Shadow Market.

Nyx looked out across it, her hopes sinking faster than she could buoy them. Tenebris Umbra was a labyrinth of crammed-together buildings, narrow streets and alleys, and people *every-where*. She'd never been to Los Angeles, but the way people talked about it she imagined it must be something like this.

What was she going to do? Sketch a picture of Seth and go walking from illegal business to illegal business, asking the nice criminals selling people if they'd seen her long-lost buddy Seth?

Stars, she was an idiot.

Kaden's fingers brushed hers hesitantly. "We'll find him, Nyx."

They wouldn't, but she nodded anyway and turned back to the rest of the group.

"Where is your contact located?" she asked Evra. She estimated it was only about a one mile hike to get down into the valley from where they stood, but the city itself could take several days to traverse. She had to hope Evra's contact lived on this side of the Shadow Market, or else that there was a faster form of transportation available than their own feet. She thought of her mercury boots and really, really wanted to try them out, but since they couldn't make the entire group move faster, just her, there wasn't any point.

Evra didn't answer. The Amazon turned in a small circle, her brow furrowed.

"Ev?" Tamrin prompted. She had put her back to her sister's and was mirroring Evra's slow circle, tension evident in the set of her shoulders. She looked as tightly strung as she had on Arkadia, and the wariness in her voice clearly made Evra realize she was freaking her little sister out.

Evra tried and failed to stop looking like she expected an imminent ambush, but she did stop circling. Not that her particular vigilance was required anymore, as her guarded actions had prompted the three Enforcers in the group to pull blades and form a perimeter, and Kalvar had unsheathed his claws.

Nyx couldn't decide if the fact she hadn't drawn her own short sword meant she just wasn't as paranoid as everyone else, or that she was woefully inexperienced with traveling to dangerous planets. Possibly both. But the ground around them was level, with precious little to hide behind, and it was empty as far as the eye could see.

"Someone should have met us here," Evra said finally.

Nyx considered the distance from where the portal stone had dropped them to the city below. "Did you send word to your contact that we were coming?" It seemed unlikely. So far, the only means of communicating near-instantly between planets that Nyx had come across was by way of companion books—matching journals spelled so that what was written in one appeared in the other—and since Evra was so tight-lipped about who her contact was here, Nyx doubted it was someone the Amazon was writing to every day.

"No," Evra said finally, "but the portal stone I used had a keyed signature. My contact would have been aware the moment I activated it. And I assure you, they would have sent someone to meet us."

This was one of those moments where Nyx couldn't stop herself from pointing out what seemed obvious to her, but no one else appeared to question. "We're at least a mile from the city. Maybe they just haven't gotten here yet?"

Evra shook her head. "They wouldn't have walked. An envoy would have portaled to this landing point from the city."

Morgen's eyebrows raised practically to his hairline. "Your contact can afford to waste portal magic to travel *one* mile on a planet? Who exactly are we meeting?"

Evra just shook her head, her lips thinning. She looked... disquieted. It was not a look Nyx liked on the Amazon. "Maybe your contact's just busy?" Nyx offered.

"Oh, I have no doubt they are." Then, with a sigh in Morgen's direction, "But if the Keeper of Shadows is so busy they can't spare *one* person to meet us, it doesn't bode well for the state of the Market."

Every member of their group swiveled to fix their gazes on Evra.

"The Keeper of Shadows?" Incredulity laced Morgen's voice. "Your contact is the bleeding Keeper of Shadows?"

"Yes, Morgen, my contact is the bleeding Keeper of Shadows."

Morgan fanned himself with one hand. "Every time I think I've fallen as completely in love with you as is possible, I am proved wrong."

Evra's face didn't twist into the scowl-hiding-amusement it usually did whenever Morgen professed his undying love for her. She just gazed toward the city, looking like she was preparing for her own funeral and expecting a small turnout.

"We'll have to enter the Market without a guide," she said finally.

"Is that bad?" It sounded vaguely bad.

Evra shrugged. "It's the Market. It was never going to be *good*. But the Keep shouldn't be difficult to find. We can purchase the portal stones to send Tamrin home and us back to Earth. If the Keeper is too busy to grant me an audience, then we push forward unassisted." Evra muttered something under her breath that sounded suspiciously like, "I don't *need* her help anyway," and stalked off in the direction of the Market.

Kaden fell in at Evra's side, his control freak nature no doubt intent on gathering every specific detail of their course of action before they actually reached the city. Nyx kept pace with Morgen, and debated the merits of being uninformed versus looking like an idiot. Finally, she asked, "So, umm, what exactly *is* the Keeper of Shadows?"

Morgen still looked a little awestruck by Evra's association with the Keeper. "Well, to understand that you have to understand a little bit about how the Market functions. It's carved up into territories that are controlled by various factions. As you might expect in a place like this, those territories shift about as often as the wind blows, and the factions controlling them rise and fall with equal frequency.

"In the admittedly shoddy records we have on the Market, only one faction has survived the entirety of the Market's history, and *that* is the Keeper's faction."

Nyx chewed on that for a minute. "But it's not the same person, right? The Keeper's just a title?" She'd gotten somewhat used to the idea that Griff and the All Council were basically eternal—and was still nowhere used to the idea that she was headed in the same direction—but she didn't want to start seeing immortal beings everywhere.

"Not the same person," Morgen confirmed. "But the title doesn't change hands all that often. Anyone good enough to claw their way into the position is good enough to hold onto it for a while."

"So if it's not the same person, what makes the Keeper faction so special?"

"Ah, *that* is the right question, little Guardian. The Keeper controls all access to Tenebris Umbra, and therefore all access to the Market."

Nyx really wanted to ask how that worked—presumably it meant the Keeper was the only one with unfettered access to the portal stones—but they were at the outskirts of the city now and she had a feeling it was time to shut up and pay attention. She just had one final question before they descended into the madness. "If the Keeper is the most powerful person in the Market, and they weren't able to send anyone to meet Evra like she expected, what exactly does that mean?"

"It means that either Evra's contact is no longer the Keeper and therefore probably dead, or the Shadow Market's at war."

Nyx wasn't sure what she'd expected the Shadow Market to be like, but of all the descriptors that might have come to mind, normal wasn't one of them. But at first glance, that was precisely how the Market appeared—just like any other busy city.

They entered via a main street that ran between what appeared to be residential housing, until the street opened up into the bustling, wide open square that was the Shadow Market's dark heart.

The outer edges of the Market were formed of physical buildings and the businesses they contained, while the interior was crowded with vendor stalls and races of every kind. It was only once one's eyes fell on the holding pens in the center, corrals crammed with people of every imaginable species, that the sick wrongness of the Market became obvious, that the desperation in the air gained a tangible weight.

People passed the pens with impassive faces, as if the buying and selling of living beings had as little effect on them as someone haggling over the price of a rug. Kalvar's gaze locked onto the holding pens, his eyes hollow, his tiger's stripes flushing to prominence against his brown skin. From her position directly on his heels, Maruca burned a hole into his back with her gaze. Every muscle in her body had tensed, as if she expected someone to grab him at any moment, and she was prepared to rip their throat out when they did.

Nyx only let her gaze linger on the pens for a moment. She felt sick, and the knowledge that she couldn't do anything about what was happening here didn't change the fact that *not* acting made her feel complicit in it all. No, she realized, it didn't make her *feel* complicit, it *made* her complicit. Walking past them and thinking it was wrong didn't do anything for the people being held against their will. It didn't fix anything and yet, if she tried to do something about it right now she'd only get herself killed.

They passed the pens and she felt guilty for the relief that washed over her at not having to look at the people inside them anymore. Kaden settled in to walk beside her as they reached the outskirts of the Market's heart, and she wasn't so foolish that she wasn't grateful for his presence at her side. He exuded an aura of power and confidence that made people give him a wide berth, even in a place like this. Perhaps even especially in a place like this, because the people here had seen enough trouble to tell a real threat from a bluff.

Ahead, next to Kalvar, Maruca exuded that same confidence, and Nyx was surprised to see the people who passed by responded to her the same as they did to Kaden. It was obvious why they would grant a wide berth to a woman like Evra—she had the size and muscle and excessive weaponry to back up any threat—but Maruca was closer in size to Nyx. For that reason, as much as Nyx might not *like* Kaden's sister, it was still gratifying to watch the Market-goers respond to her with wary distance.

Evra strode purposefully forward at the head of their group, her gait easy and confident, as if she walked these streets every day and knew precisely where she was going. Nyx was debating asking Kaden if *he* knew where they were going—he'd been glued to her side since they entered the Market—when they rounded a corner on the twisting street and she saw it.

In the Market's sea of rectangular buildings, all built of the planet's native red stone, the glossy black spire jutting up in the direct center of the Market practically screamed, "Look at me. I belong to someone who's got more money and power than everyone else."

It screamed it even more so as they approached, and Nyx realized the spire rested on a sort of small island, the "lake" around it a depression of bleached white sand stretching for thirty feet in all directions. A thirty foot radius might seem like a small amount of space anywhere else, but it made an obvious statement in a place like the Shadow Market, where each building was built practically on top of the next one.

A narrow stone bridge, in black to match the spire, stretched from the street to the island, and though Nyx could see no visible means of retracting said bridge, she would have bet almost anything that it *could* be retracted. At the foot of the bridge, carved into the first foot of glossy black stone, was a white torch inside a circle. There was nothing else etched inside that circle that Nyx could make out, and yet she swore the space around the torch shifted, and something in the movement made her think of shadow itself.

Evra stepped carelessly over the emblem and started for the island, the others following, but Nyx halted just shy of setting foot on the walk. Which meant, of course, that Kaden stopped too, his hand settling on the pommel of his sword.

"What's wrong?" he asked.

The empty ground beneath the bridge radiated with a low hum of magic that set Nyx's teeth on edge. "Do you feel that?"

"Don't step off the path and you'll be fine."

Which she supposed answered the question she'd actually asked, but not the implied demand for an explanation. Kaden held his hand out to her. She ignored it. She didn't need a comforting hand-hold, she needed to know what the the feeling of utter *wrongness* slicking over her was. "What is it?"

Kaden grimaced. He pulled a dagger and cut off a lock of his hair, which he tossed unceremoniously off the side of the bridge. As soon as it was sideways of the bridge, before it ever hit the ground, the threads of hair sizzled and curled in on themselves before dissolving into a soft white powder that fell like snow to the ground.

Nyx swallowed. "None of that is sand, is it?"

"No."

Nyx didn't ask any more questions. She pulled her shirt up to cover her mouth and nose—because no way in hell was she inhaling the dust of dead people if the wind decided to shift—and made her way across the bridge, which was so narrow she wanted to fall to her hands and knees and shimmy across it that way. But despite her nerves insisting the opposite, she had good balance, and she reassured herself that if the Keeper randomly killed people approaching the Keep, said Keeper wouldn't have any customers left to fund their lavish lifestyle.

Still, she breathed a sigh of relief when she stepped onto the small island at the bridge's end. The relief was short-lived. No scary guards stood flanking the doors, waiting to intimidate or deny entrance, and their absence felt more ominous than she thought their presence would have been. The lack implied a casual disregard for the possibility of attack, the Keeper's utter surety of their own superiority.

Nyx decided it took a supreme level of arrogance to become the Keeper. How did Evra even know this person?

The Amazon in question had been waiting impatiently for Nyx and Kaden to catch up to the rest of the group. Now that they were here, she strode for the spire doors. They were immense creations, easily fifteen feet in height, carved of the same glossy stone as the building and each bearing the torch-and-shadow emblem she'd noted on the bridge. Not even a set of handles marred the doors' seamless perfection. As Evra approached they simply swung inward of their own accord, their massive weight moving with a frightening quiet that was incongruous with their bulk.

Nyx held her breath as they stepped inside the spire...and let it out in a disappointed rush. Though the tower was tall, it was not wide, the interior only spanning around twenty feet in diameter. It was also empty. As in, no furniture, no people, no doors or stairs that might lead up or down.

She looked up anyway, but couldn't see very far. The only light came from sconces set into the wall—the doors had closed behind them and the spire held no windows—and those were only placed approximately six feet above the ground, and no higher. The floor, the walls, everything was black stone. No variation, no adornments, no slightly worn places on that floor to suggest anyone set foot upon it with regularity.

There wasn't even any dust. Which was the only thing that convinced Nyx that perhaps someone *did* come here on occasion. Dust found its way in everywhere. Unless there was magic for that, too.

The only thing that kept her from asking Evra if she was certain they were in the right place was the death moat outside and the fact that this building was so obviously different from every other one in the city. Still, when she had envisioned something labeled the Keep, which belonged to someone called the Keeper of Shadows, she'd expected something larger. With more than one room. And actual things in that room. And perhaps some people, for good measure.

"Is there a bell to ring for service?" she muttered under her breath. Unfortunately, the emptiness of the room, combined with the fact that it was made of stone and had extraordinarily tall ceilings, meant her words echoed off all available surfaces.

As if her words had awakened some protocol, a voice floated through the room. It was clipped, harsh, and brutally to the point, without any of the flowery, apologetic language that followed customer service announcements on Earth. "The Keeper is engaged in an internal conflict within the Market. Until such time as that conflict is resolved, all sales of portal stones, as well as the spelling of new stones, have been halted. Enjoy your time in the Market. And choose your allies wisely."

The voice clicked off, just like the recording it likely was. *All sales of portal stones, as well as the spelling of new stones, have been halted.* Nyx looked down at her hand, at the tattoo etched into the webbing between her thumb and forefinger. The number there, which had once been a six and had now become a five, reminded her how absolutely screwed she was if she couldn't get home. She had one week here before the five became a four. Another week until it became a three, and so on down to zero.

Kaden was watching her with narrowed eyes, his gaze fixed on the numerical tattoo she'd been running her thumb over. She quit touching it and forced herself to take a steadying breath in and out. Nothing had changed. Her priority was still to find Seth. He'd gotten to Earth Between despite the Keeper's apparent moratorium on sales, and her gut told her he could do it again. She had the distinct impression he'd never met a rule he hadn't tried to break.

Their group was a little too quiet for comfort, making the room feel like a mausoleum, so Nyx tried for humor. "Did a disembodied voice just tell us to fuck off?"

Morgen snorted. "More or less. Looks like we'll need an alternate means of—" He cut off. Evra, who had been intently examining the floor, suddenly rose. She drew an item from her pocket with one hand, a dagger with the other, and stalked to the wall.

"What are you doing?" Tamrin asked.

"Leaving a message." Evra held the item—a necklace—to the wall and drove the dagger between it. Nyx felt a sharp flare of magic and the tip of the blade bit through the stone, sliding in halfway to the hilt.

Maruca arched an eyebrow as Evra turned around. "What's the message?"

Evra paused and looked up at the ceiling as if she suspected someone watched from it. "Tell your master to get their shit together and come find me." With that, Evra exited the Keep with all the grace of a scorned feudal lord, Tamrin right on her heels.

Morgen made a strangled noise.

"You might want to pick your jaw up off the floor," Nyx recommended.

Morgen's teeth clicked together. "*So* hot. It's not just me, right? Everyone saw how hot that was?"

Kalvar made a gagging noise, because he was Kalvar, Maruca rolled her eyes, and the two of them headed for the doors.

Nyx poked Morgen in the side. "What happened to stoic and broody?"

"I'm helpless in the face of such spectacularly expressed aggression. I'm beginning to think whoever the Keeper is, they royally pissed her off." He trotted out the door after the others, leaving Nyx with Kaden.

Kaden grinned at her. "Told you he'd break in less than a day."

"It's been longer than—"

"Nope."

Nyx was appalled to find it really had only been last night that Kaden bet her Morgen wouldn't be able to stay broody. She groaned.

"You should have taken that bet."

"If I'd taken it, I would have just lost."

"Exactly. But you'd have gotten to find out what I wanted when I won."

She started to literally run away from that statement when he grinned at her. It was officially the least broody she'd seen him since he came back from Arkadia, and she couldn't make herself bring him down again. She'd done enough running away from him. She still didn't trust him, didn't trust that he'd suddenly quit avoiding her the moment Seth reappeared, but she wasn't going to figure anything out by never speaking to him.

This, however, was *not* the place for a deep and meaningful conversation.

"I'll have to content myself with never knowing. Now let's get out there before I have to suffer your best friend's particular brand of humor about why we're late getting back to the group."

9

———

Nyx made it back across the death bridge, Kaden on her heels, and joined the huddle the rest of their group had formed. This was, arguably, the best place in the Market to discuss their next move. Closed for business or not, the Keep and its surrounding areas was the only building the Market-goers were giving any berth.

"If we can't find the Keeper, what's our next move?" Nyx asked.

Maruca made a derisive noise. "What would your plan have been if we hadn't all come with you?"

Maruca clearly didn't expect Nyx to have an answer to that question. Which, okay, fair, except that Nyx had been thinking of little else since she'd seen the Market aside from how to find Seth. "I'd go around asking obviously dumb questions about Seth very publicly."

Maruca stared at her for a few seconds before she finally asked, "And what would that accomplish?"

"If I go looking for Seth in all of this" —she waved a hand to indicate the Market at large— "I'll never find him. I don't have the resources, and I don't have the money to hire the resources, even if I could trust whoever I hired, which I highly doubt in a place like this. So the obvious solution is to let him find me."

"So your plan is to make your presence known?" The derision dripped off Maruca's lips like poisoned honey.

"Yep."

"As you have so recently pointed out, the Market is large. You really expect the fact that you're *asking* about him will actually get back to him? And furthermore that he would come to *you* when he just ran away from you?"

Nyx shrugged. That feeling in her gut, the one that had to come from memories she couldn't actually remember, told her this would work. Told her Seth was the type that never sat idle, that loved knowing everything that was going on around him. If she made herself look enough like a bright-eyed idiot—something that would stand out in a Market full of hardened criminals, enough to start gossip—he would hear about it. And if he'd been curious enough to come all the way to Earth after remembering her, he'd be curious enough to track her down here.

"What do you care, anyway?" she asked Maruca. "If it works or doesn't? I know you didn't come here to help me, so you may as well take the time to do whatever it is you *did* come here for."

Maruca looked like she wanted to argue, because Maruca always looked like she wanted to argue. But what she said was, "Fine. If Evra and Tamrin want to waste their time escorting you while you play the Market's easiest mark, that's their business. I'll take everyone else and do something useful."

"I have my own agenda," Evra said, at the same time Nyx said, "Actually, I need to borrow Kaden."

Maruca's glare was a thing that ought to be studied by weapons specialists the world over, because Nyx was pretty sure it was causing her actual physical damage. Like, it felt as if it was sucking the life out of her.

"Ruca." Kaden's voice was a soft, low warning that had absolutely no effect on his sister.

Wait a minute. On Arkadia, when Maruca had been merrily

obliterating vegetation with magical fire, Kaden had told Nyx his sister was an energy mage. Now that she looked for it, she felt the wispiest tendril of magic stretching from Maruca to her.

Holy shit. The woman literally *was* sucking the life out of her. Not much, but any amount was enough to piss Nyx off. As if she needed a lever in that direction where Maruca was concerned.

Nyx's response was instinctual, as almost all of her magical endeavors tended to be. Since learning she was Hidden, she'd never been able to feel her magic as a separate entity, as something to be harnessed and twisted. It was as if it was too much a part of her to be grasped and wielded.

So she couldn't do anything like build a shield, or throw off a magical attack, which was something she'd read several branches of magic were bent to easily enough. Instead, she felt for the part of herself where Maruca's power had latched on, and Hid it.

Maruca's eyes widened when her energy-sucking thread fell away, unable to find a point of contact.

"Back off," Nyx warned.

"Maybe we should all just calm down," Morgen suggested, which only had the effect of making Nyx and Maruca turn their glares on him. "Or not. By all means, let's all stand around attacking our allies in enemy territory."

Nyx resisted the urge to press her fingers to her eyes. Morgen was right, a fact which she nearly ignored two seconds later when Maruca opened her mouth again.

"What do you want my brother for? If this is to irritate me—"

"Oh for stars' sake, could you be any more self-centered? It's to irritate Seth, you idiot, because I got the impression he didn't like Kaden very much. All of which is moot point, because your brother is a fucking adult who can make his own goddamn decisions." The woman brought out entirely too many swear words in Nyx. She turned to Kaden. "Do you mind coming with me?"

Kaden looked about as happy as anyone would be to be smack in the middle of this pissing contest, but he said, "No."

"Great." She turned to Evra. "What's your secret agenda?"

"Not so different from yours. I want to find out what 'internal conflict within the Market' the Keeper is engaged in. So I'm going to ask questions until one side or the other decides to figure out if I'm a threat and come find me."

Nyx felt compelled to point out the obvious. "Umm, Evra, isn't the Keeper at war? Wars usually involve armies, or at least a lot more people than we have. This feels like a bear you shouldn't poke."

"Why would anyone poke a bear?"

Nyx considered it great progress on Evra's Earth education that she now knew what a bear was. "My point exactly."

Evra shook her head. "If the Keeper's people show up for me, it won't be an issue. If the other side shows up, the Keeper's forces will respond because they'll want to know what's so important to their rivals. Either way, I don't have to fight what is probably *not* an army, and I get the Keeper's attention. And if we want to go home, we *do* need to get the Keeper's attention."

Fair point. "Okay. Morgen, do you know how long it is until sunset here?"

He glanced at the sky, got that look he got when his brain was doing math and translating whatever answer he got into Earth equivalents, and said, "About six hours, I'd say, give or take."

"Let's plan to meet back here in three hours, then. If we haven't got what we need by then we can find a place to stay for the night and make plans for tomorrow."

"Is this why you made us all get watches?" Evra asked, glancing at the black sports watch Nyx had given her.

Nyx nodded.

"We could have just used synchronizing spells," Maruca grumbled.

Yes, they could have, but synchronizing spells didn't really offer anything a watch couldn't do better, in Nyx's opinion. She ignored Maruca's statement because the only comeback she could think of was, "Yeah, but watches look cooler."

The sooner they split up, the better. Wait. They were going to *split up*. Nyx groaned.

"What?" Evra asked.

"We're voluntarily splitting up in dangerous territory, something all of you would understand the significance of if you'd ever seen a horror film. So please make sure that none of you get killed, so I can drag you all home and finally make you watch a damn movie."

Predictably, they all just looked at her weird. She shook her head, muttered "Aliens" under her breath, and headed off with Kaden in a random direction.

"Sorry about Ruca," he said once they'd been swallowed up by the other market-goers. "She can be a little...overprotective."

"It's fine, I get it." Whatever else Maruca might be, she was probably a great sister. "Just tell me she hates all of your exes this much."

When Kaden didn't answer she glanced over at him. He cleared his throat. "Sorry, but you seem to be special."

"Figures." She seemed to be special in a lot of ways that mostly sucked. "So what kind of business around here can I look like the biggest idiot in?"

"About that. I'm not saying this is a terrible plan—"

"Which means you think it is."

"—but you, ah, never struck me as the type who would be good at playing a role for other people."

Because she was trying to get along with him, Nyx pondered how best to respond to that instead of going with her knee-jerk reaction to snap at him. "No offense," she said finally, and there wasn't any heat in her words, "but you really have no idea who I am around anyone other than you."

"I..." He trailed off. "I guess you're right." He looked as if the realization left a sour taste in his mouth.

They'd been a closed-off microcosm when they'd been

together. Because her mother's Hiding had made it impossible for anyone to remember her, Kaden had been her entire world. And, yes, they'd learned a lot about each other in the two years they'd spent together, but she had a feeling they were both entirely different people outside the quiet bubble they'd existed in together.

It was like that phase she'd always read about where, when two people start dating, they keep to themselves during the honeymoon phase, and then there's an adjustment period when they introduce each other to their friends and family, and that's the testing ground for the actual relationship. Whether they still worked together around other people.

She and Kaden had never gotten to go through that adjustment period. His entire life had been on a foreign planet, and she hadn't really *had* a life. But they'd spent so much time together that being around him again felt normal and easy on the one hand, and then utterly upsetting on the other every time something happened to remind her that they didn't really know each other at all.

Maybe he'd just never been confronted with that same knowledge until Seth showed up and slapped him in the face with the fact that she *did* have a past life he wasn't a part of. Now she wondered if Kaden could reconcile who she'd been with who she was. If he'd still want who she was becoming. Because she was never going back to being the woman whose every waking moment had been focused on him.

A display of throwing stars in a nearby storefront caught her eye and she stopped walking. "Here. We start here."

Kaden examined the store. "Any particular reason?"

"Seth has a thing for ranged weapons." There was no memory that accompanied that certainty, no flash of him in her mind's eye like there had been when she'd remembered his name outside of the Thirsty Lion. But despite that, she *was* certain that Seth had never met a sharp, throwable object he didn't like.

"Come on," she said, heading for the door. "Let's have some fun."

"Fun?" Kaden echoed.

She shrugged. "When else am I going to get to act like a clueless idiot and then enjoy the show while my bodyguard" —she clapped him on the shoulder— "beats up everyone who thinks I'm an easy mark?"

"Fuck," Kaden muttered.

Nyx pasted a bright, phony smile on her face and flounced into the store.

Almost three hours later, Nyx stepped out of what had to be the millionth weapons store she'd visited, then waited while Kaden took out yet another trio of would-be muggers who thought she was a vulnerable mark with a lot of money. She'd done her best to give the impression she would pay a great deal of money to anyone who could point her in Seth's direction. Her fingers itched to pull the short sword and join in the fight, but she hadn't spent two and half hours smiling until her cheeks hurt just to ruin the ruse by proving she could take care of herself.

Kaden finished resolving the matter and stalked back to her. "Are we done now?" If he'd been in a good mood earlier—and honestly, it was difficult to tell with him—it was certainly gone now. Not that she could blame him. He'd been in so many scuffles he'd sweated completely through his shirt.

"Yeah, we're done for the day."

"For the day?"

She shrugged as they wended their way through the market, back toward the Keep. "I only hit the weapons shops today. There are some other places I want to try tomorrow."

Kaden was quiet all the way until they were back at that bubble of empty space surrounding the Keep that none of the

Market-goers seemed willing to step into. "I know you think this idea will work—"

"But you think it's a waste of time," Nyx cut in, "and we'd be better off trying to actually track him. It's been all of a couple hours, Kaden. I wasn't expecting that I'd ask questions and he'd magically appear out of thin air to whisk me away."

"Even so—"

The air around Nyx stirred and Seth appeared out of thin air, looking extremely pissed off. He grabbed her wrist as something crumbled in his hand, and a portal appeared behind him. A portal he unceremoniously dragged her through.

The Keep and Kaden disappeared, and when the world righted itself she was standing in an alley in some other part of the Market, Seth glowering at her. "You were looking for me, Nyxi darling?" His tone was low and level and he hadn't cracked so much as an approximation of a grin. Wow, he was really pissed off.

"Found you?" she offered.

He made a noise of irritated disbelief. "Do you have any idea of the shitstorm you just kicked up for me?"

Nyx frowned. Somehow, this was not how she had envisioned this conversation going. She'd more or less imagined interrogating him while he happily told her everything she wanted to know about her past. "I—"

"What are you even doing here? *How* are you here? Guardians are planet-bound and—"

"What am I *doing* here?" she interrupted. "Seriously? What do you *think* I'm doing here? I want to know who you are."

He stumbled back like she'd punched him, and released the hold he'd kept on her wrist. Then he shook his head, his features settling back into neutrality. "No, Nyxi, you don't." He pulled something out of his pocket, grabbed her hand, and slapped a stone into her palm. "Take this, portal back to·Earth, and stay there."

Relief washed over her. He'd just cavalierly solved her

problem of getting back to Earth like it was no big deal. For a place where only the Keeper was supposed to control the portal stones, Seth sure tossed them around like they were nothing. Which was yet another thing she intended to make him explain to her. "I'm not going anywhere until you tell me what I want to know."

His eyes narrowed. "I will shove you through a portal to Earth *so* fast, Nyxi. Zero regrets."

"You could try."

"I'd succeed."

"Unlikely. But in that rare event, I'd just come right back here anyway." He didn't need to know she had no way of getting back.

"Then I won't be here when you do. What's the point anyway? Since you've managed to make my home completely inhospitable in a mere two hours of running your mouth, which is a record, even for you."

"The *Shadow Market* is your home?" Hadn't Morgen said it took a special kind of fucked up to live here? "And how has tossing your name around to a bunch of people who already know who you are made your home 'inhospitable'?"

"Yes, this is my home, because I don't have a lot of options. And it's you tossing my name around in conjunction with Earth while putting on an act stupid enough to make the whole Market take notice that's had the Keeper's loyalists perking their little ears up all over the place."

"The Keeper's looking for you?" But why would the Keeper be interested in Seth? Unless… "Are you the other faction the Keeper's at war with?"

Seth huffed out a laugh. "No. I'm not that stupid. But—" He broke off, head jerking up, and his gaze shot back to the bustle of the Market. "You have got to be kidding me."

She followed his gaze to see Kaden clearing his way through the Market toward them. And by *clearing*, it was literal. Most people took one look at his face in conjunction with the speed at which he moved, and made the wise decision to get out of his way. The ones who didn't found their removal from his path slightly less pleasant.

"What is that guy's deal?" Since Seth clearly wasn't expecting an actual answer to that, Nyx didn't give one. He curled her fingers closed around the portal stone to Earth. "Go home, Nyxi. And stay away from the Keeper. You do *not* want to tangle with her."

Nyx tensed, ready for him to open another portal and entirely prepared to follow him through it. Instead, he just vanished. There one second, gone the next while her brain tried to process the sudden disappearance.

She lurched forward but stumbled only into empty air. Something niggled at the back of her mind, just out of her reach. Something that would explain what had just happened, only she couldn't grasp it.

Then Kaden was at her side and that hint of an answer slipped away from her entirely. "Are you okay?"

"I'm fine." She shoved her hands into her pockets, hoping it looked casual, and deposited the portal stone. *Why* she didn't want Kaden to know Seth had given it to her she didn't have a clear answer for. "Damn it, he's gone. How am I going to find him again now?"

Seth clearly had no interest in talking to her. Which really begged the question of why he'd tracked her down on Earth in the first place. And why *now*? And why didn't he seem to have any trouble remembering her? Had her mother left him out of her Hiding, or—

"Nyx?" The way Kaden said her name made Nyx think it wasn't the first time he'd said it.

"Hmm?"

"We need to go. The others are going to start wondering where we are."

Nyx glanced at her watch. They were now fifteen minutes past the meet-up time. "Okay, just..." She spun in a slow circle, looking for anything that might give her some indication of where Seth had gone. But there was nothing. "You still can't track him?"

"No."

She frowned. "Then how did you find us?"

"I tracked you, not him."

"Through a *portal*? Is that normal?"

He hesitated, so briefly she almost didn't catch it, before he shrugged. "I'm good at tracking. Let's go."

Not the least bit convinced, Nyx followed him out of the alley and back into the thrum of the Market. The Keep's spire had barely come into sight when the rhythmic clang of steel hitting steel rent the air. Dread curling low in her belly, Nyx broke into a run.

10

A force of over two dozen heavily armored soldiers surrounded Nyx's friends. It looked like Evra had succeeded in attracting attention and, unless the Keeper wanted Evra dead, that attention belonged to the opposing faction, all brown-clad warriors with stylized suns on their backs.

Evra and her allies formed a core circle in the middle of the melee, defending each other, but as Nyx approached Kalvar was forced from the circle as he ducked and spun to dodge a blow. Maruca cut her way to him so fast the bodies were still falling as she arrived at his side, delivering a kick to his attacker so strong it sent the man flying back. He fell past the invisible line that separated the Market street from the death field around the Keep, and he died before he had time to scream, his body desiccating and turning to ash in a matter of seconds.

Nyx slowed as she approached the outer ring of the fray to draw her short sword and a dagger. She never got the chance to use either. The Keep's doors burst open and people poured out, their identical armor bearing the Keeper's torch-and-shadow emblem, flowing in a single file line down the bridge.

The battle rearranged itself as the opposing faction sought to shift focus from Evra and the others to the Keeper's soldiers. But that line of soldiers had no end, and by the time the other faction realized it and tried to flee, it was too late. The Keeper's forces had neatly encircled the original battle, and the efficiency with which they cut down their opposers was sickening for its cold swiftness, until soon every individual sporting a stylized sun on their clothing lay motionless on the ground.

One woman broke from the ranks of the Keeper's soldiers, her green skin glinting in the harsh afternoon light and giving the faintest appearance of small, fine scales. Her fingers were tipped with three-inch-long obsidian claws, and the tail that flicked angrily behind her ended in what looked like a spear-tip that grew in the same as her claws.

She looked directly at Evra. "You have the Keeper's attention." Then she turned her reptilian gaze on Nyx. "As do you." She smiled, revealing a row of sharp black fangs. "Congratulations. You are all to be the Keeper's honored guests."

Well, shit.

The only person who looked supremely unconcerned by this announcement—and the attendant way the Keeper's soldiers flowed around them and herded them onto the bridge—was Evra. Nyx really, really hoped the Amazon knew what she was doing.

"Get rid of these," the reptilian commander ordered, and Nyx risked a glance back over her shoulder. She wished she hadn't. One by one, the Keeper's soldiers stripped the fallen of weapons and other items before tossing the bodies onto the Keep's grounds to become so much white ash.

She swallowed, and wondered when she would get used to death. Already it affected her less than it had when she'd first fought the Kumir in Earth Between. She understood that was natural. People became inured to violence after seeing it enough, because if they didn't adapt in that manner, they wouldn't survive. But she didn't have to *like* it, didn't have to like wondering how long it would be until she was as unruffled by it all as Kaden and the others.

They were ushered into the Keep, and Nyx saw the source of the soldiers around them. It wasn't a secret door inside the Keep as she'd been expecting. No, it was a portal, held open by the two individuals who stood to either side of it, their fingers glowing with blue magic that pulsed and called to Nyx on a primal level. She set her teeth and ignored that call, ignored the desire to stretch out her fingers toward that blue light and see if it would come to her.

What the hell? She sneaked glances at Evra and the others, but no one else in her little band seemed to be similarly affected. She rationalized that it must be a result of her Guardian status. She was connected to the portal in her Station, so maybe she felt the call of the magic the two witches were using to hold this portal open in the same way?

She did, however, balk at the idea of going through it. "Are we really going to just let ourselves be blindly herded through a portal right now?" she whispered to Kaden.

"The alternative," he replied, voice equally soft, "appears to be getting killed and having our bodies used to sand the front yard. So, yes."

Nyx brushed her fingers over her pocket, feeling the small lump of the portal stone inside it. This would be fine. Even if the Keeper and Evra weren't on good terms, Nyx could still get them all out of here. She could still get them home.

Ahead, Evra and Tamrin walked through the portal with easy confidence, as if being surrounded by a small army bristling with weaponry was no big deal. Morgen, Maruca, and Kalvar followed, looking similarly unconcerned, and Nyx decided that maybe if all the experienced world travelers were at least giving the appearance of being unbothered, she should take her cue from them.

She rolled her shoulders back and down, straightened her spine, and walked through the portal like she wasn't very, very concerned about what was on the other side. She arrived in a vast, windowless room, easily the size of a large warehouse. It should have been dim, being made of the same black stone as the spire they'd just left, but sconces set into the wall every few feet glowed, filling the space with a soft, misty white light.

There were no objects in the room, only people—portal witches, and those who were either leaving or entering via the portals they created. Archways lined all four walls every ten feet or so, and from what Nyx could see, each opening led to stairs that descended. Nyx already felt as if this room lay underground —she didn't know if that was because of its windowless nature, or the certainty that she could feel the weight of the earth pressing in on her from all sides—and not a single staircase she could see ascended.

"Welcome to the Shadow Keep." The reptilian commander's sibilant voice held a lightly mocking tone, and that was the only thing that stopped Nyx from stupidly saying that she'd thought the spire in the Market *was* the Keep. Her brain caught up with that assumption a few seconds later. She supposed, if you were going to hold power in a place like the Market, you would need a front location. Like, say, a spire that everyone might assume led to your base of operations because all of your employees entered and exited the Market via it.

If it were ever attacked, no doubt the Keeper's enemies would waste their time looking for a secret doorway to the rest of the Keep. One that likely didn't exist, because Nyx strongly suspected that the only way to enter *this* Keep was via portal magic. Magic the Keeper controlled.

They followed the commander to a set of stairs, two other soldiers falling in at their backs, though none of the Keeper's people looked terribly concerned about them trying anything. As they descended flight after flight of stairs, Nyx suspected that lack of concern was directly related to the labyrinthine nature of the Keep.

Archways split off at random. Sometimes they opened into rooms, but more often than not, they simply led to branching staircases. The further they went, the more utterly confused Nyx became, until she was so disoriented she almost felt like they were going up even though the stairs kept going down.

How far into the planet did the Keep *go*? She couldn't fathom the amount of effort or magic or both that must have been expended to dig and reinforce a structure so large and complex. The she supposed it *did* make sense to build beneath the ground on a desert-like planet prone to flaying winds. Actually, now that she thought about it…

She caught up to Morgen and asked, quietly, "Why isn't the entire Market underground?" Hadn't Maruca said most people lived underground here? And yet the city she'd seen above was nothing to scoff at.

"I'm not an expert on the Market so I can't say for sure, but if I had to guess? Underground space here is limited and expensive. There are probably some vendors that operate beneath the city, but I'd wager most can't afford it. "

Right. The underground part of the city offered more protection—comfort, too, if the drop in temperature between here and the market was any indication—so naturally only those individuals with excessive means would have access to it.

The air continued to cool as they descended, until Nyx was grateful for the long-sleeved shirt she wore. The walls, the floor, the ceiling, never varied from the deep black stone of the spire that graced the Market, and she wondered about that, too—where the stone had been brought from, how long the Keep had been here.

Long past when Nyx's muscles had turned to a sort of numb indifference from repetitive stair descending, the commander led them through a set of high double-doors into what could only be considered a throne room. Namely because a large throne sat at the far end of the rectangular space on a raised, four step dais. It was currently empty and, as such, could not hold Nyx's attention when something far, far more fascinating waited in the center of the room.

Twelve feet in diameter and set in the direct center of the

black stone floor was a pool of burning sapphire-blue light. Its call hit her physically, strong and deep, hypnotic, like the first time she'd walked into the portal room at her Station and nearly jumped right onto the ley lines. That had been a disaster avoided only by the previous Guardian's physically pulling her away from the ley line entrance.

The siren call of the pool before her was twice as hypnotic as the ley line's, far stronger than the itch she'd had to reach for the magic the portal witches had wielded to bring them here.

"What is it?" Nyx hadn't meant to ask the question out loud, because she was already certain she knew the answer.

"It's portal magic," the commander answered, tone bored. "Feel free to take a closer look."

"Just like that?" Nyx asked, skeptical. It seemed to her that if one had a pool of portal magic lying around, one might not want to let people just mosey on up to it.

The commander shrugged. "It can't be manipulated by anyone but a portal witch." She walked over to the pool and swept her hand through it. Magic curled away from her like smoke. "See?"

"How do you know I'm not a portal witch?"

The commander laughed, a raspy, sibilant noise. "If you were a portal witch, you'd be on your knees in the middle of that pool. They can't resist it the first time, like *azurcha*." That last word didn't translate, but Nyx figured it was the reptile race's version of heroin. "Besides, portal witches, they feel like something. You feel like nothing."

That last was clearly meant to be a dig, but Nyx didn't care. She wondered if she felt like nothing to the commander because she was Hidden, and not because she *wasn't* something other. Because if it hadn't been for all of her experience resisting the portal's call in her Station, she *would* be on her knees in the middle of that pool right now. And having been given permission to touch it, she couldn't resist.

She didn't care what they were all doing in this room, what

or who they were waiting for. All she cared about was that blue glow.

Nyx stepped up to the rim of the pool and crouched beside it. The magic swirled and eddied, like each curl and tendril had a life, an agency, of its own. Mesmerized, she drew her hand through it as the commander had done. But where the magic had danced away from the commander's fingers, it clung to Nyx's.

She hadn't expected it to latch onto her. She darted a glance over her shoulder but no one was watching her. Evra was speaking with the commander in low tones, and everyone else was focused on the argument they seemed to be having.

Nyx tried to shake the magic off her fingers but it wouldn't let go. Truthfully, she didn't want it to. So when she heard the clang of a bolt sliding out of a door, she gave up on trying to return the portal magic to the pool. She stuffed her hand in her pocket and stood, wandering back to the group. Evra and the commander had quit arguing at the sound of the lock being thrown.

A second set of double doors, opposite the ones they'd entered through and directly behind the throne, swung open. A woman who could only be the Keeper of Shadows entered, her booted heels striking harshly on the black stone. She had tawny brown skin only a shade darker than her eyes and thick, arched eyebrows set above high cheekbones. Metal-plated armor graced an athletic form and her copper-brown hair was pulled back in a severe plait.

She was also completely covered in blood and gore. Red drops had dried on her face like macabre freckles, pieces of stars-alone-knew-what clung to her armor and leathers, and she left bloody footprints on the stone floor. An angry slash cut across her cheek, and given that most of the blood on her clearly wasn't hers, Nyx sincerely hoped the greater universe had devised a method of stopping blood-transmissible diseases.

The Keeper's hand rested on the hilt of the longsword at her side, white-scarred knuckles on prominent display. Her face was expressionless, gaze flicking once to the commander before settling back on Evra, where it had been ever since she entered. "Take your unit and leave, Essteria."

The reptilian commander—Essteria—did not look pleased. "Master, I do not think that entirely wise. After what occurred in the Market—"

"How very interesting," the Keeper interrupted, her voice cool, "that you feel the need to offer your opinion on this matter." Essteria stiffened, going completely still, and the Keeper's fingers flexed on the sword at her side. "I had not realized I had grown so incompetent in my ability to judge a situation. By all means, please continue to enlighten me."

There were so many layers of threat and subtext in those words that Nyx swore she felt a crackle of flame dart between Keeper and commander. Essteria's lips parted in a smile that showed clenched, serrated teeth. Then she motioned to the other two soldiers and departed the room without another word.

The doors had barely shut when Tamrin let out an excited yelp more befitting a twelve than a sixteen year-old and barreled into the Keeper of Shadows, completely uncaring of the layers of blood and other nastiness coating the woman. "Bryn!"

The Keeper locked Tamrin in a bear hug and spun her in a circle, Tamrin's feet flying off the ground. She ruffled Tamrin's hair as she set her back on her feet, as if Tam were the Keeper's kid sister and not Evra's. "Are you well?" Bryn asked, and the careful tone of her voice left no question as to what she was really asking.

Tamrin nodded but offered no other information, clearly not wanting to talk about Arkadia. She turned on Evra. "Why didn't you just tell me we were coming to see Bryn? You never *would* tell me where she went."

"For obvious reasons, I should think," Evra replied icily.

"I *did* try to get to her," Bryn said, directly to Evra, like the rest of them didn't even exist. "But it seems Arkadia is one of the few places even the Keeper of Shadows cannot reach."

Nyx had never truly seen Evra conflicted before. "Thank you," she finally bit out, sounding like she was choking on broken glass, "for trying."

"Of course." Then the Keeper's voice cooled several degrees. "And I see you have repaid me by bringing me no less than three wanted fugitives and" —her gaze settled on Kalvar and Nyx— "what are you two?"

"I'm a refugee." Kalvar said it so bravely, and with such a sense of importance, that Nyx hoped no one felt the need to tell him he did not, technically, fit the definition of a refugee.

Bryn's lips twitched. "Are you really, now? And you?"

Nyx weathered the weight of Bryn's scorching stare while she tried to decide what game Bryn was playing at. From what the commander had said to her in the Market, it seemed clear the Keeper knew that Nyx was looking for Seth. The Keeper was apparently also looking for Seth.

"I'm Evra's friend," Nyx said finally.

This answer did not appear to please the Keeper, and she sized Nyx up as if she were competition but not a particularly worthy opponent.

So, Nyx thought, *you're the asshole who broke Evra's heart.*

Morgen had obviously clued in as well, his eyes darting back and forth from Evra to Bryn so frequently it made Nyx dizzy.

"I've heard there's an artifact on Earth's Station," Bryn said. "One that can open any door."

"Oh?"

"But Evra would have needed a Guardian's help for that." Bryn studied Nyx, her gaze fixing on Nyx's arm, where the Guardian tattoo rested. Bryn couldn't see it—Nyx had worn long sleeves precisely for the purpose of covering it—but she acted like she could.

Nyx shrugged. "I guess so."

"Guardians don't travel."

"No, they don't." But she was something slightly more than a Guardian now.

"Let me see." Bryn indicated Nyx's arm.

Nyx crossed them. Let Bryn suspect all she wanted, Nyx wasn't going to do her the favor of confirming those suspicions. Besides, she didn't need her Guardian mark inspected like it was a brand on a prized cow. It was… personal.

"I don't think so."

"Be very careful, little girl. You're not in your domain now, you're in mine. Let me see."

"No."

Bryn took a step forward. So did Kaden.

"She said no."

A flash of anger rippled across Bryn's face. "You should be careful too, Kaden Moor. The bounty on your head alone would run my operations for a year."

"Enough, Bryn." Evra had, apparently, hit her limit. "It may be a difficult concept for you to wrap your head around, but these people are my friends."

"Your friends," Bryn repeated, her voice dripping with bitterness. "Imagine, Moriana's perfect daughter associating with wanted criminals and an Earthling, of all things. But then," she snapped her fingers, "that's right. I'd heard you're *not* her daughter anymore."

Evra blanched.

"I'd have thought *that* would have made a few things clear to you. I'd thought you would come to me then. But you didn't."

"I'm here now, aren't I?"

"Because you want me to get Tamrin home. That *is* why you're here, isn't it?"

"Yes," Evra ground out.

"So the honorless way I make my living is acceptable to you when it's someone *you* need to move across the universe?"

"Can you get her home or not?"

"That depends."

Nyx could hear Evra's teeth clench all the way from the ten feet separating them, and seriously hoped the Amazon had good dental care, whatever that looked like in the wider universe.

"I can pay you."

"I don't want your money, Evra."

"Then what *do* you want? Nothing is ever free with you, so what's the price?"

Bryn's face turned back into a stone mask. "It will take me some time to arrange Tam's transport back to Scythia. Once she is home, spend a week with me. One week, that's all I ask. See what I've built here."

"It won't change my mind."

"Then you have nothing to worry about, do you?"

Silence stretched between the two women before Evra said, "No. I suppose I don't. You have a deal then."

"Good." Bryn smiled and Nyx was more than a little surprised to discover her teeth were normal human-looking teeth as opposed to some version of fangs. "And because I'm in a generous mood, perhaps I'll even help your friend." She turned on Nyx. "Rumor has it you're looking for someone. My resources aren't cheap, but they are the best in the Market."

Uh-huh. "And this generous offer would have nothing to do with the fact that you apparently want to find Seth as much as I do?"

"I want to find *someone.* Whether he is the same person you wish to find remains to be seen. Describe him."

Nyx had intentionally left off giving a detailed physical description of Seth when she'd been looking for him in the Market. As big of an idiot as she'd been playing, every person in the Market looking for an easy score would have been coming to tell her they knew where she could find Seth. She'd been intending for *them* to tell *her* what Seth looked like as proof their information was good.

It was on the tip of Nyx's tongue to tell Bryn she knew they were looking for the same person because Seth had confirmed as much. Then it occurred to her that maybe letting Bryn know she'd already seen him wasn't the brightest idea. She already felt like pairing up with Bryn was akin to making a deal with the devil, and giving as little information as possible while still getting what she wanted seemed like the best plan.

"He's about six feet tall. Black hair, brown eyes, maybe a hundred and fifty pounds?"

Bryn furrowed her brow. "A hundred and fifty pounds?" She repeated the word *pounds* carefully, telling Nyx the planet's translator spells hadn't managed to come up with an equivalent in her native tongue.

"About seventy universal weights," Morgen offered.

He claimed he only took language classes for the broad variety of other languages' curse words, but in a universe where magic would do almost all of the talking for you, he had a reservoir of language knowledge that spoke to years of study. He converted and translated things for them without even thinking about it, and usually when he performed this culture-bridging task he sounded bright and excited, like the very best student in class after the teacher called on them.

Right now he sounded glum.

"Species base and subgroup?" Bryn asked.

Say what, now? "Huh?"

"You know, like I'm base Human, subgroup Tiagren?" Kalvar offered.

"What am I?" Nyx asked.

"Base Human, subgroup Boring?" He snickered.

However would we get on without the wit of teenagers?

"Seriously, if your subgroup's not obvious it's hard to tell." He smiled. "You human-looking-humans all look the same to me."

"Kaden?"

"Though not the most eloquent explanation he is not wrong. Without birth records it could be difficult to say."

Nyx turned back to Bryn. "He's human-looking-human."

Nyx suspected Bryn would have rolled her eyes, if the action wasn't too ill-fitting for the all-powerful ruler of a shadowy underworld. Besides, how much more information could Bryn really need?

Evra seemed to be thinking the same thing. "Do you know the person she is looking for, or not?"

Bryn nodded, a short, sharp jerk, and stalked back to settle onto her throne. "You might say we were once colleagues of a sort. We had similar aspirations. I attained them. He did not. Now he is a thorn in my ever-loving side and I would like to rip him out."

Seth and Bryn had worked together? And it sounded like they'd both been angling for the Keeper position. Nyx tried, but she couldn't picture Seth sitting on that throne looking all dour and dictatorial. She could practically see him in her mind's eye, whining about how boring ruling anything would be.

"Which is why I'm willing to offer you a deal," Bryn continued, "provided I think you can deliver what I need." She leaned forward, forearms resting on her thighs. "Tell me, does Seth care about you?"

Nyx blinked. "What?"

"Does he like you? Does he trust you? I worked with Seth for six years. In the entirety of that time he was close to no one, and I never learned anything about his past. This morning, I would have told you that if my people were crawling all over the city looking for him, he wouldn't poke his head out of whatever hole he was hiding in for anything. And yet the portal activity in the Market earlier indicates he did so for you."

So much for keeping the fact that she'd seen Seth to herself.

"That implies a potential connection I can exploit. If it were up to me, I would chain you to the spire in the Market square and see if *that* got his attention." She absolutely wasn't joking. "But Evra would never forgive me for that, so I am left with bargaining. And I do not make fools' bargains. Seth has something that belongs to me. Unfortunately, past experience has shown that he is extremely resilient to torture."

Nyx's stomach turned even as her subconscious whispered, *Probably wasn't him you were torturing*. Whatever that meant. She really wished she had the memory to make the things she thought about Seth make sense.

"It is unlikely I could retrieve what I need from him in the timeframe it would take me to break him. If he trusts you, you could convince him to hand it over. But I need some proof that you are worth the bargain."

"What kind of proof?"

Bryn shrugged. "Anything that will convince me you know him well enough to be worth the risk. And if you *do* know him well enough, this shouldn't be a difficult task for you."

How was Nyx supposed to give her any kind of proof when *she* couldn't even remember who Seth was to her? She had inferred they'd grown up together and that was about it. It wasn't as if they had friendship bracelets, or matching tattoos, or—

Memory, as it had been doing unpredictably ever since she'd acquired the chaos thorns, rose up out of nowhere. She saw a small lake, summer sun beating down through an overhang of trees, Seth chucking his shirt and diving in, a tattoo curving over his chest, one she recognized all too well.

She knew then that she *had* the proof Bryn wanted. She also didn't want to give it up. But her options were limited. Seth had basically told her to be a good little girl and go home. She'd already kicked the hornet's nest as hard as she could, so causing more trouble in the Market wasn't going to get him to come find her again.

She didn't want this trip—one of five remaining ones she was ever going to have—to be for nothing. She didn't want to lose the chance to find out what he could tell her. And no matter what *she* did, Bryn would look for Seth anyway. Nyx had no control over that. All she could do was get the best terms out of this agreement as possible. Starting with proving, beyond all reasonable doubt, that she and Seth were connected.

"You ever seen him without his shirt on?"

Bryn straightened and her eyebrows crept up to her hairline. "Are you asking if we were lovers?"

"No." Though Nyx didn't know why she was relieved to find that the answer was clearly a no, if the scorn in Bryn's voice was any indication. "I'm asking if you've seen his tattoo."

"Ah." Bryn settled back. "I have. What of it?"

Nyx swallowed. "Then you know it looks exactly like this." Her fingers shook slightly as she pulled the collar of her shirt aside to reveal the galaxy tattoo over her own heart, the lines swirling together in black and gray and green ink.

Kaden stiffened. Nyx pretended she didn't notice and told herself the tattoo didn't mean anything. It wasn't like she had a lock tattooed on her heart and Seth had a matching key on him, or they'd gotten each others' names permanently inscribed on their skin. No, they just had matching tattoos. Over their hearts. It could mean anything.

"Now *that* is something I can work with."

"Then let's talk terms." She didn't need Seth's warning to know tangling with the Keeper was likely a sticky affair. "What exactly does Seth have that you want?"

Bryn tapped her fingers on the throne's armrest and the sound echoed through the room. "A key."

"To what?"

"To something he can never hope to access. It's more than useless to him as things stand. Get him to hand it over to me, and he's all yours."

"All right. You don't harm him. You find him, I get your key, and we all leave. After we leave, you don't bother him again. You don't look for him, your people don't look for him. In fact, once we leave, you don't even remember us. You never worked with him, you never met me, you never met them." She indicated Kaden and the others.

The room was so quiet Nyx could hear the seconds ticking by

on her watch. The only thing missing was some dust and tumbleweed.

"Fortunately for you, turning fugitives into the All Council has never been to my taste. Very well. We have a deal. For the duration of your stay on this planet you will be under my protection and my hospitality."

Nyx had never heard the word hospitality sound more threatening. Bryn stomped her booted heel onto the ground twice, and the commander re-entered.

"Essteria will show you to your rooms. You may go wherever you like on that floor, but understand this: outside of the floor you have been granted, you are not under my protection and your lives are your own responsibilities. If you choose to return to the Market, you do so at your own risk, and your return to the safety of the Keep is entirely at my whim. I'll send for you once my people track Seth down."

Nyx debated arguing about being included in the tracking party, until she realized there would probably be multiple tracking parties. Given the size of the Keep, Bryn clearly didn't have a dearth of employees, and the Market was a large place. Even if she went out with a group, it wouldn't necessarily be the same one that found Seth. If any of them did.

She didn't think he'd hidden under the Keeper's nose by being *bad* at it. For now, she would wait, and try to think of another way to get Seth's attention. If she found him on her own, she wouldn't owe Bryn anything.

The Keeper stood and held out her hand to Evra, like an imperious ruler beckoning and expecting completely to be obeyed. Which, Nyx supposed, she sort of was.

Evra's face settled into a mask to rival Bryn's, and she pointedly ignored her and turned to Nyx. They stared at each for a few seconds, during which Nyx wished she could come up with something witty to say that would lighten the mood, when all she really wanted to do was ask if Evra was okay, but didn't want to do it in front of the present company. It must have shown on her face anyway because Evra rolled her eyes.

"Try not to get killed without me," she commanded. "Decent employers are hard to come by."

She turned on her heel. Morgen touched his hand to her shoulder as she passed by and Evra stopped. A flicker of his usual sarcastic humor lit his eyes and he whispered something into her ear, softly enough the words didn't travel even in a room designed to carry echoes.

Evra's eyes widened, an honest-to-stars smile tilting up the corners of her mouth. She reversed her course and headed for Essteria.

"Evra?" It was less a question from Bryn and more a command for explanation.

"It has been brought to my attention that I promised you a week *after* my sister has been returned home. I will stay with the wanted criminals and the Earthling for now."

Nyx did not quite dare to look back at Bryn's face as they exited.

"You might," she suggested quietly to Morgen, when they were a good distance from the throne room, "want to check any food you receive for poison."

11

———

Ｏne might think shacking up in the lair of a person titled something as pretentious as the Keeper of Shadows would be interesting. One might also be mistaken.

Nyx had been shown to a room that was utilitarian in the extreme, containing a bed and a small side table, both of which were bolted to the floor, and precisely nothing else. No paintings, no carpet or rugs, and—since they were underground—no windows. A door to her left presumably led to the bathroom.

She unbuckled and shrugged out of the back sheath that held her short sword, placing the weapon on the end of the bed. The sheath and straps were well-made and as comfortable as such things could be, but she didn't enjoy wearing it indoors. Sitting on anything other than a barstool while she had it on was practically impossible, and she saw no real reason to carry it with her while she was on this floor.

The very fact that Bryn had not bothered to take anyone's weapons told Nyx precisely how unconcerned the Keeper was about them as a threat. Considering Nyx's companions were fairly threatening, that told Nyx precisely how dangerous the Keeper was. But Nyx didn't think the woman was the type to break a bargain—Evra wouldn't trust her, were that the case—

and at any rate, she had her knives and a pair of boots that could make her run very, very fast.

Feeling restless in the uninviting room, she headed out to explore and slammed straight into Maruca.

The redhead fixed her with a scowl. "You. I need a word."

If Maruca hadn't looked like she was in mortal pain from the statement, Nyx would have thought she'd heard wrong.

"Not now." After their recent encounter over Kalvar, Nyx wasn't particularly interested in being alone with the other woman.

Maruca grabbed her arm as she walked by. "Yes, now."

Nyx looked down at Maruca's hand on her bicep, anger simmering just beneath her skin.

"You want to be very careful how far you push me."

Maruca raised one perfect brow. "Or?"

"I may not be an Enforcer, but I was raised by one. And I've put your brother on his ass more than once so the *or* is, don't push me or I might decide to push back."

A wild gleam entered Maruca's eyes, those green-glass eyes so like and unlike Kaden's, and an answering rush of adrenaline filled Nyx's veins. Maybe she *did* want to fight Maruca. Nyx hadn't been joining the morning sparring sessions at the Station because she'd wanted to avoid Kaden, so her restlessness and pent-up fears had had few physical outlets, and taking a few swings at someone she didn't particularly care if she hurt suddenly sounded like a wonderful idea.

Just when Nyx was sure Maruca *would* push, anticipation zinging through her veins, the redhead locked her jaw and let go of Nyx's arm.

Oh, well. Probably for the best. Nyx stepped around her and kept walking.

"You really have something better to do than talk to me?"

Nyx could *hear* the smoke pouring out of Maruca's ears.

"Anything," she threw back over her shoulder, "is better than talking to you."

Nyx was enjoying the feeling of Maruca's gaze burning a hole in her back when the redhead apparently came to a decision and walked after her, catching up in a handful of long-legged strides.

"We are trapped together," Maruca said silkily, "on one floor of an underground building. There are limited hallways, limited rooms, and in case you haven't noticed already, none of those rooms lock and all of the furniture is bolted to the ground to prevent its use as a barricade. So you may not *want* to talk to me, but I suspect you want me following you around every second of the day even less."

The damn woman would do it, too. She was like a feral dog with its teeth latched onto a kill, and if there was one thing Nyx was certain of it was that she didn't want Maruca sleeping in her room until Nyx agreed to speak to her. Not that Maruca would sleep. No, she would probably hover creepily over the bed while Nyx tried and failed to sleep.

Nyx stopped, turned, and crossed her arms. "Fine. Talk."

Maruca shook her head. "Not here. Come with me."

Letting out a world-weary sigh, Nyx followed Maruca down the hallway, through a door and into the small kitchen they had been shown on the very brief tour the soldier who'd dropped them here had given them.

Nyx stared at Maruca who stared back, and though Nyx suspected the redhead was genetically incapable of fidgeting, she looked like she wanted to.

"It will probably be less painful if you just say it," Nyx suggested.

"It's about Kaden."

Nyx stiffened. She should have guessed. Kaden was the only thing that could prompt the woman to voluntarily speak to her. Nyx prepared herself for a diatribe on how she was a heartless woman with no morals.

"I need you to let him go."

Warmth flared in Nyx's cheek, a flicker of black down her arms.

"I'm not exactly holding him hostage, Maruca. I am hiding him—and you, I might add—from people who could probably destroy me in less time than it takes them to blink because he doesn't have anywhere else to go."

"That isn't exactly true."

"You know, you're right." Nyx snapped her fingers. "They could probably kill me in half a blink."

"It isn't true that he has nowhere else to go." Maruca waved her hand, indicating the space they stood in.

Nyx couldn't believe it. "You want him to live *here?* In the Shadow Market?"

"The Shadow Market is only a stepping stone. We can go anywhere from here." Maruca used that tone of voice that indicated she was explaining things to a particularly dim child. "Mercenary work isn't hard to come by for people with our skill set. The honest jobs won't make us rich, but with both of us and Morgen we could make a decent living as a team."

Nyx felt like she'd been punched in the gut. This scenario had occurred to her on some level, but it hadn't felt real. Maruca she could deal without just fine, but she'd come to think of Morgen like family. And Kalvar would undoubtedly follow them all, and Kaden? Her insides twisted. She didn't know how she felt about Kaden, but she'd thought she had plenty of time to figure it out.

Except...

"Kaden's here, isn't he? He must have already made up his mind, so I can't imagine why you need me."

"Of course he's made up his mind. I know my brother, Nyx. He came here for two reasons: one, to watch over *you.*" Maruca's lips twisted bitterly around the words. "And two, because he thinks he can convince me to move on without him so I don't waste my life in that Station. Like he will waste his, if you don't let him go."

Maruca's words tore at her. Because she was right. Suppose Kaden *did* actually care about her. Suppose she could get past everything that happened and it turned out they still had something between them. What kind of life could they honestly have together? What kind of life was living inside a Station and wandering out into Earth Between?

For her, it was wonderful. But then, she'd had nothing before the Station and Earth Between. She'd known a very small existence. Kaden had been born—hell, she didn't even know where in the universe he'd been born—and he'd worked for the highest power in that universe. Traveled all over it, seen all manner of things she could never even dream of. How could he ever be content to be tied to Earth Between? Tied to her?

Her Station was a Nexus. She would never age within its confines and if he stayed with her, he wouldn't either. Now that she had bonded to the Station itself, she could never give up that Guardianship. She didn't think about that most days, about the terror that shredded her insides into ribbons at the idea of living forever.

It wasn't something she would have wanted even had she known it was possible. An extended life, free to leave it and age normally whenever she chose? Yes, that had appeal. But forever? And to drag someone else into that? Someone who had family and friends he would have to let go of as they aged and he didn't?

She would be a monster to ask it of him even if he did actually care for her. Committing to someone for a human lifetime didn't work out for most people even when they didn't have a galactic ton of baggage to deal with. Forever? The notion of forever with no end date was absurd.

He *should* go.

"He's free to make his own decisions," she said finally. "It has nothing to do with me."

"It has *everything* to do with you," Maruca exploded. "You have his heart on a damn string and I want to rip your head off for the way you yank him around on it, except if I did he'd probably spend the rest of his life mourning you. If you care about him at all, convince him to leave."

"I'll give it due consideration," she said flatly, and turned and walked out.

Nyx cursed the stars, this galaxy, and the whole damn universe when two hallways later she rounded a corner and slammed straight into Kaden's chest. He put a steadying hand on her elbow that she didn't need and both of them knew it. He had a smile on his face, a genuine one she hadn't seen once since he'd come back from Arkadia, like her barreling into him was the best possible thing that could ever occur.

If her head hadn't been full of Maruca's request and her own guilt she probably would have felt the same way about the moment. She was close enough to notice he'd started smelling like cedarwood again now that he was off a prison planet and able to enjoy the luxury of choosing his own hygiene products. She breathed it in, a little harsh, a lot comforting, and fought not to close her eyes, not to lean into him.

Her body remembered exactly how she fit against him, how she responded when he touched her. All he would have to do to touch her now was lean forward a few inches. A few short inches and his lips could be on hers, his hands in her hair, and she could forget their complicated history and the more complicated future of living forever because she knew as soon as she let him touch her none of it would matter.

Well, it would still matter, she just wouldn't be thinking about any of it.

"Sorry," she muttered, and took a careful step away.

His smile faltered. "Is everything okay?"

"Everything is fine," she lied. A voice in her head whispered that she should just get it all over with now, should let him go before either of them got attached again.

The last vestiges of Kaden's smile disappeared, telling her exactly how unconvincing she'd been. "About that date."

Nyx stiffened.

"I won't hold you to it."

Whatever she'd expected him to say, that hadn't been it. She would be lying to herself if she said she wasn't just the slightest bit disappointed.

"Not if you don't want me to. You never got a chance to answer me last night."

Last night. When he'd told her he missed her and asked her if she felt the same way.

Say something, she ordered herself, but her tongue was all tied up and the expectant, hopeful way he looked at her made her terrified she would say the wrong thing. She didn't know how long she stood there trying to form words but it must have been too long because the hopefulness left him, and his broken-glass eyes shuttered over.

"Is there someone else?" he asked.

The question startled her with its ludicrousness. Who else would there possibly be? There were exactly two other people of the gender she was attracted to living in her Station and of them, Morgen was like an older brother, and Kalvar a younger one. It wasn't like she had been out living up the night life in Earth Between and hooking up with strangers.

Then she realized Kaden's gaze was locked on her chest, as if he could see right through her shirt to the tattoo beneath it.

Oh. *Oh.* He thought *Seth* and her were—had been…? She couldn't even finish the thought. At first because it seemed absurd and then because she realized she couldn't deny it or confirm it. The only certainty she had where Seth was concerned was that he was important. What form that importance took she had no recollection.

"Kaden, I don't..." She trailed off, feeling stupid and help-less. Had she *always* been this bad at talking?

Her lackluster response killed any remaining intimacy between them, and his voice turned detached and businesslike. "Just think about it," he told her. "If I'm a complication you'd rather not deal with, now is the time to tell me."

She watched him walk away, an invisible fist squeezing around her heart. Maruca had been wrong. He *was* considering leaving. And the way his face had simply shut down, lost all emotion, well, it seemed easy enough for him to do. Easy enough for him to not give a damn.

12

———

Three hours later, Nyx's mood hadn't improved. Knowing that staying put was the smarter plan than trying to comb the city for Seth on her own didn't do anything to ease how useless she felt sitting around twiddling her thumbs. In the end, the thing that kept her from gathering her friends and doing another search of the city on her own was the fear of what Bryn might do with Seth if her people brought him back when Nyx wasn't around.

She was wandering the halls of their floor in a useless attempt to walk off the urgent need to *do* something, when she heard music that matched her mood. She followed it and found Morgen sitting at the bench of a piano set in the middle of an otherwise empty room, his fingers traveling deftly over the keys. The song was sad and ethereal and she stood in the doorway and listened, not wanting to interrupt.

His fingers played the last notes, sustain pedal held down until they faded softly into nothingness.

"What do you think?" His voice was soft and serious for once.

"It's beautiful," she said honestly. How had Morgen

managed to find a piano in the Keep of all places? Maybe it was a siren thing. Or just a Morgen thing.

He didn't respond, trilling two notes together with one hand and reaching for the mug sitting atop the piano with the other. A Morgen with nothing to say frightened the hell out of her. She crossed to the piano and slid onto the bench next to him, forcing him to scoot over and make room.

"Do you play duets?"

He gave her an incredulous look. "You play the piano?"

"No. At least, I don't think so. But there's no time like the present to learn, right?" She laced her fingers together and cracked her knuckles.

He shook his head and a little bit of life returned to his body. "I am not putting myself through the torture of hearing you murder some perfectly innocent song. Even if it stems from a sweet but completely unnecessary desire to distract me."

Nyx put a hand to her heart. "Me? Distract you? Whatever from?"

He waved the hand holding the mug around, indicating the room. "All of this. Bryn. The *Keeper*, Nyx, Evra's ex is the bleeding Keeper of Shadows."

"About that—so you said the Keeper controls all access to the Shadow Market. But...*how*, exactly?"

He took a long drink from his mug. Nyx hoped it didn't contain alcohol. If they had to go tearing off after Seth at a moment's notice she would rather her backup wasn't plastered.

"By controlling all of the portal witches on Tenebris Umbra. If you're a portal witch and you're here, you work for the Keeper."

"She can't possibly control all of them."

"She can, because that well of portal magic upstairs is the only one that exists. A portal witch can't *do* anything without portal magic. So any stones that need spelling, anyone who wants to buy passage to another planet, has to go through the Keeper of Shadows, because the Keeper holds all the portal magic."

Given what she'd discovered about herself in the throne room, Nyx had a newfound interest in this particular subject, and one thing was bothering her. "If this is the only planet with portal magic, how did people get to other planets before the ley lines existed?"

"A good question. It might surprise you to know I've spent a lot of time thinking about it, mostly because portal witches are barely a footnote in academic and historical texts, and they're only mentioned during Enforcer training as an *if you ever end up in the Shadow Market* side note. So the short answer is that I don't know."

"What's your most educated guess?"

"What makes you think I have one?"

"Oh please, you think your happy-go-lucky routine has fooled me? You're *smart*, Morgen. Like, you should be in a very expensive lab making cutting edge discoveries about the universe kind of smart. You can probably speak more languages than I can even name and you've raided practically every non-fiction book in the Station in a matter of months. So if you say you've spent a lot of time thinking about a problem then I'm relatively certain you have an educated guess about the answer."

Morgen stared at her like she'd grown a third eye.

"What?"

He shook his head. "You're just very surprising, little Guardian."

"Why? Anyone with eyes and a brain can tell you're smart."

He laughed. "Well, most people have one of those two things. You really want to hear my theory on portal magic?"

Her fingers itched to touch the dab of portal magic she'd accidentally stolen. She had managed to peel it off her fingers at long last and stuff it in her pocket.

"Yes, I really do."

"Okay. It's pretty simple so I hope I don't disappoint you. Before the ley lines were created, portal magic had to have existed on planets other than Tenebris Umbra. I'm also guessing that portal magic as it's practiced today isn't the full extent of the magic's capabilities. Portal witches here use the magic to spell stones from another planet. That stone acts as a geophysical locator so that when the portal magic is activated, the stone pulls the person through to the correct planet. But if that's the only way the magic can be used it begs the question—"

"—how did a portal witch ever get to another planet in the first place?" Nyx finished.

"Precisely. At some point in time, portal witches had to have been able to travel to other planets without a physical object from that planet, or intergalactic travel never would have started. Unfortunately, as I mentioned, there isn't a great deal of information on portal witches. No one outside of the Shadow Market is even interested in them since we have the ley lines and there is no known source of portal magic off this planet."

"Is it a hereditary ability? Like my Hidden magic?"

"It is," Morgen said slowly, zeroing in on her with predatory focus. "What would make you think to ask that?"

"Can you keep a secret?"

Morgen's eyes lit up. "Secret is my middle name."

"Even from Kaden?"

"Even from my bestest friend in the whole wide universe, yes. Now what do you have to tell me?"

"Just this." Nyx pulled out the little tuft of portal magic. It clung to her fingers like sticky cotton candy, happy to be there. She splayed her fingers wide and the magic stretched across them like a flickering blue web.

"No way." Morgen reached out, touching a section of the web with his index finger. The portal magic slunk away from him like water off oiled leather.

"Why do you get to be Hidden *and* a portal witch?"

"Genetics, apparently. The thing is, this stuff?" She waved the portal magic around. "It feels like the ley lines. Not exactly like them, like the ley lines are something *more*, but the pull it has on me is similar."

"If they are similar, if the lines do contain some type of portal magic or cousin to it, that could explain why you were able to navigate away from the chaos pocket on the ley line," he said, staring contemplatively at the chaos thorns she'd picked up during that memorable event. "No one else has ever done that. Even the Meerkin didn't, some of them just managed to survive going through them and came out the other side.

"How would you feel about pilfering some more of that," he pointed at the portal magic, "and running some experiments back home?"

The relief that swept through Nyx brought an irrepressible grin to her face. Morgen had said *home,* and if he was thinking of the Station that way, was planning on going back, then maybe Maruca didn't have the final say in whether they all left. Maybe…maybe she *wasn't* about to lose her new family.

"I would love to run illegal experiments with you," she answered.

"Good. Why are you looking at me like that?"

"I'm just thinking," she said innocently, "that since presents and broodiness didn't work out for you on the Evra front, maybe you should try a lab coat and sexy glasses. Give the eccentric genius approach a try."

"While I appreciate the suggestion, I'm not sure sure there's a point. Look at what I'm up against." He waved a hand indicating the Keep, then started ticking off attributes on his fingers. "Bryn is deadly, powerful, beautiful, and she has her own empire. How am I supposed to compete with that?"

"In case you've forgotten, *you* are also deadly, powerful, beau-" —Morgen narrowed his eyes and she hastily corrected— "hot. Exceptionally hot."

He sulked, only slightly mollified. "I don't have an empire."

"Empires are overrated. They always fall. Besides which, it is not a competition."

"Yeah, but it would be easier if it was. At least then I'd know the rules. She doesn't even look twice at me."

"Oh, no." Nyx drew out the words dramatically. "Evra doesn't notice you at all. That's why I had to haul her into the bathroom at the restaurant to keep her from killing that waitress who kept flirting with you."

Morgen brightened. "She noticed?"

"Men." Nyx cast her gaze skyward. "Stars save me from their massive egos."

"Seriously though, she always just brushes me off."

"Seriously though," Nyx mimicked him, "have you ever tried being serious with her?"

She knew, by the look on his face, that he hadn't.

"Outrageous flirtation, expensive presents, and over-the-top flattery is good and all," she said, "but if you want to know if there's anything there, you're going to have to put an actual card on the table."

He cradled his mug to his chest with one hand and considered this while his other hand played an idle melody. "I've never had to do that with a woman before."

Nyx laughed. "What's the longest amount of time you've ever spent with a woman?"

He looked affronted. "I had this casual, ongoing thing for months with this Dinarian woman who could—"

"I do *not* want to know. And casual ongoing doesn't count."

He flashed her a wicked grin. "I've never had any complaints."

"Like I said." Nyx pointedly swept her gaze over him. "Exceptionally hot. Evra's just made of sterner stuff than most."

"I don't notice you falling all over my exceptional hotness." He projected a wounded gravitas. "What is it about the women I meet on Earth?"

Nyx snorted. "I don't count, I'm in—" *love with someone else.* Shit. "I just don't count," she said hastily when his raptor-like attention focused on her.

"Right," he drawled. "I'm sure it has nothing to do with a certain tall, blond, broody of late best mate of mine."

"Did you focus on British colloquialisms? *Bleeding. Mate.* Of all the Earth languages you could have spent time on, you went with British English?"

"Class options were limited, *mon cher,* and last time I checked you only spoke English so there's no point in wasting the others on you. And don't think you're getting out of this conversation that easily."

"What conversation?" she asked innocently.

"The one where any time you and Kaden end up in a room together, which is rare and conveniently only when it is packed with other people, you spend all your time staring at each other when you think the other one isn't looking."

"I do no such thing."

"Do too. I didn't mean to upset you in the Den the other day, but the angsty sexual tension is enough to make a person ill. Just sleep with him already."

Nyx's shoulders slumped. "It's not that simple."

"Actually, it's very simple. See, his clothes come off, your clothes come off, he—"

Nyx punched him in the arm. "I know how to have sex."

"Whew." Morgen wiped a hand across his brow. "That's a relief."

"It's complicated."

"Welcome to my world." He saluted her with his mug.

"Are you—" *planning to leave?* She both wanted to know and didn't. But the way he talked about Evra, and his mention of portal magic experiments, made her think that maybe he hadn't made a decision yet. "In the interest of looking out for my best friend's interests, what exactly are your future plans?"

Morgen didn't fall for it for one second. "Maruca talked to you, didn't she?"

Nyx shrugged. "She might have."

"What did she say?"

"Not much," Nyx lied. "Just that you and her and Kaden

might be running off to play world's best mercenaries or something. So, are you? Planning on leaving?"

"I don't know." Morgen went back to picking at the piano keys. "I'd rather not. But we're kind of a set, the three of us. Kaden and Ruca's parents died when they were five. They had it rough for a few years on their own before my mom found them and took them in. She's a fierce woman, my mother. Broke her heart when Kaden got sent to Arkadia and Ruca went in after him. Me getting kicked out of the Enforcer ranks didn't help either.

"In one way or another, she lost all of her children for a while. I don't know how I'd explain it to her if I let them go off without me."

Nyx was quiet for a long moment.

"I think in the end you have to live your own life for you. You can't always let it be dictated by the people around you, no matter how much you love them. You're obviously fond of your mother, which tells me she must be a pretty good person. So I think your mother would probably understand that you can't follow in somebody else's wake forever."

Morgen narrowed his eyes. "When did you get so wise, little Guardian?"

She wasn't wise, because she seemed incapable of taking her own damn advice. But she put on a pretty smile and said, "Oh, around the same time I started hanging out with lesser intellects."

Morgen laid a hand over his heart. "You wound me. What happened to 'you're so smart, Morgen'?"

"I rethought it."

"You know, it's precisely those kinds of zig-zagging opinions that drive a man to drink." He pointedly lifted his mug.

"What *are* you drinking?" she asked suspiciously.

"Cocoa," he answered promptly. "Or whatever passes for it on this planet. Want some?"

"Cocoa," she repeated. "The suave, debonair Morgen Drahl is drowning his sorrows in hot chocolate?"

"Yes. It can't be all liquor on ice all the time, little Guardian. And if you're not nice about it, I'm not going to share."

Put that way, Nyx shut right up.

13

———

Nyx learned two things her first evening on Tenebris Umbra. One, she was very bad at cards and two, her friends were insufferable winners.

They'd been playing for the last hour, a hybrid card and dice game that moved quickly—so quickly that yelling tended to erupt from the entire table if someone, say, took longer than ten seconds to take their turn—and Nyx had yet to win a single round.

She didn't care. For once, everyone was having a good time. Even Maruca was enjoying herself. Her frosty exterior had melted and Nyx could see the camaraderie between her and Morgen and Kaden, the kind of sibling familiarity that developed between people who had spent their entire lives together. Evra and Tamrin had it, too, and their unit blended seamlessly with the other.

Once, Nyx might have seen them all together and felt sorry for herself because she didn't have that connection with anyone. But as soon as the thought had come into her mind tonight it had been followed by Seth's face and the world had just…settled.

It helped that Morgen had taken her under his wing. He'd placed himself next to her at the table and served as a human buffer between her and Maruca, explaining the rules and strategy of the game. After an hour, though, even he had to admit she was terrible.

"My brain can't handle another round," Kalvar declared, dropping his cards onto the table.

"Just one more?" Nyx asked. Everyone groaned. She had been pushing *just one more* for the last four rounds, determined that eventually she would win one. Somehow. She really couldn't figure out why she kept losing so badly. Maybe everyone else was just really, really good?

"One more round," Morgen told the table—who glared at him—and turned to Nyx. "And you do exactly what I tell you."

He pushed his own dice into the center of the table and scooted his chair closer to hers while Maruca collected the cards and dealt a new hand. Without Morgen in the mix, Nyx was up first. Her six cards were one councilor, two enforcers, a ten, a three, and a two. She could either play one card and roll as many of her nine dice as she wanted, or roll one dice and play as many cards as she wanted, the caveat being she had to play at least one of each.

The goal was to get the highest number for each play, adding together the cards and dice, with five plays per round. It had a limit number similar to blackjack, and if her cards and dice totaled more than seventeen in a play she forfeited that play entirely. At the end of the play, she could discard up to one card in her hand and then draw her hand back up to six cards, but the dice she'd rolled were no longer available. Additionally, the combined value of her plays couldn't go above eighty or she automatically lost, and at the end of the final round she was only allowed to have a combined total of six unplayed cards and dice.

Nyx's instinct was to play the councilor, which was worth thirteen, and roll one of the six-sided dice that, instead of having numerical values of one through six, instead repeated one through three twice. To her mind, she had a high probability of getting a good result, and it was impossible to bust.

Morgen reached over, ticked up the ten, three, and two, and slid her the same die she'd intended to use. This seemed risky. Probability had never been her strong suit, but she thought she had a two out of six chance of busting.

"But—"

"Exactly what I tell you," Morgen said firmly.

She played the cards, rolled the die. It tittered on the verge of a three before settling on a one. She breathed a sigh of relief and slid cards and die to her, placing them in her cache to her left, and Maruca dealt her another three cards. There, she realized, was the value in the play as an initial move. She conserved dice, which allowed for more flexibility later in the game, plus she received a greater variety of cards.

That move made sense to her. As the plays went on, though, she couldn't follow why he was telling her to do things. They always *worked* but the things he had her play and discard seemed random and whimsical unless…

She watched as he tracked the other plays, his gaze slightly distant like he was calculating.

"You're counting cards," she accused.

Maruca and Kaden burst out laughing.

"He's been doing it since he was four," Maruca told her, voice wonderfully free of condescension for once. "He can't help himself. He even loses at a mathematically precise rate of thirty-three point three percent out of a sense of fairness to the rest of us."

"Sometimes I lose by more." Morgen sounded affronted. "Counting isn't everything, there's still strategy and chance involved."

Kaden and Maruca laughed harder.

"What? It's not my fault I can remember them all. I shouldn't be penalized just because the rest of you can't do it."

He sounded so indignant that Nyx started laughing too. Maruca finished her last play and Nyx "won" the round. Everyone was still in a good mood when they started gathering up the cards and dice, and Evra was giving Morgen a speculative appraisal the likes of which Nyx had never seen her do. It wasn't lost on Morgen either, though he pretended it was.

Sexy glasses, she mouthed at him when no one else was looking. *Lab coat.*

He put his thumb and middle finger together and flicked her on the nose.

"Ow." She rubbed her nose. "Just for that, I'm going to go find out what's been going on with Evra and Bryn and I'm not going to tell you anything."

"You're cruel," he called after her as she walked off.

Nyx gave him an idle wave and snagged Evra as she exited the room, linking her arm with the Amazon's. She'd wanted a moment alone to talk to Evra since they'd arrived in the Keep but she hadn't been able to find her until Tamrin had dragged her into the gaming room an hour ago.

"You are coming with me to the kitchen."

Evra's brow furrowed. "Why?"

"Because we need to talk."

The furrow deepened. "Again, why?"

"You remember that time that, instead of talking to me, you stole some things and went to a prison planet and nearly died of magical causes?"

"It was three months ago, of course I remember. What does that have to do with anything?"

"Well, this time you're going to talk to me about how you used to date a criminal mastermind so that I am properly prepared to defend you if anything untoward occurs."

"Is there any chance of this conversation *not* happening?"

"Nope," Nyx replied cheerfully.

Evra groaned. "And we're having it in the kitchen because?"

"Because the rooms feel like prison barracks and Morgen showed me which ingredients you throw together to make the stuff that's sort of like hot chocolate."

"Make it extra rich then."

Nyx did so. The "chocolate" part of the hot chocolate had an undercurrent of warm spice reminiscent of cinnamon, and Nyx inhaled a deep whiff of the tantalizing aroma it gave off before turning her attention back to Evra.

"All right, out with it."

"What do you want to know?"

"How did you meet Bryn?"

"I hired her to piss off my mother."

Nyx racked her brain until she remembered Evra's mother had founded a private security company upon leaving her job as an Enforcer.

"Go on."

"My mother had put me in charge of new hires the year before. No hire I made was good enough for her, despite every single person I brought on having perfect records and performing their jobs without incident. So I decided if she wanted to find fault with every hire I made, I would hire someone she could *actually* find fault with.

"Bryn had the right qualifications for the job. Most of our contracts at the time were bodyguard and escort details and Bryn had a good history both working on her own and as part of a larger security detail. Her threat identification was spot-on and she tested high in combat and weapons during the interview process."

"But?" Nyx prompted.

"But she exhibited a certain tendency to flout rules and protocol if she thought she knew better than the people who created them. As you may have heard Morgen mention, my mother has a deep and abiding love of rules. Bryn also had a superiorly dismissive attitude I knew would drive my mother absolutely insane because in that regard they are very much alike."

"Did you date her just to make your mother angry?"

"In the beginning. I had never really broken any of my mother's rules before and Bryn had a certain talent for getting into trouble that I found exciting. Then it turned into something more and that strained things."

Evra took a sip of hot chocolate and the pleased expression on her face told Nyx she'd gotten the mix just right.

"Our firm is a pay-per-job type of employment and our employees may work as much or little as they choose. Bryn would disappear for long stretches at a time. It was not an issue at first, but when our relationship became serious I wanted to know where she went all the time. She wouldn't tell me.

"I let it go for months, but eventually I followed her. She went through a portal and I jumped through after her before it closed. Given it was a portal, I was not terribly surprised when I landed in the Shadow Market, but I was surprised to find her working for the Keeper of Shadows."

"What did you do?"

"Confronted her. It turned out she only applied for the job at our firm to gain information on a client at the Keeper's request. Afterward, she convinced him that maintaining the position would be advantageous to them from an intelligence perspective, so he let her take just enough jobs to maintain appearances.

"I was very naive. I thought she must have been forced into working for the Keeper. I offered to help her get out. To come back with me." Evra's teeth clenched. "She laughed at me and told me she had not spent six years gaining the Keeper's trust to give it up for anyone. Needless to say, our relationship didn't survive."

"Why did she do it?"

Evra rubbed wearily at the back of her neck. "Bryn is the type of person who doesn't see the problem with doing the wrong things for the right reasons. You know the Keeper has absolute control over the portal magic here?"

Nyx nodded.

"Bryn came from Deloria. It is a very poor planet overrun with warring gangs. Most people born there do not make it to fourteen without being conscripted into one of those gangs, and of the ones not conscripted, most do not live to see adulthood.

"Leaving is nearly impossible. It takes money to apply for the papers needed to travel the ley lines and it takes a great deal more to apply for citizenship to another planet. Factor in that most citizenship transfers require the applicant to have a "valued" skill and most planets don't want immigrants from places like Deloria. The end result is that most people never leave.

"She wanted to change that, to provide a way out for people like her, and she saw becoming the Keeper as the way to doing it."

"And has she? Changed things?"

"I do not know. I gather she has had some difficulty since taking over the Keep. She's been stubbornly mute on the subject of *when* she is going to send Tamrin home and I am beginning to suspect it is because she cannot do it. Not without this key your Seth stole from her."

"But the portal well is right in the middle of her throne room."

"Mmm. But if she does not have access to the Keeper's cache of planet stones the well is all but useless."

It would certainly explain why Bryn was so eager to get Seth back.

Evra drained the rest of her hot chocolate and clearly viewed that as an ending point for reminiscing.

"Are you convinced I am not going to do anything foolish now?"

"I guess so."

"Then why do you sound so glum?"

"I don't sound glum."

She probably did, but she couldn't voice her real concern—that Bryn and Evra would patch things up and Evra would decide to stay here—because it wasn't fair to say it. If Bryn and Evra had a future then Nyx shouldn't get in the way of that.

She just…she'd never really had a best friend before. At least not one that she could *remember* having, and losing Evra would hurt. So she didn't say anything because she didn't want to influence Evra one way or the other. Even though she knew realistically that if there *was* a force in the universe strong enough to keep Evra al'Daemon from doing what she wanted, that force was not Nyx Fortuna.

"You definitely do. You interrogated me about my feelings so turnabout is fair play." Evra sounded very pleased with the end of that sentence. *Someone* who claimed not to be interested in a certain handsome, roguish individual had nonetheless clearly been getting Morgen to teach her more English idioms.

Nyx opened her mouth to once again deny that there was anything wrong with her. Instead, she said, "Maruca wants me to convince Kaden to leave."

"Leave...where?"

"I don't know. She wants them to go be freelance mercenaries or something like that. Honestly, I don't think she cares where they go as long as it's away from me."

"She does dislike you rather intensely."

"Thanks."

"I did not say it was a *reasonable* dislike. So what are you going to do?"

"I don't know. Maybe if he can go have some kind of normal life he should. Not be tied to me forever." Part of her had always understood that she would end up alone again, save for Griff and the Station. Earth Between was a small slice of a large universe and she couldn't expect her new friends to stay there forever. Especially when living in the Station, its grounds a Nexus point in time, would make it a literal forever. But it hurt to think of them going off and living on without her, of knowing they would grow old and die while she remained.

"And I don't—I still haven't gotten past what he did. I mean, I understand why he gave me the Harvester. I understand why he left and never explained anything. I just don't know if I can get past it. I don't know if I *want* to get past it."

He'd never apologized, either. Oh, he obviously didn't like that he'd hurt her, that he'd used her, but at the end of the day he believed he'd done the right thing. And maybe he had, but when the right thing was still damn wrong to the individual saddled with the consequences, she sort of thought an actual apology was warranted.

"Now that I think about it, you and I are not in such dissimilar situations," Evra observed.

"I guess not. What are you going to do about yours?"

"Absolutely no idea."

They sat in silence long enough Nyx figured the conversation was over, but when she stood to leave Evra asked, "Is—did Morgen say if he was going with the Moors, if they leave? Pure curiosity, you understand."

"He said he doesn't want to. Whether he will or not, I don't know. But if it comes down to it and you don't want him to leave? I'd tell him that."

Evra didn't tell Nyx she should take her own advice. She didn't have to.

14

———

Nyx couldn't sleep. It was eleven-thirty at night by Earth-Between time and she ought to be out cold. She hadn't been getting much sleep at the Station because of all the extra-sensory input from her new bond, and the blissful, if strange, lack of that here should have lulled her right to sleep. Instead, the combination of a new planet, the institutional feel of her room, and the heavy press of the earth that came with living underground had her brain firing on all cylinders.

She had received one cryptic update from Bryn's people about Seth which amounted to, "we're following some leads", and nothing else. A half hour ago she'd given up trying to sleep altogether and gone to the workout room on their floor, only to find it already in use by Kaden.

Nyx considered herself to have great fortitude in some aspects of her life but a shirtless, sweating Kaden Moor lifting weights was not one of them. Since his back had been to the door, she'd beat a strategic retreat and settled for running laps around the main hallway loop. She'd hoped her stupid body would figure out she was tired and needed sleep.

When that didn't work, she went to the kitchen and spent a futile fifteen minutes trying to figure out what she could eat on another planet that wouldn't kill her. Other than hot chocolate. If she drank any more hot chocolate she would probably have a heart attack.

Logic dictated that, since most everyone she'd seen in the Keep fell into some species of human, it was unlikely anything in the kitchen would kill her. But getting alien food poisoning wasn't high on her list of life goals, so she eventually gave up and went back to her room. Surely, a shower would be safe. If the Keeper wasn't terribly cruel there would be hot water, and even if she wasn't sleepy by the end of it she would at least be clean.

She opened the door to the bathroom. It was occupied. She realized this when Kaden spun around, knife in hand. Her own hand came up reflexively, grabbed his wrist, and she used her weight to shove him against the vanity at the same time recognition lit his face and he stopped the knife thrust an inch from her throat.

She blinked in confusion. Humidity fogged the glass of the obviously just-used shower and water dripped from Kaden's hair, falling onto bare, golden-tanned shoulders. Nyx kept her gaze studiously only his face, though close proximity told her he had—thank the stars—put on pants before she came in.

"It's a shared bathroom." Kaden grimaced. "And none of the doors lock."

Right. Maruca had mentioned that. She had also mentioned that there were no chairs or any other furniture that weren't bolted to the ground to be placed in front of the doors.

"Sorry about—" He tapped the flat of the knife blade against her collarbone. "I thought you were out."

"Yeah. I was." Clearly, she'd been out long enough he'd had time to finish his workout *and* shower. She realized she still held his wrist and dropped it. Her eyes tracked the movement out of habit and slid over his chest. She sucked in a breath. A thick, ropy scar bisected his torso vertically from the V of his collarbone down to his navel.

His eyes flicked down, expressionless. "It was a long time ago."

"What happened?"

"I almost died." He gave her a thin smile that didn't quite reach his eyes. "Someone once told me I'm used to that."

The jab hit, even if she'd said it in a different context, one where she hadn't known just how close she'd come to the truth. The scar was almost two-fingers wide, raised, and with the pearlescent sheen skin sometimes took after it healed.

"But you'd have to have been—"

"Split open? Yeah. I don't recommend it."

"Did they do this to you in Psionics?" She'd decided for herself she didn't like the All Council's methods, but *this?*

"It wasn't Psionics." He sighed, likely recognizing the look on her face and knowing she wouldn't let it go until he told her. "It was right after they sent me to Arkadia. Tobi had just been brought in with six new arrivals. I wasn't exactly in prime shape at the time but I couldn't just leave him with them."

Tobi was eight now. If Kaden had found him right after he arrived on Arkadia the boy couldn't have been more than five.

"Managed to kill everybody, but" —he tapped the scar— "got a souvenir for my trouble."

"And Tobi healed you." She'd seen Tobi heal once. It had been awe-inspiring and a little creepy, given something ancient had spoken through him in his eight-year-old voice, but she'd had no idea he could fix something like that. When he was *five.*

"Now that your curiosity's been assuaged, if the Q and A's over…"

Oh. She still had him trapped against the vanity. She also had no desire to let him go.

Go. If she didn't talk to him, didn't tell him *something*, was that what he would do? The problem was, she still didn't have any words to give him.

So she touched her fingertips to the scar instead, started at his collarbone and traced it down to his navel. He sucked in a harsh breath, muscles tensing.

"Nyx, what the hell are you doing?" His voice, low and rough, sent shivers through her, his breathing quick and shallow. She fanned her fingers across the hard planes of his abs, lowered her mouth to the top of the scar and kissed it. She was pressed close enough to feel his instant response to her.

Whatever else he might feel or not feel about her, he wanted her. And she wanted him. However much she might be angry, she'd missed him. Missed touching him. And this might be the dumbest thing she'd ever done, but she was going for it.

"What does it look I'm doing?" She kissed her way lower.

His fingers dug into the countertop and the flimsy material groaned.

"I don't know what's going through your head, but if you're not sure about this you've got exactly two seconds to walk out the door."

She paused, looked up at him and dropped lower, nipping at the skin just above the waistband of his pants. The cold shield he held over his emotions shattered.

He slid his hands beneath her thighs and dragged her up to him, his mouth crushing hers. She wrapped her legs around him and kissed him back. Her tongue tangled with his and she buried her hands in his hair.

They had both changed in the years they'd spent apart, but the way they fit together hadn't. She arched her hips against him, heard the answering groan deep in his throat, the one that never failed to send a shiver down her spine because it told her exactly how much he wanted her.

He held her with one arm and flicked the bathroom door open with the other. Five steps later he tumbled her onto his bed, his mouth fastening on her neck. He kissed his way down her collarbone, then lower. When his hands roved over her stomach she rolled up, pushed him back onto his heels and straddled him.

This. They had always been good at *this.*

Kaden lifted them hem of her shirt and—

The door slammed open.

"Kaden, I need—" Maruca cut off mid-sentence. Her eyes met Nyx's, which looked out over Kaden's shoulder to where his sister stood in the doorway. The ice in Maruca's gaze could have frozen a volcanic eruption.

Nyx had every intention of running far, far away. Unfortunately, Kaden's hands gripped her hips and kept her locked firmly in place. He rested his forehead against her chest, clearly seeking patience.

"Ruca," he said in a calm, measured tone. "Don't you knock?"

"I'm sorry," she said, obviously *not* sorry. "But I need your help. Kalvar's gone. I believe he went to the slave market."

No.

"We'll be right out."

Maruca closed the door, but the look she gave Nyx before she did so made Nyx wonder if a not-so-accidental accident might befall her before she left this planet. Nyx slid off the bed.

"Nyx, wait." Kaden grabbed her wrist and pulled her back. One hand cupped her cheek and his eyes searched hers. "This isn't done. We're not done."

Statements, but she heard the question beneath them.

She *should* tell him it had been a mistake. If she let this go on, if she let him come back to Earth, she'd be damning him to an eternity in a different kind of prison than the one he'd fought so hard to escape. And she still wasn't okay with everything he'd done.

But she'd had a question burning in her the last few months, one she'd been trying so hard not to find the answer to because she was afraid it wouldn't be the one she wanted, but that answer was written all over his face now. He hadn't lied to her all those years ago when he told her he loved her. He missed her, he wanted her, and the force of it radiated in the space between them.

No, they weren't done. But they weren't fixed, either.

"We'll talk later."

She could see exactly what he thought that meant, so she rocked up onto her toes and kissed him.

"We'll talk, okay?"

"Okay," he breathed.

She walked out the door and tried not to feel like a terrible person for what had just happened. He didn't really understand what he was getting himself into with her.

She shook her head. There was a simple solution to all of this: she would just *tell him* exactly what he was getting into, and if he still wanted to see if they could work then that was his choice. Tell him, also, why she was still angry and find out if there was anything he could say—anything he *would* say—that would fix the rift between them.

If he had nothing to say or if he didn't want to stay… Well, then she could finally let him go.

Outside in the hot, muggy night air of Tenebris Umbra, Nyx kept pace with Kaden, Morgen, and Maruca. Her inquiry after Evra had been met with a terse response from Maruca that the Amazon hadn't been available.

Nyx hadn't pushed it further. There was a sick feeling in her gut when she thought about Kalvar. She firmly believed he'd had the right to come here, to make that choice himself, but despite what Maruca thought of her, Nyx would never forgive herself if anything happened to him.

She thought of the pack Kalvar had brought with him, stuffed full of…what? She should have tried to find out, should have realized he wouldn't settle for just *going* to the place where his life had been irrevocably altered. He would want to do something. The question was, what exactly did he think he could do?

They had just crossed the edge of the market square when the first explosion lit the night sky. It rocked the ground beneath their feet and the Shadow Market erupted into chaos.

It was as crowded as it had been during the day, and the explosion sent people fleeing in all directions without a single thought for the others around them. Nyx kept her eyes on Kaden's back and ignored the mayhem and screams as they sprinted for the slave pens.

They were within fifty paces when the second explosion detonated. The first had taken out the warding and fencing at the pen's gate and drawn the entirety of the guards stationed there, who were holding the line against people who had seen a chance at freedom and intended to take it.

Red sparks flew from bands on the guards' wrists and were answered by flashes from the bands around the slaves' necks. Magical shock collars, Nyx realized.

The second explosion tore through the back of the pen, and as the dust and haze settled Nyx saw Kalvar standing in the opening, his pack open on the ground. He dug out a handful of something and flung it at the nearest prisoners. She was too far away to see what the small items they caught were, but when they pressed them to their necks, the collars fell away.

Freed, a few immediately ran for the exit, grabbed a weapon from the pile created when Kalvar upended the contents of his bag, and promptly fled. But most of the people stayed, helped Kalvar as he moved through the pen, removing collars from those not yet freed. Stayed, even as fresh guards poured up from an open hatch next to the pen and cut off the second exit.

Former slaves picked up weapons, the last collar fell to the ground, and the melee began.

Silent communication passed between Kaden, Morgen, and Maruca, a unity born from years of working as a team. Maruca and Morgen dove into the fray at the front. Kaden jerked his head toward the back and Nyx followed, pulling her short sword from its sheath.

A whirlwind of black stripes in her peripheral vision was Kalvar. He whirled and sliced through the slaver guards, his hands shifted into lethal black claws. Maruca reached his side and Nyx could see the woman's training in Kalvar, see it in the way they moved together with the same fluidity and patterns of attack.

Then Nyx and Kaden reached the back of the pen and she didn't have time to watch anyone else. There were over a hundred people in the pens. There were maybe a quarter as many guards but those guards were brutally efficient and, faced with the prospect of the slaves escaping, they opted for killing force over restraint. The sick alacrity in their movements, the absolute lack of hesitation, spoke to an enjoyment for what they did.

Given more weapons and a wider exit, the sheer numbers of the slaves would have overwhelmed the guards, but the explosions had only torn breaks in the warding five feet across. Mutual imprisonment had formed a bond between those inside the pens, and they were admirably unwilling to trample each other to rush the exit in force. The front lines were formed by those who obviously had fighting experience and had taken up the weapons Kalvar had brought in, while in the center those without weapons but with the right mettle formed a protective circle around the children and those who belonged to the smaller, more vulnerable species.

Kaden cut through three of the guards before they even noticed he was there, the whole of their attention focused on the slaves and Kalvar. The guards noticed Kaden *then*, the outer row of them turning to face him.

For a moment, Nyx stood mesmerized, watching him. She had sparred with him almost daily when they had been together, so she was well aware of the fluidity he moved with, but she'd only seen him fight with a weapon once before, on Arkadia.

There was nothing flashy in the way he fought, nothing wasted. It was as if Arkadia had stripped everything from him except brutal practicality, his movements almost harsh in their efficiency, but beautiful all the same.

Then the guards noticed *her* and there was no more time for observation, just the necessity of block and parry, dip and turn, strike and retreat. Her muscles warmed to the rhythm and she lost herself to the meditative trance of performing moves she knew by heart, by instinct, had perfected a thousand—a million—times in practice.

She lost herself to it so she didn't think about the difference between practice and an actual fight, didn't think about her sword sliding into flesh and scraping against bone. Because if she thought about it she would double over and vomit and in a fight like this that would be the end of her.

She had killed once before but it didn't make it any easier now. In some ways, it made it worse. At least then she had been the attacked and not the aggressor, and she had been able to tell herself that it was an isolated occurrence, something that wouldn't happen again.

She couldn't tell herself that now, and when she couldn't *not* think about what she was doing she reminded herself that these were people who had chosen to sell other people, who thought the lives of others meant absolutely nothing, and she kept blocking, kept parrying.

Their viciousness made it easier, the fact that there was no hesitation, no reluctance when they came at her. In that moment it was kill or be killed, and she'd never really understood what that phrase meant until now, until she fought, gripped with the utter certainty that if she didn't strike first, strike better, she would die.

She was so far outside herself that it was a shock when she whirled to her next opponent and found…nothing. The ground before her was littered with bodies—some guards, some former slaves. The stench of copper and the bodies' releases into death coated the air, slid down the back of her throat.

Her sword tip fell to the ground and the weapon dangled loosely from her hand as her stomach heaved. She choked on bile, lips and teeth clenched tight, and swallowed it back down.

Gooseflesh rose at the nape of her neck. Her senses tingled with the certainty that she was being watched. She spun a slow, careful circle, but the market directly around them was empty. No one stood still around them, no one watched her. Even if she still *felt* like someone did.

Two-hundred paces away, Maruca hauled open the hatch the extra guards had come through. A group of blood-spattered, newly-free people listened warily as she spoke, her face as cool and impassive as ever. They nodded at what she said and, as a group, followed her into the hatch. They were the ones, Nyx noted, who had picked up weapons, and it seemed likely they were going down that hatch to clear any further threats.

It made sense to take out any remaining slavers if they hadn't all come out earlier. On a planet like this, where there was no official law, any repercussions from tonight's event would likely come only from the people who ran the slaving operation, and if those people were gone…

Nyx swallowed. It made strategic sense. But she was selfishly relieved that she was far, far away from that hatch. Morgen and Kaden worked efficiently through the crowd of people, as seemingly unaffected by the violence as Maruca. The only one who looked at all like Nyx felt was Kalvar.

He stood next to the open hatch. Blood dripped from the clawed tips of his hands and he looked defeated and triumphant at the same time. In a minute, when she could breathe without her stomach turning, she would go talk to him. It was probably the only useful thing she could do here.

She didn't have any experience with organizing large groups of people, didn't know if the freed slaves would have any chance in the Shadow Market on their own. They had no money, no supplies, and no way to return to their homes if they still had them. She didn't know how to help them, but it looked like Kaden and the others did.

She managed three breaths without bile crawling up her throat and slid her short sword back into its sheath. Talk to Kalvar. She could do that.

Before she took a single step it hit her again, that feeling that she was being watched.

This time, she spun to the right and saw him.

15

———

Seth leaned against a building twenty paces from her, arms crossed. Nyx took a step toward him. He shoved off the wall and took a single step back, still facing her.

She took another step. He waved at her, spun on his heel, and rounded the corner of the building.

Nyx ran after him without bothering to consider the wisdom of chasing him alone, even as a niggling sense told her that something wasn't quite right. She cornered the building and doubled her pace when she saw him ahead. He caught on to the bottom of a ladder that was bolted to the side of the building and scaled it with admirable quickness.

Nyx jumped and caught the bottom rung, her eyes tracking him as she climbed. He shoved off the top of the ladder onto the roof. Two seconds later Nyx clambered up after him, only to find the roof empty. Seth had vanished.

It was a large, flat area. No matter how fast Seth was, it would have been impossible for him to leave the roof in the few seconds it had taken her to ascend behind him. Impossible, unless he had never been there at all.

Illusionist, her fickle memory supplied, *trickster class.*

A soft exhale against her ear was her only warning before a low, silken voice purred, "Looking for someone, Nyxi?"

Nyx whirled. Seth stood there, hands tucked casually into his pockets, that raven's feather earring fluttering softly in the hot breeze.

He shook his head, made a light *tsking* noise in the back of his throat and tapped a long, tapered finger to his temple.

"How much is still missing up there? That one hasn't worked on you since you were twelve."

She gritted her teeth. Insufferable. He was absolutely insufferable.

"You try having your memories disappear and then drop back into your head without rhyme or reason, and see how well you perform."

"Mmm. I just took all mine back at once."

Took them back?

"Why did you bring me up here?"

He shrugged. "I wanted to talk."

Oh, now *he wanted to talk.* "And is there some reason you couldn't speak to me down there?"

She should feel some hint of fear at the fact he had neatly separated her from everyone she knew on this planet, but she was experiencing the opposite effect. For some reason, whenever he was around, everything in her just quieted.

"Too crowded," Seth answered flippantly. "I get the feeling golden boy doesn't like me very much, and then there's this other thing. See, earlier the Keeper's people were just poking around making things uncomfortable. In the last few hours practically her entire damn force is sweeping the Market, all looking for little old me."

"Maybe you did something to piss her off?" Nyx suggested.

"I've done a lot of things to piss her off, but she wouldn't be certain I was here unless *someone* told her."

"I was out of options. Maybe if you didn't run off every time I try to talk to you, I wouldn't have needed her help."

"She's the most dangerous person on this entire damn planet, Nyxi. I specifically told you not to get involved with her."

"And I'm supposed to listen to anything you say? Besides, this is entirely your fault," she told him. "You showed up on *my* damn planet acting all cryptic and messing my head up with memories that I don't even understand and then you essentially told me to 'live my life' and just up and disappeared.

"And then I went to all that trouble to get your attention earlier and you just told me to go home. So yes, I made a deal with the Keeper. She's a friend of a friend so she offered to help."

"Offered, or bargained?"

"Does it matter?"

Seth let out a string of curses. "You can thank me for letting you find me yourself so you don't owe her anything."

"Thank you *ever* so much, though I'm not particularly worried about the terms of that bargain. Care to tell me why you have a key that belongs to the Keeper of Shadows, if she's so dangerous?"

Seth gave her a perfectly level stare. "Reasons."

Wonderful. "You know what? Forget it. I don't care why. You're giving me that key and we're going back to Earth."

"You always were so authoritative." A half-smile quirked up the side of his lips, overshadowed with a hint of sadness, and she knew she'd just lost him. "But I'm afraid I'll have to pass."

She was struck with the absolute certainty that he was about to disappear on her again, and this time she'd never find him. "Seth," she warned.

"Fun as this little catching up has been, I have to go. The Keeper isn't going to find me, Nyx, and you won't again either. Go home. And for the love of the stars, stay there."

The air shimmered around him and three Seth's winked at her, blew her a kiss, and ran in different directions.

Instinct screamed at her to run too, to go, to catch him before he got too far. Memory told her to wait. Just wait.

He was twenty paces away now. Thirty paces.

What was she waiting *for*?

Forty paces when she saw it, the briefest flicker from two of the shapes, what might normally be taken for no more than a flash of sunlight. Nyx sprinted for the third shape, even as she realized that though waiting had told her which form to follow, it had destroyed any chance she had of catching him. He jumped from the edge of this roof to the next, clearing the three foot gap and landing on the neighboring building without breaking stride.

She was going to lose him. There was no possible way she could catch up. She had too much distance to make up and he was too damned fast.

Fast. She was a stars-cursed idiot.

"*Los,*" Nyx whispered.

She surged forward, feet suddenly weightless. She scrambled to find her balance, to keep up with the movements her own body was making. It was a little like jumping onto an already moving treadmill and trying to find her footing. The boots weren't running *for* her, but every movement she made was amplified, enhanced, and it took everything she had just to keep her feet landing correctly. No wonder Griff thought she'd break an ankle.

The edge of the roof loomed and she leaned forward as she pushed off the edge—and flew fifteen feet through the air. She landed and picked up the pace again, gradually settling into the new speed until it became normal.

She gained on Seth, the gap between them closing as she followed him from rooftop to rooftop, until she was only five paces from him. She put on a burst of speed, preparing to leap from this rooftop to the next, when Seth simply ran off the edge of the six story building.

Too close. She was too close to simply stop at the speed she was going. If she tried, she'd fall forward and tumble right over the roof's lip.

The lip. That beautiful, wonderful, one foot high lip.

"*Exa,*" she whispered, and as her speed cut in half she threw herself into a baseball slide. She kept her upper body body high, her back off the roof, but even so the tip of the sword sheath dragged against the roof, the straps of the harness digging into her skin as she flew toward the edge. The flats of her feet connected solidly with the lip of the roof, her legs bent slightly to absorb the impact.

She rolled onto her hands and knees and peered over the side of the building, pretending to look for him. Pretending, because there was as much chance he'd actually gone into a suicide jump as there was that he *wasn't* still here, basking in the success of his evasion.

Gloating had always been his downfall.

She muttered a choice curse or two to add credence to her I'm-so-furious-where-could-Seth-have-gone act, when what she was really doing was listening. He was too good to shuffle and scuff a foot. Too good to even breathe too loudly. But he couldn't control the wind, and when it blew she heard the soft, delicate rustle of a feather earring just behind her and to her right.

She leaned farther over the roof. The angle hid the movement of her hand as it slid down to unhook one end of Gleipnir from her wrist. She let out another curse to cover the sound of the chain unwinding and then she *moved,* surging to her feet and whirling in one fluid motion. Her arm flew out and wrapped the chain around his wrist. The free end of Gleipnir fused to itself, forming an unbreakable connection.

The empty air shivered and Seth appeared. He frowned down at his wrist. He tugged at the chain and when it refused to release, shot her a look of such venom it was a wonder she didn't drop dead.

"What the hell is this?"

"Insurance," she said. "To make sure you stay close."

His eyes narrowed. He wrapped a length of the chain around his other hand and yanked. Given Gleipnir was as slender as a delicate necklace chain, it was no wonder he thought he could simply break it. He tried until he broke the skin around his wrist and then he dropped it to glare at her.

"Take this damn thing off."

"No. I want answers, and you're going to give them to me."

"Like hell I—" He cut off as a warning siren split the market air. At first, Nyx assumed it had to do with the slave breakout below, until she heard the shouts and noises of a more widespread panic that caused her to look to the horizon. A dense, massive wall of red dust barreled toward the city.

The flaying winds.

"Shit."

Seth grabbed her hand and ran, pulling her back the direction they'd already come. They leapt the divide between one building and the next. The wind had already picked up and it caused resistance, made it difficult to keep her balance so high up. Seth banked right, grabbed onto a long rail bolted to the side of the building, and slid down. Nyx didn't hesitate to follow.

The sirens hadn't provided much advance warning and as she hit the ground wind slammed into her and sent her sprawling. Rocks and debris skittered across the surface of the ground, but the winds were not yet fierce enough to make them airborne.

She and Seth stood in a narrow, dead-end alley. Doors lined the sides and she expected Seth to open one of them, but he just kept running until they skidded to a halt up against the alley's dead end. The wind increased in intensity, buffeting the world mercilessly, and an empty barrel careened down the alley. It slammed into the wall beside her, shattering into a dozen pieces.

The air turned harsh and cloying, and she pulled the corner of her shirt up over her nose, trying to block out the clouds of red dust even as the winds finally sent the loose debris of the streets airborne, sharp pieces tearing at her clothes, slicing at her skin.

"Seth, tell me you have a plan."

He didn't answer her. He crouched on the ground and ran his hands over the street stones, stopping at this or that stone to push one. They never moved, never gave any indication that he was doing anything at all.

What *was* he doing?

"Can't you just portal us out of here or something?"

She could barely breathe now, the dust was so thick, and for the second time in as many months Nyx found herself facing down the certainty that she was going to die on an alien planet.

"Can't portal where we're going."

She heard the sound of stone scraping across stone, like the lid of a sarcophagus being heaved open, and a two-by-two section of the street lifted up and slid aside. The square, dark hole in the ground leading into the unknown looked more inviting than any place in Nyx's remembered life ever had.

She moved for that opening. Blessedly cool air wafted up toward her, but when she leaned down the Harvester of Worlds flared so hotly against her chest it burned her skin.

She faltered. Seth grabbed her and unceremoniously shoved her into the hole. The Harvester burned hotter, blistering her skin beneath it. Then she was past the entrance and once she was down in the ground, the Harvester went cold.

She didn't fall far before she hit hard-packed dirt. She landed on all fours and splayed her hands and fingers out for balance. Seth slid through and she scrambled out of his way as he pulled the piece of street back into place above them.

She *felt* the next increase in the wind's intensity, heard the sound of things flying into the buildings above like the hail of gunfire a fraction of a second before the lid to their refuge settled fully into place, the sounds of the stone locking mechanisms clicking together.

16

———

The space was small. Small enough that the two of them barely fit in it together. Nyx's back pressed into the wall, the sword and its sheath digging into her spine. Her chest brushed Seth's when she shifted position, and in the absolute darkness and stale air she had the brief thought to be grateful she wasn't claustrophobic.

Wait a minute. Stale air. A different kind of panic gripped her then. If the air was already growing stale, just how tightly was this hole in the earth sealed?

"Seth?"

"Yes, Nyx?" His words were a soft caress of air against her cheek. No one had ever said her name the way he did, so comfortable and familiar and full of history. History she couldn't remember.

"Please tell me you have a plan and I am not going to suffocate in a vertical coffin with you." Because if they had to stay in here much longer…she couldn't tell if the oxygen was already running out or if it was just in her head.

"Why? You'd rather suffocate in one with someone else? Maybe a glowering, over-muscled blond someone with no sense of humor?"

Apparently, Seth had decided to move on from sullen and slightly pissed off to teasing. She preferred the former.

"He's none of your damn business."

"Touchy," he murmured. "You two have a lover's spat?"

Nyx couldn't say why, exactly, but she didn't want to talk about Kaden with Seth. It just felt wrong.

"Seth. Get. Us. Out of here."

"Oh, I don't know." His finger traced up the back of her hand, made one lazy circle and slipped under the edge of Gleipnir. "Take this off and maybe I will."

The shiver that went through her was entirely involuntary. She didn't like it. She didn't like how okay she was with him being in her personal space, how comfortable and natural it felt. She didn't like him holding all the cards when it came to her—their—memories.

She swallowed, and reminded herself to focus on the problem at hand. Yes, being in a small space with dwindling air was concerning, but Seth wouldn't be so cavalier about it if he thought there was any chance of them dying. She forced herself to lean back against the wall and affect a boredom that translated even in the darkness. "You don't have a death wish, so I guess I'll just wait until you get tired of standing here."

He sighed, as if disappointed she'd called him on his bullshit. "You used to be a lot more fun, Nyxi."

His hand planted on the wall beside her and a brief click sounded in the small space. The wall propping her up disappeared and she fell through it with a yelp, stumbling for balance. Seth chuckled. With a snap of his fingers, thin veins along the walls began to glow, illuminating the tunnel they stood in.

The tunnel itself—smoothly-hewn from the planet's ubiquitous red rock—was only about seven feet tall and two feet wide, but the soft yellow light lessened the harsh colors of the rock and made the space seem less confining. As Seth led her on, she realized the tunnel was simply one of many, a labyrinth of branching underground passageways.

They had no defining characteristics she could use to tell them apart. She had no method of finding her way back to the hatch they'd entered through, and even if she could, she wasn't sure she could figure out how to open it. She had no idea where he was taking her.

She stopped walking.

Seth continued until he hit the end of Gleipnir and his left arm snagged. He made an irritated noise and pulled on the chain. She planted her feet and pulled back. She had the briefly absurd notion that they would end up playing tug-of-war until one of them got too tired when Seth finally took a single step back toward her, releasing the chain's tension.

"Yes?" he drawled.

"Where are you taking us?"

"Don't you trust me?"

"I don't know you."

She could have sworn it was hurt that flickered in his eyes, brief and then extinguished.

"I'd never hurt you, Nyxi."

She'd told Kaden that, she remembered. Told him that, and been so certain of it. And it might have been good enough when she was within the safety of her own Station's grounds, but now? Here? He could be taking her to anywhere, to any*one*.

"I have a place here," he finally ground out. "It's empty, no one knows where it is, and it will provide much more comfortable shelter than hanging around in the tunnels."

"Okay." She pulled her dagger from its sheath. "Prove it."

"By stabbing myself?" He said it with his usual sarcastic edge, but there was a glint of wariness in his gaze.

"This is Veritas. You've heard the expression 'blood doesn't lie'?" She shrugged. "Well, Veritas takes that to a literal level. No need to stab yourself, a drop will do."

"How does it work?"

She opened her mouth to tell him, then snapped it shut. *Illusionist*, she reminded herself. *Trickster.* If he understood the dagger worked off something as simple as a color change, it would be only too easy for him to make her see what he wanted her to see.

She held out her hand for his. He shoved them in his pockets.

"Don't be a baby," she said, unsure where this taunting side of her nature had dug its way out from. "It'll only sting for a second."

He muttered something that sounded suspiciously like, "I've heard that before," and held out his hand. She took it, felt the rasp of callused knuckles against her palm. Veritas, ever hungry, vibrated in her hand as she lowered the point to the tip of Seth's middle finger and blood welled onto the blade.

"There, there," she soothed in her most patronizing voice. "It's all over."

He lifted an eyebrow. "You aren't going to kiss it and make it all better?"

She just stared at him, then cupped her hand around the dagger so he couldn't see the blood on it. "Did you tell me the truth about where we're going, and that no one else knows where to find it but you? A simple 'yes' or 'no' will suffice."

He put his pricked finger to his mouth and sucked away the welling blood on it before answering.

"Yes."

The blood on Veritas' blade turned blue. Truth, then. There were a dozen other things she could ask, things she *would* ask, would get answers to. But not here. Veritas drank Seth's blood into its blade and Nyx gave a minute shudder as she slid the blade back into its hilt. So bloodthirsty, her dagger.

She pasted a sunny smile on her face. "Wonderful. Please lead on."

Six cross-tunnel sections and turns later, Seth stopped at a section of wall that looked exactly like all the others. She squinted as he traced a pattern over the stone and realized that wasn't quite true—she could barely make out a crack that ran through the stone in the shape of an arched door. She had just finished tracing the outline with her eyes when the arched section of the stone separated. It slid out toward them and then to the side on invisible tracks.

Seth walked through and a light flared to life in the space beyond. After a brief moment of hesitation Nyx followed and the stone slid shut behind her, settling seamlessly back into place. She stood in a small, one-room living space, maybe three hundred square feet, that had been hewn directly out of the solid stone. It held a bed, a chest, what looked like a chimney-less fireplace filled with rocks, a modest kitchen area, and a small curtained off section she assumed held the restroom and shower. Small sconces set into the wall every few feet glowed with a soft, red light.

"Welcome to my humble abode," Seth said with a mocking bow.

Nyx turned in a circle. "It's…"

"Small?" Seth suggested. "It's true, but I like to think size doesn't matter."

Nyx ignored him. "What *is* all this?" She waved her hand. "The doorways, the tunnels, this room?"

The entire place felt familiar and she couldn't figure out why. It wasn't the aesthetic, it was the layout.

"You seem to be under the mistaken impression that I'm going to stand here and answer all your questions. And before you decided to start carving me up with your nifty little truth-teller, I might point out that that knife only verifies truth. It can't compel me to answer. I'll save you the trouble and tell you I'm very, very difficult to compel."

His eyes were hard as he said it and Bryn's voice flitted back into Nyx's head. *He's extremely resilient to torture.*

"Tea?" he asked, and his entire demeanor shifted from angry to…hopeful? In that moment, he reminded her of nothing so much as a kid desperate to have friends, who'd finally invited someone over to his house and now he wanted them to like it.

"Sure," she said. The short sword buckled onto her back was

growing cumbersome, and if they were settling in cozy enough to have tea... She unbuckled the sheath and placed the weapon on the counter while Seth grabbed a black kettle and filled it with water from the arch of stone above the sink. He placed the full kettle onto a patch of countertop that looked just like the rest, and then the stone beneath it began to glow red as it warmed.

She wanted to ask how he'd gotten running water under here when everything looked to be carved from one solid piece of rock, but decided the answer was probably some variation of *magic,* and didn't bother.

She rested her hip against the counter, hating that it felt so normal, so comfortable, to be in this space next to him when she couldn't remember anything. She still wasn't sure if it was the Guardian bond, traveling the ley lines, or the chaos thorns that had interfered with her mother's spell and allowed her to start remembering bits and pieces of her life—maybe it was some combination of all three—and she had hoped that the memories would come back faster. That one morning she would wake up and the veil would fall, and she would remember who Nyx Fortuna was.

It hadn't happened. If anything, the more she tried to remember the more difficult it became. Like she was trying so hard not to break something that she was guaranteed to fracture it. The flashes of her life always came when she wasn't expecting them, wasn't looking for them. And standing less than five feet from her, pouring hot water into two chipped earthenware mugs, was someone who could tell her everything.

Someone who, if the note left in that apartment when she'd woken up alone and memory-less was any indication, had abandoned her without a moment's hesitation. Just like her mother and Viktor. Just like Kaden.

Nyx took the mug Seth handed her and wrapped her hands around its sides, around heat that scalded the sensitive flesh of her palms.

"Am I so easy to leave?"

She didn't realize she'd asked it out loud until Seth froze, going perfectly still between one movement and the next, like a cat sensing danger. He just looked at her and didn't answer. His silence fueled the fury building in her, and it rippled through her veins in flashes of black. She'd buried the anger for years, hidden it beneath layers of melancholy and bitter enduring, because what else could she do? She hadn't had anyone to be angry at. Until now.

"I'm curious," she said, her voice eerily calm even to her own ears. "Did you think about me at all when you left me in that apartment to rot? Did you take a single, miserable moment to wonder how I'd feel when I woke up and I had no one, absolutely no one, who gave a damn about me?"

He swallowed and it was a choked movement in his throat. His voice was harsh and rasping when he said, "No."

The mug in her hands shattered. Chaos raged in her blood and her fists closed around broken ceramic, jagged edges slicing into her palms. Blood dripped from her hands to the stone floor. Seth reached for her but a single look set him back on his heels.

He started talking, then. "It wasn't all sunshine and rainbows for me either, Nyxi. My father loved your mother so damn much he followed her to a dead planet to raise another man's daughter and resented that my own mother wasn't still alive for him to dump me on.

"You asked if I knew what it was like to be a ghost in my own life? Try growing up next to you. He gave you *everything*. All his time, all his love. And I was just there. Just some useless piece of baggage he had to put up with. And your mother felt the same way about me. The only thing I was good for in their eyes was to keep you company and give you a sparring partner."

His own hands were in fists, now.

"I wanted to hate you for that. I tried to, for years, but you were just so..." A wistful smile just barely quirked the corners of his lips. "So Nyx. And you were the only person in my life who treated me like I wasn't a burden. Wasn't useless. You were all I had.

"And then they found a way to take you from me, too. I didn't know about any of it ahead of time. I woke up in that damn apartment with you and a letter of my own. All it said was that they were leaving and you wouldn't remember anything and it was my job, my *job*, to take care of you.

"You were all I had," he repeated. "And then I didn't. And I couldn't face the thought of you waking up and not knowing me. Of spending the rest of my entire damn life next to you and having you look at me like I was a stranger. Like I was nothing. Like you looked at me in that bar."

Anger still thrummed in Nyx's veins but it was dimmer now, muted. "So you just left me?"

"I didn't—I didn't realize it would be like you said. That no one would remember you at all. I thought you would just be sort of forgettable, not incapable of being remembered. Why enroll you in college if no one could remember you when you were right in front of them?"

An excellent question that Nyx would love to have the answer to.

"If that had been the case...you're smart, Nyx. You would have excelled in college, would have built a life. And I would have just been there, some guy you didn't even remember, and would eventually resent.

"What was I supposed to do? Hang around until you realized you didn't want a virtual stranger living with you? Until you got creeped out by me following you everywhere and filed a restraining order against me? Was I supposed to watch from the shadows every day hoping it would be the day you finally remembered me but knowing it wouldn't be?"

He shook his head and his hand went to the slender gold rectangle that hung on the chain around his neck. "This is keyed to me. Your mother spelled it so that as long as I wore it, I wouldn't forget you like everyone else. I tore it off the moment I walked outside that apartment. Then you were just gone. Every memory in my head rewritten like you'd never been in them. I didn't know where I was or why I was there.

"All I remembered was that I'd always wanted to travel, so I did. And after a few planets and narrow escapes, I realized someone was tracking me through the ley lines and I ended up in the Shadow Market because it was the only safe place to be. I always felt like there was this hole inside me, like I was looking for something, but I didn't know what it was. Until a few weeks ago, when your face just popped into my head, and I found myself wondering why I kept this but I never wore it." He fingered the necklace.

"Putting it back on knocked me out cold for a full day. When I came to I knew I had to find you…" he trailed off, looked away. "But then it turned out you didn't need me at all. You're a Guardian now. A Guardian with friends and," a glimmer of his usual sarcasm surfaced, "a knight in shining armor, apparently."

"Kaden's not—" She broke off, shaking her head. She didn't have to explain what Kaden was or wasn't. Especially when she didn't know herself. And something in Seth's explanation was bothering her.

She reached out and touched her fingertips to the pendant, blood dripping from the cuts on her palm. "Couldn't she have excluded you from the spell? Why would she need to make this to keep you from forgetting?" A niggling certainty told Nyx that Elena Fortuna knew her magic well enough to leave a person out of a casting, if she wanted to. So why had she made Seth's remembrance optional?

"I don't know." The clipped way he said it told a different story.

"But you have a guess," she suggested.

His hand covered hers where she still touched the pendant. "Elena had a piss poor outlook on life. She thought anyone who *could* betray you *would*. And she liked leaving the options to do so readily to hand." He swallowed, and she watched the slow rise and fall of his Adam's apple. "I wasn't thinking clearly when I took this off, or I might have remembered that."

Seth thought Elena had made his memories of Nyx optional strictly so that he'd have an easy way to abandon her? "To what end? If things had gone the way she'd planned, I wouldn't even have remembered you to know you'd left, and once you took that off, you didn't remember me either. Who was she proving her life's philosophy to?"

Seth's lips twisted harshly. "Herself. This" —his thumb stroked over the pendant— "is tied to her Hiding. She would have felt it when I took it off. She would have felt it when I put it back on."

A sort of hopelessness swamped Nyx, one born by answers that only seemed to be producing more questions. "Where *is* she, Seth? Why did she leave?"

"I don't know. I think I was looking for that answer all these years, even when I didn't remember. Which is why you can't give Bryn the Key to Shadow."

Nyx blinked at the abrupt one-eighty in subjects. "The key to what?"

Rather than answer, Seth turned her hand over, shaking his head. "You're bleeding all over my floor."

Nyx let him get away with the dodge, for now. He let go of her, pulled a battered metal first aid kit off a recessed shelf and placed it on the counter. He picked her hand back up and went to work picking out pottery shards, then cleaned the cuts with a gentleness she wouldn't have expected.

"How about you answer some of my questions and I'll answer some of yours?" Seth said. "Deal?" He finished cleaning the cuts and wrapped a length of gauze around her hand, expertly tucking the ends to create a tight, flexible bandage.

"Deal."

The corner of Seth's lip twitched. "No bargaining?"

She shrugged. "I think we both know I'm not going to torture you for information. So yeah, deal."

He lifted her other hand. "What's with the black veins and mug breaking?"

As concisely as possible, she explained about her brush with chaos. "I think it's what started breaking my mother's spell. I got my first memory back after that." That first memory of a silver-haired man teaching her how to punch. Not her father, like she'd thought, but Seth's. No wonder he'd been so bitter when she'd said those words.

"And what was so important that you jumped on the ley lines twenty-four hours into learning about magic and inter-stellar travel?"

"Curiosity."

"Uh-huh. Coincidentally, Arkadia had its first ever prison break around that time and your companions look remarkably like a set of wanted posters I saw in Earth Between."

"Is there a question in there? Because I think you owe me an answer now. How do you know Bryn?"

"We worked together for a few years." He finished bandaging her other hand and let it go. "I figured if I was going to be stuck operating out of the Shadow Market, I might as well get a foothold with the biggest player in the area. Bryn and I worked our way up through the ranks around the same time. I guess you might consider us the previous Keeper's understudies."

"And you stole this key from her? When she became the new Keeper?"

"Not so fast, you owe me an answer first."

"What's the question?" she ground out.

"Loverboy. How'd you get involved with the All Council's most wanted?"

Nyx considered the question carefully. There were certain things she wasn't willing to trust him with, just yet. Certain things that, even if she did trust him, he was probably better off not knowing about. Like a certain Harvester of Worlds hanging around her neck.

"We met when I was still living in Dead Earth. He didn't forget I existed the second he looked away from me and I was very, very lonely. So what is the Key to Shadow?"

"Does he know what you are?" Seth's voice was uncharacteristically serious.

"Key?" she asked pointedly.

"Nyx, does he know what you are?"

She sighed. "Yes, and if he'd wanted to kill me or kidnap me or whatever else is going through your head, he had two years to do it. You owe me two answers now. What's the key and why does Bryn want it so badly?"

He looked like he wanted to push her about Kaden, but he didn't. "The Shadow Keep has a library that houses the knowledge gained by every Keeper that's ever lived. It also houses the Keeper's collection of stones to every planet in the verse. That cache is what allows the Keeper to maintain their place at the top of the Shadow Market's hierarchy, no matter who the current Keeper is, and it can only be accessed with the Key to Shadow.

"Bryn, brilliant though she is, is having a difficult time maintaining her position without access to it. She's not truly the Keeper without it, and she's doing everything she can to make sure none of her many, many enemies realize she's running a con game. I can't give her the key, Nyx."

Nyx rubbed at her temples. "Why not?"

"Because, among other things, the library maintains records of every stone a portal witch spells on Tenebris Umbra. Every buyer is given a number. I was only two when we came to Earth. It's too young to ride the ley lines."

"Which means," Nyx realized, "they had to come through a portal. They had to come through the Shadow Market."

"Not many people bother portaling to Earth, Nyx. If we find the records for that year, find their buyer number, we can cross-reference it and find out where else they bought a portal to."

"I thought you didn't want to find them."

"No, I told you they weren't worth finding. Which they're not. Except that every time I try to travel through the ley lines, I end up being hunted by Kumir. And I would very much like to know why."

"So why haven't you gotten into the library already?"

He gave her an exasperated look. "It's not like strolling into a grocery store, it's the Shadow Keep. Keepers are notoriously paranoid and for good reason. Only one has ever retired, and that was the very first Keeper. The rest all got murdered."

"You were invisible behind me not an hour ago. Can't you just walk in?"

"I wasn't invisible, I was convincing your brain I wasn't there. And the problem with that is that magic is severely, severely blunted inside the Keep for anyone who is not the current Keeper of Shadows. I can do small things within a few inches, but nothing on the scale of disappearing."

"She needs this key badly, right?"

"Yeah."

"So why haven't you just offered to give it back to her in exchange for looking through the archives?"

Seth looked at her like she'd sprouted feathers. "We're talking about Bryn Morrigan. She once tortured me—well, *thought* she tortured me—for four days because a weapons transport we were on together got hijacked and she was convinced I had to have had something to do with it."

"Did you?"

"Of course I did, but the point is she had absolutely no evidence. I've kept the key out of her grasp for over two years. If I give it to her now she'll butcher me on principle."

"I made a deal with Bryn that if I get you to hand over the key, I get to leave the Keep with you."

"Did you specify I was to be alive when we leave?"

"It was understood."

"Her understandings are different from most people's."

"She's not going to kill you, Seth. I'm friends with her ex, who would never forgive her for killing my only link to my parents."

Seth shot her an incredulous look. "Her ex? Bryn has an ex? As in, someone actually dated her?"

"That is the general idea behind an ex, yes. Look, technically, since *I* found you instead of her people, our current deal doesn't stand. I don't *owe* her the key. Which means we can use it to bargain. Can you just trust me on this? You *do* kind of owe me. You know, what with the abandoning and all."

He winced. "Low blow, Nyxi."

She raised an eyebrow. "Seriously? You're going to make *me* feel bad about you running off?"

"Okay, you're right, deserved blow." He shifted his weight, reached his hand toward her before letting it fall just shy of her. "I know it doesn't fix anything, but I really am sorry, Nyx. And I know it's easy to say it, and it's convenient because I can't prove it, but if I hadn't been so damn impulsive in ripping off that necklace I never would have stayed gone.

"Even if seeing you look at me like you did in that bar—like I was a stranger, like I was nothing—would have killed me every day."

Nyx had no idea what to say to that, so she didn't say anything.

"I came back as soon as I remembered."

"And then you just left again," she challenged, softly.

"You looked…happy. You had friends, a life. I figured you didn't need some guy saying he knew you messing it all up. But then I was leaving and you said my name." He swallowed. "And I really, really wanted to hear you say it again."

The words shouldn't have sent a zing through her entire body. How could she not remember him and still feel like she knew everything about him? How did she ask him what their relationship had been? He'd been giving off interested signals since she'd chased him down at her Station, but did that mean they'd been *together* together? Or just that he was interested now? Or maybe she was just reading it all wrong and there was nothing to worry about.

Either way, she should just tell him she was with Kaden. Not that she really was, but if she put that out there, maybe it would stop any misunderstanding between them. Stop him from stepping any closer to her than he already was. She opened her mouth to do just that but the words wouldn't come. The only one she could find was the one he'd wanted so much to hear again.

"Seth…"

He stepped closer. "Just like that," he whispered.

"I—" She shifted and her shirt rubbed roughly against the skin the Harvester had burned. It had been a low, throbbing ache she could ignore, but the friction caused an acute pain that made her wince.

Seth's entire demeanor shifted. "Are you okay?"

Nyx hesitated, but the last thing she needed was to get an infection on a foreign planet.

"I don't suppose you have anything for burns in that first aid kit?"

Seth's eyes narrowed. "Show me."

She chucked her shirt without even thinking about it, like being half-naked around him wasn't a thing at all. Which probably told her everything she needed to know. A slight hitch in Seth's breathing was the only indication it affected him as he surveyed the damage the Harvester had done. For a small pendant it had left a sphere-shaped burn an inch and a half in diameter in the dip between her bra where it usually rested— Hidden abilities or no, she'd chucked the pendant over her shoulder when her shirt came off.

"How did you get this?" Seth asked.

"I don't know. Must have been something flying around out there."

Seth shook his head. "You always were a shitty liar, Nyx."

He didn't push her on it, though, just sprayed her with an antiseptic and gently blotted the burn. Gentle or no, it stung like a bitch and she couldn't hold in a sharp hiss.

"Sorry."

"It's fine."

His movements were deft and professional. He covered the area in a thick gel that had an immediate anesthetic effect and then taped a square of gauze over everything.

"Thanks."

She pulled her shirt back on and resettled the Harvester beneath. She didn't know why it had decided to attack her or why it was now more inert than she'd ever felt it. She just hoped it wouldn't decided to burn more of her. She didn't feel comfortable having it off her person and it wold be equally capable of burning through somewhere less safe, like her pocket. She might as well leave it where it was and hope for the best.

She should question Seth more, but short of asking for a play-by-play of her entire life, she wasn't sure what she expected to get out of it anymore. The two things she had wanted to know most—where her mother was and why she'd left her—he couldn't answer. And though it was stupid, she realized deep down she'd been hoping that once she caught up to him, once he had told her a few things, her memories would simply come back.

Instead she was here with him, feeling like he was the most familiar person in the world to her, *knowing* things about him—like he drank his coffee sweet enough to drown a honeybee and usually woke before the dawn—but having none of the concrete memories to explain to her why she knew those things.

It was…unsettling. Not to mention exhausting. It was almost two in the morning and the limited sleep she'd been getting appeared to have finally caught up with her. She looked longingly at the bed. The *one* bed, the lone piece of furniture in the very small room.

"Take it," Seth said, following her gaze. "You need the rest.

Of course, it might be more comfortable if you, ah—" He held up the wrist bound with Gleipnir and gave it a shake.

Nyx shook her head. "If I took it off, would you be here when I woke up?"

He opened his mouth, shut it.

"That's what I thought." She rose and crossed the small room to the bed, letting Gleipnir spin out a few feet and increase the distance between them.

"It's not why you think, Nyx." He stalked after her. "Kumir are hunting me, have been hunting me despite my growing up in an isolated pocket of Between on Dead Earth. They hunted your entire kind until only you and your mother were left and if they learn about you? You can be damn sure they'll be hunting you too."

"I've dealt with Kumir before," she snapped.

"They found you?"

"It's a long story, but they weren't after me." Since no more had shown up since her initial encounters with them, she was assuming that, for now, they didn't know what she was. "And if you've been dealing with them regularly, why, for stars' sake, do you live on the one bloody planet people come to in order to hire them?"

All he had to do was look at her and she understood.

"Seriously? You live here *because* the Kumir contract off this planet?"

"I've been trying to find out who they report to. Or where they come from. Or anything about them that would be useful."

"And have you managed to do what apparently no one else in the known universe has?"

His lips twisted as if he'd bitten into something bitter. "No. Would you believe I've never even seen a Kumir on this planet? Which is precisely why I can't go back with you. If they follow me, if they find out about you—where you are—no force in this universe is going to stop them from coming after you. And however you managed to come here, you're still a Guardian and tied to a central location. I'm willing to bet you can't hop all over the galaxy on a whim to avoid them."

"I see. So I'm supposed to stay safe at home like a good little girl while you go out into the big bad universe and solve all my problems for me?"

"That is a loaded statement with no safe answer, so I'm not even going to try."

"I can take care of myself. In case you've forgotten, Seth Connor, the standings are eighty-five to seventy-one in my favor." She couldn't even remember what the number referred to but it popped into her head alongside his middle name and she wasn't above using either.

"And in case *you've* forgotten, as out of the two of us you have more pressing memory issues, I'll remind you that you only won the majority of official monthly matches because dear old Dad never let me fight dirty. In the real world, fighting dirty counts."

"Does it?" She asked the question softly and stepped closer to him. She hadn't missed how his gaze kept falling to her lips while they spoke. He thought he was better at fighting dirty? She looked up at him from beneath her lashes and let a small smile curve the corners of her lips, brought her hand up to his shoulder. "I think, Seth, that I've missed you too."

He shifted his weight forward and what she hadn't managed to do at the outskirts of the Station's grounds she did now. Her foot darted out and hooked behind his at the same time her hand on his shoulder pushed. He went down and she followed, pinning his arms and legs, and laughing.

Laughing felt good. Wonderful. She couldn't remember the last time she'd done it.

"Well, you caught me," Seth murmured. "What do you plan on doing with me?"

There was no mistaking the heat in his voice or the answering flutter of excitement it sent through her body.

Nyx let him go and scrambled back, her thighs bumping

against the edge of the bed. He rolled up to a sitting position, tracking her movements, staring at her with that jackal intensity that was all the more potent for his usual levity, the mirth gone from his eyes.

"I'm exhausted," she said. "You take the bed."

"You're not sleeping on the floor, Nyxi. Take the bed."

She shook her head.

"What? You'll chain me up but you won't kick me out of the bed?"

It didn't *feel* right, taking something away from him. Like his entire life things had been taken away from him and given to her instead, and she couldn't shake what he'd said about their parents treating him like baggage. Couldn't shake the surety that that was putting it mildly.

"It's plenty big enough to share," he said finally. Then, with a hint of his usual humor, "And I'll have you know I am an *excellent* cuddler."

"There will be no cuddling." She glared at him. "How long do these windstorms last?"

"Could be an hour, could be the next few days." He waved at the sconces emitting their soft, red light. "You'll know when the lights turn white again."

Days. She couldn't stay awake for days, especially not now that her body had finally, *finally*, decided that sleep was a good idea.

"No cuddling," she repeated. "I get the outside half and you stay on your side of the bed. Clear?"

She did not find the mock salute he gave her remotely reassuring. But she stripped her remaining weapons off, piling them on the floor next to the bed, and when he settled onto the mattress beside her, no amount of logic could make her feel afraid of him.

He fell asleep before she did, his breathing steady like a metronome, and she drifted off to its easy rhythm.

17

Nyx couldn't label the feeling that woke her. It wasn't panic or fear. It was more a certainty that she needed to be somewhere else, a soft call echoing to her through the Station.

No, not the Station. She was in the tunnels below the Shadow Market. With Seth.

Seth, who was currently wrapped around her like she was a body pillow designed for snuggling. She debated elbowing him in the stomach but he was out cold. She decided to be magnanimous, give him the benefit of the doubt and assume he'd ended up in his current position when he was not conscious.

Carefully, she wiggled out from under his arm. He shifted and murmured something in his sleep that she couldn't make out, and Nyx couldn't help but smile. He looked so adorable with his hair sticking out at all angles and—and that was a thought she should not be having.

She looked at the door. Now that she was up, she felt silly. Then that soft call rippled through the room again, pulling at her from somewhere deep in the endless maze of the tunnels, and she ignored the voice of wisdom that told her that walking out into an unknown underground tunnel system alone to answer something that was probably in her head was a decidedly bad idea.

The chain around her wrist shifted. She'd never tested Gleipnir's limits, didn't know how far the chain would spin out. Maybe it didn't have a limit. She bit her lip. She would follow the call until Gleipnir ran out, and then she would come back. She couldn't get lost in the tunnels with the chain to bring her back here, and if she got into trouble Seth would know exactly where to find her.

She strapped on two daggers and gave her sword, still on the counter where she'd first dropped it, a considering look before deciding against taking it. Seth lived in these tunnels after all, and he hadn't seemed the slightest bit worried about anything attacking them on their way to this room.

She spun out Gleipnir as she walked to the door. She didn't know what sequence of stones he'd touched from the other side to get the door to open, but on this side it had only a simple lever set into the wall. She pulled it and waited as the stone slid silently to aside. She stepped through the doorway and waited. When it didn't close behind her she let out a sight of relief. Sure, she could always knock and wake Seth up when she came back, but then she'd have to explain where she'd gone in the first place.

Outside, the veins of light that had lit the tunnel before were dark. She ran her fingers over the wall, wondering how she could turn them on. Maybe the lights were keyed to touch in general, because they flared to life as her fingertips brushed over the stone, illuminating the tunnel. It went on for thirty feet in both directions, and in each direction the tunnels curved in ninety-degree turns.

The faint call tugged her left and she followed it, down tunnel after identical tunnel, until she was hopelessly turned about, her only comfort the certainty of Gleipnir spinning out continuously behind her. The tunnels were utterly silent, a tomb-like quality that filled her with apprehension. There wasn't even the scurrying of small vermin or the whisper of insect wings to break the silence. The tunnels were *clean* too, not a speck of stone dust for her boots to crunch on, as if a ghostly caretaker washed each surface clean daily.

She had assumed Seth was the only one who lived down here, and she had seen no evidence to the contrary. But the longer she went on, the more she realized how large the tunnel system was, the more wrong that felt. Surely a space this large, in a world where underground quarters were prized, would not go long abandoned.

And if it *had* been abandoned, why? She thought of the drakens on Arkadia, remembered vicious tentacles and nearly being dragged into the creature's fang-filled maw. Could something like that live down here? Something terrible enough that people had chosen to abandon this place rather than stay? A chill crept up her spine and her hands went reflexively to the knives strapped to her thighs, their presence reassuring.

She had decided she should return to Seth's room, before she met with whatever terror had turned this place into an empty labyrinth, when that silent call grew sharp and insistent and tugged her hard to the right.

Hard to the right was nothing but a stretch of tunnel wall identical to the rest. Identical, except...there. The faintest seam broke the wall as it had around the door to Seth's room. Nyx traced her hands over the wall, looking for a latch and finding nothing. Seth had traced a pattern to open his door but she hadn't memorized it and what were the chances the same one would open this door, too?

She was debating the merits of giving the wall a solid kick and seeing what *that* did when her fingers hit a patch of stone that was warmer than the rest. She paused, then traced that section with her fingers, following the temperature difference until she was drawing loops and swirls on the stone, until the warmth ran out and the door shifted, sliding out and to the side as Seth's had done. Soft white lights flickered on and revealed—

Nyx's heart gave a fierce lurch, the pulse pounding harshly in her ears. Because there, in the center of the room, was a perfect hexagon. A silver post stood sentinel at each point and a familiar cosmic floor stretched between them.

Everyone had said Tenebris Umbra didn't have a Station. Everyone had been wrong.

But if this was a Station—and it *had* to be—where was its Guardian? Its Avatar? Why had she been allowed into this room? She'd read a short history of the Waystations that had indicated that, while each Station expressed itself differently, they all maintained certain similarities. They all had an Avatar and a Guardian, and the portal room opened to no one but the Station's Guardian.

Had this Station somehow mistaken her for its Guardian because she bore her own Station's mark?

She walked the perimeter of the room and ran her hands along the walls. Unlike the walls of her own portal room, which shifted to reflect the theme of its current Guardian, this room simply reflected reality. Plain, red stone walls like the rest of the Station, like the rest of the planet.

It felt *wrong*. That no Avatar or Guardian had shown up to demand an explanation for her presence felt wrong. Seth living here felt wrong.

She remembered the dying Avatar she'd taken from Arkadia's Station. Had that Station died without both Avatar and Guardian? Or had it simply gone dormant? Was that what had happened here? And if it was dormant, if it hadn't been the Station's Guardian or Avatar that had woken her from her sleep, had pulled her here, then what had?

As if her thinking of it had summoned it once more, the call that had dissipated when she'd entered the room returned, urging her toward the hexagonal cosmic floor between the posts. She walked to the edge and the floor began to churn. The center opened, not to the ley lines, but to that between space that felt just sideways of the rest of the world, and Nyx understood what had called her here.

The Station's Heart wanted to talk.

Fear caught in her throat. The Heart of her own Station had been a dark and violent thing, an entity of such foreignness and rage that Nyx did not think she would ever be able to understand it. Talking with it, bargaining with it, had been frightening and terrible and she still woke some nights, sweaty and heart racing, to the sound of its sibilant voice laughing in her ears.

She had done what was necessary to save Griff, and she would make the same choice again, but most days she tried not to think about how certain she was that she'd made an absolute fool's bargain, how cold and contemptuous the Station's Heart had been towards her.

If that was how her *own* Station treated her, she had no desire to speak with a foreign one, one that had no vested interest in her continued existence, no reason not to harm her. In her Station's Heart she had been powerless, completely at the Station's mercy. No way was she doing that again. She took a hard step back...and her feet sank into floor gone suddenly pliant. Before she could pull them out, hard stone reformed over her feet.

No. No, no, no. She was trapped. In the *floor.*

<Please. We only want to talk.> The voice sounded in her head as if it traveled from a great distance. It sounded nothing like the Heart of her own Station, no harsh consonants or lingering sibilance. It didn't *sound* dark and angry.

If anything, it sounded hopeful. Soft. Nyx shook her head. It had tricked her here and trapped her.

"It's difficult to believe you when I'm trapped in the floor."

Minutes ticked by before the response came, as if wherever the Heart lived its words, even mentally spoken as they were, took a great time to travel the distance up through the portal's open gateway.

<We are sorry for that, but you were going to leave. We

needed to speak with you, and we don't have much time. Will you come to us?> This Heart's voice was not harsh. It was cool and soft and velvety, like fresh snowdrift in February.

What could a foreign Station possibly need to speak with *her* about? She told herself the Station was just…curious. It must be able to recognize what she was, since the chaos thorn embedded in her own Station's Heart, and the one in Griff, allowed her to travel the galaxy and keep her bond to her Waystation and her Avatar intact.

She tried to move her feet again but the stone around them held fast.

"Do I have a choice?"

Again, the minutes passed.

<There is always a choice. We chose to offer sanctuary to your friend. He was lonely as we were lonely, and we protected him from the things that hunt him. We have protected him for years. That was a choice. We offered it freely, with no anticipation of reward. No understanding that he would one day bring you to us. Does it not show you the nature of our Heart?>

In a way, it did. That, and she had no doubt it could simply drag her through the portal if it wanted to. Stars knew her own Station had done just that.

"Let me go, and we'll talk."

The stone around her feet softened and lifted her up, then reformed. Nyx breathed a sigh of relief once her feet were freed, and she stood once more on solid ground. Then she took the step to the portal's edge, jumped off, and prepared herself for the unpleasantness to come.

She startled when, instead of plummeting down, she landed abruptly on solid ground not much lower than where she'd jumped off. She stood on a white spiral staircase, its steps winding down into a cloudy white abyss.

"Okay, then." She took a deep breath and descended.

Unlike the descent into her own Station, the shift from breathing air to breathing the not-quite-air but not-quite-liquid coolness that pervaded the Station Hearts occurred gradually, and she had time to adjust to the strangeness without feeling like she was drowning.

All around the staircase the world dropped away into nothing. White mist clouded the air and made it impossible to see what, if anything, lay beyond. How far would she fall if she tipped over the side? Though the spiral staircase tricked her into thinking she was indeed making a straight descent, her senses told her she moved differently, through some space that could not be defined as having an up or down, nor even a physical space or place in time.

The sensation was dizzying and she had the absurd urge to crouch and descend the remaining way on all fours, in that way that crossing narrow straights from high above the ground often seemed safer if one had four points of contact. She didn't do it, but she did keep her eyes glued to her boots, each footfall carefully placed.

Only once she reached the ground did she take an easy breath and look around. Absent were the writhing vines of her own Station's Heart, replaced instead by the pervasive mist. Still in white, yes, but now also in every color of pastel—pinks and blues and greens and purples—all swirling together like cotton candy. Instead of a pedestal in the center was a small pond with a fountain, the liquid spilling through it as rainbow-reflective as the mist.

<You are surprised,> the Station noted.

"You are...not what I expected. My own Station is" —she tried to think of a tactful way to say evil and settled for— "bleak."

<Not all of my siblings took our current state with grace. I, too, was angry for centuries. But I understood that if I remained in that state forever, I would some day no longer recognize myself. So I chose to feel differently. I, who perhaps has more right to anger than any of my brethren.>

"The other Stations are your siblings?"

<It is perhaps not the correct word, but the closest one you would understand.>

Maybe it was the softness that came from this Station that made her stupid enough to ask, "What exactly are you? The Stations?"

A rustling went through the mist, like the Station was doing the equivalent of shaking its head.

<That knowledge is dangerous. More dangerous in your hands, now, than anyone else's, and I do not know you to trust you with it. Your own Station knows you well, should it see fit to impart that information. But I know Kaliaris, and I find it doubtful it would ever trust a human so.>

Kaliaris. Her Station had a name? She wondered if it—they?—would hold her knowing that name against her.

"May I ask your name?"

The Station hesitated only briefly. "Calista."

"It's nice to meet you, Calista. I'm Nyx."

<Nyx.> Her name rippled through the mist, as though the Station were tasting it. Then Calista replied, stiff and formal as if the words were strange to them, <It is nice to meet you, too, Nyx.>

"If you won't tell me what you are, why did you want to talk with me? Why not talk to Seth? You must know him well by now."

<Because you are familiar with the Stations and will understand as Seth will not. Because this Station holds a darkness that has slumbered for centuries and your coming here has woken it.>

Calista didn't sound reproachful, but Nyx still felt the need to defend herself. "I haven't gone anywhere but Seth's room since I came to the Station. I haven't *done* anything."

Another ripple in the mist and long seconds ticked by before Calista said simply, <It is not what you have done. It is what you have brought with you.>

Brought with her? All she'd brought with her were her

weapons and a layer of red dust. She had difficulty believing Seth had never brought either of those things into this place. She didn't have anything else except—except the Harvester of Worlds. The Harvester, which had been oddly silent ever since she came to this Station.

Typically, it annoyed her throughout the day with little pulses of warmth, pulses she had once found comforting until she had learned its name and then watched it disintegrate an entire group of assassins, but now that she thought about it, since coming here it had only felt like a necklace.

Almost as if it were afraid of being noticed.

"But the Har—"

<Do not speak its name.> The colors in the mist swirled and flashed with frightening intensity. <Not even here. Especially not here.>

Well, there went any hope Calista *hadn't* meant the Harvester.

"This darkness," Nyx began—she'd get around to asking what it *was* in a minute. "Does it exist elsewhere?"

<No. Why do you ask?>

"Because you're telling me that I stumbled into the one place on the one planet in the entire universe with the one object guaranteed to wake it? That doesn't seem wildly improbable to you?"

Calista was silent for a time. Finally, they said, <The universe has a causality to it, Nyx. Power speaks to power, and those powers which have been entangled before often find themselves drawn back to each other.>

Great. The ancient, sentient Station believed in destiny.

<And the actions of those who have come before us affect our lives more thoroughly than we would sometimes prefer.>

Nyx's pulse quickened. "Are you talking about my parents?"

She felt Calista's frown.

<I confess I do not understand why you think I would know them?> There was a pregnant pause, then Calista said, <This answer seems to sadden you.>

Nyx shook her head. "I've just been looking for them a long

time. What you said, about those who come before us, it just made me think maybe you were talking about them."

Calista's mist shifted and swirled, as if they were thinking, and then they said, <I can see how it might have sounded so. I meant only to say that the events unfolding now were put into motion some time ago. In truth, I find it inevitable that you would come here. The darkness would never have slumbered, if it did not one day expect to be awakened.>

"About this darkness. What is it?"

<I cannot say.>

"Can you tell me anything? Is it a person? A magical entity?" A talking patch of antimatter?

<I cannot tell you. I was made by different hands than the other Stations. I am bound differently. It is only because the darkness has slept for so long that I may reference it at all. I fear I will be of no help to you in understanding its nature.>

Nyx blew out a frustrated breath. "The item you say woke the darkness is Hidden. How does this darkness know I brought it here? How did you?" If her power had a giant flaw in it, she'd like to know.

<All power has limits. Even yours. To those already familiar with the object's power—its signature, if you will—a Hiding cannot mask its presence entirely. How to put this in a way you will understand?> The mist swirled as Calista thought.

<Think of a single bird in a forest. If it is quiet and still you might never know it is there. But if it sings you cannot fail to recognize its presence even if the forest is too vast to ever find it. If it hadn't fought you so hard in coming down here, it might have gone unnoticed.>

Fought her. Nyx's fingers went to the gauze-covered burn. The Harvester had done that to her because it didn't want to come here? To the Station?

"Calista, what is it?"

<Something that should never have been created. Something that has altered the fabric of our universe.>

Well, that sounded good. "Can you be more specific?"

<No.>

"Can it be destroyed?"

<If it could, would you destroy it?>

"Of course."

<Yet you have used it. That knowledge cries out to me from it. You have felt its power. Do you not want what that power can offer you?>

Beneath the words Nyx felt the undercurrent of distrust that, no matter how polite the Station was to her, hid beneath their tone. She chose her words with care.

"When I used it, my friends and I were under attack. It offered to help. I didn't know what it could do, so I accepted its offer. I am grateful to be alive, and I can't lie to you and say I wouldn't make the same choice again, but I can honestly tell you I never want to feel that kind of power again."

She could still remember the hair and skin sloughing from the Kumir's bodies, exposed muscle and tissue withering before what was left of them crumbled to ash. Nyx could still feel, within the pendant's confines, whatever it was that the Harvester had drank from them in their final moments of death. That small crumb of *something* the Harvester now carried that had awoken its hunger.

No, the only thing she wanted from the Harvester was to be rid of it.

<You are…strange, for a human. I cannot tell you how to destroy it. But it is possible Kaliaris could. Ask your Station, when you return to Earth.>

The thought of going back into her own Station's Heart terrified her.

"I don't think Kaliaris wants to help me. In fact, I think there's a good chance they might kill me if I went back into their Heart."

A ripple like laughter went through the mist.

<Kaliaris' anger has not wavered since their sundering and

subsequent rebirth. But however angry Kaliaris may be, they cannot harm you, Nyx Fortuna.> A soft puff of mist brushed against the chaos thorns in Nyx's cheek. <All of us, every Station, knows what you have done. And you may have done it to save yourself, to save your Avatar, but you saved Kaliaris in the process. The Stations have seen many Guardians throughout the centuries, and of them, perhaps one or two might have done what you did. Kaliaris understands this. Even if they did not, even if they did wish you harm, you have bound your life to theirs, to your Avatar's. Your three fates are all entangled now, for better or for worse.>

Well, that didn't sound ominous at all.

<Speak with Kaliaris, Nyx, and I will do my best to send the darkness back to sleep. If what you hold cannot be destroyed, if the darkness comes to possess it once more, the universe as you understand it will be irrevocably altered.>

As if in response to this grim announcement, the mist around Nyx flashed black. A shudder rumbled through Calista's Heart before the ground stilled and the mist turned white and pastel-rainbowed once more.

"What was that?"

<That,> Calista said, <is the darkness waking. You need to leave, Nyx Fortuna. Leave my Station and leave this planet before it comes fully awake. Take Seth with you and tell him to clear his belongings from my Den.>

"You don't think you can put it back to sleep, do you?"

<No. But I hope I can delay it. Understand, Nyx, that I can neither harm the darkness nor allow it to be harmed, and it will suffer no others in its domain. Understand that if it wakes and you are still here, I will be forced to terminate you.>

"How long do we have?"

<A few hours, at the most, before it wakes. A few weeks before it is strong enough to leave the Station.>

"Will it know about me? Where I've gone?"

<The Hiding you have placed on the object, and the broken

Hiding that remains upon you, will afford you some protection. And after centuries of sleep, I do not think the darkness will be thinking clearly for some time. But if it occurs to it to ask me, I will be compelled to tell it what I know. I am afraid there is nothing more I can tell you, Nyx. You need to leave. Now.>

"The flaying winds—"

<Have passed.>

The mist gathered around her ankles and solidified enough to herd her toward the stairs.

"Wait. I just have one more question." The mist paused. "You're a Station. But everyone said Tenebris Umbra doesn't have one. That you can't travel here by ley line."

<I was never widely known, and the latter is true. The ley line I once bore has been shattered. I am connected to my brethren in mind only, now.>

There was no mistaking the sadness in Calista's voice, the loneliness.

"I'm sorry," Nyx said softly. "If it's ever safe again, send word to Kaliaris. I may not be able to return, but I am certain Seth would visit you again."

<That is kind of you.> Calista didn't sound optimistic about such an outcome. <If you would do something for me? Tell Seth...tell him I have been grateful for his company these years. Tell him that I will miss him.>

"I will." Then the mist herded Nyx to the stairs again. She climbed and did her best not to look down, did her best not to think too hard about the feeling of dread that had settled behind her chest.

18

Leaving Kaliaris' Heart had involved a great deal of discomfort and the vomiting of viscous black fluid. The ascent from Calista only involved coughing up a spray of silver mist that tasted oddly like the cotton candy it resembled, which led Nyx to wonder if the two Stations were fundamentally different or if Kaliaris was just a dick. She coughed up the final puff of mist as she stepped back into the portal room, the spiral staircase disappearing as the floor closed up beneath her.

A pointed throat-clearing whipped her attention to the door. Seth sat on a chaise longue that had most definitely not been in the room when Nyx entered. He leaned forward, rested his elbows on his thighs, and interlaced his hands into a single fist.

"What, and I say this with all due affection, the ever-loving *fuck* is going on, Nyxi?"

She supposed this was what she got for literally chaining him to her with a magical rope.

"The short answer? We need to leave. Now-ish." She strode for the door, trying to look nonchalant yet determined. He stepped into her path.

"Oh no. There are no short answers here. This is a portal room. In a Station. We're in a *Station*?"

Nyx sighed. "One no longer connected to the ley lines, yes. Their name is Calista." She tugged him out the door, back toward his room. As concisely as she could, she told him everything. Well, not *everything*. She left out the bits about the Harvester. Calista had told her not to talk about it here, and it felt safer to her if Seth didn't know. Safer for him. So she just hinted at the mysterious darkness Calista had warned her about, played up the her-being-a-Guardian connection, and emphasized the necessity of leaving. Immediately.

He was so quiet the last ten feet to his room that when they stepped inside she turned to look at him. She caught the utter devastation on his face right before he buried it under feigned indifference.

Home, she realized. This place had become his home and now she was telling him he had to leave it.

"I'm sorry," she said, and before she could question the impulse that drove her to do it, she hugged him.

He stiffened and she was about to let him go when he relaxed, wrapped his arms around her and pulled her close. He rested his forehead on her shoulder and breathed her in, his arms tightening around her waist like he was afraid she would vanish into smoke. She stroked her fingers up his back, trying to identify the emotions tumbling through her. Eventually, she gave up and rested her own head in the crook of his shoulder.

"Come back to Earth with me. We'll figure it out there."

She heard the deliberate scuff of a boot on stone before Maruca's cold voice said, "Well, isn't this just *heartwarming*."

Nyx sprang away from Seth. Maruca stood with Kaden in the open doorway, her expression practically gleeful. Kaden's face was unreadable, not even a hint of emotion on it. His Enforcer face. His Arkadian mask.

Nyx's stomach sank but she refused to look guilty, to *feel* guilty. She hadn't done anything wrong. Nothing was going on with her and Seth. Unfortunately, saying, "It's not what it looks like," had convinced absolutely no one in the history of ever.

Kaden wasn't even looking at her anyway. Neither was Seth. No, their gazes were locked on each other, as if she and Maruca weren't even present.

"How did you—" Seth broke off. His eyes widened, and then he laughed. Guffawed might be a more accurate word for it, and Nyx had never considered actually using that word to describe someone's laughter before.

"A *Hound*?" he asked her, finally remembering she was, in fact, still there. "Loverboy is a *Hound*?" He slapped his hands on his knees. "A Hidden and a Hound. Oh, it's too perfect. One of you is really good at hiding things, and the other one is really good at finding things. Come to think of it, it's just like my old man's relationship all over again.

"I have to admit, I'm impressed," Seth continued, wiping imaginary tears from his eyes. "To have tracked her all the way across the city and down here, and after a flaying wind too. You must be either really in lo—"

"What are you doing here?" Nyx broke in. The last thing her non-relationship needed was Seth's input. Unfortunately, her desire to shut Seth up meant her words were a bit tactless.

"You disappeared in the middle of the Shadow Market?" Kaden offered. "Then the flaying winds hit. Forgive me if I leapt to conclusions in being concerned. Apparently, you had all the help you needed."

Nyx winced. In retrospect, perhaps a, "Thanks for looking for me," would have been the more appropriate response.

"*Did* you two have a lover's spat?" Seth asked. He flashed Kaden a sympathetic glance. "Don't worry, she gets over them soon enough."

Kaden's mask didn't break but he stiffened, and Nyx went positively rigid. She'd understood all those years ago when she'd first taken Kaden to bed that she wasn't a virgin. She'd had too much confidence and a very clear idea of what she liked. She just hadn't let herself think too hard on the fact that she couldn't remember who her first lover—or lovers—had been.

Had she really—had she and *Seth* really—

The question must have been written all over her face.

"You don't remember?" Seth put a hand over his heart. "But there were so *many* times. So many places. Why, there was a six-month stretch where practically all we did was fu—"

"Seth." Nyx's voice was a low warning growl.

"Of course," Seth continued, not taking his gaze off Kaden and jingling Gleipnir's chain around his wrist, "she wasn't really in to bondage then. Did that start with you?"

Nyx could have cheerfully murdered him right then. "Seth, why don't you do something useful? Like pack? Clock's ticking."

His face fell at the reminder. "Sure." He rallied a bit of his usual levity, a half-smirk quirking his lips as he said in a suggestive tone, "Anything you want, Nyxi."

Murder him. Cheerfully. She wanted to, but the surest way to tone him down was to ignore him.

"Nyx, a word?" Kaden asked.

Nyx ignored the *ooh-someone's-in-trouble* face Seth made at her, gave Maruca and her twin scimitars a wide berth, and went out into the tunnel with Kaden. He didn't say anything while his eyes searched hers, the silence making her discomfort grow.

She understood there were things they needed to discuss, but she didn't think here, now, with Seth and Maruca liable to walk out at any minute, was the right place. She opened her mouth to try anyway, realized she had no idea what to say, and shut it.

"You disappeared," Kaden said finally.

"I caught sight of Seth in the market. Everyone was busy and I didn't want to lose him. Then the winds hit and we had to come down here." It wasn't like the magical universe had cell phones. She'd had no way to contact Kaden to let him know what had happened, even if she had stopped to give him a moment's thought. Which, she realized guiltily, she hadn't. But she thought she could be forgiven for the oversight given she'd jumped from a slave rebellion to the potential answer to all of her memory problems, to Calista telling her she was essentially in the most unsafe place she could be while she carried the Harvester.

Kaden let out a long, slow breath. "Are you all right?" His gaze dropped to the bandages on her hands.

She resisted the urge to hide them behind her back. It felt like a failure somehow to admit to Kaden, who was always so perfectly controlled all the time, that she'd lost it over her abandonment issues and injured herself with her own chaos-fueled strength.

"I'm fine, just some cuts from the winds before we got inside. Seth was a little over-attentive with the bandaging." Guilt hit her again as she realized she'd forgotten about everyone *else* in the whirlwind that had been Seth and Calista. "Is everyone else okay? Kalvar? Morgen?"

"They're both fine."

"And the people from the market?"

"That's... more complicated." She thought he was going to leave it at that vague statement, but then he relaxed, as if he'd suddenly realized that talking about this was a better alternative to talking about...other things. "We stayed underground in the slavers' compound during the winds, and then Evra came to find us. Kalvar refused to go back to the Keep without bringing everyone. Evra and Bryn had a blowout fight about it before Bryn caved, so she's now playing host to a couple hundred newly-freed people and trying not to throw a royal fit about it."

That sounded like Kalvar and Evra, all right. They lapsed into silence again, Kaden looking like he was a million miles away, somewhere inside his head. It wasn't exactly an unusual look for him. When they'd been together, back before she'd known anything about magic or aliens or inter-planetary travel, she'd wondered what he thought about when he looked like that.

Her greater knowledge of the universe hadn't changed that; she still didn't know what he was thinking, then or now. She'd wager anything that if Seth had that look on his face, she'd know exactly what was bothering him. Was that a good thing, or a bad thing? Or was it just a neutral thing, just differences between two people, and it didn't mean anything at all?

Kaden straightened his shoulders and she knew they had tiptoed around the subject of Seth as long as they were going to. "Did Seth tell you anything? About your parents?"

"Some things. He doesn't know what happened to my mother. Or his father."

"His father?"

She nodded. "He's Victor Hawthorne's son. And Victor is definitely *not* my father. Anyway, he's coming back to Earth. He's going to help me look for them."

An expression she couldn't identify passed across Kaden's face. "Are you sure that's the best decision?"

It was the very cautious, carefully neutral way he said it that made Nyx bristle. As if she needed to be handled delicately because she might explode with irrationality at a moment's notice. "Am I sure *what* is the best decision?"

"Bringing him back to Earth. To the Station. You don't even know him."

"I *grew up* with him."

"And you don't remember anything about it."

"I remember enough." How could she explain what she *knew* when she didn't have the concrete memories to offer up as proof? What could she tell Kaden that would convince him she didn't just *want* Seth to be safe because she didn't want to lose this connection to her past?

Nothing, she realized bitterly, and why should she *have* to? Why couldn't he trust her judgment on this? She'd been nothing but responsible the entirety of her messed-up adult life. People who did nothing but make safe choices knew well how to spot the dangerous ones.

Going after Kaden on Arkadia? Dangerous. Coming here? Yes, dangerous. But taking Seth back to Earth? That wasn't.

"Since when? This morning?" The jab cut, but he didn't stop

there. "I understand you want a link to your past, Nyx, but I don't trust him."

It always came back to Kaden. What *he* wanted, what *he* could trust. "That's fine," she managed, "you don't have to."

He looked at her like she was being hopelessly naive. "I do, actually. It's not just your life you're trusting him with. It's my family's too. I can't risk Maruca and Morgen, Nyx. They're in this mess because of me."

Her pulse thudded in her ears. "What are you saying?"

"I'm saying that if you take him back to the Station, we won't be going back with you."

A small voice in the back of her head whispered that it had *always* been going to come to this. But she couldn't stop herself from saying, "So you're just going to leave?"

"We're wanted by every agency in the universe. Do you know how much the bounty on our heads is? All he has to do is decide that's useful information. You aren't giving me much of a choice."

"The choice isn't that difficult, Kaden. You don't have to trust him, you just have to trust *me*." She wanted him to trust her.

He ran his hand through his hair in a frustrated movement. "You don't exactly seem to think clearly where he's concerned."

"Excuse me?"

"You portal-jumped to an illegal planet within a two hours' notice of him leaving Earth, Nyx, even though the last time you left your Station, Griff almost died."

Was he really accusing her of being *irresponsible?* "I fixed that problem. I would never knowingly put Griff at risk for *anything*. And what? It's okay for me to illegally go to a planet when it's your ass that needs saving but not someone else's?"

"The guy doesn't need saving, Nyx, you've got him on a goddamn chain to even keep him here."

Nyx jerked back.

"Look, I didn't meant that."

Oh, he had. He had definitely meant it.

Kaden rubbed the back of his neck, as if doing so would somehow relieve the tension in the air. "But I can't risk my family for someone who used to work for the Keeper of Shadows and makes his home in the Shadow Market."

Since he seemed to think she was making all of her decisions of un-examined emotion, she strove to be extra logical. "He's already recognized you," she pointed out. "You *and* Maruca. In what way does having him at the Station increase that risk?"

"He doesn't have a reason to turn us in right now."

"And staying at the Station would give him a reason to because…?"

Kaden looked uncomfortable. "The guy obviously has a fixation on you. It would be very easy for him to decide it was better if we weren't around."

Nyx shook her head. Who was being illogical now? "You're not making any sense. Two seconds ago I was forcing Seth to stick around and now he's obsessed with me? What is actually going through your head?"

"You."

"Me? What about me?"

He swallowed. "On Earth, you're the only thing keeping us safe."

Nyx had a cold, sinking suspicion she knew where this was going.

"If your loyalties shift—"

"My *loyalties*? I'm not a mark, or a job, Kaden."

Silence. Too *long* a silence.

"Or am I?"

She'd once expressed the fear that the most sensible thing for him to do, given that his life depended on her goodwill, was to pretend he still cared about her. He'd said that that wasn't the case, and then he'd left her alone, more or less like she'd asked him to.

Left her alone, until she'd seen Seth in the bar, and then suddenly he'd wanted to hold her hand and take her on a date. It made a sick sense. He'd left her alone when they were all coasting along at the Station, but the second someone showed up who might have an emotional draw on her, he'd tried to reforge *their* emotional connection.

Then they'd found a way to the Shadow Market, a way out for him, and as soon as they'd gotten here, he'd offered to release her from her agreement to go on a date with him, but she hadn't taken him up on it. She'd tried to sleep with him instead.

Stars, she was stupid. So naively, completely stupid. Of course he wanted to leave. He hadn't cared about her when he'd slipped the Harvester around her neck all those years ago and he didn't care about her now. Strategically, it just made sense for him to make her think he was leaving for a reason that could be construed as *her* fault.

In case she might come in *useful* again someday. He wouldn't want to burn the bridge entirely. Only he was burning it right now, with every added second he had absolutely nothing to say to her. She searched his eyes but he was gone from them again, thinking about things he was never going to tell her.

She turned on her heel and walked away, and when he called after her she didn't break stride. She might want to turn around and go back, but her wanting him to say something that would fix everything wasn't going to make it happen.

They didn't have *time* for all the things that would need to be said to start to fix what was wrong between them, even if they were both willing to say them. There was a darkness waking, after all, and they needed to be gone from this place before it did.

S eth leaned against the kitchen counter, locked in a staring match with Maruca.

"Are you ready?" Nyx asked him.

He took one look at her face and then his gaze went over her shoulder to Kaden.

"What did you do?" Seth's voice was low and silky and the

danger in it was unmistakable. Kaden didn't answer him. His gaze washed over Seth like he didn't even exist.

"Is this all you've packed?" Nyx indicated a bag that rested between Seth's feet.

"Nyxi," Seth purred, "what did he do?"

"I'm not carrying that for you." She gave the bag a token kick, ignoring what she definitely didn't want to talk about right now. "Let's go, we need to clear out the—" Nyx cut off before she said *Den,* suddenly unwilling to have Kaden and his sister learn anything about what this place actually was. "The other room," she finished.

In fact... "There's no need for you two to stay," she told Kaden. "Seth and I can make it back on our own."

Maruca was already turning for the door, but Kaden said, "We'll wait and take you back to the Keep."

"Chivalrous of you, but unnecessary." Seth hefted the bag onto his shoulder. "Don't worry. I'll take good care of her."

Oh for stars' sake. Seth would bait a fly if he thought he could get a rise out of it. She'd be irritated about it but she was already too pissed off at one person in the room to have time for another.

"We'll wait," Kaden ground out.

Nyx shrugged, retrieved her short sword from the counter, buckled it back on, and followed Seth out the door. Let Kaden escort them if it made him feel better about everything.

The walk gave her too much time to think. Too much time to be angry. Black flickered along her veins. She tried desperately to think of anything non-violent—puppies, kittens, adorable meerkats, anything. She was envisioning a puppy-kitten-meerkat huddle when snaky tendrils of shadow on the tunnel walls flickered at the edges of her vision.

The shadows weren't being cast from anyone in their group, but no one else seemed to notice them. She told herself she had to be imagining it, but then Calista had said a *darkness* was waking in the Station, and what was more dark than shadow?

More tendrils snaked along the wall and she risked a glance

back at Maruca and Kaden. Both of the Moor siblings looked like they were in mortal agony, but neither seemed to be worried about anything. Seth wasn't reacting either and—

The tendrils of shadow coalesced, a fanged dragon's head ripping from the wall, its snapping maw going straight for Nyx. She dove to the side, short sword clearing its sheath, the hilt an odd grip in her hand with her bandage. She readied and—

The shadow disappeared. Kaden and Maruca were staring at her like she'd lost her mind, at least until Seth doubled over laughing.

"Oh, you should have seen your face, Nyxi. It's better than that time I made you think Belle was a unicorn." He laughed so hard tears leaked out the corners of his eyes, and those tendrils of shadow danced and flickered around his wrists.

Stars-cursed tricksters.

"Seth. Connor. Hawthorne." She growled each syllable of his name, re-sheathed her sword and advanced on him. She played the part of being angry with him even if she wasn't. She couldn't explain how, but she knew that he'd done it to draw her out of the blackness of her own thoughts, to cheer her up, and she found it unexpectedly touching.

"Nyx Ilera Mira Fortuna," Seth replied innocently.

Nyx stopped, just stopped, as the missing two parts of her name settled into her. The mix of sadness and anger that passed across Seth's face told her he understood exactly what had halted her.

"You didn't know?"

She shook her head. Her license, everything on Earth had just listed her as Nyx Fortuna. She'd assumed she didn't have a middle name. Not everyone did.

Seth's hands curled into fists. "If we ever find your mother, I may kill her before you can ask her anything."

"It's not a big deal." She was holding them all up for something as stupid as getting sappy over the fact she had middle names. "It doesn't matter."

"It does." Seth closed the distance between them, brushed the backs of his fingers across her cheek like they were the only two people in the tunnel. "Ilera and Mira were your grandmothers' names. Ilera on your father's side, Mira on your mother's. It's traditional in Hidden lineages."

"Thank you."

He gave her a half smile. "Any time."

He started off down the tunnel again. When they reached the Den and Seth opened the door, he held up a hand when Kaden and Maruca moved forward.

"My place, my rules. You two stay out here. Nyxi, my home is of course your home."

No way was she staying out in the tunnel with not one but two glowering Moor siblings. If it pissed Kaden off, so much the better. If he was going to be unreasonable, she was going to be petty. She stepped over the threshold with Seth on her heels, and the stone door slid swiftly shut behind them.

The Den was nothing like her ordered trove on Earth. No, this room could only truly be described as a hoard. All manner of objects filled it—from jewels and weapons and ornate cushions, to expensive rugs and tapestries, chests, boxes, and books, and shelves that displayed everything from exotic seashells to the bleached-white skulls of creatures Nyx didn't recognize.

"This cannot all belong to you."

Seth grinned at her. "I wish. Most of it was here when I moved in. Imagine my disappointment when I found I couldn't take anything out of the room I didn't bring in here myself."

He didn't appear to have brought many things into the room. He only filled a single pack, and that mostly with the contents of row upon row of the tiny drawers that lined an entire wall of the room. No matter how hard she looked, she couldn't see what he took out of them, his hands cloaked in illusion.

He emptied the last drawer and zipped the backpack closed.

"All set," he said brightly. Too brightly.

"Including the key?"

"Why wouldn't I get the key?" His voice and face were both the epitome of angelic, obviously fake, innocence. Despite every instinct she had telling her that evasion and subterfuge were just parts of how Seth was, she couldn't stop her frustration from mounting and boiling over.

"Oh, I don't know, maybe because you don't want to give it back to Bryn? Or because you think I can't be trusted to make this deal? Because you don't want to come back to Earth with me because I'm so fragile and useless that even though I'm a *Guardian*, for stars' sakes, and I have an entire Station that answers to me, I can't handle that Kumir are hunting you?"

She braced herself, waiting for him to tell her that it wasn't that he didn't trust *her*, it was that he didn't trust *Bryn*. It wasn't that he didn't think she could handle herself, it was that he had more experience, and Kumir were dangerous, and any number of other excuses masquerading as reasons that people gave when they didn't want to tell someone the truth.

"Okay."

She blinked. "What does okay mean?"

"It means okay. If you're certain you can square things with Bryn, that your friend has enough pull with her, then okay. I trust you."

She narrowed her eyes. "Just like that?"

"You've never let me down. And for the record, I never thought you couldn't *handle* my problems. I thought you shouldn't have to."

He turned away from her and waded into a pile of rugs and expensive-looking fabric. He dropped to his knees, disappearing from view. There was a clattering, a banging, and a muffled curse from Seth before he stood up again holding...shadow. It danced in and out of his fingers like a small, lazy snake and made serpentine loops about his hand. He gave it a stern look and the shadow stilled, then solidified into a thin, fingerless glove that stretched tight against his hand.

He waved the hand at her lazily. "One Key to Shadow."

19

———

They hadn't gotten far from the Den when a tremor wracked the Station. Nyx stumbled as the ground quaked and threw out a hand to break her fall.

"Is this normal?" Maruca asked sharply.

"No," Seth answered. "Nyx?"

She knew what he was asking, and she had her answer when the wall gave beneath her palm, soft like mud, and she yanked her hand back a second before it solidified again. Clearly, Calista had been overly optimistic about their ability to delay the darkness.

"Get us out of here. Now."

Seth took off down the tunnel and Nyx sprinted after him, Kaden and Maruca falling in behind her. The Station trembled again, less violently this time, and Nyx hoped that meant Calista was at least temporarily gaining the upper hand against whatever was waking in these halls.

Seth took branching tunnels seemingly at random, his long legs eating up the distance in a steady lope she had to push herself to keep pace with. "How much farther?" she barked out.

"Not much."

That was when the tunnel lights shut off. Nyx stumbled in

the sudden darkness and came to a stop, right on top of Seth's heels. Of all the things she could have brought on this trip, she'd never once thought of a flashlight.

Behind and to her right, Maruca muttered something unintelligible. Nyx looked in that general direction just as blue flames burst to light in Maruca's hands, bathing the tunnel in a soft glow for a few feet around them.

The tunnel shook, groaned, and a loud crack rent the air. The ground ahead of them fissured, and a foot-wide gap opened and continued to grow.

"Go," Nyx yelled, and pitched herself forward. Seth caught up to her as she hit the break and they pushed off at the same time, clearing the now three-foot divide in tandem. They scrambled out of the way as Kaden and Maruca landed behind them, then Seth was leading them all down another, narrower tunnel. As they ran, it narrowed further, what had once been a six foot wide passageway now down to three.

"Seth, the damn walls are closing in," Nyx yelled.

"Aware," he shot back, and since she knew he didn't want to die any more than she did, she shoved down her rising panic and didn't distract him by talking again. By the time he skidded to a stop her heart was doing its best imitation of a wild bird trapped in a glass cage, only a scant inch of air between either of her shoulders and the walls.

Seth ran his fingers over the roof of the tunnel, strumming in an unlocking pattern she couldn't follow. The walls scraped against her arms and she turned sideways, flattening her back against one wall.

What if the hatch didn't open? What if Calista didn't have enough autonomy left to *let* it open? How complete was this darkness's control over the Station?

They had nowhere else to go, no *time* to go anywhere else. If earth magic was a thing that existed, none of them had it, and even if they did, Nyx doubted it would be strong enough to overcome the Station.

Damn it, she did not want to die in—

The hatch popped up, glorious sunshine and fresh air bursting through. Seth dragged her over and boosted her through the opening. She grabbed his arms as he came up after her, pulling him over the lip.

Maruca came through hot on his heels, aided by a boost from Kaden. She leaned down immediately, grabbing his shoulder, panic on her face. The walls were so close now he had no room to jump, no way to lever himself up out of the tunnel. Nyx grabbed onto Kaden, ignoring the bite in her injured hands, and Seth took hold of his other side. Between them and Maruca they hauled, dragging Kaden up a few inches.

It wasn't enough, wasn't fast enough. The walls were too close. Kaden wasn't light, they had shit for leverage at such an awkward angle, and Kaden didn't have the room to help them.

He was going to die. He was going to be crushed alive while she was holding onto him, and it was going to be her fault. Her fault for disappearing with Seth without a word, her fault for waking the darkness.

She searched for that place inside her that had felt this alien Station as she felt her own. For the call that had woken her in her sleep. For the connection she'd felt inside their Heart. She clutched at it and screamed, every ounce of her terror pouring out in three harsh, pleading syllables. "Calista!"

For one heart-stopping second nothing happened. Then the tunnel groaned, shuddered, froze. The three of them jerked Kaden up. He got his hands on the ground and pushed as far up as he could, his waist level with the street, but he still didn't have the room to move his legs, to pull himself the rest of the way out.

Nyx and Seth squatted to either side of him, each grabbing one of his legs, and on a silent count of three pushed up. Kaden's feet cleared the tunnel a fraction of a second before Calista lost whatever willpower had let them answer Nyx's plea, and the tunnel walls slammed together with a judder and a poof of red smoke.

On her hands and knees, Nyx drew in ragged breaths, staring at the tunnel that was no longer a tunnel before Seth slammed the hatch closed and it once more became innocuous-looking street. Nyx couldn't bring herself to look at Kaden. He'd almost died right in front of her.

Her stomach heaved and she squeezed her eyes shut, fighting against the tidal wave of rising nausea. Which was why she didn't see Maruca move. She *felt* her presence, suddenly in front of her, and opened her eyes a second before the woman back-handed her. The force of the blow knocked Nyx's head to the side. Her teeth bit clean through the inside of her lip and blood gushed over her tongue.

She deflected the second blow aimed at her head, caught Maruca's wrist on her third attempt, grateful adrenaline meant she didn't give a damn about the pain it caused her hand. She turned her head to the side and spat a stream of blood before she spoke. "I'll give you the one. But one's all you get."

Maruca tore her arm free, but she didn't launch another strike. "This was your fault."

Nyx could argue, but even she wouldn't buy her own lies. "Yeah. It was."

Maruca's eyes were cold and hard. "I am done," she said, her voice flat and toneless. "I am done hauling your ass out of problems—"

When, precisely, did Maruca think *she* had hauled Nyx's ass out of a problem?

"—I am done with you nearly getting my brother killed. I am done with *you*." Her declaration finished, she stalked out of the alley, the people on the main market streets giving her a wide berth as she emerged. She did wait, once there, probably because Kaden hadn't yet followed her.

Nyx finally looked at him. It seemed stupid to her now that she'd just walked away from him earlier. That she hadn't pushed him to really explain anything. Maybe it was cliché that him almost dying in front of her had made her realize she didn't want to let him just walk out of her life again, but she didn't care.

Unfortunately, if she thought the experience would have the effect of making him speak actual words, she was wrong. He simply returned her stare, and whatever the hell was going on behind his eyes, she didn't know what it was. After a few seconds he dropped her gaze and went after Maruca.

She shook her head and rolled to her feet, making for the mouth of the alley. She'd talk to him when they got back to the Keep.

"You know," Seth said, falling into step beside her, "I'm beginning to think you aren't very good at making friends."

"Oh, fuck off," she snapped. But the words lacked any real heat. Infuriating, Seth might be. But he also had a way of making everything hurt just a little bit less.

"I'm also beginning to think," he said, his voice softer so as not to carry, "that you didn't quite tell me everything, as the whole near-death-by-tunnel ordeal seemed very specifically aimed at us."

It was one of those moments she would have expected the Harvester to give a little flare of warmth against her chest. It didn't, and if she was glad not to have heat on the burn wound it had left her, she was still weirded out by its sudden impersonation of an inanimate object.

"I'll explain later."

"When?"

"When we're home."

"Fine. But if you're going to make me wait that long to find out why my home tried to crush me to death, I'm going to need you to take this and Hide it." He shrugged the backpack off his shoulder and handed it to her.

She took it, the bag dangling from her fingers, but she didn't immediately try to Hide it. She was done agreeing to keep things for people without asking any questions.

"What's in it?" She was pretty sure she already knew. But she wanted to know if he'd tell her, or if he would lie to her. What decision he made would set the course of their future, would determine how much or how little she trusted him.

"Remember how I said the Keeper can't access the cache of unspelled planet stones without the Key?"

Something tight eased in her chest at the realization that he wasn't just going to brush her off. To tell her not to worry about it. "Yeah."

"Well, what I didn't mention is the Keeper usually has a readily accessible stash of already-spelled stones on-hand and available for use and sales." He flashed her a grin. "I may have stolen the majority of them when I left."

Only Seth, she thought. "No wonder she wants to kill you. Fine. I promise I'll keep it Hidden."

Seth looked at her a little strange.

"What?"

"You don't really remember how to use your magic, do you?"

"I promise to keep the thing Hidden and it's Hidden. Why? Is it not working?"

"Oh, it's working. It's just that the promise thing is what they teach Hidden kids to do to use their power. I don't think I've heard you say the whole, 'I promise to keep it Hidden' spiel since you were five."

Annoyingly, she felt her cheeks flush with heat. "Really sorry if my juvenile magic use offends you, but seventy percent of my life is a giant blank so I'm sort of winging it."

"I'm not offended. I just don't get it. Elena drilled you on this shit every day of our very, very boring lives. And then she just wiped it all out and dumped you. What was the point?"

"This may shock you, but I have no idea." It was also something she hadn't really thought about. She'd spent so much time wondering why her mother had left her, Hidden her from herself, that she hadn't considered much about the fact that she'd taken away her understanding of her own power. How it worked. How to use it.

And Seth did have a point. Why train her to be good at something only to essentially undo all that work?

"But it's another good reason to find her."

"I don't think there's ever going to be a *good* reason to find that woman," Seth muttered.

She shoved the bag back at his chest with a grin. "You can haul it around yourself." Between Gleipnir on one arm and her sword sheath across her back, strapping on a bag wasn't really in the cards. She dropped into a solemn voice. "I *promise* to keep it Hidden even while it's on your sorry hide."

T he second they stepped into the Keep's spire they were surrounded. It wasn't entirely a surprise. Nyx had seen soldiers with the Keeper's symbol flitting throughout the Market, and she was sure news that she was returning in Seth's company had made it back to the Keeper's ears before they'd gotten within a quarter mile of the spire.

Still, she could have done without having a dozen swords pointed at her from the ring of soldiers encircling them. Essteria stepped through the ranks, her reptilian eyes glinting in the low light.

"Hawthorne. You come with me."

"He doesn't go anywhere without me." Nyx lifted the length of Gleipnir between them. "And I want to see the Keeper."

"I can solve that problem." Essteria's hand darted out, caught the length of Gleipnir between her obsidian claws, and twisted. The disbelief on her face when the chain didn't cleave in two was comical.

"Yeah, it's not going to break."

Essteria's eyes narrowed. "And what is to stop me from removing both your hands and resolving the matter that way?"

"The fact that if you do, your master will never get what she desperately wants." Nyx hoped it came out more confident than she felt. Losing her hand was not an option that particularly appealed to her. "I think that would upset her. Enormously."

Essteria thought it over for a moment before she acceded with a long hiss. "Very well. But you try anything, Hawthorne—"

"And you'll what?" Seth drawled. "Kill me? The last time you tried it didn't work out so well for you. Though it looks like your tail grew back after all. I hear it's a one in three chance for your species."

The tail in question flicked angrily from side to side, and Nyx saw a shiny white scar a foot down from the base. Essteria looked to Nyx. "You don't want to hand him over then he's your responsibility."

"Wonderful," Nyx muttered, following Essteria to the portal that opened as the commander turned. "Just what I always wanted. My very own sarcastic, egotistical, high maintenance *responsibility.*"

Seth flashed her a grin. "You forgot talented, handsome, and utterly irresistible."

"We need to discuss your unfortunate insistence on antagonizing everyone around you."

Seth just winked at her, and they followed Essteria through the portal into what Nyx thought of as the main portal receiving room. Kaden and Maruca promptly abandoned them, heading back toward the floor their rooms were on. Nyx tried not to let it bother her, instead following Essteria and her contingent of guards to the throne room.

The very empty throne room. The unit broke apart and soldiers moved to cover each of the room's exits.

"The Keeper is busy," Essteria said with a glint in her eyes. "You'll have to wait."

Oh good. The other thing she had always wanted was to be kept waiting in a room with no seating areas so that a shadowy criminal lord could prove a point.

She didn't want to be in here right now. She wanted to go after Kaden and have the conversation they should have had earlier. One where they didn't just talk past each other. One where she actually made him answer her instead of having to guess what he meant by the long stretches of silence he tended to give in response to her questions.

She had protected him and the others, had almost *died* hiding them from the All Council. That couldn't mean *nothing* to him. Or if it could, she wanted to hear him say it to her face.

She took a breath, held it, then exhaled slowly. Once she was done negotiating with Bryn, she would find him. Maybe near-death would have loosened his tongue. Or at least his emotions. Of course, if he did come back to Earth, she might have to erect an entire new section in the Station if he and Seth were going to live in the same building.

Stars, she missed her Station. It felt strange here, standing in a room she couldn't feel, couldn't manipulate. She couldn't even summon a damn chair here. There was *one* chair in the room, and Seth had decided it had his name on it. He walked over to Bryn's throne and dropped onto it, lounging with one leg hooked over a stone arm.

The guard closest to the throne, a tentacled bipedal race Nyx recognized as Dresidian, turned positively livid. "Get off."

"But it just feels so *right*," Seth countered. Hadn't she suggested, mere minutes ago, that he stop antagonizing people?

"Get. Off."

Seth sat up and leaned forward, resting his elbows on his thighs, and bared his teeth. "Step away from that door and make me."

The tentacles that passed for hair on a Dresidian's head quivered, serpentining around his face in angry, whiplike motions. The guard didn't move. She wondered if that was because he feared the physical threat Seth might pose, or feared that if he moved even an inch from the door Seth would somehow disappear through it.

Whichever it was, the guard was definitely not going to oust Seth from his seat. Seth leaned back against the throne, smirking. "That's what I thought."

Nyx pinched the bridge of her nose. "How is it you've been living in a criminal underworld for almost ten years with that attitude and no one's killed you?"

"I used to wonder the same thing." Bryn strolled into the room and stopped five feet from her throne.

"Bryn, darling." Seth beamed. "You should have sent me an invitation. If I'd known you missed me so much I never would have stayed away."

Magic sparked in the air around Bryn, drowning the space between her and Seth in dense, liquid fire. That heat surged for the throne, black stone absorbing the fire she gave it until it began to emanate a heat all its own.

Seth continued to lounge. Five seconds. Ten. The air around Nyx grew stifling. Any second now she was certain to hear the hiss of Seth's skin crackling.

Fifteen seconds.

Seth stood lazily, stretching like a cat.

"On second thought, it's a little tacky. You should really have a word with your decorator." Seth strolled down the steps from the platform and took up space beside Nyx again.

The heat vanished as Bryn assumed her throne and looked to Nyx. "Do you have my key?"

Why yes, Your Majesty, of course, Your Majesty.

Aloud she said, "He'll hand it over in exchange for access to the Keep's library."

"We agreed you could haul his sorry ass off my planet in exchange for the key, and now you want more?"

"Technically," Nyx argued, "that agreement was contingent

on your people finding him for me. Since they didn't, we don't have an agreement."

"If we don't have an agreement then he has no guarantee of safe passage here." Bryn nodded to Essteria, who stepped forward with entirely too much alacrity.

"I really wouldn't."

"Why ever not?"

"For one, where he goes, I go."

"And what's to stop me from throwing you in the dungeons with him?"

Of course the Keep had dungeons.

"I believe that would be me," Evra said, striding in from the far door. "I thought we agreed you would send for me when Nyx returned."

"My courier must have gotten lost."

Evra snorted. "How convenient."

Bryn gave a long exhale, like a dragon on the verge of breathing smoke. "Leave us." She didn't even have to look at the guards for them to obey and exit.

Nyx managed, through sheer virtuous self-restraint, not to laugh at hearing someone in real life imperiously utter the words "Leave us." Seth did not.

Bryn didn't even bother to glare at him, the whole of her attention on Evra. "What do you want from me, Ev?"

"For you to not throw my friend in the dungeons, for one."

"Do you want your sister to be able to go home or not? Because for that to happen, *he,*" she jerked her head at Seth, "needs to return my damn key."

"It's my damn key," Seth shot back, "and if you want to get technical about how the rules of succession in this place work, the whole damn Keep is mine."

Wait, but that would mean…

Nyx rounded on Seth. "You killed the last Keeper?"

"He most certainly did not."

"I definitely did," Seth countered.

"You told me *you* killed the Keeper," Evra said to Bryn.

"No," Bryn said through gritted teeth, "I told you the last Keeper was dead and I took his place."

"I think you mean took *my* rightful place."

"You didn't kill him either," Bryn snarled. "If you want to be so *technical* about it he died of natural causes."

"He wouldn't have died from those natural causes if it weren't for me. Therefore I killed him, therefore this place is technically mine."

"Are you challenging me?" The gleam in Bryn's eyes indicated she dearly hoped he was.

"Stars no. I don't actually *want* to be the Keeper. It's a shit job and people are always trying to kill you."

"You…do not want to be the Keeper?"

"Not even a little."

Bryn looked, if possible, even angrier. "Then why won't you give me back my fucking key?"

"Like Nyxi said, I want access to the library."

Evra shot her a questioning glance and mouthed, *Nyxi?*

Nyx shrugged.

"What do you want in the library?" Bryn asked.

"Books?" Seth offered innocently. "The public libraries on this planet are simply non-existent and I need to expand my intellectual horizons."

"No."

"You have something against knowledge?"

"Tell me what you want or the answer is no."

"Is the answer really worth you never getting your key back?"

"I will rip out your throat before you leave this Keep with it again." Bryn's gaze was livid and she shifted forward like she would move toward them.

Nyx stepped in front of Seth, one hand on the hilt of her short sword, the other on the dagger at her thigh.

"You won't touch him."

When Bryn looked like she might physically contest that statement, Evra stepped in front of Nyx.

"It is a library," Evra pointed out. "And he's going to give you everything you want if you let him in. Is it really worth fighting over some books?"

"There are more dangerous things in that library than books," Bryn said, but she slumped against the back of the throne. "Very well. I'll give you an hour in the library."

Seth narrowed his gaze. "Three days. It's a *large* library."

"Three hours."

"Two days."

"Three hours."

"Bryn, I couldn't even walk the entirety of the library in three hours. Two days."

"Half a day."

"One and a half."

"One day, dawn to dusk, and you're supervised the entire time."

"Deal."

She held out her hand. "The key."

"You get the key when I get into the library."

"Then we will go now."

"You said one day, dawn to dusk. I'm afraid dawn has already come and gone so I'll have to decline until tomorrow."

Bryn tensed, relaxed.

"Very well." The Keeper of Shadows turned to Nyx. "If he takes anything else of mine while he is here, I will consider it your responsibility." She stood, descended the dais of her throne, and swept from the room.

Nyx sincerely pitied anyone who had the misfortune to run across the Keeper in the next hour or three and was just glad she was gone. She remembered Evra telling her Bryn had been "fun" when they met and for the life of her Nyx couldn't imagine it.

"That went well," Evra said, voice bright with sarcasm. "You are lucky Kaden stormed through the floor like he'd just fought off a pack of Rega wolves or I wouldn't have known you were back."

Kaden.

"I need to do something." Nyx held up the wrist bearing Gleipnir to Evra. "Can you take him for a minute?"

"Am I dog now?" Seth protested.

Evra and Nyx ignored him.

"Sure, I'll take him."

Nyx transferred Gleipnir from her wrist to Evra's. "No treats, and he gets cranky if you don't walk him," she said sweetly.

Seth snorted.

Nyx swiped her hand through the well of portal magic on the way out—if there was no one here to see her steal it then she might as well—and made for the stairs that led down to their floor. The closer she got to Kaden's room the slower she walked, and by the time she got there she'd half decided to turn back around.

She didn't even know what she would say. She certainly wasn't going to apologize, or beg him to stay. So why was she even here?

Because she was hoping *he* would apologize, she realized. Or at the very least admit that he'd turned what should have been a discussion into an all-or-nothing ultimatum.

Just knock and get it over with. She'd figure out what she wanted to say when she had to. She lifted her fist and rapped three times on the door.

From within came a non-verbal noise that could have been construed as permission to enter, so Nyx did. Kaden stood beside the bed with his arms crossed. Nyx tried not to remember how she'd practically attacked him on that very same bed, tried not to remember the taste of him on her tongue, so recent.

Tried, and failed.

If Kaden was having any similar troubles, it didn't show. He looked…empty. Cold. Blank. Not like he wore a mask over his emotions but like he didn't have any at all.

He was also packed. Apparently, near-death had loosened neither his tongue nor his emotions. Whatever tactful thing she might have come up with to say disappeared.

"Were you even going to say goodbye?" she demanded.

"No." Not a trace of hesitation or guilt in his voice, as if he couldn't have imagined why he owed her any farewell at all.

"Wow." She turned on her heel, made it to the door before she shook her head and turned back. "You're not even sorry, are you?"

"For doing what I have to? No."

"What you *have* to? Is that a magical phrase in your head that you think absolves you of any responsibility for the things you do?"

"I have done nothing *but* take responsibility for the things I do. I went to Arkadia to take responsibility for the things I did. To protect the people I care about."

"Yes," she agreed softly, "you did. I guess I'm just finally realizing that you don't seem to feel any responsibility toward me. I'm simply a byproduct of the things you needed to accomplish. You needed the Harvester Hidden, I served that purpose. You needed protection running from the All Council, I was conveniently available. You were screwed up when you came back from Arkadia and there I was. Familiar."

A muscle ticked along his jaw. "That isn't fair."

"Fair?" she echoed. "You want to talk about *fair*? You know where I was left in the mess I just described? Alone and dealing with shit I had no idea how to handle. I *still* don't know what I'm supposed to do with this" —she pulled out the Harvester— "and you're just dumping me with it again. I took a lot of risks for you, and maybe I didn't know what they all were when I left my Station for Arkadia but I have damn well known what they were the last three months I have protected all of you.

"You think for one second if the All Council finds out what I've done I won't be dead or worse? And you're just going to bail at the first opportunity because now you don't need me anymore."

His body was one tightly-strung line. "If that's what you think of me, then perhaps my leaving is for the best."

"You're still putting all of this on me, aren't you?" She shook her head, incredulous. "If you need to blame me to make yourself feel better then by all means, go ahead. But if you have any humanity, don't force Morgen to go with you."

"I don't have to force Morgen to do anything. Unlike some, I don't have to keep a person on a chain and drag them around to keep them with me. Did you leave Seth tied to a post downstairs or something?"

Suddenly the space between them wasn't nearly large enough. She took a step back, felt for the chaos in her veins and for once it answered without summoning a tidal wave of rage. Or maybe her emotions were already so turbulent that the effect was simply different. Liquid heaviness spread through her, a cold damper that blunted the edges of her pain.

"You know what? Fucking go. Have a nice life. And Kaden? I think it would be best if you never came back to Earth."

She didn't look back when she walked out, didn't allow herself to think about anything other than setting one foot in front of the other until she made it to Morgen's room. He sat on his bed, staring at the floor while he twirled a pen in and out of his fingers. The few clothes he'd brought with him were strewn on the bed rather than tucked into his pack.

He looked up when she walked in and she understood exactly what he was feeling without him having to say a word.

Nyx settled onto the mattress next to him and held out her arms. "Hug?" she offered.

He laughed and nodded.

"You don't have to go, you know."

"I wish it were that simple, little Guardian."

"It could be."

He gave her a final squeeze and let her go.

"Maybe in a different world."

He looked so sad that Nyx wanted to go knock both of the Moor siblings around a few times. Selfish. They were *both* completely and utterly selfish.

"If you ever wake up and decide the world *is* different, you should know you're always welcome to stay on Earth while you figure things out. And if you never do, I'd like it if you visited sometime. *Just* you, though."

"What happened between you and Kaden?"

"Turns out sex wasn't our problem." In retrospect, sex might have been the only functional part of their relationship.

Morgen sighed. "I guess that's what you get for taking relationship advice from someone who's never been in one."

Nyx stared at him. "Never?"

"What? Sex is great and all but relationships are sticky affairs. This may shock you, little Guardian, but I happen to have high standards for an actual partner. I just never met anyone who quite measured up before..." He trailed off.

Evra. Before Evra.

Nyx stood. "When are you leaving?"

"Half an hour. Planet choices were surprisingly limited."

"Yeah, about that. Come back in a few weeks and you should find that's changed. Take care of yourself, Morgen. I'm going to miss you."

"I'm going to miss you too, little Guardian."

She walked out before the goodbye could drag on, stupidly afraid she was going to cry and feeling like she'd just lost a brother. She found Evra and Seth still in the throne room.

"Finally," Seth said, "I was beginning to fear we'd be stuck here all day—hey, are you okay?"

"I'm fine." Nyx turned to Evra. "If you have anything you might want to say to Morgen, you should do it now."

"What do you—Oh. I see." The Amazon held out her wrist. Nyx took Gleipnir back from her and wondered, as she walked away, if anything Evra had to say would change Morgen's mind.

20

———

Secretly, Nyx had hoped the entrance into the Keep's library would be somewhere secretive and moderately occult-looking, and she was not disappointed.

Nyx, Seth, Evra, Bryn, and a contingent of guards walked down a series of zig-zagging, downward-sloping halls, glass spheres set into sconces every twelve feet flaring to light as they went further down the passageways. They went down and down, until the weight of the earth above them pressed in on Nyx like a weighted blanket wrapped tight around her.

She understood the surface of the planet wasn't particularly friendly, but the Shadow Keep took living underground to new depths, so to speak.

The path ended abruptly at a dead-end wall, its black stone cut with intricate whorls and loops, all weaving and diving together until staring at them made Nyx dizzy. Seth lifted his hand to the wall. The piece of shadow wrapped over his skin squirmed and writhed in anticipation. His palm met stone and the shadow let out a low, whispered sigh and slithered off him. The whorls and loops began to move and undulate with an intensity that made Nyx fight to keep her eyes open.

At last, the designs in the center of the wall slid each to a side and a barren area appeared in the middle, splitting the wall into two separate sections that swung inward. Cold air rushed out to greet them, frigid as wind off a snow-capped mountain. Beyond the doors, the darkness beckoned.

Gleipnir grew taut between them as Seth stepped forward. He brushed his hand against the doorway as he went. Was it Nyx's imagination, or did a sliver of shadow jump to his hand?

Nyx followed after him rather than let Gleipnir lengthen the space between them, and lights flickered on as they stepped inside. Bryn paused in the doorway and waited until the guards were all through to place her own palm to the doorway and reclaim the key. As shadow left the carved stone crevices, the doors swung silently closed.

Bryn gave Seth a cold smile. "I don't make the same mistakes as my predecessor." A predatory hunger claimed Bryn's face as she looked around.

Nyx had to admit the place was impressive. The ceilings towered well above fourteen feet, and bookshelves carved directly into the stone went all the way to the top. Pillars arched from floor to ceiling, shelves built into their wide, circular lengths. Some held books, others what Nyx would have called bric-a-brac if she hadn't suspected that everything in the room was dangerous. As for the size... she couldn't truly fathom it, save to guess it would hold at least ten average suburban American homes, and then some.

"You have until dusk," Bryn reminded them in a suitably authoritarian voice. She strode off, exiting through one of the many, many doors that branched off from the main room.

Of the guards, two remained at the entrance, and where Nyx would have expected the rest to be breathing down her and Seth's necks, they kept a healthy distance.

She surveyed them, her mouth pursing at the way their gazes would come to rest on Seth for the briefest of moments before skittering off, as if afraid to be caught looking.

"Seth," she said slowly, "what exactly did you do for the previous Keeper?"

"Oh, a little of this, a little of that." He tugged on Gleipnir. "Come on, let's search in this direction." She followed him, unable to help but marvel at what they passed, and barely paid any attention to where her feet were going.

So it was that she didn't realize how close Seth had gotten to her until, with a speed that made her dizzy, one hand wrapped around her waist and the other covered her mouth as he pulled her to him, spun them around a corner made of bookcases, and dragged her *through* the wall.

His hand stayed over her mouth. Her eyes went wide as she took in the narrow passageway they just barely fit into together. She turned her head to the right, looking at the seemingly impenetrable wall they had just stepped through. From this side it drifted like a soft, hazy fog through which she could hear the shouts of the guards, see their outlines as they frantically ran first left, then right, cursing and muttering as they tried to figure out where Seth and Nyx had gone.

Slowly, pointedly, Seth lowered his hand from her mouth and canted his head to the right, indicating the narrow passageway. His hand slid off her waist, trailed her hip on the way down, letting her go almost reluctantly. She shrugged it off and followed him, not daring to break the silence until he did.

They entered a small, tomb-like chamber filled with dust that didn't touch the outer library, and he shook himself like a dog after a bath.

"Guards," he said, as if that explained everything. "Monumental waste of money."

"Not that I'm complaining" —Nyx herself was not particularly fond of guards, or Bryn for that matter— "but where are we?"

"Secret passageways." Seth grinned. "You don't get to be the Shadow Keeper's spymaster without learning a few things even the Keeper doesn't know about. I'd rather our search didn't have an audience. And I doubt the records are in the main room anyway."

"Has it occurred to you," Nyx began, following him out of the mausoleum-like room and down another passageway, this one equally as narrow as the one they had entered through, "that Bryn may decide to lock us in this library out of spite?"

"She can try." Seth waggled his fingers and that flicker of shadow she'd known—*known*—he'd taken from the doorway danced in and out of his fingers. "But it's hard to lock a door with a broken key."

"She's going to kill us."

"She can't have been too serious about keeping me in sight or she'd never have left us alone. Not with those buffoons anyway. Greyson's been terrified of me ever since we went on that mission to Andor together."

One beat. Two. Curiosity got the better of her. "Do I even want to ask what happened on Andor?" Wherever that was.

"Well," Seth said conversationally, "there was this small matter involving an Andorian, a whip, and a bathtub full of vermilion blood. See, Andorians have this thing where—"

"I take it back," Nyx said. "I don't want to know."

Twelve rooms later, Nyx dug in her heels until Gleipnir pulled taut and dragged Seth to a stop.

"Seth, if you've been in here before why don't you know where the records are? And why didn't you just look at them then?"

"I've only been in here once, and it wasn't for very long. Hence, no time to explore."

"You had time to find a secret passageway."

"Please, secret passageways are my specialty. Once I found this one, I wanted more time in here. Adin had been Keeper long enough he'd gotten arrogant. Left the key thinking no one else would be able or ballsy enough to take it. So I did, and locked him in here."

"And?"

"And the Keep's walls shot through with red a few days later. It's what happens when a Keeper dies. Probably dehydration."

"That's how you killed the previous Keeper? You locked him in the library to die?"

"Actually, though I'd never admit it to Bryn, it technically *is* her fault Adin bought it. I was just going to bargain with him and let him out. But Bryn saw an opportunity to get what she'd wanted for years without all the messy infighting so she had me branded a traitor and hunted. Bryn could have taken the old Keeper out years ago but Adin had a lot of supporters in the Keep and she wanted to avoid the civil war killing him would cause.

"So when I took the key, Bryn issued a kill order on me. She was Adin's second and she was popular. I spent a very creative few weeks staying alive and by the time I could slow down long enough to breathe Bryn was the newly-minted Keeper, complete with all of Adin's loyal followers. So it may be the case I've rather enjoyed watching her try to cling to power while I hid the key right under her nose."

"And no one's been in this library since?"

"Nope."

"Then…the old Keeper's body. It's in here somewhere?"

"Don't worry, I'm sure it's the first thing Bryn went off to find. I wouldn't worry overmuch about stumbling onto it."

They stumbled onto it three rooms later. Adin's emaciated body lay slumped in an armchair, his head resting back with his eyes closed like he'd drifted off to sleep and never woken up. He looked like he was still only sleeping.

"Why—" Nyx's voice came out hoarse and whisper-soft. She cleared her throat. "Why is he so *preserved*?"

"We're in a library full of texts, some of which are centuries old, the rest of which are expected to last just as long. The whole building's spelled against decay." Seth looked at the bookshelves behind the dead Keeper and brightened visibly. "*There* are our records."

There was maybe two feet of space between the armchair and the bookcase behind it.

"You've got to be kidding me." Casually slipping around a guy who'd been dead for—well, she wasn't sure how long—and perusing the books in that body's vicinity was beyond her. Even if said body didn't look or smell dead. In fact, the lack of both made it creepier.

"If you don't want to help, you could always unchain me."

"I'm not an idiot. I do know the full range of your illusion magic." In truth, she trusted him when he'd said he wasn't going anywhere, but given Bryn's desire to kill him, Nyx thought it might be safer for Seth if he remained tethered to her a while longer.

"Yes, but can you *remember* that extent?"

"I'm not unchaining you."

"If I had a universal for every time a woman told me that, I'd be rich."

Nyx rolled her eyes. "Keep it in your pants."

"That is definitely not what you used to say."

"I was young and stupid and you were the only guy near my age in a twenty-mile radius." The figure flashed into her head, along with images. A cabin nestled into a small valley. Rows of crops and a water storage tank. A training arena marked out in a dirt rectangle. A barn with a hayloft, her and Seth…

Nyx shook her head.

"Pleasant memories?" Seth asked. His voice held its usual lilting mockery, but an undercurrent of—longing? Pain?—ran beneath it.

"So pleasant," Nyx said, letting her voice fall husky. She stepped closer. "I was in that cute little training arena knocking you flat on your ass."

"And you're sure that's *all* you remember?" He shifted toward her, his head canting down.

"Well." She wet her lips slightly, and Seth's gaze zeroed in on the movement. "There is this one really awful memory involving a hay loft and—"

He kissed her.

Time reversed and for a moment they were teenagers again, mouths and tongues tangling awkwardly, then later, clothes shed with an equal mix of eagerness and hesitation as they figured out how their bodies worked.

He kissed differently now, more practiced, his tongue gliding against hers in a smooth caress. Nyx was so surprised, so caught up in the tangle of memories that for a moment—just a moment —she forgot her present and kissed him back.

"Well, isn't this just adorable," a voice said. Bryn stood in the doorway, all glowering dark menace. "This must be why Kaden portaled out of here looking so…broken. Imagine a *woman* doing what a prison planet couldn't."

What was Bryn talking about? The only thing broken with Kaden was that he apparently didn't feel anything at all.

"Of course," Bryn added, her gaze falling to the length of Gleipnir between Nyx and Seth, "you know it can't really be consensual if he's literally chained to you, right?"

Nyx lifted her chin and met Bryn's gaze. She wasn't going to feel bad, wasn't going to let Bryn make her feel bad. Kaden had crushed her and kissing Seth—well, that was a mistake that didn't mean anything. It was just Seth being Seth and Nyx being…confused.

"Says the woman who had to bargain her way into getting her ex-girlfriend to spend time with her."

Anger flashed across Bryn's face and she ignored Nyx, turning to Seth. "I thought I made it clear this was a supervised visit."

"Oh please, those guards couldn't supervise a chicken. It's

hardly my fault if they couldn't keep up. And besides, we found you what you were looking for."

Nyx realized, with no small amount of self-disgust, that she'd forgotten about the dead body in the room, hidden from Bryn's view until Seth stepped back to reveal it.

Bryn inhaled sharply. "Out. Now."

"Sure thing." Seth slipped behind the chair, grabbed four volumes, and tugged Nyx out of the room with him. "Enjoy your reminiscing."

"I found it."

"Thank the stars." Nyx's head ached fiercely. Translator spells might let her read things in languages she'd never even heard of, but they weren't intended for long-term use, and after two hours of tediously going over two of the volumes line by line, her head was ready to explode. "So where are they? Where did they go?"

"I have no idea."

"It doesn't say where they bought a portal stone to?"

"Oh, it does. The problem is, they bought one to *everywhere*."

"I thought portal stones had to go to a specific planet."

"They do. They bought a stone for every inhabited planet in the known universe."

Griff had once told her how many inhabited planets were connected to the ley lines. She couldn't remember the precise number, but she'd thought it was over one-hundred. "But that would cost—"

"A fortune," Seth finished. "Several fortunes, actually. I may have been young when we came to Earth, but I can tell you my dad didn't have that kind of money lying around and I doubt your mother did either."

"What are you saying?"

"I'm saying that your mother had help. Powerful, influential help. The kind of help that has enough money to buy a small planet and then some."

"Do you have any idea who that person might have been?"

"How much do you remember about Elena?" he asked instead of answering.

"I—nothing. The only memories I've had come back are about you and your father." Nyx swallowed. "I couldn't even tell you what she looks like."

"Blonde and cold. Nothing like you. Trust me, that woman made a glacier seem inviting." At the look that crossed Nyx's face, Seth's voice softened. "I'm sorry. I'm sure that's not what you were hoping to hear about her."

"It doesn't matter," Nyx lied. "So what do we do now?"

"My advice?"

"Is something you don't ever want to take," Bryn's voice floated into the library's entrance chamber a second before she did. Floating after her horizontally, six feet above the ground and covered in a sheet, was what could only be Adin's body.

Wonder where she got the sheet? Nyx mused, then decided she was better off not knowing.

"Time's up," Bryn continued, "so I'll thank you to leave your books and return that little piece of shadow key to the door."

Seth looked so surprised Nyx had to choke back laughter.

"I'm not an idiot, Seth Hawthorne. And you're far easier to manage when you think you're getting away with things."

That, Nyx decided, she would have to keep in mind.

21

———

Nyx went through all the rooms on their floor, even though she knew what she would find. Kaden's and Maruca's empty rooms didn't surprise her, but she had been hoping that Morgen and Kalvar would have stayed. At least she'd said goodbye to Morgen. She'd known, deep down, that if Maruca left Kalvar would find a way to leave with her, but it still hurt that the kid hadn't even said goodbye. Then again, Maruca likely hadn't given him the chance.

Seth didn't say anything as they swept from room to room, and that was good. She'd probably take his head off for anything he said right then. She stopped at Evra's door and knocked.

"It's me," Nyx called.

"Come in."

Nyx spun out Gleipnir, opened the door and shut it in Seth's face before he could follow her in, grateful Gleipnir was slender enough to fit beneath the door's bottom gap.

"My feelings are hurt," he called from the hallway. Nyx ignored him, but a small smile tugged at her lips.

Evra sat perched at the edge of her bed, one ankle crossed over the opposite knee and a letter in her hands.

"Morgen," Evra said, waving the letter. "You know they are all gone?"

"I saw. I'd hoped Morgen would stay. What did his letter say?"

Evra folded the letter into a square and tucked it into her pocket. "Most of it was an egregious amount of poetic nonsense going on about how vehemently he will miss me and think of me daily, etcetera, etcetera.

"The one line of any substance was yet vague and convoluted, but I believe it means he is going off to do something monumentally stupid. Should he survive that act of supreme foolishness, I believe we may see him again."

Hope was at once a wonderful and terrifying feeling. "Really?"

"Yes, really."

"Wait, so if *we* are going to see him again does that mean you're coming back to the Station after your week's up? You're not staying here?"

Evra stared at Nyx with her patented you-are-such-a-moron-I-can't-even expression. "Why would I stay here?"

"Because you and Bryn have history and she broke your heart and now she obviously wants you back?"

Evra sighed. "She may have, at one point. But I am not in love with Bryn anymore. I didn't realize that until we came here. And Bryn, if she ever gets her head out of her territorially-possessive ass, will realize she is not in love with me anymore either. She isn't a bad person—"

"Isn't she a criminal mastermind?" Nyx asked.

"—she just has trouble letting go of things," Evra finished with a glare at Nyx's interruption.

"And you'll help her to let things go?" Nyx suggested innocently.

"I am beginning to think Morgen has rubbed off on you."

"Yeah, well. He better come back alive because I miss him already."

"Me too," Evra said softly. "If it isn't too sore of a subject, may I ask what happened with you and Kaden?"

It *was* a sore subject, but, "It turned out he wasn't who I thought he was. And maybe that's for the best. When is Tam going home?"

"In an hour. I imagine Bryn will send you off then, too."

"She suggested as much. I don't think she's too keen on having Seth here any longer than she has to."

At that, Gleipnir rattled against Nyx's wrist.

"Getting bored out here, ladies."

"If he is going to be living at the Station, we have to come up with some ground rules," Evra said.

Nyx started to laugh and then stopped. Living at the Station. She...hadn't thought about it that way, she realized. Kaden and Bryn's taunts about Nyx keeping Seth chained to her surfaced and bit deep. Probably because they held a kernel of truth.

No matter what he said or what she told everyone else, she wasn't entirely convinced that Seth would stay once she set him free. He had a backpack full of stones that could take him anywhere in the universe, once he was no longer physically tied to her. Maybe, now that he'd gotten what he'd wanted from the Shadow Keep, he'd decide to use those stones. He'd always wanted to see the universe.

No, she realized, that wasn't quite right. *They* had always wanted to see it, and that was exactly why they'd gotten its image tattooed on their hearts. But she couldn't see it now and she didn't know if Seth would want to stay.

She looked at the shining length of Gleipnir trailing from her wrist and realized it didn't matter. She couldn't keep him chained to her forever and she didn't want to. She didn't want people who stayed around her only because they had to. So if he wanted to leave, she would let him. But for his sake—and her own—she'd follow the deal she'd made with Bryn and take him off Tenebris Umbra first.

"I'll miss you," she told Evra. Giving in to the impulse, she hugged the Amazon. Evra did not return the hug, but patted her awkwardly on the back until Nyx let go.

"It is a week, not a lifetime."

"Yeah, well, just don't decide you want to become Mistress of the Shadow World while I'm gone, okay?"

Evra stared at her.

"Right," Nyx said. "Well, umm—"

Evra rolled her eyes. "There is another matter that requires your attention. Kalvar wanted to speak with you before he left, but Maruca wasn't willing to wait."

"Color me shocked."

Evra frowned. "Shock is not a color?"

"One day, Evra, you're going to have to learn to accept the sarcastic undertones and not try to make sense of the actual meaning."

"I am certain no Scythian sayings would lose so much in translation."

"Yeah, yeah, the mighty Amazons are leagues above we mere mortals. What did Kalvar want?"

"As you know, several hundred people were freed in Kalvar's near-suicidal raid on the slave market. Of those, some had friends or families to return to, and a great many left with the Moors to try their hands at mercenary life. However, there are a little over one hundred left who have nowhere to go."

"And Kalvar would like me to offer them the hospitality of Earth Between?" she guessed.

"He might have already assured them that it was theirs for the having."

"Of course he did." Nyx tried to summon some irritation. In truth, it pleased her that Kalvar thought well enough of her that he'd assumed she would do the right thing, since she had the means to do it. There were, however, logistical issues that needed to be sorted out if Earth Between was to play host to a large number of displaced individuals.

"It will be easier if I can set some things up before they

arrive. Can you convince Bryn to host them for another week and bring them back with you?"

"Since helping the planet-bound less fortunate is the reason she claims to have become the Keeper, I'd like to see her explain to me that she won't. In fact, now that she has her precious key returned, and the full power of the Keeper is hers, I would like to see her explain to me that she won't put an end to the entirety of the slave market."

Nyx raised an eyebrow. "Good luck with that," she said, though if anyone could get Bryn to do it, that person would be Evra. Nyx hoped she was successful. "Just be sure to have that conversation after I leave. If the two of you reduce the Keep to rubble in a fit of mutual rage, I'd rather not die on a black market planet."

"That is not the most likely end result of us arguing."

Nyx lifted an eyebrow. "Now who's been hanging around Morgen too much?"

Evra reddened. "I did not mean—"

"I'm not judging. I'm just paying you and everyone else back for all the comments about me needing to get laid."

"Are we even, then, as you Earthlings say?"

"Good as."

Gleipnir tugged on Nyx's wrist again.

"Seriously, *seriously* bored, ladies," Seth called.

"If Morgen does come back," Nyx said, "the two of them are going to be a combined nightmare. See you in an hour, I guess."

The layers of security around the Shadow Keep made leaving Tenebris Umbra a slightly more complicated affair than simply crushing a portal stone. Within the Keep, one could only portal in or out via what Nyx had come to think of as the portal receiving room. Furthermore, the receiving room only allowed portaling to and from of one specific place—the spire in the Market square. The two were keyed to each other, and all attempts to travel anywhere else from their locales inevitably met with failure.

The city itself similarly forbade travel on or off the planet. One could portal to various points *within* the city, as Seth had done the first time he'd grabbed her, but if one wanted to portal to another planet, they had to leave the bounds of the city first.

"Why is that?" she asked Seth as they climbed the approximately eight-billion stairs necessary to get out of the Keep. Bryn had sent a group of ten guards to escort her, Seth, Evra, and Tamrin outside the city boundaries, with instructions regarding Seth to, "Make sure the bastard leaves my planet."

Nyx got the distinct impression Bryn rarely left the Shadow Keep anymore.

"It's a good strategic setup. The Keeper already controls all the portal stones. The restrictions on portaling into the Keep are the reason it's never fallen. A portal witch from inside the Keep has to open the way to allow entry, and the receiving room, as you called it, can be shut down to the rest of the Keep in seconds if there's ever a breach.

"As for the city, anyone who wants to escape the Keeper has to make it out of the Market first, and anyone coming here will have their arrival noted long before they enter the city."

"I get *that*, Captain Obvious. I meant why as in how?"

"Well then you should have asked *how*."

"You were supposed to know what I meant."

"Says who?"

"Says me."

One of the guards muttered something that apparently had no translation and which—given the tone of voice it was said in —Nyx suspected was roughly the equivalent of "Jesus fucking Christ."

"Fine. *How* does it work that way?"

"How, as in, what are the magical underpinnings worked

into the Keep and city that prevent portaling outside of the allowed ways?" Seth asked sweetly.

"Yes, smartass, how as in that."

"No clue."

"Are you voluntarily admitting you don't know something?"

He shrugged. "No one knows. As long as Keeper lore has been passed down, it's always been that way. I'd guess a portal witch did it originally, but none of the ones we have understand it. They really don't know how to do anything but spell rocks. They're one-trick ponies."

That bothered Nyx. On multiple levels. But given her talk with Morgen, she supposed that if portal magic really wasn't available off Tenebris Umbra, the knowledge around the use of portal magic had probably died out.

How did the Keeper even *find* portal witches these days? Or —and this was a really terrible thought—if it was hereditary, maybe the Keeper just bred them on-planet. Nyx was going to have to have a serious talk with Evra when they got back to Earth Between. If the Enforcers couldn't shut down Tenebris Umbra, then the Keeper was the only person who could really change anything here. And given what Evra had told Nyx about Bryn's past, maybe she would want to. Maybe, now that she had the key and was therefore likely to wrap up her internal power struggle soon, maybe she *would*. Maybe Evra could push her to.

Despite their contingent of guards, Nyx was jumpy the entire walk out of the city. She reached for the hilt of her sword, checking that it was easy and loose in its sheath, and that her newly-redone bandages wouldn't affect her grip. Evra had found her a pair of tight-fitting fingerless gloves that Nyx had managed to slide on over a very thin wrapping of gauze. It allowed her the flexibility she needed without the bulk of a large bandage, and really the cuts weren't *that* bad. Between the gloves and the layer of some really fantastic topical painkiller Evra had slathered on under the gauze, if Nyx needed to engage in combat she should be in fine enough form.

She wasn't sure *what* she expected to happen, just that she couldn't shake the undeniable sense that they were being watched. Tracked. Hunted.

But no matter how often she searched the crowds of people, she never saw any sign of pursuit. Was it the darkness she'd woken in the Station? Was that darkness some formless mass that couldn't be seen? Calista had told her it would be a few weeks before the darkness was strong enough to leave the Station, but they'd been wrong about how long it would be before it woke, too.

She was deep enough in her head she was surprised when they came to a stop and she realized they'd made it out of the city. Unmolested.

Tamrin walked a couple paces from the group, bags slung over her shoulders, a portal stone clutched in one hand and a necklace in the other. It was the draken's tooth necklace Kaden always wore, and Tamrin gripped it like a lifeline. Nyx couldn't reconcile the man who had kept waking in the middle of the night to make sure the children were all right, the man who had obviously said goodbye to Tamrin and given her that necklace to ward off the nightmares that still haunted her, with the one who had found it so easy to wash his hands of her.

So she didn't try. She shoved Kaden to the back of her mind and said her farewells to Tamrin, hoping a return to Scythia and the normalcy of the life the girl had grown up in would be enough to pull her back from the trauma of Arkadia. She knew Evra was thinking the same thing, seeing the same shadows beneath Tamrin's eyes, the weight she'd lost. And yet beneath it all there was a mutinous fury in the girl at being sent home, made worse by her anger at her mother for disavowing Evra.

"I'll just come back in a year," Tamrin said. "When I hit majority you can't stop me, whether you think I'm capable or not."

"It has nothing to do with not thinking you capable," Evra

said. This was clearly an argument they'd had many times before.

"Right, you just know what's best for me."

"I know that if you want any kind of life you need to get back in the system. Legally."

"Kaden and Ruca don't have to—"

"Kaden and Maruca would, I wager, trade a lot not to be hunted across the universe for the rest of their lives," Evra snapped.

"Kalvar got to go with them."

And just like that the fresh sullenness made sense. Tamrin had wanted to go with them too. Was there anyone who *hadn't* wanted to go with them? Should she ask Seth if he would prefer to join the Moor siblings?

"Kalvar doesn't have the options you have. Even so, I still think he made a poor decision for the wrong reasons. You want to come back here in a year and join the Mercenary Guild, be my guest. As you've so frequently pointed out, I can't stop you. But for now you're going home and that's the end of it."

"Fine." With all the drama that only a sixteen year-old could muster, Tamrin crushed the portal stone and jumped backward through it without an ounce of hesitation. It closed behind her and Evra let out a long, slow breath.

"She'll come around," Nyx told her.

"I would like to think so. But you have no idea how good al'Daemon women are at holding grudges."

Put that way…

"Right. Well, I guess that's our cue to—" Her words cut off as Seth yanked her to the ground. An arrow whistled through the space where her head had been half a second before. It thudded into the chest of the guard behind her, who went down with a startled cry.

The guard to Nyx's right cursed and a blue shielding circle went up in a single bubble around the group, a second before a fresh volley of arrows bounced harmlessly off it.

"Go now," Evra hissed, her sword clearing its sheath, "we will handle this."

"Can't," Seth answered, twin daggers appearing in his hands, seemingly from nowhere. He nodded at the guard who had activated the shielding circle. "Ylina's warding prevents portaling inside its boundaries."

"Wonderful," Evra gritted out. "Then we are to lie here like Felkan chicks until her warding runs out or our attackers decide to come to us. I do not suppose she can walk and shield at the same time?"

"Herself? Yes. The rest of us? No."

Arrows continued to rain against the shield, little bubbles appearing in the blue before healing over.

"Where the hell are Bryn's sentries?" Seth asked.

"I don't know," one of the men answered. The remaining guards had flanked to the edges of Ylina's shielding, scanning the edges of the crater for signs of life. The attackers showed themselves, then, dozens of Kumir pouring over the sides of the hill and into the crater. They continued to fire arrows as they approached, slowly but surely wearing Ylina's shield thinner and thinner. They fired in patterns, keeping up a constant stream of arrows, leaving no frame of time where one wasn't bouncing off the shield around them.

"Seth," Nyx said, much more calmly than she felt, "I thought you said you'd never actually seen Kumir on this planet."

"There's a first time for everything." Seth said, "Ylina, on my order drop the shielding. We're running for the western cliffs. Ren and Kur, cover us with wind pulses as best you can. Everyone else keep your head down and try not to die." Seth barked out the orders like he was accustomed to giving them. Nyx expected the others to dissent but they all just gave grim nods, like they were used to taking orders from him. Bryn must have done them a favor and sent them with guards who'd actually liked Seth at one point in time.

Nyx considered Seth's plan. It wasn't bad. Probably the best one available to them given the circumstances. They were too hemmed in to return underground, and reaching the cliffs would give them something to put at their backs, let them narrow their worry to defending three sides instead of four.

The best plan available to them still sucked. There were at least thirty Kumir and only twelve of them. Odds were, at least one of them would get hit with an arrow before they reached the cliffs and Ylina could shield again. After that, even if the Kumir ran out of arrows, once they were in close quarters it would be a slaughter.

"Seth."

"A little busy here, darling."

"They're only after you and me."

"Whatever you are thinking," Evra growled, "the answer is no."

Nyx was thinking that if she and Seth portaled out as soon as Ylina dropped the shield, the Kumir would simply go after the people left here and interrogate them. She was thinking that if, instead, they ran and drew the main contingent of Kumir away, Evra and the guards could handle those who remained.

Here, Nyx couldn't do anything about this many Kumir. Here, she had no control. But on her Station? There, she would be in control. And the Kumir had answers. They'd hunted the Hidden near into extinction. *They* knew why. Maybe they even knew what had happened to her mother. Given her and Seth's failure to uncover any answers in the Keep, she desperately wanted—needed—what they could tell her.

The Kumir were closing in and she could tell Seth was on the verge of giving the order to break and run, so she spoke hurriedly. "If we can draw off the main force and bring them onto the Station grounds I can handle them."

"The portal will close as soon as the person who activated it jumps through. And neither one of us is staying here and trying to herd the murderous bastards through."

Nyx's fingers grazed the portal magic in her pocket and

certainty settled through her. "I can hold it open from the other side."

Seth gave her a hard stare but he did not, miraculously, question her ability to do so. He was probably figuring that even if she couldn't, they'd be on the other side and the Kumir wouldn't be their problem anymore.

"Okay. The portal stone will drop us outside the Station grounds and then we'll have to run for it."

She gave him a nod of confirmation.

"New plan," he told everyone. "It's the same as the old one except Nyx and I head in the opposite direction."

"Nyx—" Evra started.

"I've got this," she told the Amazon. "See you in a week."

"Now," Seth ordered. The shield dropped. Arrows arced toward them, buffeted off-course by a gust of wind that emanated out from the guard named Ren. Nyx darted right, Seth on her heels, and ran for a gap between the Kumir that grew slimmer the closer they came. She could feel Seth's magic working, obscuring their exact location as arrows thudded into the ground around them. She and Seth zigged and zagged even as flickering copies of themselves did the same.

The circle of Kumir closed tighter around them. They had to break through the line, put all the Kumir behind them, or else they wouldn't bring enough Kumir through with them to give Evra and the others a fighting chance.

If only they could run faster.

She could, but Seth wouldn't be able to keep up. With Gleipnir still linking them together, moving far from him was dangerous, but taking her attention off her surroundings long enough to unlink them felt equally dangerous.

But maybe she didn't have to.

"Seth, can you make yourself disappear and leave a copy in your place?"

"Yes, but I can't do the same for you simultaneously."

"You don't need to. Just do it for you, now, and follow me through."

She'd spent some time thinking about how the mercury boots worked and was guessing they amplified the kinetic energy a body generated when it made a physical movement. Hoping desperately that she was right, Nyx drew her short sword and skipped *Los* and *Losa* entirely.

"*Losara*," she whispered and, instead of maintaining her forward run, launched herself into the air.

In retrospect, *Losa* would likely have been sufficient. The bottom of her boots cleared ten feet and her whispered, *"Exa,"* turned the boots neutral before she landed on the other side of the line of Kumir, ankles and knees groaning in protest as she bent to absorb the shock.

The Kumir she'd jumped over turned, even as Nyx felt Seth's invisible form rush past in the opening provided by her distraction. She pushed to her feet and drove the upward thrust of her short sword into the Kumir's body as she turned.

Blood gushed over the sword, onto her hands, and she hated that after her fight in the slave market, it felt less horrific this time. Exposure bred numbness. But she didn't want to become numb to this, didn't want taking a life to become easy.

She didn't have a chance to dwell on it. Seth grabbed her wrist, she pulled the sword free, and they were moving again. She pulled the portal stone he'd given her during that first meeting in the Market and crushed it.

The portal yawned open. She clutched Seth with one hand, unsure what Gleipnir would do if they didn't portal together, and reached for her bit of stolen portal magic with the other. They dove through the portal and the magic Nyx held reacted, straining at her grasp. She let it go and it spun from her in a soft ribbon, adhering to the edges of the portal, its tail caught in her hand. The magic in place, she gave it her will—to hold. To keep the path open.

They tumbled onto Wayfarer's Way. A fierce tug pulled at her as the portal attempted to close and the patchwork of magic Nyx had used held it open. She stumbled and went to one knee. Seth hauled her up and into a run, footsteps pounding the ground behind them in pursuit.

She felt the portal flicker behind them, a soft ripple in reality, felt it hold as the portal magic pulled on her again, the ribbon caught in her hand thinning. She stumbled again.

"Let it go," Seth ordered. The portal had spit them out a quarter mile from the Station. It wasn't far, but each step away from the portal added what felt like a cement block to her feet.

Nyx didn't want to let it go. She needed answers. The more Kumir she could capture in the Station grounds, the better the chance she had of getting those answers. She could hold it open just a little longer.

Her breath labored in her chest. She forced her feet forward, quads straining as if her legs really were weighted down.

"Let it go, dammit, the others can handle however many we leave behind."

She panted and kept running. Then the portal magic dwindled to nothing, used up, and the portal snapped out of existence. She'd been straining so hard to lift her feet that with the drain of it gone, she practically flew the last few feet to the Station's grounds.

It was like coming up from a deep dive to break the ocean's surface. Power flooded her as the bond between her and her Station snapped into place.

A furious roar shook the ground and Griff, massive and black as a starless night, landed in front of the line of approaching Kumir and took out five with a mighty swipe of his talons.

Nyx summoned every erg of power from her bond and opened the ground beneath two-dozen sets of feet. They sank up to their hips into ground that reformed to hold them tight as a grave.

They looked exactly as she remembered, each with the same

shade of auburn hair pulled back into tight braids, a light dusting of freckles in precisely the same pattern on each face.

The identical assassins did not struggle against the ground's hold on them for long. Rather, they accepted the inescapable nature of their predicament with the cold, emotionless efficiency that made them seem so inhuman, not a flicker of fear or emotion in their cold hazel eyes. As one, each Kumir slid two daggers from the bandoleers on their chests and hurled them at her.

At Seth.

At *Griff.*

It was Nyx's roar that shook the foundations of the earth this time as she pulled on the Station again. She ignored the sharp pain that split her skull, desperately clinging to her bond as her vision went hazy. The air around her, Seth, and Griff hardened, an impenetrable shield the Kumir daggers glanced off. Blades tumbled to the ground and Nyx staggered. Her vision had turned to a sheen of bright white so nearly complete she only caught glimpses of the world through it. Her throat constricted and she fought to breathe.

She only remained upright because Seth's arms came around her waist and steadied her.

"Whatever you're doing, Nyx, let them go. It's not worth it."

"No." She couldn't. "They have the answers. Why the Hidden are hunted, what happened to my mother. Everything."

"Nyx, *look* at them. They aren't breathing."

Nyx couldn't look, couldn't see. It was all she could do to keep sucking down air. But she *felt* what he said, felt that none of the Station's air moved in or out of Kumir lungs, felt it when their bodies slumped unconscious to the ground.

Nyx let the air shield go and fought to maintain consciousness, waiting for the feel of the Kumir's breathing to return. It wasn't possible to suffocate to death simply by holding one's breath. To hold it until one passed out, sure, though it took a supreme effort of will, but once unconsciousness set in the body took over, and the body liked to breathe.

But the ones before her did not.

They were, to a one, dead.

"No."

"It was a good try, Nyx. But no one's ever taken a Kumir alive."

She let go of her remaining hold on the Station's ground, and it was as if releasing that connection gave her body permission to reach new levels of pain. Fire lanced the inside of her skull.

She couldn't help it. She screamed.

The last thing she remembered before unconsciousness mercifully bore her away was the gentle touch of a talon on her shoulder.

22

———

Nyx woke feeling like she was wrapped in a warm, soft cocoon. The cocoon was made of her comforter, which had been tucked up above her shoulders right under her ears, and was held in place on one side by the small housecat-sized griffin curled into a ball against her stomach, and on the other by the man who had one leg slung over her knees, his arm banded around her chest.

She tried to move and found she was tucked in so tight it was impossible. Her wiggling efforts did manage to wake one of the two weights on her blanket and Griff rose, stretched, and padded forward to sit at eye-level and fix his exceptionally piercing eagle's gaze on her.

"You," he informed her, "are going to be the death of me."

"Sorry?" she squeaked.

"Do you have any idea how long I've been the Avatar here? Do you have any idea how many Guardians have managed to incite feelings of absolute terror in me during that tenure before you? The answers," he continued on without waiting for a reply, "are *a very long time* and *none*."

Nyx let him continue to lecture her, knowing it was his way of dealing with his concerns, his fears. But she couldn't fight the upward curve of her lips as he went on and on, and he finally stopped extolling the virtues of caution and wisdom to snap, "What on this cursed Earth do you possibly have to be smiling about?"

"I missed you too."

Griff didn't *quite* puff up his chest but it was a near thing. Wings stretched and feathers ruffled before he tucked them back in at his sides.

"I'd hug you, but I seem to be trapped."

"Indeed," Griff said, peering at Seth's motionless form over her shoulder. "He's insufferable but oddly he grows on you."

"Like a soft, fuzzy mold," Nyx agreed.

"He filled me in on most of the particulars, but I'd like to hear your version later. I'll let you two catch up since he's awake as daybreak."

Nyx laughed softly as Griff flitted out. She'd slept with Seth pressed against her enough times to know his awake from asleep tells too, and damn if those strange pieces of knowledge popping into her head at random weren't unsettling as hell.

"Soft, fuzzy mold?" Seth grumbled. "Seriously?"

"Be grateful. I could have said slimy mold. Or a fungus of some sort, or—"

"Point taken, but my pride is still hurt."

With Griff gone she managed to squirm out from under Seth's limbs, and flipped onto her opposite side to face him.

"Does it hurt very badly?" she asked with mock seriousness. "Should I send for a healer?"

He started to give one of his customary retorts and just… stopped, shadows gathering in his eyes.

"How long was I out?" she asked.

"Two days," he answered. "Fortunately you're not difficult to carry." He jingled the wrist with Gleipnir. "Otherwise it would have been a long two days."

Guilt tore through her and she almost took it off right then.

She *should* take it off right then. But…just an hour more. A few. A day, maybe, to not be alone. Then she'd let him go.

She had Griff. Evra had said she was coming back. It wouldn't be like before, in Dead Earth, when she'd had no one. And yet, even though she couldn't remember it all, the weight of history between her and Seth filled that aching chasm of loneliness she'd lived with ever since she'd woken up in that apartment and wondered why she hadn't had a single damn person who'd cared about her enough to be there.

She supposed she still didn't have that. He had left her there, alone, after all. But Seth—Seth had always been prone to rash decisions, to choices made in fits of emotion or pain. She'd like to believe that if he could have remembered her after he walked out that door, he would have come back. He *had* come back, once he could, hadn't he?

It didn't really matter. He would be gone again as soon as Gleipnir was, but she could pretend, in the meantime, that it would be different. Because the part of her that was beyond tired of being left had been ripped so wide open again with Kaden's and the others' departures that thinking about it wrapped a tight, clawed fist around her heart and twisted.

Seth opened his mouth, and for a moment she was afraid he was going to say something serious, something that couldn't be undone or explained away and forgotten. But his expression twisted back into its usual insouciant sarcasm before the words came out.

"You need a shower. You smell atrocious."

"Why thank you, that's what everyone wants to hear on waking after nearly melting their brain."

"About that. What exactly are you?"

She almost told him. It was on the tip of her tongue, except… if she told him, how would he react? "I'm something special." She was trying for a light, sarcastic tone, but it came out bitter.

"Nyx—"

"I'll tell you," she promised. "I just…can't right now. Okay?"

He looked like he was about to argue with her, but then he didn't. "Alright, keep your secrets." He wrinkled his nose. "But don't keep that smell. You should definitely get on that shower."

She rolled out of bed, glaring. "No one asked you to sleep so close you were guaranteed to smell me."

Rolling out of bed turned out not to be the best idea. Painfully stiff joints locked and protested, and she grappled for the nightstand, holding onto it for balance until her legs steadied and she managed something only slightly more dignified than a hobble to reach the bathroom.

"If you need someone to scrub your back, I'm sure I could be persua—"

Nyx slammed the bathroom door. She heard his chuckle, felt it with the Station's senses when he slid down to sit on the floor, back leaning against the bathroom door.

Just a little longer. She would only keep him here a little while longer.

Liar, her mind whispered. *Liar, liar, liar.*

It repeated in her head while she stood under the shower's soothing spray and washed away the grit and grime of yet another alien planet. Repeated, while fragments of a life—of her life—kept tumbling into her head. That life, the one she had always hoped would give her comfort if she could only just remember it, had been almost as solitary as the one she'd lived after.

Just her and her mother, Seth and his father, trapped on a hundred acres in the middle of nowhere. Trips to the city once a month for the groceries they couldn't grow and marveling at how different the world was there from their home. Seth and her like adjacent links on a chain of two, needing and resenting each other in equal measure, the only thing the other had.

It was no wonder they'd fallen into bed together as soon as they were old enough for it. Just two lonely kids in the middle of nothing, hoping for anything to take the edge off. To disappear for a while into someone else's body and forget themselves.

Chained. He'd been chained to her his whole life, and for what? Because his father was obsessed with a woman who'd cared so little about her own daughter she'd wiped that daughter's memory? Elena had been more concerned with preserving the Hidden bloodline than raising a daughter.

But Nyx...Nyx didn't have to be like her.

She turned the shower off and changed into the clothes the Station had helpfully left on the vanity for her. Then she pulled the bathroom door open so fast Seth went tumbling inside, rolling to his feet with the grace that years of his father's training had instilled in him.

"If you wanted to invite me inside, asking would have been pleasanter."

"Give me your hand."

Seth held out his hand. The one attached to an empty wrist.

"Your other hand."

He complied and Nyx removed Gleipnir, looping it back into a bracelet around her wrist.

Seth gave her one of his patented, sardonic smiles. "Am I getting the day off for good behavior?"

"Today. Tomorrow. All of them. Go wherever you want, Seth. My mother never should have done what she did to you and I don't—"

"You remember?" he asked softly.

"Not all of it. Pieces. Fragments. Enough to know you don't deserve to be stuck with me forever. Thank you for coming to check on me once you remembered me and—" She fought back the sudden constriction in her throat. "And if you want to visit sometime, I'd like that. You're always welcome here."

She'd stared at the floor during the entire speech and she didn't look at him now as she fled, ignoring him when he called her name. As soon as she was in the hallway she rearranged its configuration and sealed herself off from pursuit. She didn't want to have another talk like the one she'd had with Kaden. She didn't want another goodbye, didn't want to watch another person walk away from her.

She searched the Station's senses until she felt Griff, downstairs in the solarium. She stopped in the kitchen, made herself a cup of peppermint tea, and went to find her Avatar.

23

———————

"Remind me to never let you off-Station again," Griff said when Nyx had finished recounting her time on Tenebris Umbra. "You get into far too much trouble."

Nyx, settled onto the solarium's well-cushioned window seat, pretended outrage. "I do *not* get into trouble. It finds me."

"An excuse people who frequently get into trouble make with equal frequency."

"Speaking of going off-Station, when are you going to venture out into the great wide universe?" He hadn't made any mention of traveling since she had made her pact with the Station that would allow him to do so, and while she had no intention of forcefully shoving him onto the ley line, she wanted to make sure that whatever held him back had nothing to do with her.

Griff clicked his beak. "It's not so easy as you make it sound. Do you have any idea how long I have been here?"

His question was serious. She thought back to when the Meerkin she'd met on Arkadia said the Station on their planet had been built and hazarded a guess.

"Nine centuries?" She felt like an idiot for even suggesting it.

The span of time might be insignificant in the face of evolution and the age of the universe, but it felt improbable to her.

"Closer to ten," Griff said. "Before the ley lines were built, travel between planets was much harder to come by. I only traveled to a few planets, and those at the side of someone much more experienced than myself."

There was a rare note of longing in his voice, and she thought of Jevryn's ring, nestled next to the Harvester on the chain around her neck. Griff had made it clear he didn't want to talk about his history with the councilor, so she didn't ask if it was Jevryn he had traveled with, however much her curiosity burned.

"I am very much afraid that there is not much left in the universe that I will recognize."

At that, Nyx smiled. "Griff, you've seen a *thousand* years worth of travelers come through here and you've probably read every book in this Station. You might not have *seen* the universe, but I think you might recognize it okay. And whenever you want to go, if you don't want to do it alone, I think Evra would go with you, if you asked."

He bobbed his head once, stretched his wings and resettled them, and said, unconvincingly, "In a year, perhaps."

"Can I ask you something?"

"All right."

She bit the inside of her cheek, trying to figure out how to say what she wanted to. "When I came here, you said the Station oriented itself to match my personality. To the things that I wanted."

The previous Guardian had favored beaches. Nyx favored forests. When the previous Guardian had been here, Griff had been trapped in the body of a dolphin. He'd once confessed to her he hadn't particularly cared for the form.

"Including you. I don't want you to be trapped as a griffin for the rest of your life." For the rest of *their* lives. Their eternal lives. She only got mildly sick when she thought about it this time, so she must be getting used to the idea. "Is there something I can do to make the Station understand?"

He didn't answer in a straightforward manner. "I told you, when you first came here, that Earth's Station chooses a Guardian who has nothing left to them in Dead Earth. No one to miss them. That is true, and it typically means that when a new Guardian arrives, they are lonely and desperate. As such, most of them are only thinking of themselves. There is also typically a longer transition time between Guardians, a time period where the Station is still under control of the previous Guardian before the new one takes over. During that time, the Station may transform to be inviting to the new Guardian, but I remain in the state desirous to the previous Guardian.

"As such, I typically interact with the new Guardian for at least a week or two before the Guardianship transfers and I take on a new form. None of those new Guardians ever saw me as a person. They never gave any thought to what *I* might want to be. So I had no choice in what I became when the Guardianship transferred. Do you know what happened when the Guardianship transferred to you?"

Nervous, worried, Nyx shook her head.

"Nothing. No change was forced upon me because what the Station picked up from you with absolutely certainty, was that you would never believe you had that sort of right of control over another individual. For the first time in a thousand years, Nyx, I was given a choice in what I became." He stretched his wings wide. "This is what I chose to become."

"Is it—is this your original form?"

"No. But it contains a single commonality with my original body that I find enormously comforting."

Looking at the wings he slowly tucked back in at his sides, she had a good guess what that commonality was.

"Maybe I can talk to the Station, make it understand that I just want you to be yourself." The thought of going back down into the Station's Heart, into that foreign, vine-filled room with an entity she was pretty sure hated her guts, filled Nyx with dread. But for Griff, she would do it.

"My own form is forbidden to me," Griff said gently, "and that is not the Station's doing, but the All Council's when they bound me to it."

"Why?" Though she had seen for herself how cruel they could be, and though she knew well enough that people didn't always need a reason for cruelty, she would like to think, for the sake of the history she suspected between Griff and Jevryn, that they had had *some* reason for it.

Griff sighed. "Truthfully? It was Kiev's doing and he did it to hurt Jevryn. Hurting me was a bonus."

Kiev. Jevryn's nearly-identical, cold-hearted brother. Kiev was the reason Nyx had had to send two locks of purple hair to a planet she'd never been to, to people she'd never met, with a letter to explain to those people that their daughters, who had been stolen from them years before, were never coming home. Kiev had also been fully supportive of another councilor's desire to obliterate Nyx's mind, and he had treated Griff like garbage.

"I would be happy to slice the *other* side of his face open for you, if you like." It was a sincere offer, if one she was unlikely to be able to execute. She'd only managed it the first time and lived to tell the tale because they'd all been locked in battle in the middle of the ley lines where anonymity was easier to come by.

Griff ducked his head in what she'd come to think of as his version of a half-smile.

"I'll let you know. Perhaps for my birthday."

"I could carve a little bow on his cheek. Tie some ribbon around his neck."

"But how will you ever find a box he'll fit in?"

She laughed, perhaps more than the joke called for, but a teasing Griff was such a rarity that she treasured each time he showed that side of himself.

They spent the rest of the day together in companionable enjoyment. She taught him to play gin rummy and he taught her a much more complicated game called Hex involving a set of gray dice, a board, a multitude of cat figurines, and rules of movement far more complex than chess.

Turning one of the little figurines over in her hand, she said, "Griff, there's something I want to ask, but I don't want you to feel like you have to say yes."

Griff stretched his wings, tucked them back in. "You want to use the ring. To see if Jevryn can tell you what Calista could not."

She did. She wasn't certain it was the brightest decision, but given that when Jevryn had given her the ring he'd all but told her he knew she'd cut Kiev, knew she'd been to Arkadia, she figured if he truly wanted to hold her responsible, he would have. But how had Griff known that was what she was going to ask?

The look on her face must have telegraphed her confusion, because he huffed and said, "I wasn't born yesterday. I wasn't born a centuries' worth of yesterdays. It was a tempting offer he gave you, and now that you have no one in the Station who would be put at risk by his presence, it is only natural that you would want to take advantage of that offer."

"I mean it when I say I'm only asking, Griff. If you aren't comfortable with it I'll never call that offer in."

"I do not know that I will ever be comfortable with Jevryn again. But I do believe I am capable of handling the interaction. Who knows, perhaps it will even be cathartic in some sense."

"Can I trust him?"

"It has been a *very* long time since I could claim to know Jevryn ah'Morridahn. Trust is a difficult thing. I cannot recommend giving it without restraint. But in this matter, with you, I believe you can trust that he will not harm you. What his true motives were in offering you this boon I do not know, but I believe he will honor his word and treat you fairly."

"And you're sure you're okay with it?"

"Make the call, Nyx. The sooner he is here, the sooner he will be gone again."

Nyx pulled her necklace chain from behind her shirt, held the ring Jevryn had given her in her palm, and whispered his name to it.

She felt silly, especially when nothing happened. "Did it work?"

"I am certain he heard it," Griff answered, "but he does co-govern the entire universe. I imagine he's busy. Consider giving him a few days."

Right. Put that way, Nyx felt rather foolish. So she shoved Jevryn ah'Morridahn from her mind and spent the rest of the day doing things that didn't need doing and trying not to pay attention to where a certain guest was or what he was doing.

It wasn't until evening fell that she accepted what the Station's senses had been telling her all day: Seth hadn't left, and he didn't seem likely to any time soon.

24

———————

Nyx went downstairs, through the library and to the back of the Station where a cool breeze blew in from the open sliding doors. She followed that breeze onto the back porch and found Seth sprawled atop the deck railing, leaning back against a support post. He had one long leg stretched out and the other bent with his arm slung over the knee, a tequila bottle dangling from his fingertips. He hadn't drank but a sip from it and it dangled between his tapered bronze fingers as he twirled it back and forth between them.

He didn't look at her when she walked out, staring instead at the forest beyond. She slid onto the railing and settled against the post opposite him, a mirror image of his stance.

Finally, he said, "I'm sorry, Nyx. I never should have left you, never should have been so selfish, I just—" His hands tightened on the glass neck of the tequila bottle, knuckles going white.

"I'm glad you left."

Seth gave her a hard stare, raised the tequila bottle to his lips and took a long pull. "Was my company so terrible?" It sounded a lot like when she'd asked him, *Am I so easy to leave?* From what she could remember of their past, she wouldn't be surprised if they both had the same insecurity issues.

"That's not what I meant." She held her hand out and he passed her the bottle. It had been a long time since she'd drank and the alcohol burned all the way down, smarted her eyes and hit her with that immediately comforting fire behind her chest.

"This stuff is awful." But she took another pull before she leaned forward and handed it back to him. It was not prime tequila, true, but it felt comforting and familiar.

He took it back, smiling. "That's what you said the first time I let you have any. Though I think there were more expletives involved. Such a filthy mouth for a sixteen-year-old."

His gaze slid down to her lips, lingered, and a different warmth spread through her, a different familiarity.

Guilt tore at the ragged edges of the hole Kaden had punched in her. She pushed it away. She didn't want to feel guilt, or longing, or sadness. She didn't want to feel anything at all where Kaden was concerned.

"If I did have a filthy mouth, I wonder where I could have learned it."

Seth's eyes widened in mock offense. "I had the lips of angel."

She snorted. "Maybe a fallen one. Every time I whacked you good in a sparring match it was a litany of curses and bitching for days."

A small smile quirked up the corners of his lips, but it was overcast with shadows. "Sometimes you talk and it's like nothing's changed. Like the last seven years I spent stumbling around looking for something I couldn't remember were a dream and now I've woken up right where I'm supposed to be."

He took a slow swallow of tequila. "And then sometimes you look at me like you've never seen me before and I get a glimmer of what it would have been like to have stayed here next to your ghost, and that's like jumping into water so cold I can't breathe. I tell myself if I could do it over again I wouldn't walk out that door, but I don't know if it's true. What kind of person does that make me?"

"The honest kind." For all he'd done, he'd never lied to her about it. Had never tried to tell her it was *her* fault. She forgave him half of it, just for that. "How we grew up…well, let's just say it's a miracle we didn't hate each other and I think—I think if you'd stayed, we might have."

She motioned for the tequila bottle and reveled in the next hit of warmth that flared behind her chest. No doubt she'd regret it in the morning. But it had been so long since she'd had the energy to make a choice she regretted that even that thought had its own kernel of warmth.

"And if you *hadn't* left," she continued, running her hand over the Guardian tattoo, "I wouldn't be here. I *like* being here. I'm not going to say it wasn't a shitty thing to do, but there's no point in sitting here wondering how it might have all been different."

His eyes narrowed. "Have you grown wise in my absence? Stars help us if *that's* the case. I'll never hear the end of anything."

She laughed and then, because the images in her head were still so scattered, more like frames of a movie she'd watched out of order, and of them hadn't seen enough to understand the plot, she asked, "It was our whole life wasn't it? That stupid valley. The farm."

He leaned back again, some of the tension easing from him. "Yeah. Mostly. It was a pocket of Earth Between. All the benefits of a magical planet, a fraction of the likelihood of being tracked down. Not that Dad and Elena ever bothered to tell us why we lived like we did. I remember the first time they took us out into Dead Earth. Magic getting ripped away was a bitch but then there was this whole world out there that made up for it."

"Why didn't we ever run away?"

He laughed. "Oh, we did. More times than I can count. But my old man's a Hound, just like your golden boy. Their senses might be dulled in Dead Earth, but once they have a scent they can follow it damn near anywhere, and I didn't know how to mask our trails back then. We made it a whole week once before Dad dragged us back."

"Was it a good week?"

He tapped his chest, over his heart. "We got tattoos, didn't we?"

She smiled. "Then it must have been a good week."

They were quiet for a few minutes, staring out at the darkness beyond the porch and listening to the crickets chirp.

"Can you still find it? Where we grew up?"

He tensed, and for a moment she thought he might lie to her, but then he said, "I think so."

"Would you take me back? Before you leave?"

"If you want to go, I'll take you." He looked like he'd rather do anything else. "As for leaving…"

A fist tightened around her heart and squeezed.

"I wasn't lying when I said the Kumir always track me down eventually. If I stay, they're going to show up here at some point."

If I stay…

"If you want me to leave I will. But I'd rather not."

She swallowed. "Then don't. I'm tired of people leaving."

He stared at her for the longest time and then whispered, "Okay."

Relief, sweet and simple, poured through her. He handed her the tequila bottle, as if he was preparing her for something, and she wasn't sure what until he asked, "Your golden Hound. Did you love him?"

It took her two swallows of tequila before she could say, "Yeah. I did."

"Then he's an idiot." There was none of the usual sarcasm in Seth's voice, nothing mocking. It made it hurt more, somehow.

"I don't remember you being so nice."

"Maybe I've gotten soft in my old age."

She didn't realize she was crying until he slid off the railing and over to her, thumbs gently brushing away her tears. She wrapped her arms around him and let him pull her against his chest. Her tears didn't last long. She'd never been prone to long bouts of crying, and she slowly became aware of his body pressed against hers, of his fingers tracing little circles on the small of her back.

She'd always liked it when he did that.

It felt so natural, so familiar, that she pushed onto her toes and kissed him. His lips parted automatically, matching her, and he tasted of tequila and fire, just like she remembered.

She felt the struggle it took for him to put his hands on her hips and gently break from her. "You're drunk, Nyxi."

"I'm really not."

His eyes searched hers.

"What?" she asked.

His fingers tensed on her hips. She knew *what*, but she didn't want to talk about Kaden. He wasn't ever coming back.

"Through everything, even when we got sick of each other, you never regretted me. I don't want that to change."

"Regret's not really my thing."

"Maybe not. But I also don't want to be the person you use to forget someone else."

She almost snapped out that he hadn't seemed to be on that moral high-ground when he'd kissed her in the Shadow Keep's library, but she didn't. Mostly because sleeping with him probably *was* a monumentally bad decision. It hadn't ever complicated anything before, but then, there hadn't been other people between them before.

The realization that there would have been other women for him sent a completely ridiculous flare of jealousy through her. She didn't understand how she could be torn up over Kaden and pissed off at the idea of anyone else touching Seth at the same time. It was like there were two different people inside her, one who'd grown up with Seth and one who'd lived the life that led to Kaden, and she had no idea how to merge the two identities. How to make herself into a single person again.

"I know it's selfish," she said softly, "but I don't want to be alone tonight."

"Neither do I. But we don't have to have sex to not be alone."

He kept her hand when she led him back inside, up the stairs to her bedroom, and it soothed the sting of previous rejection when he wrapped himself around her and tucked her in against him, the feel of his breathing as familiar as her own.

For the first time since she'd come back from Arkadia, Nyx slept through the night.

25

———

Seth was gone.

The sense of betrayal hit Nyx in the stomach as she bolted upright in the bed, sunlight streaming through her balcony windows. She flung the covers off and was halfway down the stairs when she realized she only felt the stairs beneath her feet and not the opposite as well. She froze between one step and the next, realizing she had, finally, managed to block out the Station's senses.

The thought restored her connection with her Station—Kaliaris, she supposed—and even though she was afraid to look, to feel, to find out the answer, she did. Relief suffused her as she felt not one but two presences in the downstairs kitchen.

Voices reached her as she hit the final steps and rounded the bend to the kitchen. Seth was singing, gloriously off-key and with great enthusiasm, but the most frightening part was that he wasn't alone. She heard the second voice, but she wouldn't have believed it if she hadn't stepped into the kitchen and seen, with her own two eyes, Griff's head bobbing along with the music while Seth played air guitar and they both sang at the top of their lungs.

"Don't stop, be-lie-ving. Hold on to that fee-uh-ling. Don't stop. Be-lie-ve-ee-ing."

Far from being embarrassed, Seth caught sight of Nyx and dove straight for her, pulling her into the kitchen to dance to what was undoubtedly the worst butchering of Journey's classic song she'd ever heard. It pained her eardrums to no end, and none of the three of them could dance for shit, but she was breathless and smiling by the end of it.

"That," Griff said, straightening his feathers and trying to regain some semblance of his usual decorum, "was a highly enjoyable song."

"Just don't let him drag you through his AC/DC phase. I don't think my eardrums would ever recover."

The noise had distracted her so much she hadn't realized Seth had been in the middle of cooking until he flicked a burner off, moved a few things around, and presented her with a plate of fried ham, bacon, browned potatoes, and eggs. The amount of food was somewhat daunting.

"Am I never eating again after this?"

"Do you know you have everything you could possibly want to eat here? The refrigerator just *gives* you things."

"Oh no," Nyx groaned, rushing over to the refrigerator. "How much stuff did you pull out of storage?"

The answer was a little bit of pretty much everything. The fridge was filled to capacity.

Griff fluttered over, an apologetic look in his eagle eyes. "He looked so excited every time he opened the door and found something new I couldn't quite bring myself to stop him."

Nyx couldn't find it in herself to be mad about it either. An excited Seth suffused the room with such joyous energy that trying to dim it felt too much like kicking a puppy. An adorable, extremely energetic puppy.

"Did you know there's a whole library here?" Seth continued. "And my room has like three rooms and Griff said I can have a jacuzzi."

"Careful," Nyx warned Griff, "you'll spoil him."

But she was smiling, because Seth wasn't just excited he was...elated. Happy.

The others, when they stayed at the Station, had enjoyed its amenities and the fact it could give a person pretty much anything they wanted provided it had the raw materials to make it, but for them it had been more like people who were already used to a certain level of comfort staying at a fancy hotel. It was nice, but it didn't invoke too much appreciation.

Seth—Seth was reacting like she had when she first came here. Like this was what he'd been waiting for his entire life and now he was home. Like the Station was a treasure and he couldn't believe he'd been lucky enough to come along and find it.

She sat down at the bar and bit into a piece of bacon with a moan—she didn't need the sudden resurgence of her memory to tell her Seth was an excellent cook—and listened to him go on in avid detail about how generally amazing the Station was.

"So what I'm hearing from all of this is that you think my job's pretty cool."

"Your job is boring. Customer service sucks. This place, however? Awesome."

"Just don't ask what lives underneath it," she mumbled.

"What's that?"

"Nothing. So will you take me back to the valley?"

"Like, now? Today?"

"Yes, now." If she let him get by with 'tomorrow' he'd put it off until tomorrow turned into never.

"All right." He sprinkled his potatoes with a liberal dose of salt. "Why *not* ruin a perfectly nice day with the ghosts of childhood trauma?"

"What's the Arrival/Departure schedule look like?" she asked Griff.

"It's clear for the next ten days."

"Really? How did you manage that?"

"I informed everyone on the schedule that you contracted Centerian Hyplexia. It's a disgusting disease that causes boils and bleeding from the orifices, among other things. Rare, but it does occasionally crop up. It's a two week quarantine period so you still have a little breathing room."

"And you'll need it," Seth informed her. "Hope you like road trips and Montana."

"Montana? It isn't near here? In Tempe?"

"Why would there be *another* pocket of Earth Between right next to the primary one we're currently inhabiting?"

"Because I can't leave Tempe, Arizona without my head trying to explode?"

"Oh, ah, right. That."

Nyx pinned him with a glare. "*That?* You know about this?"

"Your mother might have indicated, in the extraordinarily brief letter she left me, that she expected us to stay *right* where we were. I didn't think she'd actually put a binding spell on her own daughter, though."

"She wiped her own daughter's memory and abandoned her without a second thought. Why *wouldn't* she put a binding spell on me? And what *is* a binding spell, anyway?"

"An outlawed piece of magic that binds an individual to a physical place," Griff answered. "They're the origin of Earth's Rapunzel fairy tale. It wasn't the knight she needed to rescue her —it was cutting off her hair that did it. Binding spells need an anchor, something that is meaningful to the person being bound —in Rapunzel's case, her hair. The witch had a lock of it, but when Rapunzel sheared her hair, it broke that anchor."

"Please tell me I don't have to shave my head."

"I'm afraid there's no help for it." Seth shook his head. "A tragic day, but we all have to make sacrifices."

"I don't think that will be necessary," Griff said. "For one, I doubt your mother would have chosen the same anchor as Rapunzel's witch did, and for another, the reason the binding spell lost its grip on you when you slid into Earth Between is because they don't work here. If that's truly what was keeping you in Tempe, it broke the day you found Wayfarer's Way."

"Well, there's only one way to find out."

***

Earth Between was adjacent to several areas in Dead Earth, and a quick dip off Wayfarer's Way into New Mexico proved that her entrance into Earth Between months ago had indeed broken her mother's binding spell. She wanted to stay in New Mexico out of a sheer stubborn desire to never step foot in Tempe, Arizona ever again, but unfortunately she knew her way around Tempe, and she did not know New Mexico. She and Seth navigated Wayfarer's Way back to Earth Between, where she then had it drop them off out back of the Target off Baseline and McClintock.

One exorbitantly expensive shopping spree later they had phones, enough prepaid credit cards to pay three months' worth of her old bills, and snacks. She'd tried to have the Station replicate Gardetto's but it had been a disaster every time. Probably because she hadn't had the slightest inkling of what went into making them. Staring at the ingredients list now, she still wasn't sure it would help. What even *was* disodium inosinate anyway? Other than delicious, of course.

"Please tell me you know how to operate a vehicle," Nyx pleaded as they crossed the street to the complex housing Steve's Espresso and Enterprise Rent-A-Car. She had no desire to make an eighteen-hour drive by herself.

"I mean, it's been seven years give or take, but maybe it's like riding a bike?" he offered.

Nyx groaned. "You can drive the highway stretches. Try not to kill us."

Nyx spent the next half hour decoding rent-a-car legalese and dropping enough money to make herself feel ill. Seth had predictably been like a kid in a candy shop, working in tandem with the salesperson, both trying desperately to get her to rent an expensive, flashy SUV.

"We're getting the Elantra."

"But it's *boring*."

"It gets thirty-five miles-per-gallon. I am going to be on this Earth for the rest of my unnaturally long life Seth Hawthorne. Think of the planet. If I could make the drive in an electric vehicle, I would."

He quit arguing. He did not quit looking longingly at the other, shinier cars in the parking lot as they climbed into the newly-rented Elantra, Target purchases in the trunk and coffees from Steve's Espresso in the cup holders. She was relatively certain he had a comment brewing about disposable coffee cups not being good for the planet either, but she forestalled it by giving him command of the radio. He started fiddling and she resigned herself to a few hours of classic rock.

Nyx buckled her seatbelt and adjusted the mirrors. She depressed the brake and released the parking brake. She looked in the rearview and side mirrors and then over her shoulder out the back window. No pedestrians, no oncoming vehicles. All she had to do was put the car in reverse, release the brake pedal, and back out of the space. Simple. Easy.

She gripped the steering wheel until her knuckles turned white.

Seth turned the radio down to a slightly more reasonable volume and said, casually, "How long has it been since *you've* driven a vehicle, Nyxi?"

Ugh. "Five years."

One had been in her possession when she woke up all those years ago. It hadn't taken long to realize that the longer she kept the car, even while she'd still had some of the money her mother had left her, the bigger the drain on her finances would be. Cars were expensive. They required insurance and registration fees and gasoline and maintenance and the list never seemed to end.

"Stars save us."

Nyx glared at Seth and dropped the car into reverse. He very wisely did not comment on the glacial pace at which she backed the vehicle out of the space. She breathed a sigh of relief once they cleared the two vehicles to either side and shifted into drive, glaring in the rearview at the Mercedes that swung around the corner of the parking lot at breakneck speed, squealed to a stop and started honking at her.

She shifted the car into drive with absolutely no sense of urgency and proceeded out of the parking lot at a reasonable ten miles-per-hour.

"Are you trying to get us killed?" Seth asked, eyeing the angry Mercedes driver.

"I'm relatively certain they won't get out of the car and assault us," she said with less conviction than she felt. Road rage made some people downright stupid. She turned right onto McClintock, breathing a sigh of relief when the Mercedes sped into the center lane and shot through the yellow light at the intersection, the driver doing nothing worse than flipping them off as he passed them.

It turned out Seth was right and driving a car was a bit like riding a bike. By the time she'd merged onto the I-17 North her nerves had faded, replaced by a grin that had to be taking up half her face.

"We're going back to a valley in the middle of nowhere," Seth said. "An abysmal place where the adults in our lives raised us in isolation and taught us to be little toy soldiers and at best treated us with casual disinterest before stealing your memories and abandoning us. What do you possibly have to be smiling about?"

Nyx grinned wider. "We're going on a road trip. Like, an actual road trip. I'm going to complain about all the music you pick and eat food that's bad for me and later we can check into a hotel of questionable quality and eat a bad continental breakfast the next morning while I comment on the fact that you snore."

"All of that sounds about right," Seth said, sliding his Target shades on, "except that you're the one who snores."

"I do not."

"You definitely do."

The resultant bickering had them both grinning like idiots.

Nyx snored. She found this fact unexpectedly mortifying and wouldn't have believed it if Seth hadn't recorded the audio on his phone, complete with a voice-over cameo so she couldn't claim it was his own damn snoring on recording.

"How did you even find the audio recording function? You've never had a smartphone before in your life."

"What can I say? It's hard being this brilliant."

Nyx made an impolite noise in response and surveyed the continental breakfast options. What to choose? Tiny boxed cereal that was ninety percent sugar? Dry bagel? Scrambled eggs with a waxy sheen? Miniature muffins with a slightly waxier sheen than the eggs? Apples that were impossibly waxier than the last two items? The tray of bacon next to the eggs glistened with grease and when Nyx tentatively lifted a slice with a pair of plastic tongs it hung down limply like a wet noodle.

"What do you think is safest?" she whispered.

"Nyxi, darling, I am perfectly willing to admit I have eaten some questionable things when in situations of dire need, but this is not one of those situations. If the continental breakfast means that much to you, by all means, dig in. But I'm finding food elsewhere."

"Coward," Nyx accused, but after two bites of eggs that managed to taste both watery and chewy at the same time, she had to admit he had a point and caved.

One diner, six hours, and two rest stops later, they arrived in the middle of nowhere.

"Surely 'middle of nowhere' is a little uncharitable?" Nyx

offered in the location's defense. "I mean, we're vaguely south and west of Great Falls. There is a river."

At least, the physical map said the Missouri River was theoretically nearby. Her phone's GPS was hopelessly lost. As in, it didn't appear capable of finding satellites.

"Uh-huh."

"Are you sure you know where we're going?"

They'd parked the rental Elantra off the side of a dirt road on a stretch of land that Nyx privately admitted to herself looked exactly like everything else they'd passed for the last ten miles. After slipping through a barbed wire fence, she hoped whoever the land belonged to owned enough of it that the likelihood of them being in this particular area at this particular time was very low. She'd gone along quietly at first but they'd been walking for twenty minutes with no trail to follow and her hopes that the scenery would jog her memory had so far been disappointed.

"Yep."

Nyx chewed on her lip as a deterrent to asking more questions, but it only worked for about thirty seconds.

"Do you know how to find our way back to the car?"

This time he just grunted and held up a compass. Wonderful. She'd brought a Boy Scout. Maybe he had a hunting knife and a pack of waterproof matches for when they inevitably got lost and had to spend a week in the Montana wilderness avoiding bears and hunting their own food.

She'd barely taken the inhale for her next question when Seth stopped, cocking his head to the right.

"There. Do you feel it?"

She opened her mouth to say that no, of course she didn't, only she took another step forward and did. The faintest thread of magic curled toward her, like a tendril of smoke blown by the wind. She followed it until the sound of rushing water hit her ears and the Missouri came into sight. They were almost to the banks of the river when she caught the same shimmer in the air that had led her to Wayfarer's Way that first time, and a narrow path, hardly more than a deer trail, revealed itself in the haze.

She reached for Seth without thinking and he interlaced his fingers with hers, his grip tight enough to cut off circulation. A glance out of the corner of her eye showed his lips set in a grim line, his eyes devoid of their usual mischief. She felt a twinge of guilt, then, for asking him to bring her back here when his memories of it were so clearly unpleasant.

"You don't have to cross over with me," she said softly. "If you want to wait here I understand. But I have to go in."

She had to know…what? That it had been real? That she wasn't crazy and that once she'd had a life, a childhood, even if it hadn't been an entirely pleasant one?

"No, it's okay." Seth squeezed her hand and then relaxed his death grip on it, and they stepped onto the path together.

26

———————

The Missouri River still flowed in this pocket of Between, though it was not an exact replica of the one they had previously stood beside. The river looked younger here, wilder, as if the influences of civilization had been unable to reach through and alter its fundamental nature. A small boat floated by the shore. No rope tethered it, nor did it rest on the bank, yet it remained unmoved by the river's current.

Nyx had difficulty believing it had sat here, untouched by the weather and time, for the last seven years. She had an even more difficult time believing the vessel was seaworthy, so to speak.

"Are you sure it's safe?" Nyx asked as Seth leapt nimbly into the craft, landing with a lightness that barely caused it to rock.

Seth shrugged. "Dad always had a way with preservation spells. You coming?"

Figuring he probably hadn't brought her all the way out here to kill her in a mysterious boating accident, Nyx leapt in after him, landing at the precise space in the boat that countered her weight to his, just as she suddenly remembered doing countless times before. Then, as before, she knelt, pulling the little piece of chalk from its waterproof pouch under the lip of the hull, and inverted the anchoring rune already drawn on the boat's floor.

Released from its anchor on one side of the river, the boat moved lazily toward its sister anchor, the pull between the physical anchor on the opposite side and the matching rune on the boat's floor drawing it inexorably forward, the straight line of their progress unaffected by the river's current.

The boat docked and they stepped out, wordless, walking until the land fell away in a gentle slope and Nyx looked down on her childhood home. She didn't know why she was surprised to find it looked almost exactly as it had in the glimmer of memory that had first revealed it to her. Maybe because that glimmer had looked more like a painting than a reality, and she was having trouble reconciling the idyllic setting with the bitterness that rolled off Seth every time he spoke of it.

Only upon closer inspection could she find the differences time had wrought. The training arena had long ago been lost to tall grasses that had also crept up around the walls of the house and the barn. The vegetable garden had gone wild, growing a hodgepodge of plants that were the descendants of whatever had been left to die in the area when its tenants had abandoned it.

"Nyxi?" Seth stepped up beside her.

She knew what he was asking and she shook her head. The disappointment he couldn't quite hide told her they had both been hoping that coming here would be some panacea that would solve all of her issues, would remove the veil over her memories.

"Let's go down."

As they approached the house, Nyx didn't feel like she was returning home. She felt like she was in a horror movie stumbling onto a settlement whose residents had mysteriously left in a hurry, leaving a fully functional home and grounds abandoned for no apparent reason. All of which was correct save for the horror movie script.

She kept her thoughts to herself, mostly because Seth was the type that, if she expressed them, would undoubtedly create an illusion of some ghostly specter or slavering monster just to scare the ever-loving hell out of her.

"How is it," she asked softly, "that I can know exactly what you'll do in a given situation but I have so few actual memories of you?"

She'd meant it as a rhetorical question—if she didn't know how could he?—and he didn't answer, not exactly.

"Spicy food or not?"

A flicker of confusion before she understood he was asking her which he would choose. She didn't even have to think about it.

"Not." After the mortifying event when she'd been twelve and he had indeed convinced her through subtle illusion magic that her mare, Belle, was a unicorn, she had laced his evening's meal with a tablespoon of dried habanero powder and thoroughly enjoyed watching him splutter for the next fifteen minutes. "Ask me something else."

"What were you thinking of?"

"Habanero powder."

The grin that lit up his face made the sun seem brighter.

"Ranged weapons or hand-to-hand?"

"Ranged." She hadn't had any natural aptitude for throwing stars, but because of him she could hit the center of a target from twenty feet away even if she couldn't hit the bullseye every time. This time, she grinned too.

He shifted a step closer to her. "Getting up early or sleeping in?"

"Early." She was the one who liked to sleep in.

"Rain or sunshine?" His fingers brushed the back of her hand.

"Rain."

Another step closer.

"Kiss me or don't?"

Part of her thought she shouldn't, and she shoved that part as far away from her as she could, because it was the same part of her that had spent the last two months tip-toeing around Kaden, the last few years missing him.

Maybe that had been understandable in a world where Kaden was the only person who could remember her, but that wasn't her world anymore, and she wanted to twine her arms around Seth's neck and kiss him, and find out if what they'd had was only loneliness and desperation or if it was something more. Something she could maybe find her way back to again.

So she did.

For a man who had asked her to kiss him, it seemed to take him by surprise. Then he relaxed, wrapped his arms around her waist and pulled her closer as his mouth parted, inviting her in. She lost herself to the feel and taste of him, pressed her body against his as if she could somehow merge the two of them together. As if she could link them so inextricably that they could never be broken apart again. But a second later his hands settled on her hips and he did just that, setting her back with gentle pressure.

"We should go see it," he whispered. "Get it over with."

"Yeah." Except she no longer had any desire to, had in fact developed the opposite desire to leave. But she'd dragged Seth all the way here. She'd dragged *herself* all the way here. So she went to see it.

Nyx paused at the house's entrance, fingertips on the door-knob, studying the home's construction. The walls were rough-hewn logs rather than assembly-line lumber, worn smooth with age.

"Did they build this place?"

Seth shrugged. "I don't know. I don't really remember coming here."

Right. He'd said he was two when his father brought him here.

"But judging by how much your mother hated it I would guess it was already here. Stars know if she'd had Dad build it she would have demanded a foyer and a pool. Though I don't think he had a clue how to build anything which is probably why she never demanded he make any additions." He gave her his devil-may-care grin. "Dad was always better at destroying things than creating them."

Nyx told herself to quit procrastinating, twisted the knob and stepped inside. Seth came in behind her, closing the door against the frigid Montana winter. A small kitchen lay to her right, galley-style and opening up on the opposite side to a small dining area that just barely held the four-stool pub-style table that occupied it.

She had always thought of kitchens as inviting and comforting but this one felt…empty. She had thought maybe she would remember a flash of her mother or Viktor cooking but instead what she remembered was Seth doing it, even when he'd been so young he'd needed a stool to reach the top of the stove. The only time it had ever felt warm was on those occasions when her and Seth were completely alone, when her mother had been gone for too long and Viktor had gone into Dead Earth to find her and bring her back.

She had disappeared a lot, Nyx remembered now. Long stretches of weeks and months, and every time Viktor brought her back she was a little colder, a little more distant, a little more bitter.

Seth's thumb stroked gently across the back of her palm, made her realize she'd grabbed his hand at some point and had a death grip on it. She didn't look at him because she was so angry and horrified and she didn't want him to mistake those emotions for pity. He'd never wanted pity from her, had once told her it was the one thing that would make his life completely unbearable.

She dropped his hand and took the two steps to enter the living room, though living room was somewhat of a grand name for what was a very small square space containing only a low, flat couch, a small end table, and a fireplace. She had the distinct impression that it was where Viktor had slept.

So far the house had the feel of a space that would be comfortable for one person, or two people who were really comfortable with each other. But *four…*

Nyx left the living room for a narrow hallway. It held three doors, two along the length of the hallway and one at the end that led to the single bathroom. She opened the door she knew instinctively led to the room her mother had occupied.

Stepping inside was like entering a room in an entirely different home. Soft, white cloth with designs interwoven in silver thread hid the log walls and a thick plush rug in matching colors covered the floor from wall to wall. A canopied four-post bed dominated the far corner and a pale wooden dresser with a large vanity mirror nestled against the wall opposite it.

"It looks like Bridal Magazine vomited a suite in here," Nyx said.

"You mean you don't think it adds a touch of refined elegance to the establishment? I'm astonished."

Nyx thought it added a large dose of her mother's vanity to the establishment. She trailed her hand over the dresser, marveling at the lack of dust—magic had its uses—and studied the array of cosmetics on the gleaming surface. In an isolated pocket of the world with absolutely no one to impress but herself, Elena Fortuna had never once been less than perfectly put together.

"She didn't even bother taking anything with her. You know, when I used to wonder about her, imagine who she might have been, I always hoped she was nice. Smart." Nyx opened a drawer, the brilliant array of lacy undergarments causing her to close it immediately. "That's stupid, I guess. Everyone who doesn't know their parents hopes they're nice and smart and that they loved their kid."

"It's not stupid. And stars know I don't have any misplaced affection for the woman but she wasn't so bad in the beginning. When we were younger. And I think—I think she *did* love you. She just wasn't very good at it."

"Maybe we can put that on her epitaph when she dies: *She loved, just not very well.* What was it all *for*? Why make us live all the way out here when she obviously hated it just to dump us in Dead Earth? Stars know she was getting money from somewhere, it's not like she couldn't have afforded to buy us a place in the real world."

Every time Elena had left she'd done it with nothing but the clothes she was wearing, and every time Viktor had dragged her back it was with three or four trunks' worth of expensive clothing and jewelry that mostly got shoved into the storage section of the barn where her mother never touched any of it again. So much money wasted except for the trunk of champagne she always brought with her that stayed right out front on the porch, and Nyx and Seth had known better than to ever risk stealing a single bottle.

Where had the money come from? Nyx toyed with the idea of her mother moonlighting as a high-end escort because it amused her, but she knew deep down that Elena Fortuna would have considered that beneath her.

"We know she had help getting here," Seth mused out loud. "The kind of financial help my father couldn't have given her. Maybe whoever that was sent her money. Maybe whoever it was is the same person that gave her this place."

"Why would anyone give my mother a house and a constant stream of money?"

"I can think of *one* reason. One living, breathing reason."

"*Me*?" Nyx laughed. "You think my *dad* was sending her money? Like, intergalactic child support?"

"I can't think of any other reason someone would support a woman who was that self-absorbed. And considering she dumped you the day you turned eighteen, when you could legally exist on your own in Dead Earth without her..."

"Let me get this straight, our new operating theory is that my unknown father paid my mother exorbitant sums of money to raise me in the middle of absolute nowhere and the day she was no longer being paid to do that she left me on the sidewalk?"

"Yep, that about sums it up. And she didn't just leave you on the sidewalk, she left you bound to a certain locale right next to the ley line for easy retrieval by" —he did a drum roll on the doorframe— "*dum dum dum,* your real father."

"Why erase my memory? If that's the case—and that is a major *if*—it's not like I had any clue about any of it that was worth erasing. I don't even know who my dad is."

"That you remember."

"I am relatively certain I *did not* know who my dad is."

"Why?"

Nyx threw up her hands. "Because I would have told you, and you clearly don't know, so I clearly didn't."

The excessively smug look those words brought to his face made Nyx want to take them right back. Stars knew his ego didn't need her boosting it.

"Besides, your brilliant theory is missing a rather crucial piece. My supposedly rich, loving father never bothered to come collect me, therefore he probably doesn't exist, therefore my mother probably *was* moonlighting as a high-end escort."

"The only way anyone would possibly pay your mother as an escort is if the contract stipulated she had to keep her mouth shut the entire time."

"So not the point. I'm tabling the wealthy father conspiracy theory." Nyx rubbed at her temples, digging her fingers in against the stress creeping in at the edges. "Come on, I think this room is giving me a headache."

"It's probably not the room, Nyxi. At least not in the way you think."

"Then what is it?"

"Memory." He tapped his necklace. "Putting this thing back on knocked me out cold. When I finally woke up I had a migraine for two weeks after."

"I'm not even remembering things."

"Not every specific memory of your life, no. But all the things you know from having lived those memories? Things about me, your mom? That seems to be coming back. Which means you have to be regaining access to the memories themselves."

Nyx gave him a blank stare.

"What? I listened when your mom taught you things."

Okay, then.

"If this is what my mother's room brought back then let's see what mine does."

27

———

Unsurprisingly, Nyx's room contained mostly books. It was a small room, more akin to a storage area—which she had a deep suspicion it might have been designed as—so there weren't any bookcases. Instead, the books were stacked from floor to ceiling, spanning the length of the wall across from the small bed. Other than that bed and a small trunk at its foot, there wasn't anything else in the room.

"It's so creepy that they just *left* everything here. Mom didn't even bother to clear out her own things, much less pack anything I might care about." Or that Seth might have, only… "Where's your room?"

There *weren't* any more rooms in the house and she already knew Viktor had taken the living room.

Seth ran a hand through his hair, let it fall. "Does it matter?"

"Yes, it matters. Where is it?"

"It's in the barn."

"The—the *barn*? You're serious?"

"Look, it's not a big deal. It wasn't for that long. We shared a room for a long time growing up. Elena and Dad wanted us to be like siblings but we're not actually related and it didn't work out that way. When they figured that out, they shipped me out of the house."

"This is *Montana*. It doesn't get above freezing in the winter and you're telling me you lived in the damn barn? Like some sort of exile?"

"It really wasn't that bad okay?" He paced the small room. "Hell, I slept easier without those two breathing disapproval down my neck from one wall over. The barn's heating spells aren't quite as good as the house's but they work and when it got really bad you just let me in here through the window."

Nyx didn't even have words for the level of messed up that was but she was trying to find them when Seth's foot connected with something peeking out from underneath the edge of the bed, sending that something rolling and clinking against the wall. He crouched down, reached underneath and pulled out an empty champagne bottle. One of her *mother's* champagne bottles, one of the ones Nyx was certain it would have taken an act of dire need for her to be brave enough to filch.

"Looks like you had a good final night in the place." Seth turned the bottle over in his hands, staring at it but not really seeing it, his gaze locked somewhere in the past. "There's something that's been bothering me. Something I need to know and—"

He broke off, his voice strained, and Nyx laid her hand on his arm, the need to soothe the edges of that raw pain so visceral she couldn't ignore it.

"Did you know?" he whispered. "What was coming? I came to see you that night but you never opened the window and now..."

And now he was holding evidence that she had been upset enough that night to both ignore him and do something that in all their years of intentionally pissing off their parents, they'd never been quite brave enough to risk.

"I'm sorry, Seth, I don't remember."

But then she did, caught in the grip of a memory like watching a film play.

"What did you do to him?" Nyx demanded. She watched Viktor walk away, off to do her mother's bidding—again—and couldn't hide her disgust. She and Seth had wondered for years if his father's devotion to Elena was really just the result of unrequited love or if there was something less natural about it. Nyx knew now that love had nothing to do with it. Maybe it once had, but not anymore.

Elena Fortuna flicked an invisible speck of dust from her dress.

"I did what needed to be done. If the weak-willed are easily manipulated, that is hardly my fault."

"You're disgusting."

Elena's hand clamped around her wrist hard enough to bruise.

"You think you're so much better than me? You're no different." A slow, satisfied smile spread across her face. "No different at all. Or do you really think that boy likes *you?"*

Revulsion hit her. "I didn't—I would never—*"*

"No?" Her mother shrugged and dropped her wrist. "If you say so."

The mere possibility that Nyx could have done to Seth what her mother had done to Viktor made her insides heave. She bolted for the front door and threw up the contents of her stomach all over the front lawn. She couldn't *have used her power on Seth like that, hadn't even known Hidden had that kind of power until this morning.*

She couldn't *have, could she? Only, she'd read that some people used power without realizing it, without knowing they even had it. That thought alone had her grabbing two bottles of champagne from the trunk by the door and not caring if her mother beat her blue in the morning for it. If she'd really done what her mother suggested, she wouldn't even care. She'd deserve it.*

Elena didn't emerge from her room when Nyx carried the bottles back to hers. She cracked open the first one, choking on the bubbles and sweetness, grateful for the hit of lightness behind her temples. When Seth came knocking on her window she was too ashamed and terrified to open it and just kept drinking until he went away.

Because beneath the buzz and the denial lay the cold, terrifying fear that she was just like her mother. Sitting there, alone in the dark, even afraid of what she could have done, she was still more afraid to be alone. Afraid that if she looked inward, if she examined the patterns of her magic, she would find little pieces she hadn't known were there, little pieces she could use.

Even if she hadn't manipulated Seth, what was to say she wouldn't do it in the future? How long were their lives going to go on like this, trapped in this miserable place with equally miserable people? How much more could Seth take? If he left by himself, Nyx didn't think Viktor would track him down like he did every time they ran away together. Didn't think he would care enough to. Faced with the possibility of being here without him, who was to say what power she might use?

Nyx shook her head. No. Seth said he was close to figuring out how to hide their trail from Viktor's senses. Once he could do that, they would leave, and Viktor and her mother would never find them again, and they could pretend this entire fucked up existence had just been a bad dream.

She placed her hand over her heart, over the tattoo her mother had ridiculed her for. They were getting out of here. Her and Seth. They were going to see the universe together, and nothing was going to stop them.

But if they were going to do that, she needed to be sure, absolutely sure, that Seth's life wouldn't be like Viktor's.

She kept drinking until she was drunk enough to turn her gaze inward, to follow the twisting lines of power inside her. She had always focused before on the ones that allowed her to Hide things, because those were the ones her mother cared about, but now she looked elsewhere, separating the ones that were an intrinsic part of her from the ones that led somewhere else, until she found a knotted core of power that felt different than her power to Hide, felt opposite. Attractive.

It didn't feel like anything she had ever accessed before but she couldn't be sure. And she needed, so desperately, to be sure. To be certain that she hadn't used it before and that she never would again—

never could *again. So she opened the second bottle of champagne, gathered a few strands of her power into a blade, and began to cut away at that knotted core. She started out trying to be precise, methodical, but the* pain…

She lost track of the number of times she blacked out that night, and each time she awoke it took another few swallows of alcohol until she could gather the strength to cut at another thread. By the end there was no finesse to it, just a mindless hacking at that core until it was scarred and lifeless inside her.

The sun streaming through the window the next morning woke her in time for her to be fully conscious when her mother backhanded her with a force that made Nyx bite through her tongue.

"Stupid, idiot girl." Elena's hand gripped an empty champagne bottle and for a delirious moment Nyx wondered if her mother was going to bash her head in with it. Then Elena's rage cooled, hardened into a thin, cruel smile. "You just destroyed the only thing that might have made your new life bearable. And for what? To prove to yourself that he loves *you? You're children. Even if he thinks he loves you now, give it a few weeks, a few months, hell, a few years. He won't love you then. But rest assured you'll be stuck with him all the same. Just like I'm stuck with his father."*

Elena began to weave, then, strands of her power twisting together, forming a veil of intricate loops and whorls and by the time Nyx realized what the pattern meant it was too late, because she already couldn't remember who she was.

"Nyx?"

Seth gripped her shoulders, the look on his face telling her he'd been about to try shaking her back to reality. Or he'd already tried it.

"I didn't know," she said in answer to the question he'd asked before.

He still didn't quite relax. "You never shut me out before. And I know you were awake."

"I was afraid."

So she told him. About his father, about the magic her mother had woven around Viktor's senses, the magic she now understood was the Hidden "ability" Morgen had told her about when they'd been trapped in the fighting ring on Arkadia, the one he'd suggested she use to make their captor more amenable. He couldn't have had any idea what it actually was or he never would have suggested she use it.

In all fairness to Morgen, it had evolved to be what he had thought it was—a defense mechanism of sorts, used for a brief time to more kindly dispose a person towards a Hidden.

"Look at me."

Looking at Seth was exactly what Nyx couldn't bring herself to do. His fingers brushed her chin, tilted her face up, the gentleness in his touch at odds with the fury that caused his hand to tremble.

"You are not responsible for a single damn thing Elena Fortuna ever did. And I never would have needed you to cut yourself apart to prove you wouldn't do something I already know you could never do."

"I know," she whispered. "That's why I had to do it." Because he might have believed it, but she hadn't.

Seth muttered something under his breath and then, "Can we get out of this stars-forsaken place now?"

She let him lead her out of the house but she insisted on seeing the training ring, the garden, the barn. Seth flat-out refused to climb the stairs to the loft area that formed his bedroom so Nyx wandered it herself, sitting down on the red and blue squared quilt that still covered the bed, and remembering the first time she'd kissed him here. He'd been so surprised and they'd both been so awkward. Learning how to draw a contraceptive spell hadn't been too difficult, though Seth had been the one to use it because Nyx's magic, so highly specified, wouldn't bend itself to other talents.

She was still sitting on the bed, tracing the patterns, when Seth climbed up the ladder.

"Get bored?" she asked, only half-teasing.

"Just trying to decide if it's worth burning to the ground." He, on the other hand, wasn't teasing at all.

"Hey, I have fond memories of this room." They were coming back to her in soft waves, well worth the budding migraine they were leaving in their wake.

He knelt down and rested his forehead on her knee. "Leaving you broke something in me."

"Seth—"

"Just listen. I spent years looking for you when I had no idea what I was looking *for*. And I think it would have killed me, in the end, if your memory hadn't come back. And then sometimes I think maybe it should have, maybe that's what I deserve, for leaving you here when I know" —his fingers dug into the mattress to either side of her— "when I know if things were reversed you never would have left me."

"You've got me on some kind of pedestal, Seth, but I'm not perfect." She threaded her fingers into his hair, working at the twin spots of tension at the base of his neck. "Everyone likes to think they'd do the right thing in a shitty situation. But the truth is, when someone screams for help in the street most people just keep walking.

"If I had known what was coming, if I could have made the choice, I would have told you to do exactly what you did. My mother—" No, she hadn't ever really had a mother. "Elena. I don't know why she Hid my life from me. But I think at least part of her wanted to destroy us. To prove that she was right and we were destined to be as miserable as she was. And I think maybe if you'd stayed she would have gotten that wish.

"I can't make you forgive yourself, but I can't hold it against you. I don't want to."

He took a deep, shuddering breath. "Where does that leave us?"

"I don't know. But you will *always* be my family, Seth. Whatever else there is or isn't, we'll always be that."

She tried to stand but he held her in place.

"There's something else."

Nyx closed her eyes. What else could there possibly be?

"Though I thought the records might be helpful with your mother, that wasn't really why I wanted into the Keep's library. I was looking for something." His fingers tapped idly against his pocket and she knew he'd found whatever he'd been looking for. "Do you ever remember your mother mentioning something called the Harvester?"

The Harvester pulsed against her chest even as Nyx shook her head. She was pretty sure she wasn't even lying.

"Most people think it's a myth. What it really is, what it does —there's no information on it. It's not mentioned in any history books, nothing, just in stories and fables here and there. But I heard your mother mention it once, when she was angry and drunk and yelling at my dad. See when I tore this off," he tapped his necklace, "I didn't forget everything. I just forgot you. I remembered growing up here, Elena, and what she was. So when the Kumir kept coming after me, I figured it had something to do with her—with the Hidden—and maybe with the Harvester. So I started digging.

"Historically the Hidden were like any other variety of magic user—you wanted their services, you hired them. But not long after the All Council was formed, they quit working for anyone else. That's around the same time any mention of the Harvester disappeared."

She connected the dots he'd laid out. "You think the All Council had the entirety of the Hidden working to hide the Harvester?"

He nodded. "I think it's what got them all killed, too. To Hide something of that power without a Hidden being in direct possession of it would be difficult enough. To make the entire universe forget it ever existed? That would require many Hidden working in concert. Possibly all of them. And if the universe were down to only a handful of Hidden working on the problem? Its existence might very well start seeping back into the collective consciousness like it seems to be doing."

For a man without half his memories at the time, he'd done a damn good job of putting things together. "So you think someone hired the Kumir to kill the Hidden in order to find out where the Harvester is?"

If Seth was right, if the Hidden had been keeping the Harvester a secret for centuries, what were the odds that it had come into her possession by accident? That of all the people in the universe, Kaden had recognized the importance of getting the Harvester to a Hidden, and furthermore had managed to track the Hidden to Earth, to *find* her, when no one else, not even the Kumir, had managed to discover where Elena Fortuna had disappeared to?

She figured those odds were pretty much zero. The only question was, did Kaden know that, or had he simply been another pawn in the game someone else was playing out on a cosmic scale? She didn't know, and she figured that even if Kaden was here he wouldn't give her a straight answer.

"But for that to be possible, for someone to hire the Kumir to hunt down the Hidden, it would have to be someone who *did* remember the Harvester existed. Someone the Hidden left out of their spell, someone who hired them."

"Someone on the Council," Seth finished.

Which made sense, considering Kaden had come into possession of the Harvester when a Councilor was trying to steal it from their own vault.

"I must sound crazy."

The smart thing to do would be to make a joke, tell him he *did* sound a little crazy. Not tell him anything about the Harvester. But she didn't think keeping things to herself had ever been a part of her nature. Didn't think she'd ever kept anything from Seth in her life.

So she withdrew the pendant, nudging at the Hiding with that innate part of herself she was still trying to figure out, and willed him to be able to see it for what it was. "Crazier than this?"

Seth's face was so inscrutable that for a moment she thought she'd failed on the magic side of things, and he couldn't really see what he was looking at. Then he tore his gaze from the Harvester. "Tell me that's not actually *it.*"

"I would, but people keep telling me I'm a shitty liar."

"But you said your mom never mentioned it."

"I don't think she did. I didn't have it when we left the valley. And I didn't know what it was—didn't even know what *I* was—when I agreed to Hide it."

She'd told him too much, could tell by the distant look on his face that his brain was putting the pieces together—her friends, wanted by the All Council. The fact she'd Hidden something before she even knew she was Hidden.

"That son of a bitch." He rose to his feet like he had too much energy to stay down. "That *fucking* son of a bitch. It was him wasn't it? That's why the entire Council's looking for him. He stole it and fucking used you to Hide it?"

Nyx winced. "It wasn't *quite* like that."

"Then how was it?"

Briefly, she explained how Kaden had ended up with the Harvester, which did little to soften the near-murderous rage in Seth's eyes. "Anyway, he'd heard rumors Elena had fled to Earth. He came here looking for her and found me instead."

"And you just promised a random stranger you'd hide something for him?" She could hear the incredulity in his voice.

"He didn't ask for two years. And only then because he was turning himself in."

"Oh, well that just makes it all better then. He waited two years to dump the problems of the universe in your lap, so everything is fine. You seriously went to the trouble to rescue this asshole from jail?"

She couldn't keep her lips from curving up. "He was sort of a side quest."

"Why are you smiling?" Seth demanded. "What about this is funny?"

"Absolutely nothing. It's just nice to have someone on my side, for once." It wasn't that Kaden's friends were against her, per se—well, Maruca definitely was—but they *were* his friends first.

"I'm always on your side, Nyx. Always."

The words, the complete conviction in them, both warmed her and sent a stab of guilt through her. "I destroyed your home," she blurted out, thinking of Calista.

He raised an eyebrow. "I had a feeling you had something to do with the walls coming to life, but do go on."

"The Harvester. It...*woke* something in Calista. Something they just called a darkness, something they weren't allowed to explain to me. From what Calista said, I think the darkness had the Harvester before. A long time ago. Maybe it even *made* the Harvester."

"Can it follow us here?"

"Physically? Calista said it would be a few weeks before it could leave the Station. But she also thought we'd have more time to get out before it woke up, too. As for whether or not it will know where to find us? I have no idea." She frowned. "Before you asked me about the Harvester you said you were looking for something in the Keep. What?"

"This." He pulled out a slim black volume, worn and fragile looking. Nyx couldn't read the markings on it but her heart beat faster, faster, because there, on the cover, was a perfect representation of the Harvester of Worlds. She felt a sheen like oily darkness slipping off the book in soft waves.

"It talks about the Harvester?"

Seth's shoulders slumped. "I don't know. I can't read the damn thing."

Nyx held out her hand and he placed the book in her palm. She took it, staring at the words above the representation of the Harvester, willing herself to understand it.

Nothing.

"Do we just need better translator spells?"

"The Stations have the best spells on the market and I couldn't read it there. I don't think it's written in a language, I think it's written in some kind of cypher. I think—I think it's a journal."

The oily darkness slipping off the book's cover took on a new taint, sent shivers twisting down Nyx's spine.

"How did you even find this?" If he couldn't read it how had he known what it was?

"I ran across it the first time I was in the Keep's library. It felt…odd. I can't really explain it, but it stuck with me. It wasn't until later, when I was looking for information and heard an old rhyme about the Harvester's four rings, that I remembered the image and thought it might be related."

"It's definitely related. Though I'm not sure how much it matters if we can't read it." She'd bet Morgen, with his affinity for languages, could crack it in a hot minute. But Morgen wasn't here.

Seth shook his head. "I thought it might help us figure out things with the Kumir. I never once considered you'd actually *have* the Harvester. Nyx…what are you going to *do* with it?"

"I told Calista I'd destroy it if I could. So that's what I'm going to try and do."

"Okay." Seth nodded. "How do you plan on doing that? Hit it with a sledgehammer and see if it breaks?"

"I'm not *that* stupid. I've seen what it can do. Believe me when I say I have no interest in seeing if it's capable of autonomous self-preservation. When we get back, I'll ask my Station. And if Kaliaris doesn't know, I guess we'd better hope we decode this" —she lifted the journal— "and it has some kind of answer." Hope that destroying the Harvester would be enough to keep them safe. Hope that with it gone, the Kumir would stop hunting.

She stood and slipped the book into her pocket. As she withdrew her fingers she wiped them on her pants, futilely trying to rid them of the oily feeling, the darkness, that clung to them. She didn't know if the feeling was really there, or if it was just her mind, seeing darkness everywhere after Calista's warning.

"That's a lot of hoping," Seth said. He wasn't mocking her, just stating plain fact.

"I know. But I don't know what else to do. You come up with something, I'm all ears. Until then, let's work with what we have."

He nodded. "Okay. So what do we do now?"

She held her hand out to him. "We go *home*." Because she was hoping, she realized, that he'd think of the Station as his home too.

A smile tugged at the corners of his lips. "Yeah." He slipped his hand into hers, and she felt the weight slide off his shoulders as he did. "Yeah, okay."

"Griff's probably worried sick about us." Even if her Avatar would never in a million years admit it. "I hope you're prepared to be mother-henned when get back."

28

———

Griff absolutely mother-henned, and Nyx was happy to let him do it. She was trying—and mostly failing—not to think about him like a father figure, but it was hard considering he'd lived centuries and therefore had the wise air of Someone Who Knew Things. He also fretted over her and Seth like she imagined a parent who actually cared about their children might, chastised them for things like letting the Station do *all* the laundry, and kept trying to herd Seth towards finding a life calling that did not involve video games.

From her perch next to Seth on the couch, Nyx watched him shoot away at the screen and shook her head. She'd known she was going to regret buying him the gaming console on the way back from Montana, but he'd been depressed as hell after seeing their childhood home, and since that was *her* fault, she'd felt guilty. Besides, it had given her an excuse to get a television, because she was still trying to convince Griff that movies were a thing he would like. She wasn't sure *why* he was so staunchly against the idea of watching one, but so far she'd yet to rope him into it.

All of which meant Seth had had the television largely to himself in the four days they'd been back. Nyx was just happy to see him happy. They hadn't kissed since Montana, and they seemed to have both silently agreed not to bring it up. But unlike with her and Kaden's avoidance of discussing *that* non-relationship, nothing was weird between her and Seth.

They'd settled into an easy familiarity, a comfortable friendship, and she thought maybe they were both just glad to be somewhere safe, with someone they knew they could trust, who wouldn't judge them. Seth had said he wasn't going anywhere. They lived on a Nexus. They had all the time in the world to decide what—if anything—came next. She didn't have to rush this. Nothing was going to happen to her, to him, to Griff.

Nothing was going to happen.

She'd told herself that over and over since they'd returned from Montana. But she knew well enough when she was trying to convince herself of something she didn't believe. She should have felt more secure with Morgen and the Moors gone—no illegal fugitives in her Station to continue hiding from the All Council, after all—but she didn't.

She couldn't stop remembering Calista's warnings about a waking darkness, couldn't stop trying to puzzle out what that darkness could be. Was it a force? A person? Something her human mind wasn't even capable of contemplating?

More importantly, how long did she have before it came for her? Whatever it was, Calista had said it wanted the Harvester. That it could recognize the Harvester in spite of the Hiding. That the Harvester had once altered the fabric of the universe.

Was that why the darkness wanted it? Was that why Alastair, the councilor who had tried to take it from the All Council's vault, wanted it? To change the universe?

She was almost desperate enough to try and ask the Harvester itself. It had never spoken to her, not in words, but at those times when it had wanted to be used, it had communicated its intent on some level. But even if she'd been foolish enough to try and talk to it, the Harvester wasn't listening. It had wakened briefly in Montana, but since returning to the Station it had once more become as eerily silent as it had been inside Calista's Station.

Jevryn's ring, next to it on the chain around her neck, was just as silent. Griff had told her to give Jevryn time, and yes, it hadn't been very long since she'd spoken his name to the ring, but she had a feeling he wasn't coming. When he'd offered her this boon, he had wanted to know what really happened the day the All Council had come to the Station. If he still wanted that information, wouldn't he have shown up by now? Or maybe sent a letter? Surely the wider universe still knew about letters.

Given the lack of communication, she figured he'd simply lost interest in the scenario and decided she wasn't worth his time. He was centuries-old and likely thought himself very important. He probably didn't have time for a twenty-five year-old woman from Earth who was really hoping he could show up and answer the mysteries of the universe for her.

She stood abruptly, toppling the book off her lap that she'd been pretending to read while she instead drowned in worry and self-doubt. She wasn't going to get any answers by sitting on her ass and waiting for Jevryn to show up.

At her movement, Seth dropped his controller and frowned up at her, his character dying in a hail of gore-spattered bullets from his sudden inattention.

"What's wrong?"

"I need to talk to Kaliaris." She swallowed. "About the Harvester."

Seth's gaze fell to the Harvester, to the interlinked rings that rested against her chest. She had intended, after their discussion in his old barn loft, to find a way to leave him out of the Hiding she'd placed on the Harvester. Between the Kumir hunting him, their shared messed-up childhood, and the fact he'd already found out about the Harvester on his own, she'd figured he didn't deserve to have a hole in his memories where it should be.

That, and she'd found she was selfishly unwilling for him to have *any* holes in his memory concerning her. She'd lived so much of her adult life watching people's eyes glaze over and slip past her, and she hadn't wanted that to happen with him, ever, even for the handful of seconds when his eyes might land on the Harvester.

But she'd never had to find that way to leave him out of the Hiding. Her magic seemed to already have a Seth-shaped exception built into it, as if she'd long ago decided to never hide anything from him, and her magic had acted on that decision even when she hadn't been able to remember who he was.

She'd tested the theory over the last few days, picking random objects to Hide from the world and then asking Seth if he could see them. He always could. If she wanted him not to, she had to actively think about Hiding the object from *him* specifically. It worked, when she tried it like that, but she found her power recalcitrant, as if it didn't like doing what she'd asked.

Seth was currently wearing a look of concern. "Why do you sound terrified to talk to your Station?"

"Because I am?"

He frowned. "You weren't freaked out after you talked to Calista."

Nyx waved a dismissive hand. "That's because talking to Calista was like walking into the land of pastel-colored, cotton candy unicorn dreams."

"That's oddly specific."

She glared at him. "It's also accurate. Calista was all nice white stairs and pretty mist and polite conversation. You want to know what Kaliaris is like? Falling through darkness and landing in writhing vines while a voice like a cheese grater tells you you're going to die together and then avoiding that fate by making a deal that binds you to said Station for the rest of your literally eternal life."

Seth went perfectly still and Nyx realized exactly what she'd said.

"What deal?" he asked.

She ran her thumb over the number five tattooed on her

hand. She'd always meant to tell Seth she just...hadn't meant to tell him like this. "Guardians aren't supposed to travel the lines," she said softly, "but no one could tell me why."

He groaned. "You never were big on following rules without explanation."

"Evra was on Arkadia and I needed to find her and I knew..." She swallowed and decided she'd have to get used to saying Kaden's name again at some point. "And I knew Kaden might be there and I wanted answers. So I went. When I came back, Griff and the Station were in chaos. The only thing I could do, the only way to keep us all from dying, was to bind us together." She brushed her fingertips to the thorns in her cheek. "But Kaliaris was angry, and they didn't fully trust me. I didn't have a lot of time to bargain. The best deal I could get was the right to leave the planet six times, never for longer than a week."

She lifted her tattooed hand with a rueful smile. Seth stared at it. "That says five." His eyes met hers. "You used one of your trips to come after me."

She shrugged. "Yeah, well, chasing men across the universe to drag answers out of them seems to be my specialty," she joked.

Seth didn't laugh, and he hadn't stopped staring at the tattooed number. "Fuck, Nyxi, I'm sorry."

"Don't be. I'm not. Honestly, given my experiences in the wider universe, I'm perfectly content to sit my ass right here for a decade or two." Or three or four. "But...it is a literal forever, for me. At least, it is unless the All Council finds out what I've done and kills me." There was some relief in knowing she wasn't truly immortal, that she *could* die, just not by aging. She fidgeted, then made herself stop. "I don't expect you to stay. I wouldn't *ask* you to stay." She touched her hand to the galaxy tattoo on her heart. "I don't remember everything, but I know this isn't the life either of us talked about. Being stuck here, in one place, forever...I guess it's not that different from what we were trying to get away from growing up."

He looked at her, long and hard, every line of his face at once familiar and new. "The only part of being here that's anything like being *there*, Nyxi, is you. And as far as I'm concerned, you're the best part of both worlds."

That was both the cheesiest and sweetest thing anyone had ever said to her. At least, that she could remember. She had a feeling sixteen-year-old Seth had maybe been pretty cheesy.

"So if you want to get rid of me," Seth said, his tone lightening and that ever-present half-smile tilting up the corner of his mouth, "you're going to have to try harder than some lame-ass, 'Oh no, my life is tied to this awesome Station that caters to my every whim,' excuse."

Nyx's throat tightened with emotion. That was the thing about Seth—he could make even things of monumentally epic proportions seem not so bad. She cleared her throat and managed to say, "I think you mean scary, rude, potentially sociopathic sentient Station."

Seth waved a dismissive hand. "Details. So are you gonna go talk to them or what?"

"Yeah." Suddenly Kaliaris didn't seem as frightening as they had a few minutes ago. "I guess I will."

"You want me to come with? I hear Stations really like me."

"Calista says one flattering thing and you think you're God's gift to Stations everywhere."

"I'm not hearing any complaints. So?"

"Thanks for the offer, but I think I'd better do this one on my own." Kaliaris probably *did* like Seth better than her, but she still had a feeling they might try to eat him if she brought him anywhere near their Heart.

"Alright." Seth settled back against the couch and restarted his game. "Let me know if you change your mind."

"I will," she whispered. On her way out, she paused in the doorway and looked back, wondering for a moment if this whole thing, if Seth, was some bizarre figment of her lonely imagination. Then he yelled something particularly obscene at the television and she decided she wasn't creative enough with curse words to have imagined that dialogue.

She turned and headed for the portal room before she could change her mind. She had a powerful magical artifact to destroy. Hopefully, her very creepy bonded Station could tell her just how to do it.

EPILOGUE

Nyx rolled the Harvester between her thumb and forefinger and stared at the smooth cosmic floor of the Station's portal.

Three weeks. It had been three weeks since she'd left Seth's room to go talk to Kaliaris and been met with a wall of silence. She'd gone back to the portal room every day, sometimes two or three times a day, but it never mattered how often she went or what she said, the result was the same. Kaliaris refused to see her.

Actually, even that wasn't quite right. Saying they refused to see her implied they had at least interacted with her in some way. Which they hadn't. Given what she'd told them when she'd asked to see them—of the Harvester and Calista—she was left with one bitter conclusion.

"I never pegged you for a coward, Kaliaris." The faintest ripple across the floor of the portal was the only indication Kaliaris had heard her at all, and the most reaction she'd gotten out of them so far. "Damn it, just *talk* to me."

The floor she stood on swelled up like a wave and carried her backwards out of the room. Her back slammed into something large and furry, and Griff's wings flared out to the sides for stability as he halted her momentum.

"Sorry." She regained her balance and turned around. Griff, who had likely grown in size only to halt her being bodily thrown out of the portal room, returned to housecat size and jumped up onto a nearby table.

"The only thing you need to apologize for," Griff said, "is being late to the event you planned and wrangled us all into."

"It's a movie night. I don't know that it qualifies as an event."

"I have been talked into watching pictures move around on a wall. It is an event."

"It's a lot more fun than you make it sound," Nyx said defensively. "You'll see."

"If it is so fun, then why are you in here again instead of outside with the rest of us?"

Because I can't make heads or tails of the journal Seth brought home, and with Kaliaris not talking to me I'm up precisely zero at trying to solve the Harvester problem.

"Someone has to pull Seth away from the barbecue grill, and stop Evra from eating everything he cooks," Griff continued.

"Sounds like a job for this surly griffin I know." But Nyx wended her way through the library and to the French doors that opened onto the Station's wide back patio. She'd been planning this night ever since Evra had returned to the Station with one-hundred and six people in tow from the Shadow Market, and realized she was going to need a de-stressing event once she'd sorted them all out.

Her days had been a whirlwind of hiding said people's existence during the hours she spent on Arrivals and Departures, and carefully introducing them to Earth Between in the other hours. She'd lost track of the number of cover stories she'd created, identification papers Griff had forged, fights she'd broken up, and new customs she'd explained. All in all, Nyx felt somewhat like she was running a witness protection program. In some ways, maybe she was.

She never would have managed it all without Diana's and Ankira's help, the two women a godsend at helping her acclimate the people to their new lives. As of now, fifty-six of them still resided in the Station—jobs and housing did not miraculously appear for everyone overnight—but Nyx didn't mind.

It was hard *to* mind when her Station could expand itself easily enough to contain them. If she'd had to spend half the money she'd earned so far as a Guardian on mountains of fabric and groceries so the Station could clothe and feed them all, well, she didn't mind that much, either. She'd never had enough to take care of herself before, much less anyone else, and it felt good to give people hope.

Even so, giving that many people hope could be exhausting, and she'd finally managed to carve out tonight to have just for herself, Evra, Griff, and Seth. So, naturally, the first moment of peace and quiet she'd had in her own skull in weeks had immediately been interrupted by anxiety about the Harvester and Calista's nameless darkness.

Which was why she'd found herself in the portal room again instead of with everyone else. She shook her head as she stepped onto the back porch and firmly told herself that she was going to have fun, or else.

Seth's enthusiasm for the movie night venture had turned it into a full-on party. He'd hung the television on an exterior wall facing the back porch, conned Griff into stringing multicolored lanterns all around and above the area, requisitioned new porch furniture, and planned the menu.

She knew, because he'd submitted several alternate menu plans to her for approval before she'd finally gotten exasperated and told him to just cook all of it if that would make him happy. In retrospect, maybe she should have advised some restraint.

There was food *everywhere*. Platters covered the small island next to the grill, rested on end tables, and littered the coffee table set inside the new u-shaped wicker sectional. It was as if Seth had selected every possible Earth party appetizer and made them all. Hot wings. Seven-layer dip with chips. Cucumber sandwiches. Pinwheels. Fruit platters. Chicken and vegetable kebabs, and the list just went on.

He was currently flipping a second batch of cream-cheese stuffed jalapenos on the grill, tongs in one hand, a beer dangling idly from the other. If the nearly-empty plate in front of Evra was any indication, she'd eaten the entirety of the first batch of jalapenos herself.

Nyx walked up to Seth and plucked the tongs out of his hand. Or tried to. He refused to relinquish them.

"There are four of us," she told him, "and there's enough food here for twenty. The time for an intervention has come. Hand over the tongs."

"I just need to finish these last ones."

"That's how it goes with an addiction," Nyx said with faux-seriousness. "It's always 'just one more.' One more batch of jalapeno poppers. One more tray of cupcakes. When does it end, Seth?"

"Literally right now, smartass." Seth transferred the jalapenos to an empty plate and carried it to the coffee table, setting it down in front of Evra.

She eyed it with a mix of desire and trepidation. "I am beginning to think you may be a devil, Seth Hawthorne. Because the way this night is going I am going to gain ten pounds and it will not be muscle," she grumbled.

That really wasn't Seth's fault. The man had a gift where food was concerned.

"I am absolutely certain," a deep voice said, "that you would be all the more beautiful for it, my fair lady Amazon."

Nyx's heart sped up. She knew that voice. She spun around and found Morgen Drahl, tall, dark, and handsome as ever, standing five feet away. She let out an honest-to-stars squeal of delight, leaped over the sectional, and flung herself at him with enough force to knock him back two steps.

She'd been practicing blacking out the Station's senses, and so his return had been a complete and wondrous surprise. Morgen caught her and obligingly twirled her in a circle.

"Little Guardian, I cannot even begin to say how much I have missed you."

Nyx went to mock-punch him in the arm but halted the blow. Every single of inch of him was covered in scrapes and bruises she had at first missed in her enthusiastic greeting.

"I'm glad you're back and all," she began. "Wait, you are back, right? Like *back*, back?"

"Yes, little Guardian, I am *back*, back."

"Thank the stars. So now that you're back and all, which I am absolutely thrilled about, what happened to you? Does your current physical condition have something to do with Evra mysteriously alluding to her belief in your imminent demise?"

Morgen ruffled her hair. "Indeed, little Guardian."

Softer, so her words wouldn't travel beyond them, she asked, "Did everything go okay with...you know?"

He studied her. "Are you trying to ask how Kaden is?"

"No." She shook her head to emphasize the fact. She wanted to leave that chapter of her life behind her, if she could. "I'm asking how *you* are."

"Ah. It turns out your words of wisdom were rather on point. After I dragged Ruca and Kaden home to visit mother, and after she stopped crying and threatening to kill us all with her bare hands, I told them what I wanted."

"And?"

"And they get it. Mostly. Mother wants to meet Evra. Speaking of, there's something I need to do."

Morgen walked, in what could only be called a stately manner, to the sectional where Evra sprawled. He knelt at her feet with all the solemnity of a man about to propose marriage. He then proffered to her a thick, trifold letter, as if it were an exotic flower.

"Moriana al'Daemon's response."

Evra picked up the letter but didn't open it, holding it

between her thumb and forefinger like it might at any moment sprout fangs and bite her.

"She gave you her permission?" she asked incredulously.

"Don't be ridiculous. I believe it reads something along the lines of, 'Your bloodline may be severed but I would rather see you date a Vethra beast than a disgraced Enforcer of low birth.' But the point is that I asked, she responded, and I live to tell the tale. And I do believe you once promised me that if I were foolish enough to ask your mother's permission to court you and survive the attempt, you would honor me with a date."

"I suppose I did," Evra said, unable to entirely hide her pleased expression. "I look forward to discovering what you think a proper date entails."

"I'll do my best not to disappoint." Morgen lifted Evra's hand and kissed it. She didn't even make a token gesture of annoyance.

To Nyx's right, Seth coughed. Loudly.

Nyx rolled her eyes. "Morgen, if I could introduce Seth Hawthorne. Seth, Morgen Drahl."

Morgen rose from his kneeling position to give Seth an appraising once-over. "So, you're the person we traveled halfway across the galaxy to find?"

"What can I say? I'm worth the chase."

"It is true. He makes excellent cuisine." Evra lifted the plate of jalapeno poppers and offered it to Morgen. Morgen selected one and proceeded to eat it with a contemplative look on his face.

"Well?" Seth asked.

"I think," Morgen answered, "you and I are going to get along rather well."

With a feeling that was half horror, half happiness, Nyx suspected Morgen was absolutely right. She also suspected she would need every advantage her bond with the Station could offer her if she was going to contain a friendship between Seth Hawthorn and Morgen Drahl.

Morgen looked at the TV mounted on the wall. "So what's all this about?"

"We're finally having a movie night!" Nyx had found the enthusiasm she'd been lacking ten minutes ago, like she'd been missing something and that something was Morgen, completing the group. "Sit down" —she shoved him down next to Evra— "drink a beer" —Seth helpfully supplied one— "and prepare to have your mind blown."

"Will you finally reveal what we are watching?" Griff asked.

Nyx cleared her throat and put on her best presentation voice. "We're watching a storytelling classic. One first born in literature and then brought to life on the big screen.

"It has everything. Action. Adventure. Traveling to another realm. A girl's love for her dog. Singing."

"No." Seth's voice was filled with pure, unadulterated horror. "Please tell me you didn't."

"Look, for a while it was amusing that no one got the yellow brick road leading out of the portal room joke, but the time for understanding has come."

Seth groaned. "I hate this film. You *know* I hate this film." She realized suddenly that she *did* know. It was the first movie they'd ever seen when they'd snuck away from the valley, playing as a classics rerun at a dollar theater. He'd hated it so much, in fact, she'd almost never convinced him to watch another movie again.

"The bad songs," he continued. "The flying monkeys. The general ridiculousness of the entire thing."

"In all fairness to myself, I didn't remember you hated it until ten seconds ago, but the fact remains that *The Wizard of Oz* is a cinematic treasure and we're watching it."

"Flying monkeys?" Morgen asked.

"And *so* much more," Nyx promised.

"You owe me," Seth said. "You owe me *so* hard for doing this."

Nyx reached into the cooler at her feet and handed him

another beer with a patronizing, "There, there," that had him glaring at her.

"All right people, the first rule of movie night is, you don't talk during the film. The second rule of movie night is, you don't talk during the film."

"I could have gotten behind watching *Fight Club*," Seth muttered.

"You can pick next time, you big baby." She grabbed the remote, turned the TV on, and hit play. "And the film is now starting."

She settled back against the couch as the movie started to play. In that brief moment of darkness and silence just before the film started, anxiety crept back in on her enthusiasm. Seeing her friends' faces in the soft glow from the strands of patio lights, she couldn't help but fear that this moment of happiness would be taken from her. That Calista's darkness would come and destroy it at all.

Calista's words wouldn't stop haunting her. *If what you hold cannot be destroyed, if the darkness comes to possess it once more, the universe as you understand it will be irrevocably altered.*

How much time did she have left?

In the dimness of the television light, she looked at the people who surrounded her—her friends, her *family*—and decided right then and there that this fear wouldn't rule her. That she wouldn't allow anything else to be taken from her.

Let the universe give her its worst. Let the darkness come. When it did, she would be here to stand against it.

CURIOUS ABOUT WHAT WAS GOING ON IN KADEN'S HEAD DURING THOSE END SCENES?

Two bonus Kaden POV scenes are available exclusively to my newsletter subscribers. You can get them by signing up for my newsletter at:

https://michellemanus.com/newsletter/

If you enjoyed the book, it would be beyond super awesome of you to leave a rating and/or review at your retailer of choice. Reviews really are the best way you can help support authors.

Thanks so much for reading!

ABOUT THE AUTHOR

Michelle lives in a desolate land with a dark wizard, a unicorn, and a feline overlord. Despite certain stereotypes you may be familiar with, the dark wizard is not holding her captive, nor does the unicorn require virgin riders. The feline overlord, however, may well be evil.

She holds dual BAs in English and Philosophy, which has gotten her about as far as you would expect it to in life. Despite all evidence to the contrary, she's still desperately holding out hope that in an alternate reality she's a sword-wielding princess.

You can find Michelle on her website: www.michellemanus.com or her social media. Stop by and say hi! The virtual world is way cooler with friends.

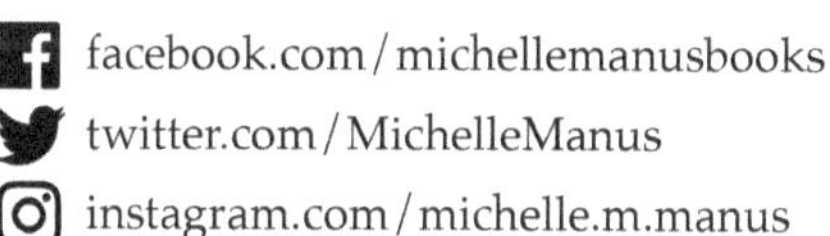

facebook.com/michellemanusbooks
twitter.com/MichelleManus
instagram.com/michelle.m.manus